The Rex

Rick Lawton

Sasha Press
San Francisco, CA
www.sashapress.com

Published 2007

Published by Sasha Press
P.O. Box 410990, #274
San Francisco, CA 94141-0990
www.sashapress.com

ISBN-10: 0-9788862-0-8
ISBN-13: 978-0-9788862-0-2

Library of Congress Control Number: 2006932308

Printed in the United States of America

Goodbye to all that.

Robert Graves
Book Title

The Rex

1

Frieda Berg tossed, turned, woke up, lit cigarettes, stabbed them into her brass man-in-the-moon ashtray, closed her eyes, and stayed half-awake all night.

Then there was the nightmare.

Frenchie, her father, dead thirty years, watched her, mournfully. Then his wavering image was cut off by the unwavering image of Stella, her mother, and her mother's crazy sisters—the Korsokoff sisters, her aunts, Anna and Libby. She wanted her father, but the Sisters blocked him out, erased him, as they'd done in life. Stella said, "Look how you repaid us! Look!"

A crowd. Old lovers, Ron, her crazed ex-husband, Ron's sneering prune-faced mother. It was a flying wedge of accusers. Ron gesticulated, his face a ball of sweat.

Ron poked a trembling finger at her, as if he was the ghost of Christmas past. "I hate you," he screamed. "Die, DIE, DIE."

Frieda groaned.

"Bad Seed," intoned the chorus. "Bad daughter. Bad wife. Bad lover. Bad seed."

Frieda whipped her head back and forth on her pillow. "Yes. Yes."

"It's not enough," shouted Ron.

He beat her with Iron John.

Thump, thump, thump.

Bad seed. Bad seed.

Thump, thump, thump.

Frieda's eyes snapped open.

Thump, thump, thump.

Her hand fumbled for the clock on the night stand. She picked over her glasses, the smooth Gallimard cover of the *La Peste*, the sharp edges of an ashtray, a handful of coins. Finally she picked up her metal gray Braun clock and focused. Eight-thirty. She frowned. "Wait a minute."

In the dim light, the edges of a thousand objects balanced on the rim of her sight. Beyond her round Art Deco table, her handbag of yesterday—purple, used, and needing an overhaul—sat in her stuffed chair like a bloated frog, spilling out its change purses, lighters, smokes, lipsticks and accessories, as if it had performed hara-kiri. The floor was a garage sale of purple shoes, black dresses, and naughty nighties. Scarves and clothes bulged out of the closet and books balanced precariously from every nook, cranny, and cubbyhole.

Iron John was about to fall from the bookcase. It must have come out when she took out *La Peste*. No wonder she had nightmares of Ron. He'd sent her the book two years ago in one of his crazed amphetamine phases. And he'd sent it because of what? To show how far he'd come? To show that despite Frieda ripping his psyche and slashing off his testicles he could still shout his frail Jewish manhood into the void? At least crank kept him thin.

And she'd kept it for...for what? A symbol of their wasted marriage? A testament to the greedy ego-centric eighties? A sign of the nineties? Homage to Gutenberg?

Thump, thump, thump.

"Quit pounding on that door."

"It's Rose Tutweiler."

"I don't care if it's God. Quit that goddamn pounding."

Frieda picked up her rose-tinted sunglasses, flicked out the frames, and put them on. The jumble turned sepia. She got up slowly and navigated bare-footed towards the light rimming the blind of her bedroom/living room. She paused briefly in her passage, pulled *Iron John* off the shelf, and dropped it in the wastebasket on the side of her stuffed chair.

Andahone, andahtwo, andahthree.

The blind snapped up. Light flooded her brain. She blinked once, twice, three times. Sepia Manhattan, East Side, Kip's Bay. Past vines and morning glories tangling off towards the roof from her planter, the sun limned the edges of the Olympia, the pretentious, modernist monstrosity across Lexington. She saw opaque reflections of Rex windows in its windows. What did the reflections hide? An early morning grope? Spilling coffee on the hotplate? The disasters of the Republic on NPR?

Frieda turned and picked her way through the tangle of garments to the door. She put on her robe and cinched it up. She paused before she opened that door. She didn't believe in ghosts, heavens, hells, or other worlds. And she didn't believe in presentiments or premonitions. But at that moment, she felt a premonition. The timing was wrong. She didn't know Rose well. She wasn't sure she liked her. And Rose was pounding on her door at eight-thirty in the morning. Something was going to happen that morning that would change everything.

She didn't know *how* she knew, she just knew.

She cracked open the door and saw it *was* Rose Tutweiler, a sepia Rose Tutweiler. She opened the door wider.

"What's up, Rose."

Rose Tutweiler lived on the sixth floor. She was sharp-nosed, diminutive, and lean. She wore a simple shift and a black beret from which an errant gray curl invariably crawled down towards her right ear. When she wasn't writing dark, death-oriented poetry à la Sylvia Plath, she was writing fan letters to Dr. Kervorkian. She was a vocal member of New York City's Hemlock Society and once a week took the subway to Queens where she was an equally vocal member of the death group Concern for Dying. Rose had a plan for "leaving" which included a last supper at Plato's Diner of fresh spinach pie, apple pie à la mode, 40 Seconal and two, possibly three, glasses of Christian Brother's Tawny Port. Rose was also on SSI and welfare, in part because of her obsession.

"This is up." She thrust a paper in front of Frieda's eyes. The sepia paper was a form from Frieda's own department, Human Resources Administration, HRA, the city's labyrinthine welfare department.

"It's too early to focus," Frieda said. "You have a problem, go to your worker."

A door cracked open behind Rose. White hair, ice-blue eyes, and wrinkles appeared in the cracked door. Sven Bjorn was a painter and teacher of retirees at the First Presbyterian Church. Frieda gave him a quick I-don't-have-a-remote-idea shrug. Sven frowned and closed the door.

"It's an IMD 209. It says my welfare has stopped. Cut off. Zip. No reason."

"Hum." Frieda tried to focus on the paper and failed.

"I've never gotten one of these," said Rose, fuming. "It doesn't say why. It's blank!"

It *was* blank, which *was* odd. "Give it here. I'll see—if I have time."

Rose let her take the form. She scowled as she tried to tuck the curl back under her beret. "I wrote my worker's name up here." She pointed a rigid, thin finger at the top of the form. "I know *you* can help. The

9

others are morons."

"I told you I'd see. Right now I'm in the middle of a bad dream."

Rose turned and stormed—Rose stormed more than anyone Frieda knew—down the hallway past Sven's tiny paintings, which he'd placed between and above the doors, around the fire extinguisher, and around the floor telephone making the eighth floor of the Rex more a gallery than a hallway.

Frieda shut the door, shook her head, and headed towards her bathroom in the other room. After using the bathroom and opening the blinds in that room, she dug in her small refrigerator for a carton of orange juice. She extracted a blue glass from a sink that was a disaster zone of knives, forks, plates, and glasses. She poured a glass of juice and a few seconds later picked up her bag from the stuffed chair and dropped it on the floor. She sat, sifted through her bag, and extracted a lighter and an Old Gold.

She lit the cigarette and watched the smoke drift away. She ran over the events of last night in her head. Nothing was interesting or remarkable. She'd listened to Meryl, a phone tree lady, and her litany of health problems; she'd thought of calling Harry, her occasional lover. They were on the outs, had been for a week. She didn't call. Typical. Boring.

Frieda plucked her Art Nouveau mirror off the wall behind her and looked critically at her image. She expected a sepia Ava Gardner. The cheekbones were still high, the hair a tumble of raven curls, the eyes, partially hidden behind rose-colored reflections, sloed and mysterious. That morning her face seemed to sag, to droop like a melting hepatic ovoid.

Frieda stubbed out the cigarette and hauled herself out of her chair. Fifteen minutes later, showered and freshly scrubbed, she started comparing dresses and purses and shoes. She chose a flowing paisley in purple, a burgundy bag, and her red shoes with their fantasy touch of Arabic tracery. She donned her mother's ring, the square obsidian one with the diamond in the middle, and her watch with its soft tiger's eye face—wheedled from an ex-lover, a romance writer she met in the Cave two years ago. Hoop earrings. A dash of blush. The rose-colored glasses.

She bent over and scrutinized her image, again. That same mirror, where half an hour before she'd found a wasted, early-morning Frieda, now showed her at top form. She was over forty—sure there were a few lines; who didn't have them—slightly overweight, but with a solid frame, good legs, firm breasts, and—she had to say after all those years and some of them very bad years—stunning good looks. Her looks had gotten her in trouble, too. After the divorce, before actually, she was needy, too needy. It led to bars, men, searching and mostly not finding. She ended up in dicey spots with violent, usually drunken men. She was surprised she'd come out of those personal dark ages intact.

Miss Movie Star. Our little Frieda.

The movie star business started with her mother and aunts. But over the years she decided she didn't care how she looked. It was about what counted as an accessory. Looks were another accessory. Something to use. Something which, when pressed, never touched inside. Sometimes when she was really down, after a long day sorting out welfare screwups or worrying why the men passed through her life like phantoms, she doubted her queer stamina, the hard quasi-existential exterior, the random shot of cynicism. Inside, deep inside her spirit, was the hollow worm of insecurity; her secret life was about a long grope towards the unchangeable. Always was, always would be.

Frieda shrugged, opened, and locked her door. Sven's gallery. Since his stroke, his portraits had gotten tinier and tinier. That morning, his gallery, her morning chorus, felt like a jury. It was the wailing of the Sisters, the stabbing finger of her ex, an echo of her nightmare.

Frieda walked around the elevator housing, pushed open the fire doors, and stopped in front of the red elevator. She looked longingly at the stairs up to the roof. No, she'd play in her garden after work. She punched the button and waited. A few seconds later, the elevator rattled to a stop and she got in, closed the accordion door, and pushed one.

The elevator almost made it in one whirring fall, past all those floors of Rex residents peeing, showering, or firing up their hotplates. The express jerked to a stop on four. Frieda frowned. A pale face flashed in the elevator's window. The flash assembled itself as Carly Darling, singer and Crazy Eddie saleswoman. Carly opened the door, then the accordion gate, and edged her way into the elevator.

Carly was a Cybill Shepherd double with a full mouth, full body, knowing smile, and long, straight blond hair. Carly sang blues, was cynical about men, but pining, waiting for a rescuer. Carly had given her a Bleeding Heart for the garden.

"Think it will make it," said Carly, shaking her hair so it swirled around her neck.

"If we wanted to make it, we'd walk."

Carly punched one. "It was a three-in-the-morning night. Funny how we say morning night. A three-in-the-morning morning doesn't sound right."

"I dreamt my ex was right."

"Yuck. That's a night stallion."

Frieda laughed. "Come up to roof, tonight. I'll buy you a drink."

"Date. I love it up there. Whoops, got to go."

Carly opened the accordion gates, then the elevator door, and sped through the lobby. Frieda held the accordion gate, angled through the closing door, and walked into the lobby. The sun streamed in the open door of the Rex; Rudi, the Rex's diminutive manager and part owner, hunched over his green much-used ledger.

Frieda walked to the half-oval and propped her bag on the ledge. "Rudi."

Rudi shoved his coke bottle glasses in his salt-and-pepper hair and adopted an expression of intense suffering. "What?"

She dug into her purse and found a cigarette and her Art Nouveau lighter. She snatched the lighter, flicked it open, and lit her cigarette in one movement. She carefully blew a plume away from Rudi. Behind Rudi, letter boxes rose halfway to the ceiling. A small fan she couldn't see fluttered the edges of the ledger. She wasn't sure why she stopped. "Most things are more than the sum of parts. You know that, of course. Take the Rex. What is it? A random collection of individuals? No. It's a spiritual ship of fools, a magic mountain, and Oran, the city of plague, all rolled into one." Frieda frowned. "I guess that makes more than one sum."

Rudi shook his head. "Always the romantic. It's a hotel. People pay money. They have rooms. It's not a secret. Aren't you late?"

Frieda shook her head no. "I can get in when I please. Of course, if I looked at my watch, which I'm not going to do, I'd see the express will reach Thirty-fourth Street in ten minutes and I'll start rushing to catch it. Odd how we're built." She plucked a tissue out of her bag, bent to the side, and dabbed a ragged line of sweat trailing out of her curls.

"I have so many worries," Rudi said, despondently. "The list already runs from your sagging roof of illegal plants to the prehistoric boiler.

They have a saying: No good deed goes—"

"Please, no witticisms this morning. When's Harry on?"

Rudi shrugged. "You know already."

"I know. I know. I'm reinforcing my own craziness. Keep the ship afloat, captain."

Frieda grabbed her bag, turned, and in a few seconds she was on a street alive with yuppies, tourists, and worker bees. Cars and cabs sped towards Lexington Avenue and runners jogged up Twenty-eighth Street the neon strips on their cross trainers flashing like police sirens.

She was halfway up the street when she thought about Ron and her nightmare. It brought up all the rest, the Bronx, the Korsokoff Sisters—truly Chekhov's "Three Sisters" pining, always pining—tentative steps in the real world, marriage, the West Side apartment, and the looping trajectory that landed her in the Rex.

She turned and shaded her eyes against the piercing sun. The Rex—her ship of fools—was a holdout on the western border of Kip's Bay. Except for The Moat, the basement bar in the rundown house flat up against the Rex on the west, they were surrounded. Remodeled townhouses. Tall buildings up-and-down the block, the Olympia across Lexington, the Giltmore, catty-corner. Every day when she came back and turned down Twenty-eighth, she was surprised the Rex was still piercing the East Side skyline. She almost thought that they, whoever *they* were, could raze the Rex and put up a high-rise while she was at work.

She hesitated as a black limousine stopped at the door of the Olympia. It was sleek, intimidating. The door cracked open. A hand grabbed the top of the door, then an oily head edged into the triangle between the car and the door. But the head dipped back in the car, as if the owner were angry. She would have waited to see who got out, but she didn't have time.

Frieda turned and rushed towards Park Avenue.

If she hurried, she'd catch the express.

2

Frieda Berg stopped across the street from IM66, welfare center, a square three-story building with steel shutters on the corner of Livingston Street, Brooklyn. Two blocks to the north, the board fence with the square-cut holes hid the busy pit of the huge MetroTec development, which would, eventually, be the home of Bear Stearns, IBM, and other escapees from Manhattan commercial rents. Frieda couldn't see the pit but she could hear the noise and the random shout and imagined knots of workers standing, smoking, and watching the cranes and earth movers pushing dirt and shoring up forms. To the south, through the heavy morning sunlight, blocks unraveled past a few tenanted apartments, boarded-up buildings, small bodegas, and, a few blocks away, an Art Deco movie theatre with broken windows and missing chunks of stucco.

Frieda rummaged through her bag, found a cigarette and her lighter, and lit a cigarette. She watched the smoke drift towards the center entrance. Boyfriends and kids huddled around the entrance most waiting for women inside to straighten out the paperwork. A few waited in line for the pay phone, a metal midget scrawled with numbers and graffiti.

She always paused. Inside was okay, but the transition from out here to in there, the flight from sanity to arcane rules and hopelessness, was tough. Social welfare was in her blood, part of her DNA, part of the dubious inheritance from the Korsokoff sisters and their strident unionism and depression-era politics. But the illusion of the quaint terms of "social welfare" or "social justice" had fallen away like dead leaves long ago.

After the divorce, after she'd lost her apartment, after she'd moved into the Rex for what was supposed to be a week, she decided to quit. But Tobius Minus, an old drinking buddy, citing her drive and bumptious character, said she'd make an ace internal investigator. *Bumptious? Internal investigator?* Should she be offended or proud? After stewing on the barren roof of the Rex that night, she decided it would be a diversion. After years of running down absent fathers, counseling grieving mothers of dead teenagers, and trying to shoe-horn clients into under-funded programs she became an official thorn in the side of the department. She tried not to think of the multiple ironies.

She had keys. She could go in the back door. But that morning, she decided on the whole catastrophe. She flicked her cigarette into the gutter and crossed the street. She navigated through jive boyfriends, husbands, and haggard women with kids attached like tentacles. Inside, she got the usual reaction when she headed towards the elevators. The heads turned, the gazes settled like moths over her clothes. People expected a black, run-down, mopey worker or black, run-down mopey client and they got a neurotic Jewish dervish with a talent for confrontation.

She waved to the loungers borrowing butts and trading jibes at the elevators but stopped at a distracted woman who held out a piece of paper as if it were a death sentence.

"Let's see, dahling."

"Here," she said, handing her the notice. She was skinny, bent, and with brown hangdog eyes, as if she were a spiritual Atlas carrying the woes of the planet.

"Right in there, dear," she said, handing the paper back. "Line 3. Tell them Frieda sent you. If that doesn't frighten them into helping, come see me in Liaison & Adjustment on three."

Frieda turned and caught an almost full elevator. She puttered around her bag, checking her keys, smokes, and accessories. On three, she walked the few short steps to the third floor intake room where clients shuffled towards their caseworkers like zombies.

She navigated through the noise and clatter waving to the few workers who tolerated her. On the far side of the room, she walked briskly through the open door into a gray room of unrelieved florescent lighting and her temporary home, IM66's L & A section.

Three grade one supervisors—Johnny Malik, forty, white, and lanky; Mike Jones, thirty-five, white and stocky; Adrian Peoples, thirty, black and cornrowed—lined up at desks on her left. They swiveled their heads towards her. She tried, when she first arrived, to make nice, to help them out, but Johnny was the only one who was halfway pleasant and that was because he was an incipient depressive. No, they'd never accepted her. Why should they? She found their mistakes.

"Morning boys."

They nodded and mumbled their hellos. Rodriguez, grade two supervisor, was standing in the doorway of the small room he called an office. Rodriguez looked up, frowning.

"Mr. Rodriguez," she said, not stopping to chat.

Rodriguez, hefty, square-jawed with glossy rippled hair and toffee-shaded skin, despised her, and was not subtle about it. She thought he was incompetent and anti-client. According to the little she heard on the IM66 grapevine, Rodriguez fancied himself a ladies' man. But a throw-back ladies' man, who wore, at least once a week and to the consternation of most female workers, a Playboy tie, usually featuring an endowed shiksa in bunny drag, red lips parted, wide hips bunched high at some winged phallus.

Rodriguez looked grim as gravy. He sneered at her greeting, turned on his heel, and disappeared into his office.

She cut across the barren landscape to a large gray desk near the window and dropped her bag next to her desk. She fussed with the Frieda Berg Traveling Circus. Terrarium of Venus Flytraps, pots of ivy, philodendron, and schefflera, postcards of her three Ks: Klimt, Kandinsky, and Kafka, and a strong but slender Tanzanian Makonde "Tree of Life" sculpture, a jumble of elongated limbs, bodies, and smiling faces all supporting each other.

Finally, she sat and hitched her chair up to the desk. She plucked Rose's IMD 209 out of her bag. She smoothed out the form. She frowned at the closing code of 333. The same premonition she had that morning before she saw Rose came back. She couldn't see how that form meant anything more than another HRA foul-up, but it did.

Frieda propped her phone between her chin and shoulder and called IM33. After being shunted to two other workers, Mindy Jenkins, Rose's caseworker, came on the line.

"Mindy. Frieda Berg, IM Investigations. Rose Tutweiler. What's going on?"

"I don't know. I didn't send out the IMD 209. And she's erased from the system. Gone."

Frieda frowned, then looked at the mystery code 333 again. "*Nothing* in the system?"

"Zip."

"Shizer. Get someone to type in her case record."

Frieda frowned at the silence on the line. Finally Mindy said, "I can't find it. I've checked with Records Management and it's gone."

"Christ," said Frieda. "The whole record?"

"That's what I'm saying."

"What are you doing about it?"

"There's not a lot I can do. Talk to Condi Maxwell in L & A."

Frieda sighed. The system didn't reward initiative. Problems were there to be passed to someone else. "If you find anything else about Rose's case, call me at 638-4509."

Frieda stared at Rose's code 333. The department lived on forms and codes. The rules were strict, fussy, often insane, the essence of bureaucratic anality. A mystery code: not very likely.

Frieda called Condi Maxwell and nudged her into working on Rose's case without supporting docs. Then she called the Rex and told Rose to go into IM33 and talk to Condi. At least Rose wouldn't hammer on her door tomorrow morning. Frieda went on to the other items stacked in her in box. She flipped through forms, made notes, called caseworkers. IM66 was a disaster when she arrived. Missing forms, inexperienced workers, weird ad hoc rules. She'd fixed the worst ones, but when she thought she was done, she found something else.

She took a break at three in Sam's Diner, where she had a quick lunch of Reuben and pickle and watched MetroTec construction workers leaning on shovels and scratching their balls.

When she came back, she realized that what she'd done for Rose wasn't enough. That weird code *was* part of her job.

"Johnny, have you heard of cases closed with a code 333?" She held the IMD 209 in the air and waved it back and forth.

Johnny frowned and then said, "Ask Mona."

"Hum."

Frieda called Mona Talbot, one of the few workers she could talk to in IM66.

"Oh yeah," said Mona.

"What?"

"Got ten. And there's probably more out there."

That got her attention. Frieda got up and sortied into the intake room. She walked through a bedlam of yelling, typing, terminals, stern-faced workers, clients poised on the edges of metal chairs, and papers, papers, papers.

She recognized most of the workers and a handful of clients in the sprawling workplace. A hard luck story about an absent father, a lost check, and a pregnancy filtered through the noise. She'd heard the story a thousand times. Meeting, mating, poverty, and the grim trickling off.

Mona Talbot was a gay black woman with a butch cut and nose-ring.

"Ten cases, really?"

Mona put her finger on a folder. The label said, "Code 333 cases." "They're scattered. A few in Brooklyn and Manhattan; all Home Relief. Singles, probably live in SROs. I called a friend at IM34 and she had a few. I looked them up in the database and they're not there—not a trace."

"Case record?"

"They complained to L & A in their centers. And L & A couldn't find their case records. They've vanished. Without their docs—"

"Rent receipts, letter from the landlord, bank account statements, letters from Employment, UIB, and filled out IMD 110, 124, 137, and 206 forms. Paper, paper, paper. What a fucking waste. Workers don't lose this goddamn many cases."

"You said it. The case record is a lot of paper. A DELETE key won't touch it."

"I can't believe this," she said, too sharply. "Why didn't you report it?"

Mona looked hurt. "I did. To Rodriguez, months ago."

Frieda felt the lines in her face tighten. She calmed herself down. "I'll take these," she said, picking up the folder. Frieda patted Mona on the hand. "Thanks dear."

"Are you—"?

"—going to be calm and reasonable?"

Mona snickered.

Frieda turned, and picked her way through gray desks and harried workers. She knew she should put off talking to Rodriguez. But she'd never cooled down before. Besides, she knew the asshole was crooked, not that she'd ever prove it.

Rodriguez had on a blue sports coat and tie, which fortunately did not feature a Vargas nude. His office was barren, except for a few chairs against the far wall near the window. His desk was bare. He was intent on scribbling something, his head canted over his desk. He pursed his lips and wrote.

She reviewed what she knew of him. Missing forms, weird rules, which he'd never corrected. He wasn't there half the time. Said he was at Central Office. That was odd for an L & A Supe 2. They were all in the trenches and most L & A supes had desks full of problems. She'd already had a handful of run-ins with him. It looked like she was going to have another.

When he looked up and saw her, a ghost of distaste passed over his face. He turned what he was writing face down.

He said, "What's the problem today? Coffee stains on a record?"

She smiled back. "I've watched you for a month. I've never seen a Supe 2 do so little. You're never here. When you are, you don't supervise worth a damn. Fortunately, there are good people working here to cover your mistakes."

Rodriguez's false smile hardened. "I have work to do. If you came to insult me—"

"Not at all. I came because I have ten IMD 209s with code 333. What are they?"

She thought later his reaction was odd. It started when he heard the words "Code 333." He started backtracking. "I reported them. The head of IM told me to ignore them, that it has something to do with Special Projects. I have too much to do without—"

"What? Leaving clients to dangle in the wind? They've been wiped out of the database. And what happened to their paper records? You had to follow up. What's going on?"

"You might be right this time. Give me the cases and I'll find out."

"Not good enough, Mr. Rodriguez. *I'm* going to find out."

Rodriguez looked sick. She wondered, later, about his reaction.

"Whatever you want, but I won't let you disrupt our office. We—"

She laughed. "Your office? It has one of the worst records in the city. And it aint because of Johnny, Mike, and Adrian."

Frieda turned and walked back to her desk. The asshole. Rodriguez knew about those cases. If he were involved in some kickback scheme, she would staple his ass to the wall.

Frieda opened the folder, stared at the form. But the words became meaningless. It wasn't her run-in with Rodriguez, or the code 333 cases. It was another anomaly she would research, pigeonhole, and forget. She stared at the boys scratching their heads and plowing through forms.

She dug in her bag, found her cigarettes. She walked over to the window, lit a cigarette, and blew the smoke out into Brooklyn. MetroTec workers tried to look busy as a crane lowered a giant funnel of concrete into a long square wooden form.

It was time for Frieda Berg's daily dose of the past.

Her mother, her aunts, Ron. The chorus had always been shrill. The soft voice of Frenchie, her father, had been banished almost as soon as she was born.

Frenchie was a handsome, funny, engaging Swiss Jew who spoke ten languages, most fluently, had lived in Paris for five years, and made money playing chess and giving tennis lessons. Her mother, the saint, was a staunch leftist of Internationale stripe, a union organizer who loved to fight more than eat. How her parents managed to get into the same room was inconceivable. But conceive her mother did. And soon after, her mother threw Frenchie out on his ass.

Little Frieda, Miss Movie Star. She had always been an uneasy amalgam of romantic yearning and fighting for underdogs. The spirit of her father was with her at City College when she soaked up international literature in five languages, the spirit of her mother when she started fighting for peoples' rights in HRA.

She fell for Ron Steiner because, subliminally, she recognized the same competing pressures. Ron was first an anarchist, then a crank addict, then a corporate lawyer. She'd liked the anarchist, tolerated the addict, and wanted to kill the corporate lawyer. She'd called him once in the late eighties when she was short. That's when he yelled "Die, die, die," into the phone. Yes, she'd left bodies in her wake.

The only problem was that she was tired of the sine wave. She needed a grand accommodation, where the competing voices of her past, her fractured psyche, could sit down and agree on a cease-fire.

Frieda stubbed her cigarette on the windowsill and flicked it out on the street. She watched its flight, watched it bounce on the sidewalk, and into the gutter.

Then, eyes hooded, contemplative, she turned and walked slowly back to her desk.

3

Gray edged the window shade. Ratty worn chair, abused desk, a brown open suitcase with a jumble of clothes. Room 103 seemed like a cell in a prison. Marcy Benaventura hated that room. She got up and used the common bathroom, which was close enough to the lobby to hear Ivan, the desk clerk trying to explain something in broken English. Back in room 103, she dug through her duffel bag and found a clean bra and pair of panties. She dressed quickly, glanced at her beetle brows and rim of auburn hair in the small mirror, and got out. She stopped in the lobby to tell Ivan she was staying a week, but he was already knee-deep in a crowd of residents complaining about this or that or trying to get their mail, so she headed to the Odyssey.

Last night, when she dragged her brown suitcase into the Rex lobby, she was almost out of money and flat out of ideas. She was exhausted from a two-day cross-country trip on Greyhound. The first person she saw, thankfully, was Rudi. He was there when she left over a year ago and he was still there, would always be there. He propped his glasses in his hair and ran his finger down his ledger and helped her, even though he wondered what it would be like to have two Benaventuras in the Rex. The last time she and her mother were there, it was impossible for a handful of reasons. He gave her the room, then, just as he was leaving, he mentioned that a Greek diner, the Odyssey, had an opening as a dishwasher, or a waitress. He didn't remember which.

While taking a shower, she decided to try the Odyssey. She changed and hiked over there. Wee bit of chaos last night. A cook and a waitress had a fight early that day and they needed both a dishwasher *and* a waitress. Last night, she put on a spare uniform, washed dishes, and took orders. It happened so fast, she didn't have time to fuck up.

She wasn't sure about that morning. She felt Nikos, the owner, liked her. But he could have called someone who had a lot more experience.

She walked the few blocks to the Odyssey quickly, took a deep breath, and opened the shiny aluminum doors. The Odyssey was a big Greek diner with a long counter right of the entrance, a central maze of Masonite tables and faux Tiffany lamps, and a rim of booths along the far wall and under the picture windows. Above the booths on the far wall was a huge faux-fresco of the Greek hero Odysseus leading a band of not-too-happy sailors towards the crowds on Lexington Avenue.

She waited, edgily, for Nikos to finish making change for a customer. Nikos was a short animated Greek with dark hair, a big fleshy nose, and the warmest smile she'd seen in weeks. He looked up at her. She saw ambivalence in his soft, brown eyes. If *he* was worried...

"I'm glad you're back," said Nikos. "You never worked waitress before."

"I did okay last night."

"You did good for not having experience. It's okay. Alice likes you and says she'd rather work with you than anybody. You're smart and got quick hands. You'll learn fast. You got to be more easy with people."

He'd seen something, maybe the way she looked at customers, or the way she'd come close to getting in a fight with one of the cooks. "Thanks, Nikos."

"Use the same uniform. Okay, it's busy. You're on."

On stage, he meant. It was more like being in a play that morning than the helter-skelter war last night. She felt like an actress in the maze of booths, sorting specials, cleaning messes, and trying to remember the serving order. She had the script, but was still memorizing the lines.

And the Rex carnival followed her. She recognized—greeted and served—black-haired Ric, the cab driver, white-haired bow-legged Sven, who had coffee before he taught his painting class, the feuding Farmers—John and Melissa—Mary, Jeb, Petey, and a host of others who messed with their eggs and Danish and jolted themselves with Odyssey coffee before chasing jobs, firing up cabs, or straightening TV antennas at the Rex.

They almost acted liked everybody else.

Rudi came in at ten. She thanked him for the tip about the Odyssey and told him she'd probably stay at the Rex a week while she found another place. He said that was fine with him.

The waitressing part got easy that afternoon. When she left, Nikos made out her schedule. It was too cool. She held the shiny door partly open. She glanced back over the maze of booths, at Nikos frowning at receipts at the register. Yes, it was going to work. She felt—what was that word?—grounded. For the first time in a year.

She turned, her heart light, and tripped down Lexington. She got supplies at the Emporium on Lexington and went back to the Rex. A few men she didn't recognize walked down the steps and into the Moat. Brucie Melton was in front, in the same position when she left. Brucie was squat, bald, and walleyed. He wore a baseball cap, shorts, and tennis shoes, and listened to his Walkman most of the day in front of the Rex.

"Brucie."

Brucie turned down his Walkman and let the headset drop to his neck. "Hey, it's good to see ya," said Brucie. "You back for good?"

"A week maybe. How are those Yankees?"

"Same old, same old. They're brilliant, then stumblebums. Say, it's good to see ya, again."

"Later."

She hopped up the worn steps of the Rex and a few seconds later stopped in front of the desk clerk's half oval, where she was surprised to see Mario Sotto, her mother's boyfriend. Mario was a six foot two ex-marine a tad on the heavy side with soft brown eyes and a tangle of brown curly hair. Marcy liked Mario. He was a bright, tough guy who would do anything for you. But he was too much like her father. They both loved fighting and booze—although her father was a dynamite artist, when he was sober—and Bel had taken up with Mario after Ray died. When she thought of it, they'd formed the same triangle Marcy had with her parents. Drop one, add one.

She wasn't sure she wanted to see Mario yet. But she played it out.

"Marcy, my favorite artist," said Mario. He leaned through the half-oval and they pecked each other on the cheek.

"Way too kind. Why are you doing desk clerk?"

"I started filling in when Ivan has a class, Harry an interview, or Rudi needs a break."

"You still have the Circle?"

Mario shrugged. "It's an institution. Verbal repartee, keen observations on the passing scene, Dionysian fun. It keeps us sharp."

"Up most of the night, you mean."

"Depends on your point of view."

She talked to Mario for a few minutes and found he was still working as head cook at Luigi's, still had his Circles, and, she gathered, still liked to drink too much. She didn't expect that to change while she was gone. She was surprised at how good it felt connecting to something besides her trip, although when they started talking about Bel, her heart lodged in her throat.

She took a big breath. "She around?"

"On the roof an hour ago."

"I guess it's time to say hello."

"She's mellowed some," said Mario, lowering his eyes in a quick conspiracy.

"That I have to see."

Marcy went to her room and stored her groceries in the fridge. She didn't want to see Bel. Last year, Shannon, a high school friend, told her she'd gotten her talent from Ray, her brains from Bel, and her trip temper from both of them. A Bel and Marcy dialogue was like Mrs. Nitro talking to Ms. C-4.

"Fuck it," she said. She grabbed a can of MGD, walked back into the lobby, and took the elevator to eight. She walked up the dark narrow stairs cluttered with Frieda's garden tools, dirt, and fertilizers, to the roof. The top of those stairs glowed with July sun. Marcy paused for a moment, then walked out onto the roof. Across from her was a trellis of red and yellow roses. She saw Bel out of her peripheral vision sitting under a yellow umbrella at Frieda's deck table.

She shrugged inwardly; then, sweat trickling down her neck and her heart racing, she turned and walked down the central black path bordered by Frieda's pallets of plants and flowers. Bel was in the shadow of the umbrella, one shapely leg stretched out on a chair rung, the other, half-bent, on the seat, her hand near a half-empty glass on the table. Bel's auburn hair and dark brows matched Marcy's. Her green eyes were lowered, focusing on some intangible spot west towards Frieda's vegetable nook of tomatoes, zucchini, radishes, and beans.

"Ma."

Bel looked up, shocked. Her eyes narrowed, then she frowned. Finally, her face relaxed. "Marcy, my peripatetic girl. Rudi told me you were back." Bel debated what to do, but finally she untangled herself from the chair and got up. They hugged. At forty, Bel was still dynamite looking and light on her feet. Marcy couldn't remember if they'd ever hugged. She supposed that at a certain age people did it for show.

Bel stepped back and looked at her. "What's changed?"

"Got rid of the nose-ring and most of the earrings. I'm letting my hair grow. Thought I'd try on a different character."

"It's what inside that counts," Bel said.

Marcy shrugged. "That takes longer."

The sun boiled down on them. They both started to fidget. "Well let's not die of sunstroke." Bel sat back down. Marcy hesitated, then pulled the other chair around, and sat opposite Bel in the shade.

The sun up there hit you like a hammer in the summer and it was windless. Heat waves eddied around the roof and made the Olympia waver, as if it were a mirage. Frieda's garden spread in front of them, a kaleidoscope of pastels anchored by those trellis roses.

Bel glanced at her and said, "The story of Marcy Benaventura. You left when you got your inheritance, moved in with Mickey, a guitar player for the Something Monkeys, got pregnant, got an abortion, went on Marcy's Wanderjahre, and blew your inheritance. That's a fuck of a lot of experience for one year. What now?"

Marcy felt her lips go straight-line, her back stiffened. Whenever she did that, she was close to blowing up. She got up. "Trying to stay as far away from you as possible."

Bel looked shocked. She sighed, shook her head. "That inheritance shit still pisses me off. Sit down. I'll behave."

She didn't want to. Half an hour ago, she felt great. Now she was in a death struggle with her mother. Marcy looked at her can of beer, shrugged, and sat. She took a healthy swallow of her beer and set it on the table. "I'll give it a few more minutes. How did you know that stuff?"

A smile teased Bel's mouth into a curve. "Brenda."

"Figured." Marcy took a pull on her MGD, and set it down on table. Marcy watched a bee disappear in a flower that was large and orange with petals that dove inward. Brenda, her aunt, and Bel didn't talk, at all. It could only have been about one thing. She had to talk to somebody besides her asshole boyfriend and she'd asked Brenda about periods, doctors, and what she'd do. She made her promise not to call Bel. But she knew, deep down, she would.

She watched Bel closely. Bel returned her stare. "You could have come to me."

Marcy laughed. "And what would you have said?"

"Why blame me," said Bel, angrily, "for something that didn't happen. You figured it out."

"I suppose I did. Did you and Brenda talk, really talk?"

"Fuck her. She got the money; I got zip." A ghost of sadness flicked across Bel's face. "Okay, we've opened the closets, exhumed the graves, and doused salt on the wounds. What's next? School?"

Marcy thought about that. She shook her head. "Don't think so."

"You're smart enough to go anywhere. I could get you into Vassar."

Bel had gone to Vassar. At one time, she liked to flaunt it. She hadn't since Ray died. Marcy shook her head. She held up her index finger and thumb. She rubbed them together. "Money."

"Scholarships." Bel frowned. "We're talking past each other. What *are* you going to do?"

They'd always talked past each other, but that was the first time Bel noticed it. "Work, sketch, paint, do caricatures at the Seaport, Pier 17."

"Fuck me," Bel snorted. "Another starving artist. Like father, like daughter."

"You married him. What happened there?"

Bel was wearing shorts and a red halter-top and looked thinner than Marcy remembered. She'd never seen much likeness, but she did that day, especially around the mouth. It was a good mouth, entrancing, but thin, too ready to purse and etch a straight line across the face.

Bel sighed, looked her over critically, and then shook her head. "You have time."

"What about you? Things the same? Mario?"

Bel shrugged. "The same. I edit manuscripts, go to movies, catch a symphony, and stare at the fetishes in the Met's Oceania collection. Play with Mario. It even sounds like fun, sometimes."

"You don't make it sound like fun," said Marcy, uneasily.

Bel grimaced. "Maybe I need you around. Makes me dissatisfied. Are you staying here?"

Marcy felt a surge of feeling. Bel wasn't happy, at all. A year ago, she wouldn't have cared. "I'm not sure. A week, maybe. It's stop-gap."

"Ha!" Bel said, laughing. Bel held up her drink. She drew her finger through the condensation. Tiny drops snaked towards the bottom of the glass. Two larger drops formed and dropped in Bel's lap. Bel looked at the splotches, as if she wondered how they got there.

"Why did you laugh?"

"At us. We need a new definition of 'temporary' for people who crash land in the Rex. We linger like those graduate students who work on their Ph.D. for twenty years."

"Maybe I did crash land," said Marcy, wondering about that. "But I'm still alive."

Bel made another slash on the side of her glass. She watched the drops form, race towards the bottom of the glass, and then fall on her shorts. "Fuck school," said Bel, looking at her directly. "No one can take away your talent or brains. Pretty soon, you'll be living on Park, on another 'A' list."

It was the closest Bel had ever come to a compliment. "Right now I'm glad to have a room for a few nights."

"If you stay, get off one."

"I don't know about staying, but right now I don't know where else to go." Marcy got up. She looked directly at Bel. Their connection, without her doing anything, had changed. "I'm glad you're okay, Ma. I've got to wash clothes, eat, and sleep."

"Some fun. It's good to see you too, dear."

Marcy picked up her beer and walked towards the door. She knew Bel was staring at her, at her hair, at her legs. She felt rigid, contrived, as if she were learning to walk. When she reached the darkness of the stairs, she let out a sigh.

It was almost cold inside, after the heat. A few minutes later, she was in the elevator.

Bel and Marcy. It was bad, then not that bad. She didn't expect they would become loving mother and daughter. If they never did, it was still better than last year.

"Rudi, I gotta get off one. It's freakin' me out."

Marcy had begun feeling settled after a week sashaying through the maze of booths at the Odyssey, a week at the Rex, and a one late afternoon spent drawing caricatures of tourists at Pier 17. Bel was okay as long as she didn't see her often. And the Rex, especially the residents she knew like Mario and Frieda, even Brucie, made her feel secure. Besides, there was no way she could afford a real apartment—yet.

The hint of a smile cracked Rudi's normal harried expression. "Some people like one."

Marcy frowned. "Yeah, the ones who aren't staying."

"I remember someone saying they were only staying—"

"Right, right. So we're all liars."

Rudi turned and stared at the mailboxes. He flipped through the ledger. "Hum. Seems I have an opening on four. It's a double room, too. What do you know."

Marcy's heart beat faster. "That's too cool. People hold on to those rooms until they die."

"Last week, Whitey Zero said he was moving to Queens. I was shocked. But he's gone."

"Hi." A man, unshaven, thick-lipped with a mop of greasy hair, stuck his head in the other side of the half-oval.

Rudi frowned. "What?"

"I'll take it."

"*What* are you going to take?" said Rudi, puzzled.

He fumbled in his pocket. He took out a paper and peered at it. "Room 408."

Marcy frowned. Rudi frowned too. Rudi said, "How do you know about 408?"

"Can I have it or not?" the man said, abruptly.

"Not," said Rudi, turning away. "It's taken."

"Fuckin' taken? It only opened up."

"Who the fuck are you?" said Marcy, sticking in her two cents. "It's my room."

The guy measured her with his eyes. His breath smelled of cigarettes and coffee. He shook his head. "You shouldn't talk that way little girl. It's not nice."

"You shouldn't be such a shithead. It's my room."

The guy backed up and looked at both of them. "Yeah, okay. Misunderstanding. Name's Lew Cranston. I'd appreciate if you'd put me down for a room, when one opens up."

Rudi looked at Lew suspiciously, then shrugged. "I'll put you on the list. Number."

"621-5631."

Lew hesitated a second, then turned and loped through the open door. He hustled down the worn steps and disappeared down Twenty-

28

eighth. Rudi balled up the piece of paper with Lew's phone number and flipped it into the wastebasket.

"Super weird," said Marcy. "The guy knew about the room before you did."

"Practically," said Rudi.

Rudi popped his glasses off his head, leaned down and made a mark in his ledger. "I haven't had time to clean, yet. You won't be able to—"

"Don't worry. I'll clean it."

Rudi looked at the key board, plucked off a key, and slid it to Marcy. "Okay. You need help, ask Mario or Ivan."

"Thanks Rudi. I'd better get up there before Lew moves in."

Four was sleepy, laid-back, domestic, definitely in the slow lane compared to five with the Freak Brothers, Crazy Ritchie, and Joey, a reputed drug dealer, or seven and Mario's Circle. Her new room was one room shy of the fire escape and came equipped with the standard art nouveau sconces, white arched ceilings, elegant, tangled leaf trim, and hardwood floor. The smaller room had a sink, small frig, and a small bathroom with a turn-of-the century marble sink whose mirror had reflected a million faces. She had space and light. As you went up in the Rex, you went from hell to heaven, from Ben and his burrow to Frieda and her garden. She couldn't explain it, exactly, that health and life were up, sickness and death down.

Over the space of a few days, she cleaned, painted, buffed the floors, moved out the standard furnishings and moved in her own, which included a futon, a director's chair, brick-and-board bookshelves, and a chest-of-drawers. She found a bedspread for her futon with a pattern of gold vines, which matched the tangle of leaves around the lights. When it was all done, Marcy smiled to herself. She had a job. She felt safe for the first time in a year. Perimeters secure, sir. Shall we continue with the operation? Good question, she thought.

She picked up her sketch pad. She had gone through a lifetime with her last pad and it showed in the coffee stains, splotches, blood, and traces of body and mind-altering substances.

She took her pad to the window and leaned against the sill.

She stared past the Olympia, past Kip's Bay. She was caught for a second by the smallest movement of the East River, which inched between two buildings. The cluttered space made her feel small and delicate.

Closer, she had a quick desire to draw the reflections of the Rex's rooms in the Olympia windows. She saw half-drawn blinds, single chairs, framed photos, and beds. It was like M. C. Escher, the overlapping of lines making a new perspective. But Escher was precise and tricky, almost mathematical. She wasn't. She had her own style, similar to her father's. She sketched the reflections, and then added the ominous bulk of the Olympia.

Finally, she added the two men leaning over the side in the penthouse. Mutt and Jeff. She added what looked like drops of blood to Mutt's hands, which were gesticulating, as if he were having a fit. She added worry to Jeff, the tall man, who seemed more arch and distant, although she couldn't see his face. She quit drawing and tried to pick out more details.

After a few seconds, she saw they were staring at her.

She cocked her head and stared back at them. She felt they meant something, something predatory and bad, something beyond her own style, which freely warped most of her subjects. Then she thought of Lew, the bad-breathed gangly guy who almost got her room. What was that about? He had a slip of paper, a room number.

Who gave it to him?

4

Brucie flicked off his Walkman and let the headphones slide down to his neck. He shook his head mournfully, as if he were ruminating on a cosmic curse. The Yankees let another game slip through their fingers. Fucking Yankees. They were brilliant, then not. What happened to consistency?

Brucie yanked off his baseball cap. He ran his hand over his sweaty scalp twice and wiped his hand on his shorts. The Rex stoop was his favorite spot, his power spot. Raised voices from the Moat, Rex tenants entering and exiting, street action—he saw it all. Frieda called him their gargoyle-in-residence. He supposed he was.

Someone brushed by and knocked his cap out of his hand. "Hey."

There were two of them. The skinny guy just moved onto two. 202 or 201. The beefy one, the one who knocked his cap off, with the dirty Snoopy T-shirt, was on three. Brucie had seen them in the McDonald's on Park. He didn't like them.

"Hey what?" said the big guy. "You shouldn't hang around here all the time. You a statue?"

"Watch where you're going," said Brucie, pissed. He stooped to pick up his cap.

"Guess we got a live one," said the heavy guy. He backed up and stood in front of Brucie. He pushed his thick-featured face close to Brucie's. His eyes were hard points. His breath smelled of grease, butts, and booze. "Let's go. You and me, right here baldy."

Brucie, trembling, put his hat on. "You're too touchy, man."

The skinny guy grabbed the other's arm. "Ace, not here."

Ace shook off his arm, but started to walk away. He pointed his finger at Brucie. "You're at the top of my list, buddy."

Ace snapped off his stare. The two navigated the steep steps down into the Moat and disappeared in the darkness. Brucie realized his heart was beating hard. He breathed slowly once, twice. What was that about? New guys. There were at least four of them. They weren't friendly and they all knew each other. It was peculiar, too peculiar.

Brucie took a last glance at the street and walked up the steps of the

31

Rex. Mario was subbing for another fifteen minutes. He was going to hear about the latest Yankees disaster whether he wanted to or not. He was also going to hear about Ace and the new guys. There was something about them that wasn't right.

Light from the street struggled into the Moat, but gave up a few feet from the table in the corner. Max Best flipped the hair out of his right eye and watched Ace, Bert, and Truck.

"Listen up," said Max. "I don't know if it's a good idea we all meet. You know, if there are complaints, they could start fingering us. George said we'd know who the other guys are, but to keep it cool."

Bert was tall and sallow, his skin the color of paste. Thick veins snaked over his arms and legs like sickly blue vines. He'd written "love" and "hate" on his knuckles with a Bic ballpoint. He'd just moved into a room on eight. Bert said, "Nobody's gonna figure it out now. We're just a bunch of guys havin' a beer. How many of us do ya think later?"

Max took a sip of his Bud. "Don said seven, maybe eight. We're gonna need a hall."

They chuckled at that. Truck—he was heavy and sloppy and had just moved into a room on four—took a long draw on his beer and belched. He looked at Max. "George said something about an enforcer type. Who's that?"

Max knew. "Some hard ass. Don said his name's Kramer or some such shit."

"The klutz on Seinfeld?" said Truck, emitting a croak.

"Not hardly," said Max. "Don said he's a big guy. A stone killer."

They all nodded. They knew the Kramer-type.

Bert said, "What's the deal here? Like he wants us to hold down rooms and do little stuff, harassment stuff, but no strong-arm. What shit is that?"

"Cuz it worked at the Amsterdam," said Max, scratching the scar under his hair. He'd gotten the scar in a knife fight a thousand years ago. It was out of sight under his hair, but he liked to touch it, to scratch it. Sometimes he scratched it too much and it looked like a thin, red smile. "I was there for six months. It was hit-or-miss. Then George stepped in. You pick your targets, find their weak points, work on their heads. It's like aerobics. There's high impact and low impact. This is low impact."

"Fuck psychology," said Bert. "I'm tired of being nice."

Ace guzzled his Bud, belched. "Fuck yes."

Max shook his head at Bert, "And we haven't even started."

The light from the door became a shadow, then the light returned, as if someone had thrown a switch. Mario and Bel walked into the Moat. She had a medium build and an erect carriage, but looked small next to Mario. Mario was burly, but his gait suggested a lightness on his feet belied by his size. They sat at the bar and Mario ordered a beer and a glass of white wine. After a few minutes, Mario glanced at the group in the corner. Worry passed like a cloud over his face. He whispered in Bel's ear. Bel turned and glanced at the corner.

Max tried to get the other guys back to their conversation, but Ace stared at Mario. Ace started to get up. Max caught him by the sleeve. "Stay cool," he whispered. "We don't want any trouble. It's too early."

Ace shook his hand off. "Stuff cool. Nobody messes with."

Max wondered if it was a mistake to make friends with Ace. He remembered what happened to Whitey Zero. He'd gone in thinking that he, Max, was going to mess up Whitey. But Ace had his hands around him before he could say boo. Ace had a flip temper and it looked like he was going after Mario. Max shrugged. If Mario left, another room would free up. Jack would move another agent in and they'd be closer to starting. Problem was that Ace didn't look like he could take Mario. If it took a couple of them that might get back to Jack, which might...Max shook his head mournfully.

Ace strode across to the bar. Larry quit wiping glasses.

Ace stopped between Mario and Bel. "Hey, jerkface. You talkin' about us?"

Mario turned slowly. He regarded Ace. He glanced at the three in the corner and shrugged. "I have better things to do than talk about shitass losers. You sharing a brain cell?"

Ace blinked. It wasn't supposed to happen that way. When he challenged guys, they were supposed to slink away, or make excuses. If they were small enough, sometimes he beat 'em up; sometimes he just scared 'em. Mario was big, his short-sleeves revealed muscular arms. He looked like a brawler. Ace glanced into the corner. He couldn't back down. He hesitated a beat, set himself to throw a punch, and grabbed Mario's shoulder to turn him around.

Mario didn't move much. He seemed to huddle on himself almost as if he were cold. Then his left fist shot out. It slammed into Ace's throat. The blow rocked Ace back on his heels. He grabbed his throat.

"Ach. Ach. Ach."

Ace staggered. He stumbled and crashed to the floor. He tried to turn his head towards the trio in the corner, but he felt something crushing his fingers and throat. He found himself staring at the laces of Mario's shoe.

Larry, frightened, leaned over the bar. "Mario, take it outside."

Max, Truck, and Bert pushed their chairs back and hurried into a semicircle in front of Mario. A can of Mace appeared magically in Bel's hand. She aimed it at Max and said, "You'd better be sure boys."

The three stared at Mario and Bel.

Max glanced at Bert, then Truck. Max said, "Sorry. My friend's a little hotheaded. Didn't mean anything. All over."

Mario lifted his foot off Ace's fingers and neck. He squatted next to him. His face was a foot from Ace's. "I think you're asshole and your friends are assholes too. If you're going to live here, you're going to behave, or you're going to get hurt. Capece?" Ace looked at Max, then back to Mario. Ace nodded. "Good. Now get the fuck out of here."

Max and Bert struggled to help Ace up. Ace was still trying to breathe when they led him away. Bert turned before they got to the door. "This aint over. Believe me, before we're done, you're all leavin'."

Mario stepped towards them and Bert scrambled up the steps. Mario laughed.

Mario rubbed his knuckles. "Who are these guys? They act like a fraternity."

Larry let out a long breath. "Some fraternity. I've seen 'em with this other guy, Don. Short, fat guy. You're right though, they're up to something."

Bel dropped the Mace into her bag. "I've been thinking," she said. "Every time we've had a vacancy, one of these guys has been right there to take the room. And what was that crack about leaving? No clichés about rooms in hospitals or getting out of town or getting your lights put out. He said 'leave'. What does that mean?"

Mario said, "What if we had to leave? I haven't thought about that for a year."

Bel patted him on the hand. "Yes we have, dear; you just don't remember. Time creeps in its petty pace—"

"From day to day, from hour to hour, from minute to—"

Bel laughed. "It's definitely drain bandage. Right now, I want another drink. So do you. You just punched a guy out. You must be mainlining testosterone."

5

Frieda cleared the lump in her throat, snatched up the phone, and dialed the Rex desk.

"Hello Harry." Her voice sounded high and twitchy.

She'd avoided him lately, but she couldn't anymore. As long as she was busy, as long as she was rooting out welfare screwups or rooting in her garden, she was okay. As soon as she stopped or closed her eyes to sleep, she was dead lonely. The line was silent. She read chapters of subtext into that pause. Their last fight was gigantic, a knockdown drag-out about nothing.

Finally, he said, "What do you want?"

"Dinner. You and me. Luigi's. I'll pay."

The line was silent again. "We can't act like kids forever. Dutch."

Frieda smiled. That was good. "Seven?"

"See you there."

Easy phone. But the phone wasn't the hard part.

After work, she took the subway to the Village and fortified herself with a Campari in the Cave, her long-time favorite dark, smoky, basement bar. Peggy, the blond, pony-tailed, super efficient bartender/owner, talked to her for a few minutes, but when she turned to wait on other customers, Frieda zoned out. She stared out the small, grated window in front, and watched the shoes and calves of passersby flick by.

Flats. High heels. Espadrilles. Birkenstocks. Wingtips.

The procession led her to think of things transitory, transients, and Harry. That was all one subtext. She guessed, knew, Harry would leave. Why prolong the agony? Why stack up more regrets? She'd met Harry in the lobby of the Rex last spring. Harry was big, half-Swedish, half-German, and bright as a tack. He got his MD degree from the University of Wisconsin and interned at King's County. That is, he interned until he turned himself in for using ER drugs.

ER drugs?

Harry explained what happened, sometimes too often, almost as if he were seeking absolution. He'd started out a young idealistic intern from the Midwest bent on giving back to society. But the ER's thirty-

36

hour days, knifings, shootings, and the constant stream of human misery exacted too heavy a toll. He'd used the drugs to cope, then, remorseful, he'd turned himself in. Then he was fired, then he was blackballed.

It didn't matter to her. She knew about trashed ideals. It didn't take long after that first meeting to get together. And it didn't take long after that to discover the push-pull. There were fights, the last one a classic with yelling, accusations, and slammed doors. But she'd reached the point, a point she'd reached before, when the loneliness was too great. She missed seeing him on the roof, missed talking about Times' editorials, missed going to the summer Shakespeare Festival; she missed the sex and she missed having someone to take the edge off her days.

She drank the last of her bittersweet Campari, waved to Peggy, and eyes blinking against the accumulating smoke of the Cave, exited up the worn linoleum steps into the fading light. The air was warm, the night full of the buzzing of Villagers and tourists. She hailed a cab, and fifteen minutes later saw Harry standing in front of Luigi's looking like a Junker. She paid the driver, and walked, hesitantly, up to him.

They were both edgy. She smiled and he smiled back.

"Darling," she rose up and kissed him quickly on the cheek.

Harry said, "I've forgotten how beautiful you are."

"Compliments will get you everywhere."

"Shall we?"

Harry held the door and they scanned Luigi's. It was crowded, but there was a table near the window. Rudolpho waved his hand at the table. By the time they sat down, Rudolpho was there with the menus. Rudolpho was a competent, vinegary man, who that night had two red sauce spots on his ill-fitting jacket. She'd been coming there for years, but despite her winning manner, Rudolpho refused to be friendly. Beyond Rudolpho, fake grapes tangled in a ceiling trellis suspended over checkerboard tablecloths. White candles flickered in straw-dressed Chianti bottles.

She said, "Is Mario working tonight."

"No, no. His night off," said Rudolpho, starchly.

"Just as well. He always makes me something delicious and heavy. I'll have the pesto."

Harry said, "And I'll have the eggplant parm. Is the house Chianti okay, Frieda?"

"Fine. A bottle."

After Rudolpho left, Frieda scanned the crowd again. "It's good to see people here," she said finally. "I thought those new places would cut into their business."

Harry said, "I recognize some of the people. They've probably been coming here for years. They wouldn't go to Pasquale's or the Trattoria if you paid them."

"And as soon as they die, so will Luigi's."

"It's happened before."

Frieda shook her head, half-mournfully. "And we're right back talking about the fabled Kip's Bay renaissance. It's as if no one lived here before the gentry arrived."

Rudolpho arrived with the Chianti. He uncorked the bottle and left.

Harry filled both their wine glasses, and they both had a healthy gulp. The heat spread and she felt calmer. Harry looked good too—strong face, ice-blue eyes, long blond hair combed straight back. Still, she couldn't read him.

Frieda said, "Thanks for tonight."

"As I said, we can't act like kids forever. I still have reservations," Harry said, pleasantly.

"We both do. Should I ask you how it's going, or not?"

Harry frowned, shrugged. "You just asked. Two interviews yesterday. I sent out two more CVs today. So far nada. Today was a down day. I felt positive I'd never make it back."

Making it back—that was the theme. Whenever he talked about it, she always thought of where she would make it back to. Pre-psychotic ex-husband? Pre-HRA? Pre-college? The Bronx? Did she want to channel back to the Russian stetle where her grandfather, the architect, was born to the pigs, grime, and potatoes?

Harry would make it back. She knew it. He would rise through Kip's Bay like a phoenix, spread his middle-class wings, and fly back to his stolid destiny. Harry was positive and competent, definitely foreign to the HRA moms with the kids tugging on their skirts, blank-faced, worried their worker was going to stick it to them again.

She put her right hand over his. "You will make it. I know it and you know it."

Harry looked at her hand, turned it over, and stroked her fingers. It gave her a thrill she hadn't expected. "It better work out soon. I'm going crazy at the front desk."

"Was it worse than usual today?"

She could see Harry was relieved he could talk about something other than his job search. He took his hand away and took a sip of Chianti. He set his glass down. "What's there to say? It's a circus and Rudi's the ringmaster. I'm a stand-in."

"Rudi is a Polish Jewish watchmaker; the Rex is an anachronism. It's a perfect symbiosis."

"You think you know everyone's gripes and habits, then they change on you. A rash of people have left. Whitey Zero a week ago, Jane Burrows a few days ago. Who ever thought either would leave."

"One day we'll all leave."

"That's optimistic." Harry pulled back as Rudolpho slipped the eggplant in front of him. "We talk about it all the time. Few are chosen."

Frieda laughed. "The Rex is always good for a story."

Rudolpho slid the pesto in front of her. She took another sip of wine and watched Harry. Harry sliced up his eggplant, speared a square, and shoveled it into his mouth. Harry chewed, swallowed, then said, "How are the forms, welfare moms, and absent dads?"

She shrugged. "You don't want to know. That was our last fight, remember?"

"We didn't have many people on welfare in Wisconsin. Here it's an occupation."

Frieda backed away from that. "I just reread *The Plague*. Dr. Rieux reminds me of you."

"Naïve?"

"Not at all. An Arrowsmith, perhaps. Dedicated, hardworking, idealistic."

Harry laughed. "And egotistical, and a researcher. You don't know what kind of a doctor I was. I could have been clumsy, incompetent, and left forceps in my patients."

"I know you have a great bedside manner."

Harry laughed, and then frowned, as if he were thinking about why he laughed.

She finally got into her pesto. They ate silently for a few minutes.

Finally, she quit eating. She wasn't hungry anyway. She poured another glass of Chianti and watched the street. It was busy, still busy. A young well-dressed couple stopped outside Luigi's and read the menu tacked to the door. They glanced in Luigi's, squinted, and walked away.

"Take the rest," Frieda said. She pushed her plate towards Harry.

"You know me better than I do," said Harry. He made room for her plate, and then drew it towards him. He twirled his fork in the pesto.

She took a healthy swallow of Chianti. "Could we forget what happened last time? I miss talking to you, movies, the theatre."

"I don't know," said Harry. He watched her, his knife held like a lance.

She shook her head. "I guess I was trying to say that I miss *you*."

Harry looked sheepish. "I thought of calling, then didn't. You'd think I'd be assertive."

"The problems wouldn't go away," she said, surprising herself.

"Everyone has them. Maybe that's all we can expect."

She put her hand over his free one. "There won't be any problems tonight. Promise." Good. It was going to work—for a while. Maybe that's all she could expect.

Frieda made a pot of coffee. She was happy, upbeat, and smiling. It wasn't just Harry. A lot of it was of course. They'd become bed buddies, again. Rex sex. It was hot, harried, and comedic. Narrow beds, scuffling to get everything in sync. Groans. The random gasp of fulfillment. Frieda could almost see Sven across the hall, Ivan underneath, Mario and his Circle shaking their heads and smiling in their beers.

It wasn't just sex. She chatted with Harry at the desk and on the roof as she deadheaded wilting flowers, dug out stray weeds, and fertilized in her garden. It felt good to have some kind of certainty, some small bit of elusive security, some evasive iota of what her mother called creature comfort.

No, it wasn't just Harry that made her upbeat that morning. Yesterday, late in the afternoon, her boss, Tobius Minus called. He wanted to see her. Fleeing the centers was a vacation, although Central Office had its own brand of craziness. At least she wouldn't see the welfare grimness first hand. And she was going to take her time and relax in her garden. She hummed as she walked up the stairs to the roof past potting soil, garden implements, pots and seeds, careful not to spill the pot of coffee.

She stepped out onto the roof and into her garden.

Roof gardens had popped up all over Manhattan. But at the Rex, she couldn't chance a full-fledged garden with its multiple layers of sealers, trappers, gravels, and special soils. She was Frieda the Container Lady. Most plants were on raised pallets in large square wooden boxes, but she liked to improvise. She smiled at her shock troops across from the door—red and yellow roses—snarling up a verdigris trellis. She turned and walked slowly down the black tar beach path past plants wound elegantly around grinning cement satyrs and cupids, rusty railroad plates, and clay planters full of annuals. At the far end, the water tower was a kaleidoscope of white and purple morning glories, hooting orange trumpet flowers, and moon flowers, which hadn't at that time opened for business.

My baby, she thought. Crass, but true. For years, she was one with Woody Allen who said he and nature were two. She moved in a verbal space of neurotic, psychosomatic events, of time warped by personal craziness and crazy history until a run-of-the-mill geranium spit open in front of her, its pink poking through the bracts like a cat's nose. Since then, her garden had become her baby, her Zen, an oasis of peace in a strife-filled world.

The deck table with its bright yellow umbrella, which was square in the middle of the roof, looked clean and the yellow garbage pail was empty. That was good. She sat and poured herself a mug. Then she propped her feet on another deck chair and gave herself up to the morning. The sky was a pulsing golden cap over the city, the air thick and heavy. She smelled humus, roses, and a show-off honeysuckle. She could stay there all morning and night and let the crises out there build up and blow over. It didn't matter in the big picture. Why did she have to insert herself into the monotonous and irritating sine wave of welfare boondoggles?

The door swung open.

Ric Montes, paranoid Cuban cab driver, blinked at the sun and walked down the central path. He sat across from her. His restless brown eyes swung back-and-forth nervously under his straight brown hair like an erratic pendulum. Ric moved into the Rex a couple years before she did. It didn't take her long to get his story. It started with the high drama of the Bay of Pigs, and tapered off to Ric's paranoia about the CIA.

She'd put on her social worker cap and tried to talk him out of it. But no go. Thirty years after the Bay of Pigs his paranoia had become an old friend, the casting of daily events into the mold of disguise and surveillance Ric's status quo.

"Have some coffee," she said. "I'll get you a mug."

Ric glanced at the coffeepot. "No thanks."

Ric stared at the door to the roof, but he was quiet. Frieda convinced herself she could deal with him. Then that same door swung wide again. Mario and Bel held coffee mugs in one hand and shielded their eyes from the blazing sun with the other. They stumbled towards her table. The sounds of Mario's Circle had drifted through the Rex at midnight pawing at her sleep like a cat.

"Okay, you win," she said, getting up. She addressed the three. "I know you want to help, but don't water during the day, and please stay on the paths and pick up when you leave." She felt like a mother. She had found weird things in her garden. Besides the occasional wine bottle, beer can, or cigarette butt in her Gerber daisies, she'd found parts of dolls, and, once, a shrine made of pieces of blue cloth and glass, as if misplaced Bower Bird was trying to attract a mate.

"I couldn't water if I had to," said Mario, sitting down. He held his head with both hands. "I promise myself each day, it'll be different. Then at night—"

"Ditto," said Bel. "It's called a rut." Bel flopped down opposite Ric. She balanced her head on her hand. Her dark brows drooped; her eyes were cracked, red marbles.

"Help yourself," said Frieda. "I'll get the pot later."

Frieda was barely able to hide her disappointment. She took a last look at the southern end of her garden and the water tower, turned, and walked down the central path and then down the stairs.

It took her half an hour to dress. Then she walked through Sven's gallery for the third time that morning. Elevator. Lobby. She raced through the lobby and turned towards Park Avenue. She was in the morning groove and the letdown on the roof was replaced with a cheery feeling. She liked seeing Toby. She called him every few days, but saw him infrequently. She knew one thing: She had to tell him about the code 333 cases. She would have researched those cases without bothering him, except Rodriguez was in a frenzy. He asked people—Mona and

Johnny—what she was doing with them, what she'd found out. It was time Toby knew about them.

She started to walk—it would have been a pleasant cross-town hike—but the heat changed her mind in the short block to Park Avenue. She waved down a cab. Ten minutes later she stood in front of Central Office.

The CO building was a sprawling thirty-story Art Deco building. It housed warrens of shifting departments with sub-warrens of cubicles where scribes shifted paperwork ceaselessly from box to box. HRA Investigations and Toby' office—and a desk she shared with Ramon Menes, whom she'd seen twice—was located on the twelfth floor where they had a view of the bustle of Fourteenth Street and of Eighth Avenue.

She got coffee from the Lego Café. She took the elevator—full of office workers, managers, assistant managers, gold trim, and chevrons—to twelve. There were differences between the intake room at IM66 and that huge piss yellow room at CO with its smell of just-sharpened pencils, gray desks, and busy people with loud voices. The most obvious was that almost all the workers at IM66 were black or Hispanic, and the program heads, managers, and supervisors at CO were white. The irony was not lost on her. She'd given up trying to justify her own position, or complicity. It was unfair when she got there twenty years ago and it would be unfair when she left.

She walked around the periphery of the room, past several conference rooms, where people waved their hands and talked of some welfare Armageddon or another. Finally, she walked into Toby's office ready for another skirmish in the unending war pitting human nature against bureaucratic inefficiency.

"Mr. Minus." She pulled up a chair and dropped her bag next to it.

Toby swiveled in his chair and regarded her from behind a desk that was a garbage dump of papers and forms. "Frieda."

Toby always looked rumpled and he looked rumpled that day. His flop of graying hair was alternately spiky and matted and was set off by an untrimmed moustache that hung past his chin like dark stalactites. His clothes looked slept in and a striped shirt ballooned out of an open vest and suspenders. Toby was a bachelor with a Ph.D. in English from Columbia. He'd tried teaching and didn't like it. He tried the rat race and didn't like that. And he ended up, like many of her friends, in HRA, where after many years of infighting and politics he became Director of HRA Investigations, which he did like, sometimes.

Toby was politic, calm, saw clients as pawns in a big game chess game, and liked solving problems. She was explosive, thought clients were people, and used intuition to feel which center director was teetering on the edge of sanity, or who was engineering a food stamp kickback. They were a perfect couple. If nothing else, Toby was on the right side.

Toby rested his arms on his belly and pyramided his fingers. "IM66," he said, as if it were a complete statement.

"Why?" she said, curious. She let that sit between them, while she dug in her bag for smokes. She found one, took it out, and lit it. She blew a stream of smoke away from him. It rolled out then settled in the air like a cloud on a windless day. "It was to park me, wasn't it?"

Toby shook his head and deflected her question. "Please."

"I know it's about Waverly."

Toby was testy. "You—we—walk on a razor's edge. When you find things are wrong you go off like a bulldog on meth. You have to sift, find the right course. Getting HRA into the papers again and getting a center director fired is not the right way. If we'd waited, we could have pressured her to make changes."

Frieda felt testy herself. "Right. The department covers up what it's been doing, the director gets a reprimand, then goes right back to doing what he or she did before."

Toby's grimace told her she was right, but it didn't make her feel better. "Not all the time."

"She deserved it. Besides, I'm honing my diplomatic skills. I have Rodriguez, after all. That man is not right. I have a feeling."

"Your fabled intuition." Toby stared over her head. "Fishing is much easier. I wait for hours, even days before I catch anything. It's called patience. Then I throw them back."

Frieda coughed to get his attention. Toby quit musing and looked at her. "HRA Investigations is not a sport," she said, too primly. "We're not supposed to nail idiots who make their own rules, let them go, and then compliment ourselves on our expertise."

Toby grunted. "I'm reassigning you to IM34."

She cocked her head at him, stunned. "What? Why? Is that why you wanted to see me?"

Toby shook his head, tiredly. "Please. I quote Frieda Berg. 'Toby, please reassign me. The commute is a killer and they treat me like hot death.'"

"True," she said, relaxing into the chair. He'd caught her that time. But she wasn't ready to go. "Thanks. But I have to solve a riddle first."

"Even if I tell you to go?"

That surprised her. "Are you?"

Toby sighed. "Of course not. I try to do things for you and I get harassed. Okay, I sent you to IM66 because of its closure rate. What's the riddle?"

"It may not be about IM66 at all. It may be about Rodriguez."

Toby picked up his coffee and took a sip. He tilted his mug and stared at the bottom as if he were staring at tea leaves. His hands were large, almost pudgy. He had thick cuticles, one dirty nail, and two that needed paring. "You've told me about the harsh protocols and the weird center rules such as that missing Fair Hearing form. What else?"

Behind her, she heard the crackle of papers, and the pontificating tones of HRA managers. She supposed there was a meeting next door on how to implement a new federal directive on food stamps or the latest crisis in the field or, more likely, what the new org chart would look like when a sub-manager retired. The phrase "blowing in the wind" stuck in her mind. She had signed on with HRA in the seventies before she met Ron. She was eager to help people, to get them into programs, to fight for their rights. Her idealism had been remorselessly eroded since, if not by the attitudes, if not by Reagan/Bush, then by the bureaucracy and everyone roping off their tiny piece of turf. She felt hope with Clinton, but he would fail too. She knew it.

She told Toby about the IMD 209 Rose handed her, the mystery code, the deletions from the database, and the missing case records. She told him that Rodriguez tried to get those cases away from her. "I've talked to everyone from Fulvous Meridian to Jerry Marguiles and no one knows a thing. You know Jerry, he's a liaison to Computer Operations."

Toby started looking grave. "I know him."

"Guess what he said."

Minus lidded his eyes. "Quit playing games. What?"

"'Which database?'"

Toby frowned. "What does that mean?"

45

"The Money Management Monitor, the Triple M, HRA's new computer system."

Toby stared at her. She had his attention. "What about converting cases or parallel testing?"

"Said he didn't know one iota about the new system. Contracted out to Oracle and IBM. All our programmers do is clip coupons, fix the old system, and play games."

She'd visited Computer Operations. There were many posters of Dilbert, many games of Mortal Kombat and Myst. Molecules of programmers stood around talking bits, bytes, baseball, and the latest Detroit tank. Farming out the new system might have been a good thing.

Toby reached into his desk, took out his pipe, and turned it over in his hands. Finally, he looked at her. "Outsourcing, new systems no one knows a rat's ass about." Toby wrinkled his nose, as if he'd smelled sulfur. "You know it's time to retire, when you can *feel* things are wrong."

"That's what I'm supposed to say. Special Projects is working with the new system. Isn't that where that fuck Morty Bennet landed?"

Toby's eyes rotated to a spot on the wall behind her. He was silent for a good ten seconds. "I think so," said Toby. "Morty and a few hand-picked friends, Theo Dryseck, someone Milan."

Morty Bennet was anti-client, mayoral shill, a cutthroat PR man. "I thought he resigned two years ago, but he pops up in the weirdest places like a jack-in-the-box. How did he get there?"

Toby waved her smoke away. "Kelso is a good man, but sometimes has poor judgment."

She reserved her opinion of Kelso. He was the head of IM, an ex-Army bureaucrat who knew exactly squat about welfare. "Judas Priest. If Morty's involved, I'll—"

"Don't worry about what you can't help. This code 333 could be a conversion issue. If it's not and if the intent is to wipe Joan Q out of the system, why send out a form?"

Frieda shrugged. "A mistake or a show of following routine."

Toby shook his head no. "We don't have a conspiracy yet."

"But the real case record is gone—ten of them." For the first time in weeks, Frieda felt jazzed. Routine fuckups were one thing; mysteries added a spark to her day. "There might be a log-jam of HR recipients with mystery codes and missing records."

Toby shook his head in agreement. "If they don't have case records and they're not in the database, it will be tough. We have to wait for clients to complain."

"What about an ad in the paper?"

Toby snapped his suspenders. His stare made her feel guilty. "Please. We have suspicions and a few scraps of paper."

"I know, go slow," Frieda said. She tried to mask her irritation.

"Don't go to the papers," Toby said, leaning on "don't." He hunched his trunk forward and the bristles on his shaggy eyebrows almost disguised eyes, which were steady, serious. "Everyone is in an uproar for a day and then it's over and nothing has changed."

"It seems to work that way. You see how important this is."

"I can see it's important without you telling me," said Toby. Toby relaxed in his chair, as if he'd just settled a dispute and was ready to be rational and reasonable. "We can still flail our aged limbs. I'll check with the rest of our staff and Computer Operations. Don't give up on making IM66 toe the line. They're one of the worse centers, if not the worst."

Frieda grimaced. "Okay." She dropped her cigarette into what was left of her coffee, and dropped the cup in the wastebasket. As she was getting up, she noticed the Catskills Real Estate brochure tucked in a pile on Toby's desk. She'd checked that real estate company years ago with Ron, when they were thinking of buying upstate. Seeing it sitting there brought back the debacle of her marriage. She picked up her bag, vaguely depressed, saluted Toby, turned, and trooped out. Two weeks ago, she would have killed to get back to Manhattan. And she'd stuck herself back in IM66. Rose, code 333. She had a feeling code 333 was linked to something else, something important. She would find what it was.

Outside, she watched a flotilla of cabs bunch up on red. They seemed angry, bursting with unfocussed energy. Explosion, release. The rhythm of life. From time to time, she thought she understood that rhythm. Other times, understanding eluded her. Then there was the practical part, the doing part. Perhaps, she thought, as she walked slowly and deliberately towards the Number 3 at Fourteenth Street, solving HRA messes, her grab bag of routines, certainly her garden, were substitutes, not-too-subtle decoys of her failure to hook into that rhythm.

Frieda shrugged that thought off as she dropped her token in the tollbooth.

47

6

"D istortion," said Bel Benaventura. She sipped a whiskey and soda and set the glass carefully on the end table. "My life has been a distortion from beginning to end. I shouldn't be here, but here I am. 'Bel Benaventura: The Hope and the Pity.' Right after Oprah."

Mario was right, Bel had mellowed. It didn't mean she wanted to hang out with her. But that day was different. As for Bel's story, Marcy had always felt incidental to it. Bel's mother, Martha, had died so quickly all Marcy remembered was graying auburn hair, powdered pink skin, big rings, and Martha's Bichon Frisee, Claire. The estate was divided between Brenda, Bel's sister, a small bequest to Marcy, and a batch of charities and nonprofits, including a hefty donation to the SPCA. The one thing Marcy remembered about Martha and Bel, explaining en passant Bel's being cut out of the will, was that Martha didn't like Ray or his art, at all. "He's an angry drunk," she'd told Bel. "And those stinking, ugly paintings. Why doesn't he paint something nice?" Bel never gave an inch in those run-ins. "Like a wall?" Bel used to say. "Or Long Island sunsets?"

Stubbornness and a trip temper were Martha's legacy, and it looked like Bel had passed them on to Marcy. But she hadn't dropped by room 602 to listen to Bel tap the one-note. Bel was sitting in a burgundy-colored stuffed chair wedged between the alcove and a table, on which was a pile of manuscripts and a note Marcy couldn't read. The alcove was messy with dirty cups and a stray spoon. Marcy had taken the single bed with its burgundy and burnt orange patchwork quilt. Bel lit a cigarette and the powder puffs of smoke matched, above Bel's shoulder and out the window, cotton ball clouds in the pale blue sky past the Olympia.

Bel's room was full of time bombs. There were photos of Bel and Ray in the Hamptons on the chest-of-drawers in the corner, and, of course, Ray's self-portrait, in reds and oranges, a vintage Ivan Albright, which made Ray seem more Dorian Gray than Ray Benaventura. It hung over the bed and was the spiritual center of that room. Whenever she glanced at it, she felt a tremor, as if the murky history of the Benaventuras had landed in her head. It wasn't just the photos and painting. The closet was

48

stuffed with flapper dresses, white sheaths, black feather boas, fantasy pumps, and stiletto heels, none of which had been worn in years. Bel and Ray had been a fun couple—on the tag end of some "A" list once—who barely thought of themselves as a family. Marcy Benaventura was a bauble trotted out on stage for a brief display, then hurriedly sequestered in their huge flat.

Booze was a big part of their act in their glory years. But two years after Ray died, Ray was still there, a spirit linking those old times with Bel's drinking. Marcy wondered, vaguely, whether her own temptations, the drugs and booze and wild times last year, weren't a physical offshoot, or spiritual eddy, of the rise and fall of Bel and Ray Benaventura.

"I was guessing when I said you'd blown your inheritance on your trip. Any left?" said Bel, glancing at her quickly. Bel picked up her glass, took a sip, and carefully put it back on the table.

"It wasn't much," said Marcy. "The trip helped me clear my head."

She was just talking, the words floating out without volition. She was antsy, full of trepidation one minute, anticipation the next. Her breasts felt jelly-loose and her sex itched. She had a date with Butch, a sculptor she'd met at the Seaport. Bel was just a roadblock she'd put between herself and committing herself to the night.

"I think that happened to me," Bel said. "Now I don't remember. Something wonderful happens, the stars line up, and just as it's coming together, it slips away like a phantom. I could blame Ray. He was handsome, fun, a dynamite painter, and dirt-poor. I'd be on Park Avenue right now, if I hadn't married him. Our love was 'in a hut, with water and a crust.'"

"Ray shouldn't have died so young." Shit. She wanted a dull, normal conversation and she ended up face-to-face with the specter of her father. He was a strong rangy man, violent when he drank, but never with her. But the cancer. She remembered a thin frame, rivulets of lank, dark hair, which spilled over his wasted handsome face, a green bottle of oxygen framed against an apartment that was huge and full of Ray's paintings. She'd spent time roaming through that apartment alone. Then, in a few months—the worst months for the Benaventuras—Ray died, they lost the apartment, most of Ray's paintings got lost in a moving van fiasco, and she and Bel moved to the Rex.

"Starting and ending points. You worry when they feel the same."

Marcy knew she should shut up. "Talk to Brenda."

Bel gave her a venomous glance; her hand shook as she took another sip. "I suppose I'd be as greedy as she is. But I don't have that option."

"You could move. Start over."

"It always comes up. Right now, I'm trapped here. I try to be philosophical, but then spite or hate or whatever steps in and I find myself crying in my beer. I know it's counter-productive—isn't that the buzzword de jour—but I can't help it. Maybe it's what I'm about. Wouldn't it be boring if we were all alike, everyone as calm, well-adjusted, and productive as a colony of bees."

"That sounds like Ray."

"It's my rationalization now. It makes me feel fine and spiteful. Why not? I'm good at it. At least I can say that about something." Bel took a long swallow and placed it on a coaster.

Marcy remembered what Mario said. "What about those guys."

"They're a bunch of morons. They've been invisible since their run-in with Mario. Still."

"Maybe Rudi let his standards slip. I told you about this guy who wanted my room."

Bel frowned. "We talked about that. But nothing else has happened. I can't think what would happen. Rudi runs the hotel. Forget about it. It's Mario's Circle time. Come up, you can play Edna Ferber to my Dorothy Parker. Just don't mention Brenda."

Marcy thought about the Circle and what it would be like to watch Mario and Bel go into their booze routine. If she had time, she wouldn't go. "I don't have time."

"Where are you going?

Marcy looked at Bel and decided it didn't matter. "I've got a date."

"Tell me, so I can gossip."

Marcy shrugged. "A sculptor I met at the Seaport." She'd been doing sketches, caricatures of tourists, at Pier 17. The Pier was a small mall with three stories of shops and restaurants, but the view of the Brooklyn Bridge and river made it a tourist magnet. She'd hung out there before her trip and knew some of the artists. The Pier staff let them keep their gear in a small maintenance room near the main entrance. It took a few days before she knew everybody and they seemed to accept her, although she didn't exactly do their kind of sketches. Hers were more imaginative with what Mindy, who always did smiling caricatures of her subjects striding across the New York skyline, called a hint of the bizarre or grotesque. Lone pine over the shoulder. Bleak landscapes. Any weird costumes that came into her head. The others were surprised she made money. But a certain kind of person liked her skewed Scarfe faces or grotesque Steadman landscapes.

She'd just put down her charcoal to watch Donna, who did caricatures at parties, whip out five-minute caricatures of a family from Dallas, when she noticed Butch. He was negotiating for a pile of scrap metal with a construction foreman across Fulton. She liked the way he looked, his muscles, and his trimness. The metal deal didn't work out and he must have sensed her interest. He watched the other street artists for a few minutes. Then he watched her. She wasn't sure what they talked about when he came over, except that when he asked her out she said yes.

"You're too old to take advice. I suppose," said Bel, glancing at her.

Marcy laughed, grimly. "An advice column is *way* too late."

Bel winced. "At least you've gotten away from that guitar player."

She thought about Mickey, about getting pregnant, what he said. "Mickey was a creep."

"And knocked you up. It's an old story. Time to go."

Marcy flushed, glanced quickly at Bel. Bel didn't care about the abortion. A wave of regret washed over her.

Marcy took the elevator to one. She glanced at the guy sitting in the chair across from the desk clerk's half-oval. He was fat, hairy and stared at her. It was a bug-eyed, hostile stare. She almost marched back and asked him what his problem was, but she didn't want to start the night on the wrong note. She ignored him and slipped out the door of the Rex. But despite the thrill of the night, the anticipation, she couldn't quite get rid of that scene in the lobby. It hooked up later, much later, with a fight in the Moat, and with the guy who wanted her room. She wasn't sure what it was, but she was starting to feel edgy when she walked into the Rex.

Marcy took the subway to Astor Place, and hiked through the East Village towards the Alphabet avenues and the Zoo, a bar between Avenue A and B across from Thompkins Square. The Zoo had been there since the pre-Cambrian. You could sit in the second-hand stuffed chairs or sofas and look out big plate glass windows onto the park, and wonder which side was the zoo.

One last glance in the Zoo's window on First Avenue. Burgundy lipstick, a hint of blush, boobs nice and jutting—if he wanted melons, he was shit of out luck—super-short shorts, showing her slender knock-out legs, black pumps. If he didn't have an erection in the first minute, he was gay. She gulped, shouldered her brown, beaded bag, and took the leap.

It was an old bar and still attracted serious artist-cum-drunks who mixed with the scraggly punk crowds. The bar was full and Butch wasn't in front. She headed towards the back where a punk band, the Black Mambos, were setting up. She found Butch on a sofa across from a plate-glass window. You couldn't tell he was over six feet the way he hunched down in the sofa. He had a square head, short black hair and beard, straight sharp nose, brown eyes, which she remembered were amused or serious, never flat, and a single gold earring. His skinny T showed off muscles, which she supposed he got by wrestling metal into sculpture.

She went back to the bar and got a beer. A few minutes later, she sat down on her end of the sofa. Butch looked at her with a crooked smile. Then he took a swig of beer, balanced the pint on the arm of the sofa, and settled into the cushions. "I forgot what you looked like," he said.

"I remembered the outlines, the body, the black hair. I remember now," said Marcy.

"At least we were able to find each other." He smiled mischievously and glanced at her breasts and bare legs. Inspection over, he watched her expectantly.

She felt examined, but wasn't that what this was about? Her sex started itching again. She wanted to leave or jump him and get it over with. "I've been coming here since I borrowed my first ID. You can make stories of people in the square, living there, walking through, having fights, or copping drugs. Something's always happening." Marcy tucked her legs underneath her, took a sip of beer. A couple with red spiky hair watched her their faces pressed against the window.

"People in Manhattan are seduced by the surface," said Butch. "I like to dig deeper, find out what's happening with me, or with people. Or you."

She returned his stare. "What about me."

Butch raised a dark eyebrow. "Your sketches are weird, grotesque, that's what. You must be projecting your own dark background."

Butch was a syllable away from pissing her off. What was behind her sketches? She'd always thought she was imitating her father—his art had always been grotesque, an American Roger Bacon—but then there was her footloose history last year. The other street artists thought she was Steadman, Scarfe, or Taylor Jones incarnate, that she had a streak of Brit bitchiness. It was more than that. "People are blasé, ready to sugar-coat who they are or what they've done."

"You're talking in the abstract," said Butch, laughing. "What is *your* dark side?"

"That'll wait for date number two. Do you always grill people you've just met?"

"I don't like to waste time. Sometimes—too often really—the relationship stays on the surface, meaningless talk time makes important."

"I'll settle for small talk, tonight. Who are you? Where do you come from? It doesn't have to be a dissertation."

"This one time." He told her, in that voice people use when they're reciting, about his parents, about dropping-out of the San Francisco Art Institute, an art school in LA, and Cooper Union. He didn't like taking orders or being pushed in any direction and he'd never fit in those places. He was happy being on his own, living with his own obsessions. As he talked, she began to like him again, to feel what those what-if stares at Pier 17 were about.

Then it was her turn. She gave him the essentials of growing up in Kip's Bay, of her edgy connection to her mother, of Bel being cut out of her mother's will. "When dad died, we moved to an old hotel called the Rex. When I got my inheritance, I left, played in the East Village for a year. Then I got pregnant and left."

Butch looked puzzled. "Are you still pregnant?"

"Does it look like it? I took care of it. Problem?"

Butch looked abashed, then amused. "Do you take prisoners?"

"No place to put 'em."

Everything was going wrong. She was too hard and so was he. She supposed it would have ended there, if the Black Mambos hadn't started warming up and Butch upped the stakes.

"You want to see my studio? You'll like it."

She could have said no. She could have arranged another date, seen a movie, or eaten dinner, but she wanted something to happen. Right then. "Let's go."

He looked at her, as if he expected her to say no. Then he smiled. She started feeling a lot better about the night. They killed their drinks and wound their way through what had become a typical Zoo crowd of punks and dreadlocks. A man with a beard at the end of the bar glanced at the crowd, and wrote furiously in his journal.

Outside it was warm, the streets crowded, the glow from the street-lights in Thompkins Square covering it like a dome. They walked through the square, which was reaching its own boozy, drugged peak, and out of the glow into the dark alphabet avenues. A few blocks in, they stopped in front of a barn of a place, which she used to pass on her way to different points in the avenues. It looked like an old service garage. Marcy crossed her mental fingers, as she'd done a couple of times that night, and took the plunge.

Inside, it was full of junk. It was a maze of tanks, welders, and an A-frame hoist. But Butch's junk had more organization than your average dump. There were thin Giacometti-like figures, Henry Moore-type bio-morphic pieces, abstract iron sculptures with cutout circles and spidery legs. It looked like he couldn't make up his mind on a style.

Butch looked her over and said. "Mind helping me move a piece?"

The piece was a soft painted lump, half-Moore, half-pornographic. It looked like a big limp cock. It was even called "Soft Cock." Looking at it got her hot. She supposed that was the point. It was bulky, not heavy, and they placed it near a sofa, which anchored what looked like a bunch of rooms laid out along a wall.

She was trying to get the feel for the studio/living space when Butch lit a candle, which made spiky shadows near his bed. He produced designer vodka, poured two shots, and they sat on a sofa, which looked out over his field of junk. Car lights shone in the garage door windows and rotated shadows through rebar, fenders, and a stand of steel plate. She had to pay attention to what was going on between her and Butch, but the light and shadows mesmerized her. There was a black sheet on the side of windows, which, she supposed, he used to block out the light.

"You want to stay," said Butch, looking her up and down and grinning. He tossed back a shot. His face turned pale in the light from a passing car.

Her legs glowed in the half-light. She tried to imagine what it would be like to have them spread, to have Butch inside her, to have his body pressing down on her. Trying to imagine it made her too hot. She picked up the shot glass and downed her shot in one gesture. She felt the vodka burn all the way down. The vodka was vile, but she liked the gesture. She was sure she would remember that vodka and shot glass beyond Butch, down some far-off road snatching at memories, the way Bel snatched at memories of Ray or of some distant Bel full of piss and hope. She'd already decided that Butch was not a mass murderer, a serial killer, or a deviant. She wanted it, but she was afraid of it. She wanted excitement, but not melodrama.

"Why not," she said.

She put down her shot glass, slipped off her shoes, which surprised Butch, and crawled over the sofa, which seemed to surprise him even more. She grabbed him by the sides of his neck and kissed him. He kissed back. Then her tongue was in his mouth. His mouth was a strange mixture of beer and an iron-like taste, as if he'd been eating metal. He put his hand on her breast and kneaded it and she felt herself getting off on it.

His sex got hard against the side of her hip and she reached down and stroked it. Good. Seemed big and hard enough for a good fuck. His beard was rough, his tongue wet, his head a shadow on the wall. He took his mouth off hers and gently stroked the curve of her breast. Her nipples strained against her blouse. "You can take the bed and I'll sleep here, if you want," he said.

She laughed. "Are you kidding? Let's go Romeo."

She untangled herself, took his hand, and walked past a wall of books, a stereo system hemmed in by racks of CDs, towards what looked like a bed near the far wall. Waterbed. Cool. She hadn't seen one for years. Then there was the play of tugging and poking, the stray giggle—wasn't it funny, after all, cocks and pussies collaborating as if they were pulling off a cosmic act. But it felt good being back in the saddle after that finger fantasizing. Besides, "Soft Cock" was close enough to prick her imagination.

After the foreplay, there was the real thing. She felt his cock thick in her sex, his muscles, and his stroke, which started out slow and came hard and fast. She knew he was going to come before she did, and planted her finger under his stomach, and pushed her G spot.

She jerked and screamed. She held him tight, forcing him to come. But he wanted to play. He backed up, slowed down, then pumped her for another five minutes. Then he came on strong again. She clasped him tighter and tighter and finally he came in one lancing thrust.

When he quieted down, she saw her pale legs over his back, ankles crossed, pointed to the right and left of the candle which burned bright on a shelf. She unhooked herself and they grinned at each other. It looked like they both got what they wanted. Butch came out, rolled off, and went to bathroom. When he came back he tugged on her foot so she could use the bathroom too.

She didn't remember much of the rest of the night, except, after they fell asleep, she woke up. The candle threw spiky shadows through piles and piles of junk and art.

She walked naked past "Soft Cock." The junk fascinated her. Junk, garbage, detritus was about what was beyond the spiffy surface. What was unreal was thinking that life is a wedding cake that never gets old, stale, and full of bugs. Or that couples stay glued together forever. Or that fender would stay shiny and new and not become old, rusted, and bent. Garbage was a slap of reality. Why did it fascinate her? Of course in Butch's case junk was just the beginning. He was the ultimate recycler.

She wandered through Butch's junk. She felt the rusty edges of his pipe and felt the A-frame hoist he used to boss the big stuff around. It was like walking through the inside of his head, trying to feel where all that re-bar and six-inch pipe fit into a grand scheme. She supposed if she were around more than a night, she would guess about what he was going to do with each piece.

Butch hadn't decided on one style, but he wasn't linear. He liked to bend metal into soft shapes. He had a full deck of testosterone and a lady's touch. Butch puzzled her, but she decided it was a good puzzlement. As for Marcy Benaventura, the grand sum of that night, the punch line, was that she'd planted another piling deep in the spiritual bedrock. The Odyssey, the Rex, Butch.

She felt good about that, about all of it. Her heart was light and she almost felt like singing. Especially about Butch. Marcy Benaventura was back. She was back in the game, a sex game, and a connection game. It was a game she knew was fraught with problems, missteps, and mistakes.

It was better than no game at all.

7

W hy so secretive," said Jeanie Jarvis. "What does 'hotel management' mean anyway?"

Jack Kuhl wanted Jeanie to go away. He had a lot of work that day.
He had to call his agents, hire another one, and see Lansky. He'd gotten
up early, padded down the condo's staircase, made coffee, and opened the
drapes. The light had illuminated the Tribeca condo in all its modernist,
spare glory with its white walls, hardwood floors, white leather sofa, and
blond-and-silver kitchen. It was a far cry from the warm Spanish colors of
his house in San Diego. Of course, it was even further from his boxy room
at the Amsterdam hotel. The only splashes of color were an elephant palm
near the door, and a garish LeRoy Neiman, "Olympic Track," in flashing
reds and yellows in the work nook.

He'd headed to the nook, took out Sammy's file, and sifted résumés. "Résumés"—that was rich. He was sure Sammy wasn't his real
name. From what Lansky told him, Sammy was a lawyer who had connections in the underworld and supplied ex-cons for everything from
murder to mayhem. For the Rex project, Sammy had given him twenty
résumés—read rap sheets—of older, white ex-cons who needed a bit of
money. He'd already interviewed and hired seven. He hoped to hire the
last one that day.

He'd found a good prospect for his last agent, when he heard the
shower. He knew Jeanie would soon turn on the dryer, come down, press
her lips against his forehead, and leave. But no. She came down, grabbed
the paper, and set up at the table under the staircase, as if she were going
to stay a week. He'd covered the résumé he'd chosen, poured another cup
of coffee, sat on the sofa, and told her he had a lot to do. So far she hadn't
fielded the clue. So far she'd done a yeoman's job of harassing him.

Jack sipped coffee and stared at the window. His reflection showed
him fashionably rumpled, his hair mussed, his profile strong. He supposed if he checked a mirror, he'd see the details—the straight nose,
the lambent brown eyes, the waves of brown hair, and the casual arched
eyebrows. He looked the same as he did last week, last year, three years
ago. The Club Fed at Lompoc hadn't taken his looks away.

"Jack are you still here."

Jack turned and glanced at Jeanie. She was in her bathrobe, her hair puffed out like a sea urchin, her muscular legs tucked up, and her high-arched feet hidden. She looked tousled, the haystack marred by a single curl edging towards her neck.

He forgot it was his turn. What had she said? Hotel management consultant. That's what Lansky called it. Jack called his goons "agents." They all played games with words. He supposed he could come up with a security reason for calling them agents, but it was mostly to assuage his own conscience. "I'm defining the job. It's the latest trend."

Jeanie looked up, frowned. "Is it investment counseling like KAM?"

When he first met Jeanie, he was vague about his past. Then, gradually, the whole tawdry tale of Kuhl Asset Management emerged. The heady times with millions of dollars in the bank, the wife, the expensive vacations, the Jaguar, the house in San Diego, the getaway in the Sierras were, very reluctantly, matched with the downfall, the trial for fraud, the sentencing, and finally the two years in Lompoc. Oddly, she loved it, especially the part about being in Lompoc, the same Club Fed as Ivan Boesky and Michael Milkin. "No Jeanie. It's management...of hotels that have problems. How's the horoscope?"

"First you ignore me, then I'm predictable." Jeanie rustled the papers. Her bright red fingernail scratched down the column.

"Horoscopes are worse than fortune cookies." Jack hooked his ankles on the table. His reflected image balanced between his crossed feet. A smokestack on the far side of the Hudson jutted out of his right toe. "They should add in broken legs and car accidents."

"Who wants to read about broken legs? Mine says, 'Gemini. This is your lucky day. Keep options open'." Jeanie looked up. A challenging expression spread over her face. "I guess that means options in men."

Jeanie was a hostess at Carismo's, a chic restaurant near Times Square. When she wasn't working, she danced for Muriel Dankin's Troupe on the upper West Side a couple of blocks from her apartment. She'd appeared in two off-Broadway musicals. She was an accessory he couldn't have afforded two months ago. "This early," Jack said. "We hardly know each other."

Jeanie folded the paper. "Don't worry yet, Jack. You've got a couple of good days left."

"Speaking of jobs and titles. You're free, you're emancipated, you're a nineties woman. 'Options' means you should ask Bobo to be manager." Carismo's owner liked Jeanie. He would have asked already.

"What a laugh."

"So he says no."

"It wouldn't work. I know it," said Jeanie, frowning.

"You pretend you're free and emancipated, but you stay on the bottom."

"Only with you, Jack," she said, licking her lips.

Jack snickered. "Then walk up and tell him you want it."

Jeanie shook her head no. "What are you doing today?"

"I'll decide when you leave." Jack said, hoping she'd take the hint.

"I should get ready," said Jeanie, looking up. Jeanie made a face at him, got up, and clattered up the stairs. Jack watched her buttocks sway, the material bunching on the upswing and releasing on the down. He almost followed her up, but then he went back to staring at his crossed feet, the thread of New Jersey connecting his little toes.

Jeanie's heels clacked down the staircase. He felt her lips on the side of his forehead.

"You want to meet for lunch at Carismo's?" Jack said, impulsively.

Jeanie brightened. "Love to, lover."

Jeanie sauntered to the door, and waved goodbye, as if she'd dismissed other "options."

Jack got up and strolled to the work nook. He popped open the laptop—it was the one thing they hadn't taken in KAM's bankruptcy; he had his father send it when Lansky tapped him for the Rex—booted it, and brought up the Rex Project. The Rex. After Lew missed the room on four, they got lucky when two long-term residents left. A week ago, Truck and Bert moved in. Yesterday, he'd sent Tim and Jimmy to get rooms. One more agent and he could start. It looked like it was going to be Wayne "Blondie" Reynolds. According to his résumé, he was a reformed crackhead and a hacker. A programmer. Blondie had spent time upstate and a couple years on Riker's for misdemeanor drug charges.

He let the details of the Rex diagram marinate in his head for a few minutes. Then he called Ace and Max. Since they beat up Whitey Zero, he called them every day and made sure they behaved. Then he called Bert and Truck. They funneled him more details on residents, who they were, what they did. Lots of duplication. Don and the others had already done their job.

He spent a couple hours tweaking the project. Tap, tap, tap. One room, two rooms, three...a floor. The floors were filling out. Phase 2. That's when he'd see if the project was going to work.

Towards noon, feeling expansive, he closed the laptop and strolled to the window. A boat made a sluggish trough up the Hudson. He felt like that boat a few months ago, laboring against the current, fighting waves of depression and hopelessness. But that was over, except, he cautioned himself, his new start depended on the Rex project working. First he had doubts about the project and then he couldn't wait for it to start.

Jack showered and dressed in Docker khakis, a white shirt, and new Mephisto street shoes. He looked casual and he looked good. He narrowed his eyes and pursed his lips. His long molded face looked perfect. It was pure conceit, but he'd always wondered where he'd be if his father, Leo, had made it as an actor. He would have been an actor's son. He'd have connections. He'd be a star. Wasn't that the dream?

Could I have your autograph, Jack?

Jack smirked at his conceit.

He locked the door and left. At the last minute, he turned towards Duane Park. At noon, the park was a going concern. The homeless woman with the brown wool cap rummaged through her shopping cart touching pots, a broom, tin cans, a hula-hoop, and two Starbucks coffee cups. A dozen office workers from the buildings around Duane Square juggled sandwiches in their laps. A band of pigeons, iridescent necks flicking on and off, roamed beneath the benches pecking at scraps. A sleepy tourist mouth open in an "o" dozed in the sun. The tourist kept his arm tight around his packages—*he'd* heard about thieves in New York.

When he reached Hudson Street, Jack raised his hand and snapped his fingers. A cab veered across the street towards him. Fifteen minutes later, he told the cab to park down the street from the Rex. He turned and watched the entrance. On the steps leading to the open door a big guy with a tangle of curly hair talked to a serious small man with glasses propped in his hair. A woman with short hair, dark brows, and good legs walked out of the Moat and joined the men.

The small man was probably Rudi Lopwitz, part owner and manager. Soon, he'd know who the others were. Soon, they'd have a room in his Rex diagram. Soon, he would know more about them than they knew about their neighbors.

Jack ordered the cab driver to Carismo's. He glanced in the driver's rear view mirror as the cab sped up Twenty-eighth Street. The Rex wavered and disappeared.

If only it were that easy.

Jack ate a late lunch at Carismo's. Jeanie was busy, so Bobo, the owner, came over and chatted. Baseball, the weather, global warming, Clinton's cabinet, and blah, blah, blah. It was a smorgasbord of topics, which made him feel good, more substantial. Carismo's, Jeanie, Bobo were the real world, real businesses, real bottom-lines, and real profits. How real was hotel management consulting?

Towards the end of lunch, he started thinking about the rest of the afternoon. He had to interview Wayne Reynolds and see Lansky. He had a lot on his plate.

Ten minutes after he finished lunch, he walked into Harrington's.

Harrington's was only a few blocks from Carismo's, but the contrast couldn't have been greater. Harrington's was a little Irish bar full of winos and drunken Irishmen. Frank Sinatra was on the juke, the sawdust dirty and ratty. A couple of drunks had passed out on the bar and now and then the bartender would poke one of them to see if they were alive. It shocked Jack to remember that *he'd* sat at a table in back, watched the action in the bar—which was mostly inaction—and tried to extrapolate his history into some future. Score that one of the worst times of his life.

Jack got a beer and sat at a table near the entrance. Five minutes later, Wayne "Blondie" Reynolds appeared in the open door. Blondie had a big thatch of fine blond hair, big blue eyes, and pink, round cheeks. The rest of him was pudgy, except he looked more cherubic than fat. He had a bad feeling about Blondie. If he had better prospects, he'd pass.

Blondie saw him, waved, then went to the bar, and got himself a beer. A few minutes later, he pulled out a seat, and sat down.

"Is it 'Wayne' or 'Blondie,'" said Jack.

"Most people call me Blondie."

Mentally, Jack ticked off the points in Blondie's résumé. Crackhead.

Programmer? That part blew him away. If nothing else, he wanted to see what a white ex-con programmer looked like.

"Your résumé said you're a programmer. How'd you end up—"

"Résumé—that's funny," said Blondie, looking up. "You mean how did I end up smoking crack for a living?" Blondie shrugged. "I don't know. First, there's a lot of crack in suburbia. Second, people want to try it. A shrink in Auburn said it was because my parents split up. I've given up trying to explain it. It happened."

"And you want to stay out this time."

Blondie laughed. It wasn't a pleasant laugh. "Right-o."

That's what they all said. They all had a scheme to stay out, which evaporated as soon as they *were* out. Blondie seemed to know about the problem of staying out. "You still program?"

"Everybody needs something, a project. I work on games."

"Games?" said Jack.

"I started designing computer games when I was in Auburn."

Software in the Rex? The others couldn't tie their shoes without going to jail. "What kind?"

"Mystery/adventure. You know a search, a confused hero who's not sure he is a hero."

Jack smirked. "It must be about you."

"It probably is," said Blondie, irked.

"It only matters if you want other people to like it. People don't like question marks; they like black and white. Boy gets girl, boy loses girl, boy finds girl, and lives happily ever after. Of course, add hot sex and ten car wrecks." Jack took another sip of beer and set it down on squarely on the circle another beer bottle made a century ago. "I guess that sounded too cynical. But we're not here to talk about movies or games." Jack hiked his chair closer to the table and trotted out his rap about the Rex. He could have done it in his sleep. "Okay, this is the proposition. We want to raze an old hotel on the East Side, but we can't because people still live there."

Blondie frowned. "And?"

"I'll pay you to move into the hotel. You'll wait until I tell you, and then make life tough on the people who live there. We want them out."

Blondie's frown deepened. "What does 'tough' mean?"

"Make yourself a nuisance. Pound on the walls. Listen to rap. Slip notes under their doors. I'll tell you who to work on and how. This is

62

important: No rough stuff. There will be complaints, but we don't want incidents or cops. If we have to, we'll take care of that later. We pay your room and you get $125 a week. I'll give you more details, when you start."

Blondie let out a sigh. "That's the gig, harassing people?"

"You don't seem too warm about the proposition."

"What about later? I've read the papers about cleaning tenants out of buildings. Somebody always gets hurt or dies. "

Jack thought of what happened at the Amsterdam, Kragen. He'd avoided thinking about that part, but Blondie was right. Jack sighed inwardly, but forged ahead. "It may not reach that stage. Besides, at a certain point, we won't need you anymore. Look at it this way: You'll have money in your pocket and a free place to stay for awhile."

Blondie rolled the bottom of the bottle around on the table. A hundred years of winos, and drunks must have done the same thing. The top of the table looked like an alcoholic's war zone. Blondie shrugged. "I wasn't ready for it, but I'll do it."

"You don't look the type," said Jack. "But that's a good thing. My other agents *do* look the type." Jack watched Blondie. Crackhead from the burbs, programmer. Normally it wouldn't fit; it seemed to fit with Blondie. "Are you sure you want to do this?"

Blondie seemed thoughtful. "Right now I live at home and it's impossible. I need a job and a place to live. I'm in."

"It covers the basics." Jack got up. "I'll call you."

"Great."

Jack dug in his pocket, found his wallet, and fished out a fifty. He threw it on the table. "Here's a fifty bucks for listening to me."

Blondie looked surprised. "Thanks."

"I have another appointment. Take your time."

Jack walked to the door, then, curious, he turned and glanced at Blondie. Blondie seemed troubled, distant, almost lost. Jack couldn't shake the feeling that all was not right with this new agent. Of course, every agent was a question mark. He had no idea whether they'd go back to drugs, get violent, steal. Every one was a question mark and a risk.

Jack opened the door and let it swing shut. He watched the heavy traffic on Forty-second Street for a few minutes. Then he waved down a cab.

Whenever he saw Lansky, which wasn't that often, he felt queasy. That time wasn't any different. The cab stopped in front of the Olympia, a half block from the Rex. Jack paid the driver, turned, and walked down the driveway into the parking lot under the building. Jack had never gone in the front entrance. At first, he felt irritated, as if he were a second-class citizen. But considering what he was there for, anonymity was a good thing. Two curvy women in white headbands, tennis racquets, and shorts got out of an Isuzu Trooper. Jack smiled at the tall one and got a quick smile back.

He said hello to the uniformed guard in the garage, and got in the service elevator and punched in the penthouse. A minute later, the doors opened into a small lobby, where he saw Rod, one of Lansky's two body-guards. Rod looked up from the New York Times.

Jack smiled. "Hey, Rod."

Rod was over six-three, muscular, a former college linebacker. He inclined his square crew cut and cracked a smile. He nodded towards the inside. "Michael's out by the pool."

Lansky's penthouse was laid out like a wheel. The axle was a huge living room with clusters of leather chairs, ornate tables, Persian rugs, a fireplace, two bars, and a dining room. The spokes were the lobby, a handful of bedrooms to the south, a kitchen, and a huge terrace. The terrace fronted north and west and gave a mogul's view of prime New York real estate. When you were out there, you felt, truly, you were on Mount Olympus, gods treading on an airy firmament.

The terrace had its own swimming pool, and that day featured two women in lounge chairs at the far end sipping drinks as if they were on a beach in the Bahamas.

"Jack."

"Michael."

Lansky was Jewish, short, and had a pampered belly stuffed with pates, cheeses, steaks, and lox he had flown in from Scandinavia. His head was broad; his thinning wavy hair was matted close to his skull and his eyes were small and black. He had three or four rings on his thick fingers and when he ate and drank, which he did whenever Jack saw him, the diamonds flashed in the sun as if his hands were shooting sparks. That day he wore a pale blue sports shirt, slacks, and brown Gucci loafers without socks.

Three months ago, Jack Kuhl lived in the Amsterdam, the SRO hotel on Forty-second Street. It was the worst time of his life. Kuhl Assets Management, KAM, his company was a memory. His career as an investment counselor was dead. His friends in New York shunned him. To top things off, he found that the owner of the Amsterdam was trying to kick everybody into the street. One day, curious, he spent an afternoon in a branch library in Chelsea rooting out details on the owner of the Amsterdam. The official Lansky was a rags-to-riches American success story with houses in New York, the Hamptons, Bermuda, still married to his first wife, two daughters married to...and blah, blah, blah. The real Lansky was a ruthless slumlord. Thousands of housing violations, rent gouging, unfair evictions. In the Bronx, he divided basements into six-by-six rooms—barely enough for a bed—and rented them to immigrant Chinese for $600/month.

Lansky was a poster boy in Landlord/Tenant court, a busy Civil Court division. Tenants, the city, state, and feds had all sued him. Lansky's army of lawyers got him off all the time, *almost*. The one time he hadn't was when the feds invoked the RICO statute and Lansky, rather than go to trial, gave up the Rincon building, which he'd renovated with HUD subsidies, but rented as luxury flats.

What interested him most immediately about Lansky's methods were the reports of thugs, beatings, and intimidation. Fighting for your rights was one thing, getting your arm broken another.

After he'd finished his research, Jack knew one thing: His time in the Amsterdam was about up. Lansky's goons hadn't pounded on his door, but they were close. Sharon, an out-of-work actress and occasional bedmate, had already kissed him a last time and left for a hotel in Brooklyn. Jack still wasn't sure how the stars had lined up, but one day, a few days before he was going to move, he came up with an idea. The idea came to him in the Markee, the sprawling Forty-second Street movie house with a thousand seats, litter, rats, and roaches.

"Drink?" said Lansky.

"A glass of white wine."

"Always the sensitive, nineties type." Lansky signaled his butler, Moran, and a few minutes later they sat at a white table under a yellow umbrella with two glasses of Chateauneuf du Pape. They both took a sip. Then Lansky dug a piece of ice out of the ice bucket and held it up as if it were a diamond. He flicked it back in the bucket. "Why did I call you, Jack?"

Jack frowned. It was the Mensa riddle. Where does the game start and stop? What game is it? Are we playing now, or are we in a time-out? But he was good at guessing. Lansky wanted dates, times, progress. Lansky was in a constant state of anxiety over time. It should have been done yesterday. Why hasn't the building been demolished? Why are you so slow? "Because you want to know about the Rex. It's only been weeks that—"

"I know. I know," said Lansky, frowning. "I have to watch you, Jack."

Jack glanced quickly at Lansky. "How so?"

"Oh, I've checked."

Lansky had hinted about finding out before. Jack knew it could be bad. What did Lansky think of what had happened to Jack Kuhl, ex-investment counselor, ex-CEO of his own company, Kuhl Asset Management, convicted of fraud, the two years in Lompoc? Of course, Lansky was a slumlord. "A few errors of judgment."

"Forget that. Let's talk about the Rex." Lansky smiled conspiratorially. Jack had a bad feeling about that meeting. He knew he couldn't trust Lansky. In a pinch, Lansky would feed him to the wolves, the police, or his connections in the underworld. No, Jack wouldn't forget it—that was Lansky's point in bringing it up.

Lansky got up. Jack shrugged and got up too. He knew where they were going. Lansky had obsessed about the Rex for over a year. As they strolled to the side of the penthouse terrace, Jack felt the women sunbathing watching him. He turned his head a fraction and smiled reflexively. One gave him a simper; the other spread her legs slightly.

They had a view towards Park Avenue. The day was hot and heat waves rippled the thin yellow cloud over midtown. Closer, Murray Hill and the edge of Kip's Bay spread out like a circuit board. Lansky already owned the two-story townhouse on the corner. Behind it was the Rex, the target, the old brick building with the heavy stone façade, and the hotel in his diagrams. They hadn't built hotels like that for a century.

Lansky gestured towards the Rex. "Old buildings, aging residents, new high-rises. It beats trying to crowbar the rent out of scum in the Bronx. Hit and run, Jack. Hit and run."

Jack glanced at the Rex, then the surrounding townhouses and high-rises. Doubts crowded out his wavering optimism about the project. "We have to be very careful. Nobody cared about the Amsterdam except a handful of reporters, do-gooder social workers, and the West Side SRO Law Project. The Rex is an anachronism, but it's not rundown and it's in the middle of gentryville."

Lansky paused; his head fell towards his chest. He shook his broad head slowly as if a friend had died. "I know it seems like a stupid idea. But the Cardiff and the Amsterdam taught me about how much I can make. Every time I see that building, the possibilities string themselves out like pearls on a necklace."

"You're working on the other owners?"

"Every day," said Lansky, frowning. His eyebrows lifted slightly, his small black eyes seemed to glitter. "They're immigrant Polish Jews. They're holding on like it's their homeland. Don't worry about that. The big problem is the residents."

"Like the Amsterdam," said Jack. The Amsterdam was old, dirty, worn, the residents a paycheck from the street. *He* was a few hundred dollars from the street.

Lansky's eyes glazed over, as he rushed on. "It will be easier than the Amsterdam."

"I don't see how. These people will fight. You'll have every tenant advocacy group, ACLU lawyer, poverty lawyer, and the police fighting to break down your penthouse door."

Lansky shrugged dismissively. "C'mon Jack, these are the nineties. The city supports—wants—upscale housing, luxury rentals, conversions. Ex-developers staff the Department of Buildings. I have contacts with the police and the welfare department. We got the tools."

There was no way to be diplomatic. "We've had this conversation."

Lansky frowned, then looked at him sharply. "And I get this idea you have cold feet."

"No Michael. It's just—"

"Let me outline your position in more detail, Jack," Lansky said, taking a quick sip of wine. Lansky stared at him, his black eyes unblinking. "You have a record. The SEC has barred you from the securities industry. Investment counseling is out. You're living on my money. If I wanted to kick you out of that tony condo in Tribeca, I could pick up the phone. You would be back at another Amsterdam tomorrow. Get it?"

The heat hit Jack. Perspiration flowed down his neck and coursed along the ridge in his backbone. He raised the glass to take a sip, but felt his shirt sticking to his arm under the jacket. He lowered the glass. It had started out okay, then Lansky was on him. A black cloud settled in his head. He blinked. "If you want the condo back. You can have it."

Jack turned and started walking stiffly towards the table, when Lansky's hand encircled his arm. "Now, now, Jack. Forgive my little temper tantrum. We're in this together. Your my protégé. Let's talk it out."

"Okay," Jack said, nervously. He breathed slowly. He turned towards Lansky. He was hot standing in the sun, but he felt he couldn't move unless Lansky moved.

"I'm worried about you Jack. Once you commit to the project, you have to see it through. That means digging out the hard core. That means vetting more agents. That means Wing Attack Plan R. Go straight to the goal. Have moral jitters later."

How had he ended here? Jack began to see where his inspiration—it wasn't even that, it was more an offhand analogy—had led him.

"I need you, Jack. I'd still be twiddling my thumbs waiting for the last resident to pack up, if you hadn't come along. You have that drive, that instinct of whom to push, when, and how." Lansky smiled as if he were imagining what he would get for that corner of Lexington and Twenty-eighth. Then he turned and headed back to the shade of the umbrella.

Jack followed Lansky. Lansky waved to a chair and Jack sat down. He hadn't realized how hot he was, until the shade of the umbrella enveloped him. Vetting ex-cons, kicking people out of their rooms, pointing a half-crazed killer at the holdouts. Jack took a quick gulp of wine.

How had he ended up here?

Mid-morning. The Coffee Shoppe in Midtown.

An ash-blond waitress eyed the three men sitting at the Formica table tucked behind the Art Deco glass-and-metal entrance. They looked scruffy: Mr. Slob, Mr. Weasel, and Scarface. Small tippers. Probably wanted coffee. She shrugged inwardly, picked up the coffee pot, and walked over to her least favorite table. Three coffees. Figured. She poured, asked if they wanted cream, or anything else, and when they'd shaken their heads no, she left to wait on tables on the other side of the door.

Don Breem waited until she was out of earshot. He took a small sip of coffee. He thought about chewing on a cigar and decided to wait. Since he started working for Dombry at the Cardiff, then Jack, he'd detected a change in the way he dealt with people. The other night, watching Raul Vasquez and "Face Off" on the tube, he decided it was about maturity, prudence, being a manager. Or maybe he was just getting old.

Don pulled a small notebook out of his pocket, pulled the stub of a pencil from the wire loops holding it together, and wetted the end of the stub with his thick pink tongue. He glanced at the small man across the table. "Let's see," said Don. "Which room did you get?"

Tim Gaskins was smallish with quick nervous eyes and quicker nervous hands. He wore a short-sleeved yellow shirt with a faded Toucan on the front, a pair of old Dockers, and heavy, square-cut black shoes with elevated heels. "First floor, one-oh-five."

"Cool," said Don. He wrote that down and turned a page with his finger. "Jimmy?"

Jimmy Rankin was of medium height; he was muscular with a shaved head on which a skewed square of light twisted when he leaned to drink his coffee. He wore a black T-shirt, jeans, and a pair of flip-flops. A scar ran diagonally across his face from under his right eye to his left cheek. "Seventh floor. Seven-oh-four."

Don squinted at the small notebook, and then wrote Jimmy's name and room number. When he finished, he looked at Tim. "First floor should be easy. It's the transient floor, although some people have been there forever. I don't know about everybody. There's a doc who lives next to you—Harry. A couple of old-timers near the fire escape. Get as much on them as possible. George will call you. He's a bear for details."

"What about seven?" said Jimmy.

"Seven's tough," said Don. "Russians near the fire escape, the guy who hangs out in front, Brucie, Mario, an ex-marine. Mario has this party a couple times a week. Shit, he even asked me! Get as many details as you can for George, but be careful. I'd guess he'd want you to work on six. We aint got anybody there, yet, and it will be a helluva lot easier."

"Where's the money," said Tim.

Jimmy and Tim had gone to the Rex a few hours ago and gotten in. It was good luck. Smooth running. Don didn't want any more slip-ups like the one with Whitey Zero. Don reached inside the billowing jacket he wore when he paid off agents. His hand fumbled across slips of paper, matches, and a phone bill, and finally felt the firm edges of the two small envelopes. He took them out, looked at them, and slid one to Tim, the other to Jimmy.

Tim snatched at his envelope and tore off one end.

Jimmy glanced casually around the diner. Satisfied, he pulled his envelope over slowly, saw it wasn't sealed, and opened it.

They both counted the bills inside.

Tim looked up at Don, frowning. "Two fifty?"

Don stared at Tim. Same fucking routine. Same fucking mentality. It should've been more. It should've been earlier. And each time he paid them, he wondered. *Is this one going to turn asshole and rob me? Fuck, they're all ex-cons. Assault and battery, theft, breaking-and-entering. It was in their fuckin' blood.* But of the six agents Jack hired, they all seemed to be working out. Not that there weren't question marks. Max and Ace. Ace had a trigger temper and Max was devious. Max had been okay at the Amsterdam, but he knew he'd come up with the scheme about messing up Whitey Zero, which had gotten them *exactly* zero. Bert was too stupid to hatch a plan and Truck too slow and tired. As for these two, Jimmy seemed okay. He'd watch Tim.

Don glanced at Jimmy, then Tim. He explained. "A hundred twenty-five is for this week's rent. A hundred twenty-five is your pay for a week. At the end of the month, your pay adds up to five hundred."

"Can't I get it all now," said Tim. "I got—"

"Tim," said Don, trying to be friendly. "Everybody gets it the same way. We can't change the routine for one guy. Besides, I don't have the money. I'd have to ask Jack and he'd say, *fuck no.*"

Jimmy put his hands over his envelope, turned to Tim, and said, "That's the way the man explained it."

Tim frowned, leaned over his coffee. His right hand jiggled his coffee cup and coffee splashed on the table. He jutted his head close to Jimmy. "You sayin' I didn't get it?"

Fuck, thought Don. He glanced at Jimmy.

Jimmy smiled. It wasn't a good smile, especially with that scar running through it. The smile said if you don't get out of my face, I will rip it off. "No, asshole. I'm saying that's what the man said. It's an easy fucking gig. Why fuck with the rules?"

Don couldn't have said it better. Tim measured Jimmy with his eyes and decided it wasn't worth it. He eased back in his seat. He grabbed the envelope, and stuffed it in his pocket. "Right. But who's Jack?"

Don sighed. He tried to use "George" all the time, and then forgot. "George is Jack. He uses 'George' for security."

Tim and Jimmy both laughed.

"Some security," said Jimmy. He stuffed the envelope in his jeans. "What's his deal?"

Don shrugged. "You know as much as I do. He's the manager. He tells you who to work on and what to do. Besides that, it's better not knowing. Anything happens, you know shit."

Jimmy shrugged. "I just wanted the skinny."

"When do we start the real shit?" said Tim.

Don asked himself the same question. Jack better start soon. He was catching bad vibes from the residents. He was getting the bad eye from the holdover hippies in 506 and Joey, the dealer, across the hall. Whispering in the lobby. He had coffee with Petey, the guy on one, and Max and Ace's run-in with Mario had made it into the Rex grapevine. He called all the agents. Low profile, he said. Quit meeting in fucking groups. Sure, they said. Fuck, he knew better. His agents banded together like Chinese immigrants. He knew they drank together in the Cave, and he'd seen all four together at McDonald's on Park. If Rudi or any residents guessed what was happening, they'd need a crowbar to get residents out of their rooms.

The kicker—the real kicker—was that he wasn't sure it would work. He could tell Jack wasn't sure either. That bugged him batty. The Cardiff and Amsterdam were walks in the park; Lansky had half of the residents out one way or another before Dombry hired anybody! At the Rex, Jack and his troops were at the starting line picking their noses.

Don said, "Soon. Real soon. There are seven of us. I think George—Jack—wants one more, maybe two. I'll call you." Don took a quick sip of his coffee and hunched forward. He tried to be the nice guy. He didn't want conspiracies or the guys ganging up on him. But—big but—he was making it up as he went. "Listen, I guess this will last six months, maybe. It's an easy gig. You sit on your butts until we start. Then you harass people. Do little shit here and there. Might be another gig."

Tim shrugged. "Shitty single rooms are as small as in prison."

Jimmy said, "Big difference is you can walk out when you want."

"Amen to that," said Don.

71

8

Frieda Berg loved the Catskills. She knew all the little towns along the Beaverkill and the East Branch of the Delaware, all the -kills, -tons, and -villes with their hard, crusty, inbred natives. Grossinger's, the Borscht Belt. She had history upstate. Sex, for example. First time. It was in a barn with hay, manure, and yellow clouds of dust. She was sure Seymour Katz still felt guilty.

It must have been seeing the Catskills Real Estate brochure on Toby's desk. It was way past time for a holiday, not that a weekend was much more than a fast retreat from Manhattan. Harry rented a car and they drove up Friday. Friday night, in a cabin literally on the bank of the Beaverkill, they drank wine and conspired to make sticky messes on the bed. Saturday, it was a cozy lodge with lacquered pine and high-backed booths, blueberry pancakes, real maple syrup, rich coffee and real cream, and strolling along the West Branch of the Delaware.

Sunday, they drove to Woodstock where they cruised the galleries and shops. She bought an antique weather vane for her garden. It was a rooster vane, cock perched on top, chest inflated, beak opened. She supposed she bought it as a paean to Harry, the cock. But as she handled the rusty tail and tried to get less than the fifty bucks the sharp-eyed cock-seller wanted, she thought Harry the cock was a mixed bag. The sex was as good; the rest was iffy before their latest détente and was still iffy. The problem wasn't Harry's permanent grace note of unhappiness; it was the cover-up. It was his default Type A personality. When he talked about his interviews, he danced around them, pausing, sorting out the question and response, how to cover the gap in his CV. He never went for the gut, never talked about how he felt or any goal beyond being a success again. If he could only see success or not, why did she care?

Sunday brunch. The Alders, Woodstock.

The view out the floor-to-ceiling windows was bucolic and peaceful. A bridge was partially hidden a half-mile up Briar Creek. Humid undergrowth spread along the banks in front of them and sunlight played a shimmery hide-and-seek in the water. The room was big and airy and noisy with brunch-goers. On the side away from the windows hung the heads of unlucky moose, deer, and mountain lion. The curly, blond-haired waiter wanted them to leave so he could seat a quartet of yuppies making sounds at the door. But she paid rent on their table with another Mimosa and felt like staying a week.

The Sunday Times, her cultural retreat, was mostly a habit and well-tooled ads for Bergdorf-Goodman, Gucci, Tiffany, and Steuben leapt out at her. How could a paper be liberal, unbiased, brilliant, and plutocratic at the same time? Of course, New York was the town of Astors and union leaders, Rockefellers and welfare, Bernstein and Panthers. She knew that without the social, cultural, and economic chasms the city would be too blah. So she read and tut-tutted about this idiocy and that occasionally pausing to think about where in her garden she'd put that rusty cock, or to watch the ripples in Briar Creek.

She was flipping through the Metro section, when an article brought her up short. It was about the Amsterdam, the hotel on Times Square, being readied for the wrecking ball. She read the article twice, and then sat back. She sipped Mimosa and watched the light on the stream. Ideas formed and dissolved. What bothered her? Why did she pause over that article? Was it the names? It *was*.

"Harry?"

"Yep?" Harry had finished his Denver omelet and then her heavy and forbidden Eggs Benedict and was deep in the Want Ads.

"Did you read about the Amsterdam?"

"What's that?" Harry said, not looking up.

"The hotel on Times Square," said Frieda.

"The one they're tearing down?"

"You know those people I talked about last week with the weird closing code?"

"Vaguely." Harry fastened thumb and forefingers to the top of the paper and tore it down the middle. He did the same from the side making a ragged square. He could have done it later. Was he trying to irritate her?

"I think two of those people were evicted from the Amsterdam."

"Hummm. Interesting connection."

"Fine connection," she said, acidly. "Or maybe no connection."

Harry seemed to wake up, then thought about what she said. "Is our time-out over?"

"You're reading the Want Ads."

Harry thought, diced, synthesized. He checked the table. It was ravaged, the plates taken away, the diversion of food gone. "It's a coincidence, not a conspiracy."

Frieda felt her frown deepen and two thin lines wrinkle her forehead. She gave Harry a disgusted look, which she didn't quite mean. She re-read the article for a third time. Old building. Evicted clients. New high-rises. Code 333. The code 333 mystery would have been just another welfare screwup, except that someone pulled the real case record. That meant they wanted those people to go away. And that led in lockstep to the question of motive. Why? And there it was. Tenants, residents in old hotels. The connection was slim, she granted that.

The Amsterdam being readied for the big ball, code 333, and missing case records troubled her last Mimosa and stayed with her through an afternoon of driving through hot Catskill villages and watching kids float the Beaverkill their pale legs flopped over gray inner tubes.

It stayed with her during the long, hot ride in bumper-to-bumper Sunday traffic along the Palisades Parkway en route to the George Washington Bridge. Harry was anxious to get the rental back, but he took the wrong off-ramp and got lost in the malls of New Jersey.

They had to pay more for the rental, and they fought in the cab back to the Rex. They were in that tense, foaming state, which made them both horny as toads. He plowed and she serviced the male beast. She supposed everyone on eight and under her on seven heard every groan, creak, and cry. It was the Rex. She'd given up being discreet years ago.

Frieda Berg stumbled through her room. Why was she up this early? Her right foot snarled in a bra strap and she adroitly flicked her foot and watched, in a room barely illuminated by light sneaking around the shade, the bra bounce off her bookshelves. It lay on the ground like monstrous black ant. Frieda tried to assemble her thoughts, of what she did the night before. The scenes crowded dizzily into her head. Harry, the sexual beast with its lathering openings and sweet musk—no, that was nights ago. Late night gardening.

She flipped open the shade, recovered from the blinding light, stumbled into the other room, and stumbled back to plop in her chair.

She balanced a glass of orange juice on the arm. What happened to that fucking week?

She had big plans. Tuesday, she was going to the library. Wednesday, she was going to track down more code 333 cases. Thursday she was going to nail Rodriguez' ass to the wall. She knew—knew!—he was behind those cases. Big plans. Sure. Well nothing worked out that way. Monday morning, when she trudged into IM66, there was a note on her desk from Toby. There were two serious crises: mass closings in Food Stamps in two Brooklyn centers, and a backlog disaster at IM65. At IM65, a caseworker had retired—*retirement?!* What a concept!—and the new worker had discovered fifty active cases stuffed in a drawer.

She'd watered her plants, tipped her hat to her postcard of Kafka, picked up her bag, and left for IM65. She spent half that week deep in the heart of Brooklyn helping new workers straighten out the cases stuffed in that drawer, the other half tackling IM63 and 64's Food Stamp closings, which was mostly the fault of their antediluvian computer system.

That morning, Friday, was the first time she could get back to those code 333 cases. And she was going to get to IM66 before Rodriguez. She knew he had his dirty hands deep in the shit of those cases. And she was going to prove it. She lurched out of the chair and headed towards her closet. An hour later, she was about to unlock the doors of IM66, when she saw Mr. Williams, the janitor. He frowned, as if he'd never seen anyone that early. He was right about her: Give up her quiet time in her garden? Race off to IM66 at 7:00 in the morning? Was she crazy?

She hurried through an empty intake room to a deserted L & A office. She scattered stuff over her desk and stepped into Rodriguez's office. She had a vague idea of finding something—a paper, a note, a missing record—which would implicate him. But she was fishing.

Rodriguez was crapulous, not stupid.

Fortunately, he didn't lock his desk. Inside the first drawer was a cache of Playboy magazines, Stud, Penthouse. Did he jack off at his desk? She rummaged through the other drawers and found nothing. She looked in the middle drawer. It was full of office accessories and a small pile of folders. She glanced in the folders. Official this, official that. Evaluations. She was about to give up, when she saw a folder shoved behind the others. She drew it out and looked inside. Inside, were two lists of clients with a scrawled X' in the upper right corner. She glanced at her watch. She had time. She hurried to the copy room. Workers were filtering in for the coming day of confrontations. She made a copy, hurried back, stuffed the original back in its folder, and stuck it back in the middle drawer.

Back at her desk, she'd just stuffed the papers in her code 333 folder, when Rodriguez walked in.

He frowned. He walked over to her desk. "You haven't been this early since you came here," he said, squaring off over her terrarium. If only her Venus flytraps were bigger. He would squirm, the spidery fingers would close over the head, and Rodriguez would scream. Then the glabrous fingers would tighten, his scream become a whimper. Rodriguez, consumable protein.

"I have a lot of work, unlike some people."

He leered at her. "Really? And what are we working on this early?" He leaned over her desk. "Code 333, code 333, your new obsession. From one neurosis to the next, from one scatterbrained idea to a dozen."

She was obsessed—it was true. It was how she got anything done. On the other hand, every time Rodriguez said something about those cases, she knew she was onto something. He didn't have enough brains to ignore her. "And what's your job, bucko? Shuffling forms, gutting clients?"

Rodriguez stepped around the desk. He was too close. He leaned down. "I've had enough of you. You're a failed caseworker, a throwback, and a lifer. If you don't give up those cases, we'll write up a complaint. Understand? Capece?" His eyes darkened, his face formed a rictus mask. The little moustache twitched and a glob of spittle detached itself from Rodriguez' mouth and dug a tiny channel down his chin.

Rodriguez was explosively hot. But so was she. Her eyes went hard. Her high eyebrows arched higher. She leaned towards him. "I can't imagine you qualifying for case worker. I find your mistakes, you correct them. Then you thank me and slink back to your burrow."

The corner of Rodriguez' mouth twitched into a sneer, then beyond the hard lines of his mouth, a thin seep of hatred made her blink. His hands made fists. Rodriguez' face inched closer.

Johnny appeared in a corner of her vision. "Johnny," she said. "We've got to talk."

Johnny looked at them, puzzled. "As soon as I get settled."

Rodriguez hesitated and glanced at Johnny. He straightened up, turned, and walked stiffly into his office. She watched Johnny arrang-

76

ing his desk and considered the threat or rather a re-issued threat. What nastiness could descend on her if she kept going? In her twenty-some year career in welfare, she'd been threatened by experts, by mothers with meat cleavers, fathers with golf clubs, sneering punks with knives, and armed police and security guards.

Rodriguez was stupid, if he thought he could intimidate her.

That afternoon, Frieda felt hot and humid. Despite the air conditioning, sweat trickled past her black curls. She dabbed her brow and flipped through the code 333 cases absently. Clients cashiered at the Amsterdam. Lists of code 333 cases. Lists from Rodriguez's office. She'd found matches, but how did it work? Who could be doing it? Why?

She watched Johnny arrange himself after taking a mid-afternoon break. Johnny pulled out his drawer, picked out his favorite pen, then carefully closed the drawer, and squared his green desk mat. "Johnny, it's depressing," she said.

"What?" said Johnny, carefully. Johnny was always wary with her. She had found two of his mistakes, after all. But he'd warmed up. Once he'd told her about his depressions. It looked like he was gearing up for another, about to descend into Styron's darkness visible. She'd been there. She'd taken loads of antidepressants after Ron, after Dugan, after affairs that left her hiding in her room.

"Code 333 cases, missing records, clients wiped off the database."

Johnny thought for a few seconds. "Mona told me what you were doing. Maybe they're test cases for the Triple M."

"Been down that road. They're not testing. Of course, we don't know for sure, because they—who are *they* anyway?—aren't using our programmers. It's tied up in Special Projects."

Johnny lowered his voice and nodded at Rodriguez' office. "He used it yesterday."

"Don't kid."

"I'd just come back from lunch. I asked him if it was up, and he said no. But it looked to me as if he'd filled in a screen."

"Has he used it before?"

"I'm not sure. Once, I swear he'd signed on. When he saw me, he turned it off."

Johnny looked at her, as if he wanted to find out why she was interested and Frieda realized her hand was shaking. New code, new system. Jerry Marguiles had said, "which database." Maybe she should have believed him. "Thanks, Johnny."

Johnny drew a folder towards him and opened it up. "Tell me, if you find anything."

Maybe she would; probably not. "Sure."

Rodriguez left late that afternoon. Johnny, Mike, and Adrian had drifted into the big hall to hassle cases with caseworkers. She went to the new terminal. It was a dull gray plastic with a big black screen.

She sat and stared at it. She aimed her forefinger at the "On" button and punched it. A blue background sprang at her with a box in the middle with "Password" underneath.

That was bad. She should have expected it. She tried several passwords, including Rod, Rodriguez, IM66, 333, and a few others. Then she looked around the rim of the monitor and under it. She'd been around enough computers to know that people kept their passwords handy. Apparently Rodriguez knew his, or kept it in his office.

She'd found a secret door, but it was locked and she didn't have the key. She was about to switch it off, when she thought of the list from Rodriguez' office and that doodled X'.

She plugged an "X" then a "" into the password field. The screen flashed blue, then green, and then filled up with a menu.

Hello.

Frieda got up and glanced out the door. The guys were still out there. She closed the door and hurried back to the Triple M terminal. She was in, but where was that? The screen was labeled "Conversion." After scanning the eight options from Convert to Exit, she tried the Search page. She was surprised to see the Search page was almost intuitive. She put in Rose Tutweiler's name and hit the ENTER key. She always thought that something dramatic would happen when she did that, that a siren would go off, or a line of Rockettes would pop up behind the terminal. She wasn't surprised when Rose's old case flashed on the screen.

Rose was in Triple M purgatory.

She took Rose's old case number down and went back to the main menu and tried the Restore option. The screen that came up was also intuitive and she plugged in Rose's number, checked the Restore radio button, and hit the ENTER key. A blip flickered on the screen. She didn't expect it to work. If the point was to delete—convert—cases, why restore? If it did, Rose would end up with two cases. The new one Condi opened for her and her old case.

She walked to Johnny's terminal. In a few seconds, she was staring at its old, green screen. She typed in Rose's old case number. The last time she'd done it, it wasn't there. She held her breath. The screen filled up with Rose's welfare life history.

Check, mate, and game!

She found the folder of code 333 cases and went back to the Triple M. She typed in the names on the paper she'd copied from Rodriguez' office. They were all in Triple M limbo. Frieda flicked off the Triple M. She stared at the two terminals. She'd found a crucial and significant fact about a mechanism. But what about the real case record? Then there was the sixty-four dollar question. Why? Were they targeting residents of old hotels, or was that incidental?

There were lots of questions. And certainly more digging. But a checkmark had been tallied for her side. She picked up the phone to call Harry. Drinks in Chumley's, dinner at Joe's. She didn't win many wars. She could celebrate winning the occasional skirmish.

9

It was another deadly hot day in Manhattan. Waves of heat pulsed from sidewalks. From Harlem to the Lower East Side, kids screamed and danced in rainbows of hydrant fountains. Central Park carriage horses were given the day off after one flopped over across from the Plaza and died. It was a day you sat in front of an air conditioner and ordered in.

Marcy Benaventura had found a new groove. She hipped her way through a maze of booths at the Odyssey, drew caricatures of tourists at Pier 17, and spent as many nights as she could at Butch's. She was still trying to figure out how Butch and his studio fit into Marcy World. Sometimes logistics were tough, other times she wondered exactly who Butch was.

That Saturday morning was a logistics morning. Friday night, she'd gone to Butch's after her stint at the Odyssey, but Saturdays she spent at Pier 17. She was racing—in shorts, skinny T-shirt, and flip-flops—back from Butch's, when she found herself spun around and her backpack on the ground. She turned angry and pissed and saw Frieda's hand on her throat.

"Dahling, we have to quit running into each other like this," Frieda said, frowning. Frieda wore a flowing mauve-colored dress, pearls, espadrilles, and one of the largest mauve bags she'd ever seen. She always looked like an out-of-breath Auntie Mame late for a curtain call.

"You okay?" Marcy said.

"You're such a slip. You make me feel like a hippo."

"Where are you going?"

"I should be planting, potting, and poking."

"And instead you're going..."

"To the library. It's about good guys and bad guys, us and them, Hopalong and Legree," Frieda said. She shifted her huge bag from one shoulder to the other.

"It's never *that* easy. I'll walk with you. Wait while I get my pack."

"C'mon then."

Frieda dabbed at sweat on her neck while Marcy hopped up the steps into the Rex.

Upstairs, she made up her backpack and a few minutes later, jumped onto the sidewalk. Frieda was smoking a cigarette and talking to Brucie, Yankee fan and perpetual adolescent. Voices rose and fell from the Moat. She heard Bel and Mario. "Ready?"

"Let's go before I implode."

They walked down Twenty-eighth to Park Avenue and then started walking up Park towards Grand Central. The night with Butch had followed routine. They ate, talked about what they were doing artistically, and fucked. The sex was still as good as the first night and, according to plan, he dropped out early, because he spent his day roaming the city buying junk and hassling six-inch pipe. After he fell out, it was her turn to roam. She drifted through his junkyard, looking at edges and shapes, and wondering how they would be transformed. She sat down in a little chair on the side away from Butch and sketched in the faint moonlight.

That night, late, there was less musing and sketching and more worry about whether there was a problem with Butch. Did he have someone on the side? He didn't have time in that whirlwind he called a day. But she'd started to find signs. Too bad. She liked the guy, a lot.

"What's your mystery? Those cases?"

Frieda told her, again and breathlessly, about the connection she'd made to the closings at the Amsterdam. "I need more ammunition. I'm going to spend this beautiful day inside a microfiche reader."

"Who would we be without schemes?" said Marcy. She hitched her pack further up her shoulder and shifted the weight so it was closer to her neck.

"You worry too much about the down side. That's very romantic. I suppose I do the same. I should be looking for rare victories, not obsessing about massive failures. What's appalling is that once you start digging you can't stop. One tawdry fact leads to another until you find yourself at someone's black heart, or the distaff heart of the species."

"And all they have is you."

Frieda trained her brows at her. "Sometimes I feel it's just me."

They reached the library and she waved goodbye to Frieda. Marcy started towards the subway, but then stopped. She'd been touched unexpectedly by Frieda's resolve. She watched Frieda trudge past the impassive lions, up the steps, and disappear in the blackness of the massive open door. She had an image of Frieda challenging immense powers, giants, but doing it unswayed and unswerving. She felt a quick sense of envy. She shrugged it off, and then she turned towards the yawning, congested subway steps.

Marcy settled in at Pier 17 and drew whopper noses on tourists—with her own twist of course. While she drew, though, she came back to the sight of Frieda trudging up the library steps, a lone figure battling immense powers-that-be. That image bothered her while she sketched and it bothered her when she took her breaks and sipped lemonade on a bench near her set-up. Or was it something about *what* Frieda was researching. She thought of Mario and Bel's run-in in the Moat. That could have been Mario and Bel's fault. Her mother was not the soul of diplomacy. But then old hotels. The Rex. Frieda's connection. She shrugged it off.

Later that night, she dragged by the Rex desk drained by the long day, the heat and the subway. She waited like an automaton while the elevator creaked slowly towards four. On four, she pushed her way through the fire doors. Carly was closing her door.

Carly saw her. She pushed her door open wider. "You look beat."

"I work all day and draw at night. In between, I fuck up my life with men, or one man."

"Butch?" said Carly, arching her eyebrow. She and Carly had a drink in Sullivan's a few days ago, where they talked about men, the neighborhood, and life at the Rex.

"Driving me crazy. How's your search for the perfect guy?"

Carly laughed. "We know that's an oxymoron. Come in, I'll buy you a drink."

"Let me drop my stuff."

A few minutes later, Marcy stared at Carly's room. In the crack in her closet door, she saw neat stacks of sweaters, blouses on plastic hangars, and a tree of polished shoes. There was a brass bed and gooseneck lamp on her right. Two chairs with padded burgundy arms anchored a Victorian claw-leg table under the window. The view west took in a few townhouses on Twenty-eighth and a monolithic high-rise on Park Avenue dotted with lights. There was a Maxfield Parrish print over her bed of a dreamy boy in a fantasy setting with gold enameled vines.

Marcy sat in one of the chairs.

"Chardonnay or designer beer?" said Carly.

"Chardonnay."

A few minutes later, Carly set a glass in front of her and sat down. Carly tapped her glass against Marcy's. "Here's to life."

"And success. It's cozy here. My place is a desert."

"My cave by Carly. You can see, despite the cynicism, I hold onto the past." Carly gestured to the dreamy boy in the Parrish print. "It makes me feel there is a real fantasy out there, something lost I'll find again. I suppose we're all like that."

Marcy realized she liked looking at Carly. Through the thin, flowered housedress, Carly was voluptuous, encompassing, and hot. Marcy felt a thrill, as if she'd felt something forbidden.

Carly flicked on her stereo. She took a CD out of its jacket and inserted it. The room filled with "Long Ago and Faraway."

"Know who this is?" said Carly.

"The voice is familiar," said Marcy. "I like it, a lot."

"It should be obvious on this cut." Carly advanced it to "Never Will I Marry."

"This is frustrating," said Marcy. "Help me."

"It's yours truly."

"You're kidding."

"Two CDs and not a pot to piss in. I'm just another frustrated Manhattan artist." Carly reached behind her, dug out a CD, and slid it across the table. "It's my best."

The cover showed a blurred nightclub scene, a singer, and a mike. "Thanks."

Carly looked good, but she always looked good. Carly crossed her legs and her housedress bunched up to show off her legs. Marcy felt strong, determined, no-nonsense, but there were some people who stopped her by their presence, or magnetism.

"Say what do you think of these new guys," Carly said, worried.

"Which new guys?"

"A guy on one—Max—Don Something on Five, this guy Truck down the hall. I've seen them together. They don't act friendly."

There it was again. That glimmer of a connection. Mario and Bel's run-in in the Moat. Truck was the one sneering at her in the lobby. New guys. Old hotels. Frieda. "Don't know, now that you mention it. You know

Mario had a run-in with one of them in the Moat. Guy named Ace."

"He's on three. Something's going on. I'm good with feelings. Oh well. More wine?" She smiled with a mischievous twist to her lip.

"Sure," said Marcy. Carly was singing "The Sun Died." The wine had warmed Marcy and she felt a languorous tiredness, despite the talk of the new guys. She thought of her room, its barrenness. "I could stay here all night."

"Why don't you," said Carly, laughing.

A thrill raced through Marcy's body. Yes, that was what she felt earlier. Forbidden love. She'd had a few flings with Shannon before her trip. She felt guilty about it the first time, but not later. Odd, she liked it, but knew it wouldn't last. Butch? Butch was a big boy. It was time for an adventure. Carly's eyes were open, frank. Marcy read what they could do there. "I'm so far from home, I might have to."

Carly laughed again. She reached over and dialed up "The Sun Died." "You might not get much sleep."

"I don't think that will matter."

10

Don Breem crushed the empty can of Bud, squinted at the overflowing waste can near the door, cocked his arm, and let it fly. The can hit square in the middle of a nest of cans, pirouetted, and tumbled to the floor.

Don grunted.

Don was sitting next to the window in room 502 of the Rex. On his left, an end table supported a clock, a phone, an ashtray overflowing with cigar butts, a scotch-taped TV remote, and a picture of his mother—a Don in homely drag. On his right, a breeze ruffled the drab tan curtains he'd bought at the Second Time Around thrift store on Church. The Giltmore and the Olympia filled the right and left sides of the window. If he craned his neck and looked out the window, which he didn't do often, he had a view down Twenty-eighth Street. Across from him, on a diagonal on an old chest of drawers and against the wall, was a used Panasonic TV.

Don picked up the six-pack from the floor, twisted the last beer out of the plastic, and dropped the plastic on the floor. He popped open the beer, put it to his lips, and chugged half of it. It felt good in the heat. Don had been thinking about the project, about what his agents had reported. Jack was a bear when it came to reports. Report this, report that. He was always after him for something. But he was getting tired of *reporting* details about the Rex residents. Millie went here. Petey's got diabetes. Jeb gets a pension from a jockey's union from an accident where, according the Jeb, a horse made mincemeat of his leg on a home stretch railing. Jack had spent a wheelbarrow full of money on gossip.

A timer went off in Don's head. He rested the beer against his round stomach and checked the clock on the night stand. Seven. Time for Raul Vasquez and "Face Off."

Don picked the remote off the table, stared at the buttons for a second, and then punched on the TV. Glow and noise filled the small room. Don flipped through the channels until fast-talking, wavy-haired, big-nosed Raul filled the screen. Funny. A spic on TV. Oh, excuse me thought Don. A Latino-Mexicano-Chicano-Americano. Thought they'd never make it on TV. Course they had enough kids. One of 'em had to make it. Fuckin' law of averages.

Don squinted at the screen. He sorted out who was facing off.

There were two groups on the stage, not counting Raul's guards. Raul pranced across the stage and before you could say boo was in the face of a transgender ex-NFL tackle named Gwen who raised rabbits—bunnies, she called them—and who was stroking Sweetie, her favorite bunny with long thick fingers. Five feet away, barely controlled by Raul's guards, was a homophobic—transgenderaphobic?—sneering tattooed skinhead, who was trying to restrain Rage, his Presa Canario, who was two times the size of a pit bull and twice as ferocious.

Animals on "Face Off." Cool.

Bring. Bring. Bring.

Don stared at the phone. The only people who called him regularly were Jack and Mom. He'd told the agents not to. 'Cept Tim, the dick-less wonder, always called about his money.

Don snatched up the phone. It was Jack.

"Hey Jack, what's up?"

"Blondie got a room on three. We've got enough agents. It's time to kick off Phase 2."

Don dialed the volume down on the TV.

Rage bounded across the stage. He skidded and stopped in front of Gwen. Gwen backed up tucking Sweetie under her arm. Rage stuck his huge maw at Sweetie. Now he was nose to nose with Sweetie. Time for a little blood and guts. Bye, bye, bunny. "Say Jack, can I call you back. I'm kinda—"

"This will take a second. I'll call each agent with instructions."

"Right. Sure, Jack."

"*You* report everything and I mean *everything*. Ace acts up, you tell me."

All the fuckin' dog has to do is open his mouth and the fuckin' bunny would die of fuckin' fright. Open your mouth, sissy.

"Are you there Don?"

"Sure, Jack, sure. Got it. Phase 2. Report everything."

Don leaned forward. *Rage was close. He sniffed Sweetie! The dog turned mournful eyes on Raul. He turned back to Sweetie. He licked him!*

"What the fuck! Kill 'em. Rip his fuckin' throat out! What kinda fuckin' mutt are you?"

86

"Don!"

"I'm here, Jack. I'm here."

"What the fuck are you doing?"

"Little tube, Jack. That's all."

"What did I say?"

Rage licked Sweetie again! Raul yelled at the dog. The skinhead bounded across the stage, snarled, and clipped Raul with a right. That was better. He didn't watch "Face Off" to see group hugs.

"Got it, Jack. Phase 2. I'm there. Got my thumb on the guys."

"Like shit you do. I'm checking on *you* tomorrow."

"Sure Jack."

Don hung up, dialed up the volume, and leaned towards the tube. The stage was a chaos of fists, snarling dogs, guards, and Raul. Fucker finally got tapped. Nose bleeding, maybe a cracked tooth. Phase 2! Chaos. Bleeding residents. It was a good omen.

Then Don saw Sweetie. He hopped over Raul. His nose twitched once at the camera, then he turned and hopped off stage.

Don shook his head mournfully.

That better not be an omen.

11

Frieda bundled ten rolls of microfiche into the microfiche reading room. It took her five minutes to get the first film threaded. Then she propped her head on her left hand and started scrolling. What she was doing was way beyond the call of duty. She had an inkling of what was going on with the code 333 cases. Toby might think she was chasing chimeras—it had happened before—but the more she dug, the worse it smelled.

After three hours, her head felt like the inside of a scanner.

She'd taken five pages of notes. She turned in her rolls. Then she dragged herself down the great marble hallways, past a depressing display of Kathy Kollwitz prints of hollow-eyed mothers and dying children, and walked out the small side entrance of the library. She walked towards Times Square and veered off into Bryant Park behind the library. The park had signs about an upcoming renovation, but it was still open. People moved slowly in the heat across the parched grass. Along the sides, chess players in shorts and T-shirts moved pieces and jabbed at clocks, and a scattering of homeless shared paper-bagged drinks or slept. The bustle and noise from Forty-second Street and Times Square created a shifting wall of shouts, horns, screeching tires, and buses revving up or gearing down.

She sat on an iron chair in the shade of a sycamore, dabbed the sweat off her forehead and opened the top button on her blouse. She knew she looked bedraggled. The heat destroyed any attempt to look good. She watched two black chess players flicking at pieces and stabbing at clocks for a few minutes. Then she sifted what she'd found.

Michael Lansky. Slumlord. He owned the Amsterdam and another hotel, the Cardiff. Lousy conditions, residents leaving, intimidation. The Cardiff was history, the Amsterdam about to be history. There were a handful of reports of welfare clients evicted for non-payment of rent. She had a motive—greed, naturally—and a mechanism, the Triple M, a computerized welfare system designed for slumlords.

She had facts, lists, and a theory. She knew it wasn't enough for Toby or anyone else in the department. She also had the name of a reporter,

Sean Borgan. He'd done a Pulitzer-nominated series on the Cardiff residents. From what she'd read, he was her kind of people. She needed someone on her side who didn't think she was crazy.

She picked up her bag and plucked out her change purse. She counted out change then walked out of the park to the bank of phones, which fronted on Forty-second Street. She found one that was free, dropped in her money, dialed the Times' number, and when she got Borgan's number, was about to leave a message, when Sean Borgan answered the phone.

She explained, briefly, what she wanted and he sounded interested. But he was about to leave and needed a drink. Could she meet him in twenty minutes at the Pen on Forty-fourth and Broadway? She said yes and that was that.

Frieda walked down Forty-fourth Street. The Pen was located across from ranks of New York Times delivery vans. And what news today? Megalomania in the Middle East? Bombs in Northern Ireland? Ethnic cleansing in Serbia? An oil spill in California? Clinton taking on the health insurance industry? She would feel the relative importance of those messages and the usual feeling of impotence. And why was *she* there? Where did her mission fit in the grand scheme? At most it was a footnote, a tiny eddy in a vast flood.

The Pen was a huge sprawling bar with lots of polished wood, a buffed hardwood floor, and a swarm of solid oak tables and chairs. At that time of day, it was packed and noisy. It was hot and still outside, cool and chaotic within. It was the perfect place where reporters could down shots and trade lies out loud. The walls were hung with photos of writers and reporters, the centerpiece, one of Hemingway. There was also a photo of Clark Gable, a screen reporter.

She angled her way through the crowd. She didn't see him; then she felt a hand on her shoulder. On the phone, Sean Borgan described himself as a diminutive hyperactive Irishman. And that's what she got. He was a red-haired Yorky with a small frame, freckles, and agitated blue eyes. "You should have told me you looked like Ava Gardner," he said, taking her arm.

"Believe me, it's never helped," said Frieda.

"I'm over here."

She let Sean lead her through the mass of reporters, editors, stringers, copy boys, and whoever else put out whatever was fit to print to a relatively quiet table against the wall with two glasses on it. One was empty and the other looked half-full of whiskey or scotch and water.

"This is ours for a few minutes," he said, pulling out a chair.

"I'm beginning to see everything as a struggle over property," she said, sitting down. She sat, dropped her bag on a chair, took off her glasses, and posed them on the table. "Are you a real reporter or the movie version?"

Borgan laughed. "Rose-colored glasses?"

Frieda grinned. "I don't have any illusions left. I just like the color."

A harried waitress—tall with a thin, angular nose—hipped her way through the crowd and stood over her. "A gin and tonic, dear."

She watched the waitress take a few more orders.

"So what's up," said Borgan.

"Give me a second. My head's been inside a microfiche reader all afternoon and my temperature is over two hundred."

Sean smiled and picked up his drink. "Fair enough."

She dug in her bag for her smokes and found them and her lighter. She lit up and scanned the crowd. Lots of conversation, lots of noise. It made her feel, briefly, what she felt outside, that her welfare career was a tiny eddy in a backwash, definitely out of the mainstream.

She turned to Sean. "I like this place. In another lifetime, I was an aficionado of old bars."

"Sometimes I like it too much," said Sean.

The waitress came with a tray of drinks, extracted hers from the middle, and set it down in front of her. "Thanks, darling. You saved my life."

"That'll be five bucks."

Frieda paid and tipped her. She sipped her drink and looked at Sean Borgan. Despite his size, he looked solid, dependable. His article on the Cardiff was poignant, caring. She decided she liked him. "Let's start at the top. I'm an old school HRA caseworker nudged into working for HRA Investigations. We look for fraud, poor procedures, kick-back schemes."

Sean smiled wryly. "Internal investigations?"

"Believe me, they hide when they see me coming. In the last few weeks I've come across welfare clients evicted from old hotels with a code that's not in our current system. Some of those clients lived in the Cardiff and another hotel, the Amsterdam. I want to know more, a lot more."

"I didn't write about the Amsterdam, although I know about it. What kind of more?"

"Links to welfare. Any kind."

Borgan looked into his drink, then at her. "We all have the same usual illusion about time—that it's going to stand still. I felt for those people at the Cardiff and I thought I had something to say about change and greed and our inability to sympathize."

"Fighting change is a terminal condition."

"After I published the series, I spent six months in the Sierras in a cabin making those real stories fiction. When I came back, the Cardiff was closed, draped in bumblebee tape."

"I read about it," said Frieda. Mentally, she ticked off what she'd read at the library about the Cardiff, who owned it, the stories about goons. "There was a fire."

"That was the last straw. It killed two people, injured others. It left the building a shell."

"What about the welfare clients."

Borgan frowned. "What exactly are you looking for?"

Frieda gathered her thoughts. "Clients have their case records filched, their case cancelled with a mystery code, and they're wiped out of the HRA database."

"And they lose their benefits."

"If they're smart, they reapply right away. But without an electronic case or a paper one, they have to go through the application and certification process. It can take months. During that time, unless they prove a dire need, they don't receive benefits and they're kicked out."

Borgan glanced at her, and then thought for a few seconds. "You'd think eviction *would* be a dire need. I saw clients evicted. I thought they'd done something to jeopardize their cases. I can dig welfare cases out of my notes."

"That would be great help."

"Do you know about the owner of the Cardiff?"

"I got a headache from seeing Michael Lansky's name in that microfiche reader."

"He's a piece of work. Ruthless, a money-making machine."

"Then it's a matter of time before his statue adorns the lobby of a new high-rise."

"You're almost as cynical as I am," said Sean, laughing.

"Was he the only owner?"

"I think there were others, but I'd have to run them down. Listen, I'd like to do another story, but right now there's no definite link between what you've said and the Amsterdam or the Cardiff. If Lansky targeted another hotel, that would be different."

Frieda stifled a laugh. She was going to say something witty, another one-liner, but then she thought of what he'd said. Target? "I'd hate to have him target another hotel just to be right."

Borgan tipped up his shot glass, and thrust two fingers at the waitress. "Talk of schemes and scandals lasts only so long. I'll buy you a drink and we can trade stories. You tell me the Frieda Berg story. I'll relate the exciting journey of Sean Borgan."

Frieda laughed. "Mine will be a tale told by a fool of the Bronx, signifying—"

"I'd like to hear it anyway."

"Then it's a go."

It felt better talking about something normal. She talked of the Bronx, her history, her garden, the Rex, Sean about his tough life growing up in Hell's Kitchen, his scholarship to Columbia, being shot at in Brooklyn, and a book of short stories, which she promised to read. But later, after the crowds and noise grew less and after watching the Times delivery vans come and go out the window, she began seeing the scheme she'd uncovered—she *knew* it was a scheme—against a broader background of nations, peoples, and ethnicity, of grudges building up, of impulses to Machiavellian manipulation, of schemes and plots. She started feeling despair that people spent their intelligence and time piecing together schemes at all.

Frieda needed a day off. She'd spent another day in the library sifting through reports of clients being evicted. Sean Borgan called with the names and phone numbers of three clients evicted from the Cardiff. She called them. Yes they'd received code 333s. Yes their entire record was missing. And yes they were evicted. She was getting evidence, a lot of it, and it was pointing right at the Triple M. She'd also called Fulvous Meridian in IM complaints and found more code 333s. She called Jerry Marguiles in

Computer Operations again and found there were no Triple M terminals hooked up at Central Office and as far he could tell, the only live terminal was at IM66.

It all pointed to that playboy scumbag Rodriguez. She was going to nail his ass to the wall if it was her last breath.

But not that day. She was staying in and playing in her garden.

Tap, tap, tap.

Frieda glanced at her door, sighed. "This better be good."

She got out of bed, opened the blinds, recovered from the shock of all that light, then walked to the door and put on her robe. It was hot already, which meant it was going to be a scorcher. She couldn't garden; it was probably a hundred degrees up there already.

She felt grumpy. She looked at the clock. Nine.

She opened the door. Raquel Jones stood there looking cowed. Frieda felt guilty right away. Poor Raquel. She was skinny and bent with short, kinky hair edged with gray. She'd worked for years in a clothing store in midtown. One afternoon, she'd slipped, fallen, and dislocated her arm. When workman's comp and UIB ran out, they wouldn't hire her back. She looked—always looked—frail.

Frieda smiled. "What's up, Raquel."

"I'm real sorry to bother you."

"That's okay."

"Rose said you'd helped her and I was wondering."

Frieda's frowned. "About?"

"This." Raquel picked through her housecoat with a graceful, brown hand. She pulled out a carefully folded piece of paper and held it out.

Frieda unfolded the paper. It was an IMD 209 with a code 333 embossed on it.

"Fuck. Excuse my French, Raquel. Come in. Sit down."

"I don't want to—"

"You're not, darling." Frieda walked over to her chair. She picked up her bag and dropped it on the floor. "Come on, I won't bite."

"All right."

Raquel sat down on the chair and folded her hands in her lap. Frieda looked at the IMD 209 closely. It was identical with Rose's, except the date was a few days ago. It hit her, finally. Rose. Raquel. "Do you know about Sid or Jeb? Did they get these?"

Raquel shrugged. "I don't know."

"I'll check."

She was puzzled, deeply puzzled. And when she started sorting what she knew and what she'd been doing, it still didn't make sense. "Has anything peculiar been going on here?"

Raquel frowned. "You mean at the Rex?"

"Yes, dear. Anything unusual?"

"Well, I wasn't going to say anything..."

"Tell me."

Raquel took a slip of paper out of the pocket of her housecoat. She handed it to her.

Frieda read, "Leave the Rex now!"

"Jesus Christ. Who sent this?"

"I don't know. But there's a man at the end of the hall. Mario said his name is Jimmy. He's bald with a scar."

"I've seen him," Frieda said, grimly. She snatched up her pack of Old Golds, but didn't shake out a cigarette. It came together, finally. Rose, code 333, Rodriguez, old hotels. The Rex.

"I'm not sure why, but I think he might have done it. Of course, I couldn't swear to it."

"Damn, damn, damn."

Raquel watched her, frowned. "You know something else?"

"It fate, Raquel; it's a coda for my life."

"Just yours?"

Frieda shook her head. "Ours, or most of ours, dear."

"I guess it's not supposed to last," Raquel said, sadly. Raquel shrugged, got up, walked slowly to the door, and shut it behind her.

Frieda watched the bags heaped on the door. Then, abruptly, she turned and opened her closet. She dressed, made up her bag, and left. In the lobby, she thought of stopping and talking to Rudi—she had a lot to ask him—but she had work to do at IM66.

Frieda Berg paused at the corner of Park Avenue and Twenty-eighth Street. She had been rushing. Her fingers held a cigarette lit in haste as she climbed the subway steps into the waves of heat, cars, and noise of Park Avenue. The Rex was small and dark overshadowed by the Olympia. It looked like a timid David standing up to a hulking Goliath. The town house on the corner of Lexington and Twenty-eighth had been locked for months. She'd wondered why they hadn't tried to rent or sell it. Now it made sense. Coming soon: Olympia II.

It all started with Rose Tutweiler banging on her door. That was the premonition. This was the punch line. She felt grim, grimmer than she'd felt in years.

She walked down Twenty-eighth Street, but paused outside the Rex. Brucie, welded to one of the Rex's pillars, raised his hand in greeting. A BMW sped down Twenty-eighth Street, then a Land Rover. She felt, as she'd never felt before, what "Kip's Bay renewal" meant. The dying strains of "Beat the Devil" leaked out of the Moat. She heard Mario, then Bel. Instead of walking up the worn steps of the Rex, she walked down into the Moat.

She waited a few seconds for her eyes to adjust to the dark. The Moat, with its smoke and locals perched like lumps of coal on their stools and in their chairs, seemed as inevitable and fragile as the Rex. She saw Mario and Bel at the bar and walked over.

Larry came over and she said, "G and T, Larry. Double the gin."

Mario and Bel stared at her. Mario said, "Rough day at the office?"

Frieda shrugged. "You have no idea, but you will soon enough."

"Sounds serious," said Bel, frowning. "I'd better have another,"

"Me three," said Mario. He killed his drink, cocked his head in her direction. "Now, what drove you to a double?"

"The Rex," said Frieda. "We may have a war on our hands."

Mario's frown matched Bel's. "How so."

Frieda took a long pull on her drink. The drink made her feel high, but not much better. The Moat was convenient, certainly, but not her kind of bar. The Cave had its share of drunks and locals, but it also had a ripe crowd of poets, writers, and artists. People she could talk to about something besides boozy personal stories and drinking.

"Where to start." She took a healthy pull on her drink and took a deep breath. Then she gave them the digest version of cancelled welfare benefits, goons, and Lansky. It took longer than she expected. "Right now, the welfare cases are okay, because I restored them this afternoon. But the real problem is going to be here, the Rex, the front lines."

"It fits," said Mario, staring at the rim of his drink. "We've been wondering who these guys are. They act like a fucking secret club."

"We know exactly who they are," said Bel, eyes narrowed. "There's Ace, Max, Truck, Tim, Jimmy...most of the guys who rented rooms in the last three weeks. Bert on your floor. Two of them tried to pick a fight with Mario a week ago."

"How did that go?" said Frieda, frowning.

"Not good for them," said Mario. "But now—"

"I can't fucking believe this was going on under my nose. Raquel got a note saying that she had to leave."

"Fuck," said Mario.

"I'd guess they'll start on the weaker ones first," said Frieda.

Bel looked at Mario and said, "What are we going to do."

"That's the sixty-four dollar question," said Frieda. "Do we stay and fight, or slink off to Queens or Jersey City?"

Bel grunted. "*Those* are our options?"

Frieda laughed. "I was exaggerating."

"What about Rudi?" said Mario, frowning.

Frieda looked at her drink, grabbed it, and gulped the rest. "I'm sure he doesn't know what they're planning. I talked to him earlier. When he told me Michael Lansky bought out Shem two weeks ago, my heart stopped for the umpteenth time today. And Lansky lives in the Olympia penthouse. He watches me prune my roses."

"Fuck," said Mario.

"I can't think," said Frieda. "If you have any bright ideas, call me."

Frieda moped past Sven's tiny portraits, changed her clothes, and a few minutes later was in her garden. She had neglected her garden in the last few days and she had pests. Whiteflies, mealy bugs, aphids, the whole shooting match. But that day, as she worked up and down the pallets spraying, rubbing, coating, pulling, deadheading, and digging, she found the Zen Gardening state elusive. The Rex had been invaded; the pests were on every floor, every closet, and every bathroom. She would get up in the morning and wonder what Bert would do when she walked down the hallway.

She glanced at the Olympia. Lights popped on. A rim of lights illuminated the penthouse. A thick shadowy figure leaned, watching her.

Lansky!

She shuddered. She walked slowly down the central path. She felt his eyes on her back. In her room, she found an open bottle of Chardonnay, poured a glass, then settled in her favorite chair. She was too antsy to sit still.

She snapped up the phone and punched Harry's number. "Harry? Let's go out. I need real people, talk of symphonies and art galleries."

Harry sounded diffident, offish. "Why?"

"Don't be difficult. I haven't seen you in days."

"Right. I'll meet you outside in fifteen minutes."

Fifteen minutes later, she walked into the hot night. Brucie was there. He was talking to Petey. It was too normal. Where were the thugs?

They walked slowly down Twenty-eighth Street towards Second Avenue. At the service entrance of the Olympia, Frieda glanced into the underground garage. She saw several cars angling for position, a service elevator, a guard, and a couple walking to their car. The woman had a false, brittle laugh; the man looked subdued, worried. Frieda could march down there and ride the service elevator to the penthouse. She could brace Lansky and expose his scheme.

Harry wanted to go to Pasquale's and she was too preoccupied to protest. It was new, blond, and barren. The prices were too high, but the waiters young and friendly.

They ordered dinner and a bottle of Rosé and soon had glasses in front of them. She went for the wine and a few minutes later Harry went for the food. She drank and he ate. She watched Harry apply himself to his pasta his knife and fork dipping in and out like a strange animal with metallic limbs. She thought of the Rex, of what happened, of what they could do.

"Why did you want to go out tonight," Harry said, finally.

Frieda gave in. "Today has been a disaster. A handful of Rex residents have been cashiered with my mystery code. The slumlord who owned the Amsterdam and the Cardiff now owns part of the Rex. I mean it's the Rex!"

Harry stopped eating. "You're kidding."

"Bel and Mario fingered the goons." She told Harry who they were.

"I've watched them. I wondered what was going on."

"Why didn't you mention it," Frieda said, sourly.

"Do you have to know everything?"

Harry finished his plate. He pushed it towards the center of the table. Frieda grabbed a bunch of curls and released them. She watched Harry settle into his chair. In a few minutes he would ask her for what she hadn't eaten. When it was over, when Harry dragged his boots through the dust and his fly-image flicked off the horizon, she would remember settings in Italian, Mexican, French, and Japanese and a mechanical eating monster rising through the steam.

Harry ran his hand through his straight blond hair, then propped his elbows on the table. He looked at her as if it was time to have a real talk. "Okay. This guy Lansky wants to gut the Rex. It's inconceivable, outré, and another entree in your ill-fated life. So what?"

If she'd been wise, she would have changed the subject. Frieda felt her mouth tighten and her eyebrows push up. She tried to be rational. "We don't let it happen, that's what. We form residents' committee. We contact tenant advocacy groups. We find tenant lawyers. We take Lansky to court. There's the West Side SRO Law Project. There's—"

"And when Rose gets hurt? Or Petey is pushed downstairs and breaks his leg?"

"I haven't doped out everything that *could* happen. But you can't just sit there like a lump on a log and flip out cynical one-liners."

Harry looked thoughtful, then said, "Everyone will find another place."

"Your fine conservative philosophy rears its head. The Jebs and Peteys don't have your options. They'll never find a place in New York."

Harry shook his head. "You're not their guardian angel."

"Soon you'll be redeemed, a solid member of your favorite class," said Frieda, tapping her cigarette on the ashtray. The ash crumpled off and lay on the white tablecloth. She flicked the ash with her finger leaving a gray curl on the tablecloth.

Harry put his fork down. "And the downtrodden and social misfits are the only people important. As they say, it's a one-trick pony."

"You had more chances than the moms standing in line at IM66."

"What a great fucking idea," he said, biting out each word. "My life is over. Now I can be a desk clerk at the Rex for the pleasure of trading barbs with you. Fat fucking chance."

"You blew *your* fucking chance."

Harry shot her a withering look, reached into his pocket, and came out with a twenty, which he threw down on the table. Then he got up, turned without looking at her, and left.

Frieda watched Harry's back with a stone in her throat.

Frieda poured the rest of the Rosé into her glass and took a healthy gulp. She trashed her reconciliation with Harry in record time. Frieda Berg, confrontation expert. She knew it went back to the Korsokoff sisters, to her mother, but after a certain point you had to learn. She'd never learned, or had learned badly.

When Harry had his tantrum, fortunately, Pasquale's was emptying. Shadows deepened in the restaurant. The waiter turned the "Open" sign around. Outside, Ben, the Rex's gaunt and solitary basement dweller, edged into a Hopper view of Second Avenue. He paused at the street light for two cycles, then after getting the nod from a cosmic code-maker, walked slowly across the street. Often Ben was so angry that his speech was a torrent of babble about everything from Jews to sliced bread to baseball. The problem was that if sometimes when you were feeling a little off, or down, and you listened closely enough, his word salad started making sense.

That night she felt like wandering the streets and standing at stop-lights herself.

12

Jack Kuhl woke up juiced. No Jeanie. No morning sex. No small talk.

The Rex project shimmered on the wall pulling him in. The jockeys were ready, their mounts pushing against the bar. Jack vaulted out of bed, grabbed his black robe, and put it on as he skipped down the stairs. He walked quickly to the curtains, opened the drapes, and then retreated, half-blinded, to the kitchen.

Coffee, mug, desk.

Jack booted up the laptop. The Rex project bloomed on the screen. He'd typed the four phases in bold:

Phase 1. Move in agents. Gather information about tenants.

Phase 2. Start harassment. Evict welfare clients. Block off rooms.

Phase 3. Send in construction crews to "renovate" rooms.

Phase 4. Dig out the hard core.

Cost:

8-10 agents X 1000/month X six months. $50-60,000.

Payments to tenants. $30-50,000.

My salary. $50,000.

Kragen (if necessary). $10,000.

Construction costs?

Buying the Rex?

Lansky figured it would cost a quarter million to get the residents out, another two million to buy out the owners. When Jack last talked to him, Lansky saw a three million dollar profit.

Nice work if you could get it.

He'd called Don and told him to start the harassment. Don was weird, into some freak television show. Did he get it? Did he understand low key? Did he get the meaning of "low profile?" The word was *control*. That would work. Not letting a bunch of baboons run wild through the Rex; they'd end up picking their noses on Riker's Island before you could say boo.

Jack called Don. He took a sip of coffee while he waited for Don to come on. Where was he? His room could fit in the condo's kitchen.

"Don, Jack. Let's meet."

"Yeah, sure Jack. Factory?"

"Not anymore. I've got a list of out-of-the-way places, not that it makes a rat's ass difference. Black Bar, West Side, near the piers off Twenty-second." Jack looked at his notes. "Next time it'll be the Odessa, East Village, opposite Thompkins Square. I'll give you a list. Pretend you're a tourist."

Don chuckled. "Black Bar. Yeah sure. I'll find it."

"See you at six. And I want reports."

"Sure Jack, sure."

Jack hung up. Don was the only person he knew who said "sure" just the way he said "hello." He'd make sure Don knew exactly what to do.

Jack moved the cursor through his model. Transient floor. Drug floor. Jack tapped out "police?" in the "Comments" column. Carly Darling, Marcy, Sid—full names, nicknames. They were like circus names, the Rex a ragged traveling show, which had a permanent—that would change—location. Weak spots everywhere. Residents on welfare, residents fired from jobs, residents who were old, crippled, and weak. Many would snap at a thousand bucks to leave.

After figuring out who were the weakest, he called his agents and told them who to work on and how. If they kept a low profile, the cops wouldn't be a problem. The cops didn't give a flying turd about tenant/landlord problems. He'd seen that. They did give a shit about people getting hurt, especially in high rent districts. Jack typed a note about checking his agents every few days. Playing it cool wasn't what they did best.

He called Lansky. He said they'd started Phase 2. A couple of residents were ready to pack their bags. When he got off the phone, he faxed Lansky the names of two more welfare recipients.

Lansky called him back after getting the fax. "It sounds good, Jack. But early on it's always easy. I want you thinking about later and by later I mean six months or less."

"It's working, Michael. Let me do my job. It worked at the Amsterdam."

When it came to making money, Lansky was a pit bull. "Brendel doesn't want to sell, but he will when things get tight. Right now, I convinced him to renovate. Rooms open up, we'll close them for my crews.

That means you have to get them open. Right?"

"That's what I'm here for. I can pay four residents to leave. It might cost $4-5,000."

"Cheap at three times the price. I'll send checks for you, your agents, and a separate one for the buyouts. Go for it, Jack. Get those rooms. And keep up the pressure!"

"Of course," Jack said, wearily.

At six, Jack got ready to see Don. He dressed down in jeans and white shirt. He stuffed two disposable cameras in a small backpack, checked his cards and money, and a few minutes later locked the door. He walked up the West Side Highway. Past the meat district, the landscape was full of abandoned warehouses, run-down bars. A few streets were full of trash, garbage, flies, the quick flip of a rat in the sewer; other streets were swept clean, as if they were complying with a city ordinance. It was an odd juxtaposition of the squeaky-clean surface and backed-up sewer.

The Black Bar seemed like an intrusion from the East Village. It was a punk bar done entirely in black. Framed posters of scraggy rock bands like Kiss livened up the atmosphere. He got a Bloody Mary and found a seat near a window. Darkness and light chased each other over that urban desert, the deep gloom of a shadow suddenly forgotten in the metallic sheen of a passing car. Ideas of hope and despair chased themselves through his consciousness.

He lost his thought when Don's blobbish figure appeared next to his table. "Don, how are you?" he said, masking a quick irritation.

"Fine, fine. Let me get a drink." Don went to the bar and got a beer. Don looked like a seedier version of Lansky. He was about the same size, but his double chin was unshaved, his shirt worn and smudged, his ear hair bushy, his thinning hair too long in the back. Don sat down and took a long pull of his beer. The drink left a slight curve of foam above Don's full lips. Don stretched, took out a cigar, and clamped it into a corner of his mouth.

Jack leaned over the table. He watched Don closely. "Sorry I was so uptight the other day. Everything okay?"

"Fine, just fine," said Don. "I get wrapped up in this show. At least I used to. Hasn't been the same since that fuckin' bunny."

Jack didn't pretend to understand that. "The agents?"

Don rubbed the side of his nose leaving an oil sheen on his nail. Don half-lidded his eyes, as if he were testing Jack's reaction. "Good bunch of boys. You just hafta stay on 'em."

"How so?" said Jack, frowning. That was exactly what he didn't want. Don was good with the money, gossip, and relaying messages. He wasn't good for much else. He'd heard something about Ace, but not from Don.

"They got this habit of meeting, you know. For a beer or coffee."

Jack ran his hand through his hair. "Christ. You have to tell me these things. I'll talk to them. I don't want the whisper of a thought of a conspiracy. This has to be done in phases."

"I understand, but they're guys," said Don. He glanced at Jack surreptitiously. "You know five is gonna be tough. If Joey or Ritchie catch me—"

"Go after the ones I told you to go after." There were scores of weak spots in the Rex, but then others weren't. He'd told Don to focus on John Brent and Judy Morro, two of the older, long-term residents. The Freak Brothers, Joey, and Ritchie were too young and potentially violent for his agents. He didn't think they could be bought out. "Don't worry, it's early. Watch for drug deals. A few discreet calls to the police will do wonders."

Don guffawed. "Us callin' the cops. I love it."

"I want photos of the tough ones. Helps me think. Be careful, especially with Joey and Ritchie. I don't want to lose my right hand man." Right hand man. If only he would concentrate. If only he would tell him when his agents acted up. Jack showed Don the disposable cameras, then put them back in the backpack and handed it to Don. "Ask if you need more."

The Black Bar was full of sneering punks with multi-colored hair and metal protruding from available soft tissue. The street had filled up in the last thirty minutes with a mix of punks heading towards the Black Bar and transvestite whores in short leather skirts and stiletto heels. Jack made out the name of the hotel that stared over the Hudson like a sentinel. A few people hung around the entrance of the Jane, as if they were waiting for their ticket out, a drug drop-off, or the Second Coming.

A feeling of vulnerability stabbed through his dialog with Don. The common sense efficiency he applied to the Amsterdam and was applying to the Rex masked fragile props. Don wasn't the most brilliant second-in-command—what could he expect? But brilliance had nothing to do with it. Jack knew his only real control over Don or the other agents was the promise of more money. It wasn't a premise on which to build a life, although everyone did. Safety was a big bank account. Lansky had insulation, he didn't. Yet.

"How's Blondie," Jack said, finally.

"Ah, he's okay. Keeps to himself. Works on his game."

Jack knew. Programmer. His other agents couldn't tie their shoes without going to jail. "At least he's not in an agent kaffeeklatsch." Jack pulled out an envelope and shoved it across the table. "Four thousand for the agents and a thousand for you. This is something extra." Jack threw down a second envelope.

"What's this?" said Don, smiling.

It was a game they played. "Open it."

Don opened it and saw two hundred-dollar bills. "Man, I love this job."

That was the hope, that Don would keep coming back, that Don would tell him if anything went wrong, that Don might be there if there was real trouble. "For doing such a good job. Listen, I have to meet someone in a few minutes."

"Okay." Don chugged the rest of his beer, picked up the backpack, saluted Jack, and left.

Outside, Don shook his head at a transvestite, and vanished.

It was early in the project, but Jack couldn't shake the feeling that all was not right, that he was casually, and without thought, already in over his head.

"Everything's going smooth as silk," he said.

"Everything?" Jeanie said, taking her eyes off the remote and looking at him.

Jeanie was curled up on the sofa next to him. They'd had drinks at Oak's, and then eaten dinner at Capriccio. It was a good night, but they were full, languorous, and tired. They'd reached the point in the night when they needed a diversion, any diversion. He supposed that was why

TV was such a wasteland.

"Problems are inevitable. You have to be flexible."

Jeanie straightened up and leaned back into the sofa. "I can't believe what your doing. Rousting people out of where they live. Jack Kuhl, efficiency expert. Whenever I think of it, I have this image of a little old lady with a knapsack on her back."

He told himself not to talk about the project, then did. He had to talk to somebody. "It's like any business. That little old lady will find a place just like the one she left. Think of me as a catalyst. I'm shaking people up, making them think about where they are, what they're doing."

Jeanie laughed. "I've heard rationalizations, but that takes the cake. Tell me, Jack." She tucked her legs under her and watched him closely. "Is there anything you wouldn't do to make it?"

A week ago, Bobo, Carismo's owner made Jeanie a manager. And in the space of a few days, she started acting like one. It was human nature. He was glad to call her manager. Yes, this is Jeanie, manager of Carismo's. She's cool, with it, fast track. Can't you tell? "Why ask that?"

"Since I became a manager, I feel more aggressive. On a continuum of aggression, or competition, I've just started, but you're way up the scale. You've got to be ruthless to throw people out on the street."

Jack saw she was serious. "I'm not ruthless, just efficient. I'm just speeding up the capitalist evolutionary process. It's like social Darwinism."

"Don't be obscure," she said, untucking her legs. She flexed one leg, tightened her muscles, and then scrutinized her muscular leg.

"I was dumb and idealistic once," he said, too seriously. "At UCLA, I thought things were run by good intentions and planning, charts and numbers, boom and bust cycles, Laski curves, supply-side economics, Keynes, Galbraith, Tobin, Friedman. It's a tidy world. It left out the most important ingredient—more. And after that 'more' even more."

"And that keeps you going." She leaned over and examined a toenail critically, then bunched the muscles in her legs and crossed them.

"Greed drives the system, although only Ivan Boesky called it by its real name. It also takes brains, insight, and a feel for what you're doing. I'm doing it for that 'more,' for money, the apartment, a car, vacations." He was doing it for "more" and to get the good life back, but then it always came down to what the good life was. You couldn't question *that* too closely.

"Isn't it funny that mothers and fathers across America tell little Dick to share with little Timmy in the sandbox. Then when they grow up little Timmy is the competition or the kid on welfare you don't want to give your tax dollars to."

"We're built that way," said Jack.

"It doesn't seem human."

"It's quintessentially human."

"Where is this hotel?"

She already knew a lot. It was something he couldn't help. It was another worry: the sixth degree of implication. *Jeanie, how long did you know the suspect? Who did he meet? What exactly was the project?* "I have a straight job lined up. Soon, I'll be squeaky clean."

Jeanie shook her head. "I'm not sure I wanted to know. Responsibility, more money—you get invested in the system. You're a cool guy, Jackums, bright, drop-dead handsome, but I don't want you to get in over your head. Shit happens."

"Not on this project."

Jack ran through a mental list of what he'd seen in the TV guide. Soap operas, sitcoms, okay series spinning off unwatchable ones, unending commercials. He grabbed the remote. "Let's watch 'Scarface.'"

Jeanie settled into the sofa, miffed. "I love Pacino, but it's so violent."

"At least it's well-crafted. A few minutes. It's all I can take anyway." Outside, lights from Jersey drew streaks across the water.

"Scarface" bloomed on the TV. It was the torture scene, the one with the chain saw. Might makes right. The strong inherit the earth. The weak inherit sickness, death, and babies. He'd avoided Jeanie's question, but it came back while he watched the bloodletting on the tube.

It was a simple question, even simplistic. But there were simple questions you couldn't avoid.

How far would he go when the project heated up?

13

Rudi Lopwitz sat behind his desk. It was a big desk, which made him seem small. He liked the desk. It held everything he needed to know about the Rex. Old ledgers, tax forms, the addresses of construction companies, elevator repairmen. Behind him perched loosely in the window was an ancient and disabled air conditioner. A breeze slipped through the crack between the air conditioner and the bottom of the window and ruffled the pages of the open ledger near his hand making them stiff in the draft, then fall slowly.

The door to the small room was open and beyond his large and perspiring partner, Brendel, who sat in front of him, was the crowded Rex office.

Brendel wiped his head with a large handkerchief. He tucked the handkerchief in his pocket and then glanced at his watch. He watched Rudi. He said, "You see it's a natural development. It's something we've wanted for years."

Rudi's glasses were poised in his salt-and-pepper hair. He frowned, pyramided his hands, and fixed Brendel with an icy stare. "We know Lansky's reputation," Rudi said. He pointed to a wad of papers on his desk, which Frieda Berg had given him. "Newspaper reports, articles, quotes from the police. They're not made up. We knew some of it when we met him."

"Slanders from people who don't like him. He's not like that."

Rudi smiled, sardonically. "So now you're his brother? When did this happen?"

"I didn't want to say this. I think you're jealous."

"What!"

"He's one of the big boys. He makes big deals. Last weekend at his house on Long Island, he told me about a deal in Brooklyn. He wants me in. This is the big time."

Brendel was smart. Rudi had always known that. Brendel had brought him into part ownership of the Rex. Brendel had seen the opportunities. Rudi worked hard, but Brendel had the brains. "You're a bright man. But this is a snow job. You know what a snow job is? He wines and dines you, blows you up like a doll in the Macy's parade. Then it's time for the needle. Pssssss. Pssssss. There goes Brendel. See, now he's a pile of plastic."

There was an accent of worry in Brendel's eyes, then Brendel set his jaw. Rudi had seen that before. Brendel had brains, but uncertainty made him obstinate. Brendel dismissed Rudi with a wave of his hand. "I say you're jealous. These renovations are what we need. The hotel has to be part of the Twentieth Century."

"I don't mind renovations," said Rudi. "We do them, not him."

"He has resources," said Brendel, testily. "Why look for them, when he has them?"

"Because he's not going to renovate the rooms." Rudi slapped his hand on the papers. "It's here in black and white. He did the same thing at the Amsterdam. He doesn't renovate, he destroys. What about those guys he's moved in? What about them? They're here to get the other residents out. And for what? He takes over hotels. He razes them and sells them to a developer or puts up a high-rise himself. That's what he does."

"You keep talking about a conspiracy," said Brendel. "Residents always have problems with neighbors. It's a law of nature."

"What about these renovations?" said Rudi. "We do them."

"I can't talk to you," said Brendel, getting up. "Michael and I have the controlling interest in the Rex. We vote to renovate. If you don't like it, we'll buy you out. When rooms come up, don't rent them. You'll see. I'm trying to make you rich. All you want to do is live in the past."

"At least it's a past that I know."

Brendel shook his head dismissing Rudi with a wave of his hand.

Brendel walked through the open door, then his heavy form appeared in the desk clerk's half-oval. Then he was gone.

Rudi stared at the pile of papers. Their margin was thin enough without letting rooms stand vacant. According to Frieda, Lansky owned seven or eight of the Rex's residents. Residents had started complaining about notes and threats. His list of Rex ailments, formidable in the best of times, was already twice as long. And now he couldn't rent rooms.

Rudi didn't know how long the Rex would last, or how long Rudi Lopwitz would last. When he first started working at the Rex, he told his wife it was an albatross. After ten years, it was still an albatross, but he'd grown fond of its leaks and windy spaces in winter and oven-like heat in summer. He liked the people. It felt more like a home than his cookie-cutter two-bedroom house in Queens. No, he didn't want to give it up, or think of giving it up. But it looked more and more that was what he should do.

Max knew that the second floor was going to be easy, one of the easiest. And it was. There was black homo Sid, the blond, husky, but shy Calvin, crippled Maury with his goat's head cane, the two homos, Mark and George. That is, a real George, not Jack's George. Max laughed every time he thought of Jack's name game. He told the others the homo floor was easy, although not many homos had actually left. Bonnie, she'd lived near the fire escape for years, was the closest to actually packing it in. Didn't take long there. He called her a couple times from outside and whispered threats like he was Max the Ripper. He'd left notes. Sneered at her in lobby. Tracked her with his eyes, as if he were an alley cat stalking a house mouse.

The others would be tougher. But Jack knew what to do, who to work on, what to say, what to write. The other guys were doing OK too. Don was on five, but five was tough, so he was helping Truck on four. Jimmy—he was the type who let things build up, then exploded—did what he was told, but not much more, at least from what Ace and Tim said. Blondie—fuck, a programmer!—stayed in his room diddling his computer most of the time, but Don said he'd done his share on the Farmers, a couple, and Lester an old guy who lived near the fire escape.

He didn't hear much about Bert, but he had a tough floor. Everyone knew about Frieda, the Jewish bitch, and her garden. That's what he'd do, if he was Bert. Fuck up her garden, fuck up her. Max made a mental note to mention it to Jack. Oh, excuse me—George!

It was time to work on Sid, poor fuck. He'd followed him a week ago. Sid had gone to an old bar on First full of old queers. Funny to see them all together. Could wipe them out with a bomb. He'd reported it to Jack although he wasn't sure what he could do with it. Max flipped his hair out of his eyes, leaned over the paper, and wrote, laboriously, "Get out now nigger queen!!" He carefully folded the note in two. A few seconds later, he locked his door, and walked quickly down the hallway.

A door opened, shut. Calvin—blond and blue-eyed in black jeans, blue button-down shirt, a light sports coat—hurried past him towards the fire doors.

Max turned and watched Calvin's retreating form.

"You'd better hurry," Max said. Calvin shot a scared look back as he opened the fire door. Max made a slash across his neck with his forefinger. Calvin's eyes did a dance number, then he hurried through the open door. A few seconds later, the door closed slowly. Max laughed. Then he waited, listened. Convinced no one was about to come out, he slipped the note under Sid's door. Max paused, smiled to himself, and rapped loudly on Sid's door. Then he turned and walked to the fire doors, opened them, then skipped down the stairs into the lobby.

He gave Rudi his best ear-to-ear smiles. Rudi shook his head.

Max felt Rudi knew what he was doing. But what could Rudi do?

Max watched the traffic on the street, scratched his head, and decided to go to McDonald's. Getting paid for staying in a room, for living—it didn't get much better. It was like the rich guys, the bond clippers. They didn't work either.

Ace wiped the sweat off his face. He left the damp handkerchief on the desk. Outside, over the roof of the townhouse, pigeons settled on Olympia ledges. He'd had one inside Riker's. A pet. He fed him every day for six months. Then one day, he brought his birdseed to the same workout area and the pigeon was dead. Head torn off. Body crushed. He knew Winton, a beefy guard, had done it. He felt like shit for a week. Told himself that if he ever saw Winton outside, he would kill him *and* his family.

Ace tore a paper in two, then tore one of the halves in two. He squared the paper on the desk, picked up a pencil, and wrote: "Get out now, asshole!!!" He folded the paper clumsily. He looked around the room. Unmade bed, dirty laundry, beer cans, full ashtray. He got to his feet and stuffed his handkerchief in his pocket.

At the door, he felt the dull pain in his throat. He massaged it with a beefy hand. It was still sore. Mario had nailed him when he wasn't looking. Yes, he'd get his rounds in. Yes, they'd have to carry Mario out in a box. Fuck Jack. Fuck playing by Jack's fucking rules.

Except he did it, at least for now. He wasn't a moron. He needed the money and for the first time in years, he was staying out of jail. But he sure didn't like to play chicken shit. Phone calls, notes under doors, givin' the eye to old ladies, clogging drains. It was kid stuff. What he wanted to do was grab Lester Abado by the throat, take his wiggling body through the lobby of the Rex, and throw it down the steps. Fuck you Lester. I want your room.

Fantasies of violence had always haunted him. Course his truck driver father beat the shit out of him, and mom. He knew what the shrinks said. He beat me, I beat them.

Fuck that shit. It felt good.

Yesterday, for no reason, he felt lousy. It was the Rex, the single room. The heat. Back to go. Back to square fucking one. The last time he lived in one of those places was right before he met Marie, his ex-wife. Life seemed so easy. They were tight, really tight. Marie wasn't a great looker, but she had a nice smile and liked him, told him he was her protector. Moved out of that single room to a one bedroom near Coney Island. They were both working. He worked construction for the Nicolli Brothers. Shit they were thinkin' of havin' kids! Then...well what happened was what always happened. Got drunk one night in the Nightcap. Decided it was time to make some real money. Called Jimmy Dix. Did a couple of jobs, had more money. It was a good time, a great time. Then he got caught; then he did time. And then he was angry all the time...at his rotten life, at everything.

Marie. He wanted to call her, but knew—knew!—he shouldn't. He paced to the window, then back to the door. He smoked. He had a beer. He knew he had one chance. One chance to get the job; one chance to make it outside. If he blew it, he couldn't call her again.

Late in the afternoon, he had another beer, and punched out her number. He held his breath as he recognized her voice. She didn't hang up. He knew it would work. She listened to his shuckin' and jivin'. Then when she didn't say anything, he started bailing. He made up stories. Working in trucking; going straight. Might buy a car. Could she meet him for a beer, for old times? He'd pay.

There was a longer silence. Too long.

Then she said, fuck no. Remember the beatings? Remember the broken nose? Remember the divorce? Remember the restraining order?

And didn't she hear he was wanted?

He said no and hung up fast.

He wasn't exactly enjoying life, but it was a million times better than Riker's.

Ace opened and closed his door. At the end of the hallway, the sun shone through the fire escape making bars on the carpet. It was going to be a scorcher. He hated that room. It was a fucking inferno. All his fan did was push the heat around.

Lester's room was right across the hall. He walked over to Lester's door. He saw the corner of a note sticking out. Blondie must have been busy. But weren't two better than one? Ace bent down and stuffed the note under the door, but the crumpled note wedged in the small space and bunched up. It pissed him off. He reached up to pound on the door, but stopped.

Ace shrugged and left the note crammed under the door. He walked towards the fire doors. It was early. He supposed he might as well go up to McDonald's. Max was always there and sometimes other guys were too. He might as well find out what they were doing.

Tim Ramsey checked the hallway. Empty. He walked to the bathroom near the fire doors, closed, and locked the door. He flicked his zipper down with small nervous hands. He left the lid down, then peed. Some of it got into the stained toilet bowl, but not much. Then, a smile tugging up the corners of his small face, he picked up the spare roll of toilet paper. He turned it this way and that, then seemed to agree with himself that it was just right. He dropped the roll of toilet paper into the toilet. He picked up the plunger behind the toilet and aimed the plunger at the roll. He punched it until it wedged in the back of the toilet.

Flush time at the OK Corral.

He watched the water rise, then crest over the rim of the toilet. Tim smiled, flipped his cigarette in the pool of water, and threw the plunger to the back of the bathroom. Yellow water spread over the floor like olive oil on a hot skillet.

It was going to be a wet morning for somebody.

Tim unlocked the washroom, checked the hallway, and then hurried back to his room. Inside, he contemplated the sorry state of his personal items. You couldn't have anything in prison. Outside, his room filled up with junk.

Stuff, stuff, stuff.

Tim was unshaven with a wan, thin face and a full head of hair, which was mostly black, but in the last year streaked with silver. He wore—always wore—elevator shoes, which made him reach the height of five feet seven inches.

Tim was born in Iowa on a farm. After Tim's third goround with his stepfather Glen, he left for good. Never looked back. Two years after he left the farm he was sleeping in a culvert in Illinois, begging, going hungry most of the time. Then he was in jail for shoplifting. Five years later it was Riker's Island for stealing, Attica for burglary. Six months ago, it was back to Riker's. Like a lot of his friends on the inside, he couldn't seem to stay out of jail.

Until he paid Sammy to get on the list and George—Jack Kuhl—hired him.

Funny. Workin' at the Rex gave him a sense of accomplishment he never felt. And it was legitimate. Sort of.

The problem was that he liked the Rex—living there that is. Never thought that would happen. Last night, in Greg's Bar in midtown, he talked about it with Truck.

Truck was sloppy, smelled like damp cloth, but knew the score. Truck said, "Where you goin' after we finish."

Tim shook his head and said, "Don't know."

"Me neither. Livin' here sure beats livin' with my brother, but—"

Tim knew. "But everybody treats you like a fuckin' leper."

They both nodded. Truck said, "Course if somebody threatened me every time I opened my door, stopped up my toilets, ran me batty with rap music..."

They tapped cigarettes into the ashtray. "Hate livin' around 'em."

Truck took a long swallow of his beer. "Gottcha."

"You steal from somebody, you don't usually see 'em again."

Truck nodded, and said, "Here they're right there starin' at ya like you're a rat."

"Or a sack full of shit."

Truck shrugged. "Shouldn't bother me, but does."

"Say, you got the best lookin' gals on your floor. They should be easy."

"Think again. They're fuckin' poison. They aint got no respect. I'll get this round."

Truck was okay. They'd had a couple more beers, shot the shit. They'd known some of the same guys in Riker's. Riker's was huge, but there weren't many white guys.

Tim looked at the mess in his room and decided it was time to go to McDonald's. Time to compare notes. Sometimes it was okay, but he didn't like being around Max and Ace that much. Max was a wise guy, Ace a firecracker. He sure didn't want to be around when Ace got drunk and decided to take off after one of the residents.

Shit, he thought, it might ruin the job for all of us.

14

Get out or els. I meen it.

It didn't take long for Marcy Benaventura to find out what was going on. Someone named Lansky bought out Shem, one of the owners, and he wanted to get rid of the residents. It happened everywhere else. It couldn't happen at the Rex. But it was. The greasy-haired goon, or thug, or creep, at the end of the hall was part of what Frieda called an invasion. First there were phone calls, then the notes. The phone calls didn't bother her, she just unhooked her phone. She left instructions at the desk not to put through calls on the room buzzer. That left the notes, those mashed up slips of paper Truck jammed under the door. She knew one thing: She wasn't leaving, if the creeps' best shot was an illiterate fucking note.

Neither was Carly.

Marcy opened her door. Carly's door was open. Carly's room was light, impeccably clean, full, and hot. Carly, in jeans, her shoulder length hair brushing the top of a frilly white blouse, was staring in her brown leather bag, her hand on her chin. It was eight. In a few minutes they'd both be on the elevator, or running down the stairs.

Marcy said, "Anything new?"

Carly looked up, guessed what she meant. "You hear things. The Rex grapevine is fast, but almost never gets it right." Carly motioned her into the room. Marcy walked in a few steps. Carly whispered, "Larry the Moat bartender knows everything. The goons are all blabbermouths when they get drunk. Don talked about getting money from a George whose real name is Jack."

"That's almost complicated. We know about Don. I guess somebody has to pay him."

"We know a lot," said Carly. "'We'—thought I'd never say that about the folks here. But there is a fledgling esprit."

"Mostly because of Frieda. Guess that doesn't extend to a residents' committee."

Carly checked a black purse, and dropped it in her bag. "At least she tried."

"I better get ready," said Marcy.

She was halfway across the hall, when their goon's door opened.

Truck—the residents knew their names, and traded stories of what they'd done, and what they might have done—said, "Packin' up?"

Marcy felt Carly behind her. Marcy said, "God you're ugly. Is this the only job you can get? I mean really."

Carly put her finger to her chin and looked puzzled. "We shouldn't blame him. Brainless, dickless. What else *could* he do?"

Truck walked closer to them, then stopped. He seemed to think about what he was doing. "You're both on my list, sweeties. You'd leave if you knew what was good for you."

"We're sooooo frightened of the big, fat slob," cooed Marcy. "Wish I could chat, but I gotta work."

Carly said, "Me too."

Truck glared at them, then turned, walked back into his room, and slammed his door.

And that was that. Except Marcy knew that not all the residents reacted quite the same way. Many knew about the goons, Lansky, and the rest. Most had an inkling of some sort of the big picture. And most felt there wasn't much they could do about it.

And Marcy Benaventura had another life, just as she'd hoped. She and Butch had become a two-to-three times a week couple. She'd gone to openings in the East Village and gotten to know his studio, the way he did things. She wasn't sure what effect thugs in the Rex was going to have on her other life. She was about to find out.

That day, after work and drawing at Pier 17, she went to Butch's. He'd been out of town for almost a week visiting his parents in Chicago. She was sure ready to see him. The garage doors were open. She angled through the iron, A-frames, and sculpture. Butch was working on a new piece, helmet down, dropping a bead along a seam.

"Hey," she said, waving her hand.

Butch waved back, then snapped off the torch, and pushed his helmet up. "Hey yourself, plutonium thighs."

She smiled, dropped her pack, and collapsed on the sofa.

Butch walked through the mess, stopped at the refrigerator, and pulled out two beers. He popped both of them, and walked over to the sofa.

He leaned down and they kissed.

"How was Chicago," she said.

"My parents treat me like I'm fifteen. I go along with it. I suppose everyone does."

"Bel never treated me like I was fifteen," she said, shaking her head.

"You look pooped," said Butch.

"Am I ever. But it's not work or Pier 17. It's something else."

"At least relax." Butch handed her a beer, then sat down on the couch. He propped his feet on the ancient luggage case/table. He looked at her somberly. "Whip it on me."

She shucked her tennies off and curled up on the sofa. The sofa was turned towards the front of the garage. It let her mind wander in the art and junk, fondle a piece with her eyes, see skewed lines of perspective. She steeled herself. "Guess what's going down at the hotel."

Butch shrugged. "A party? Somebody die? A drug bust?"

"All good guesses. Nope. Some guy, Lansky, bought part of the Rex and is trying to kick the residents into the street. He hired a bunch of thugs and a guy named George or Jack to do it. I've already got three notes telling me to get out, or else. And he can't spell 'or else'."

"Fuck me," said Butch, eyes widening. "What are you—"

"Going to do? Isn't it obvious? I'm moving in here."

Butch frowned, then looked stunned. He rubbed his head, flipping the bristles forward and back. He always did that when he felt nervous. "Why didn't I think of that?"

She had an edge, if she knew how to play it. "I was kidding, just kidding. If we were around each other 24/7, we'd kill each other."

Butch's frown deepened. "I don't know about that. It's nice having you here, cuz I dig you. And I mean it. It's also nice not seeing you all the time."

"I know exactly what you mean." And she did.

"Where are you going to stay? You want me to ask around?"

Marcy thought about that. She could find another hotel, maybe a small studio in the East Village. "I haven't thought much about it. But I'm leaning towards staying right where I am."

Butch took a quick sip of beer, then said, "And the thugs?"

"They whisper asthmatic threats into the phone. They leave notes.

They stare at us. I think they've done other stuff, hassled people, broken shit. They're a bunch of morons."

"You don't know what might happen."

"Everybody asks the same question," she said. "Frieda Berg—I've mentioned her before; she lives on eight, has the garden."

"Jewish, neurotic, works in welfare."

"Most times you don't look like you're paying attention."

"One of my many gifts."

Marcy smiled wryly. "Anyway, she thinks they already forced a couple people out. You know, did more than threaten them."

"You don't want to wait around to find out, do you?" Butch said. "You don't want to get hurt. *I* don't want to you to get hurt."

"If that's as close to saying I love you, I'll take it."

"We've only known each other—"

"Kidding again. I guess I got that from mom. She's the smart, distant, alcoholic type. Whenever it got emotional, she started kidding. Dad called her the needle. She never told me she loved me. Dad did. How'd we end up talking about this shit?"

Butch shook his head. "I'll come over and look around. You can point out the thugs."

Marcy snorted. "Right. A fucking war."

"I've read landlords leave scaffolding up, blow fumes into apartments, beat people up, start fires. If this Lansky wants it, he'll get it."

"You're sure encouraging." She got up and stepped over his outstretched legs. She bent down and kissed him on the forehead. "Stay up if you want. I'm dead tired. At least I won't have to worry about the Rex tonight."

"I'll be right there."

She was anxious when she got in bed, but she was afraid of sleep. Grossly, she found Butch on her, his hair looking like a black sculpture against the dark ceiling, his muscles rock-hard. And it made her forget the Rex. Sex. Sometimes it felt like the only answer.

Later she heard Butch rumbling and banging around his studio. She saw a light pop on in the middle, then the torches. Sex had, once again, jump-started his creative juices.

The next morning, she left Butch snoring on his waterbed. If she remembered, he crashed about four, the creative and animal juices pumped into an angst-ridden piece with penis.

Weenie, weenie, who's got the peenie?

Outside Butch's, with its thin light and cool, dank space, was a typical August inferno. The dog walkers and joggers in Thompkins Square Park, most from the more respectable sections of the East Village, moved in slow motion. The camp of homeless was starting to stir. She walked through the park slowly then more briskly away from a bum with ratty Rasputin hair and beard and a huge red nose, planted in the middle of the sidewalk like a pillar. He seemed stunned, his puffy thrust-out hand calcified.

She was walking across from the Odessa, a prime East Village breakfast spot about a half-block from the Zoo, when she saw Don, the blob of a goon from the Rex. He sat at the window seat in the Odessa talking to a handsome man in a blue blazer and white shirt. She about-faced and walked back into the park, sat on a bench and watched.

After a few minutes, Don finished his coffee, got up, and left. The blazer stayed. George/Jack—she assumed it was Jack—would look out the window, then appear reflective, as if he were trying to find meaning in what he'd seen.

Marcy wondered what to do. She could be way off base about who he was. What if he was George/Jack? She was in a tizzy of ambivalence, but then she felt angry. She was already hot and sweating, but that anger made her head feel super hot. When she tried to analyze it later, she thought it was about people getting away with shit, about people fucking with Marcy Benaventura's new start, about a bunch of assholes who thought they could push people around.

Fuck him. She got up, hitched up her shorts, rubbed the bristles on her head roughly—for the first time she realized she was imitating Butch—picked up her pack, and headed for the Odessa.

She glanced in the window as she passed. He was still there. She grimaced as if she were about to cut open a fish, or stick her hand in a sack of garbage, and pushed open the door. Inside was a typical East Village crowd of punks, writers, and musicians with pastel hair, facial hardware, and hard, laughing faces, dreaming of breakout CDs and big bucks.

Marcy hesitated, turned on her heel, and stood in front of him.

He felt her watching him and looked up. "Yes?" said Jack, pleasantly. He was handsome with a long face, wavy brown hair, straight nose, and wide brown eyes. He had a half-full cup of coffee in front of him and a notebook open to "Seventh Floor."

That made her sure he was Jack. "Hey asshole."

"I don't know you," he stuttered.

She took a step closer. "Let's see if I can be clearer. Your name is George, or is that 'Jack', and you're trying to kick residents out of the Rex. I can be even clearer. Don and your goons rattle peoples' doors, pound on walls, and stuff illiterate notes under doors."

He frowned, and then scanned the crowd. By the time he got back to her, he'd composed himself. The corners of his mouth lifted and a line of straight, white teeth appeared. "I have friends who stay at the Rex. I'm not sure I'm behind anything."

She was relieved he admitted it; even with that notebook entry, she could have custard pie on her face. "Okay Jack, if you're not behind anything, why talk to me?"

Jack laughed. He moved his spoon around his coffee in circles. "I don't have much choice, do I?" Jack smiled again, as if he'd found the thread. "If I were behind anything I'd try to find out as much as I could about the people who live there. If you lived there, for example, I would try to find out where you worked and where you went. I'd try to find out if you were a waitress at a place called the Odyssey, or if you liked to go to Pier 17 to draw caricatures of Tommy Tourist. Gotta make the right management decisions."

The skin crawled on her back and then it felt like a full body shock. People she didn't know watched her, knew about her. She looked down the counter. Everyone seemed happy, boisterous, messing with their breakfast or eyeing snowy wedges of pie and cake in the revolving cases behind the counter. She turned and looked at Jack. Her face felt drawn tight. "Are you insane? What the fuck does *management* decisions mean?"

Jack screwed his face into what was an ingratiating, puzzled expression, then folded his hands as if he were thinking deeply. "I like good movies and good food. I read books and I vote for green candidates. I suppose that's my California heritage. We all have to do something with our lives. Right now, I'm a hotel management consultant."

"You're a fucking goon, that's what you are."

Jack looked abashed. He stammered, "I feel for the Rex residents. I lived in a hotel myself. But there are other hotels, other places to live, other things to do with your life."

"What a crock of shit. You're just another fucking self-serving goon." She could tell the people in the booth behind her were staring. She could tell he didn't like being called a "goon."

Jack frowned. "That high-rise on Thirtieth, the Giltmore, the Olympia, renovated town houses. Your hotel is dead in the center of Gentry City. The residents feel displaced already. It's not Mario's or Sven's Kip's Bay or Murray Hill. They're strangers in a strange land."

There it was again. Bits-and-pieces about the residents. It was almost as if he had video cameras in the rooms. She was close to blowing up. She could grab the coffee cup and...calm down Benaventura. Attacking Jack in the Odessa will get you precisely zero. Rattling him might do just as good. She sifted through what she knew about the goons, Jack, Lansky. "How did Lansky find you? A want ad?"

Jack's frown told her she'd registered a hit. Jack squared himself up, as if he had to compose himself to reply to her. "I don't have to answer your questions."

She watched him watching her. They had all the guns on their side. Jack acted like he knew he was going to win. The anger bubbled up again. "Threats, intimidation, notes under the door, petty vandalism. Is all that on your fucking résumé?"

A waitress appeared on her right.

"Is everything all right here," she said, glancing at her, then Jack.

"No, it's not all right," said Marcy. "This asshole is trying to kick me out of my room."

Marcy felt the silence around her.

"She was just leaving," said Jack.

"All right," the waitress said. To her: "Come on. It's bad enough with bums from the park hassling customers."

Marcy said, "I don't want to cause *you* problems." She turned back to Jack. "One last thing. You may know about us, but we know about you. We know about Truck and Ace and Max, and we know about Don, you, and Lansky. We won't roll over and play dead."

Jack was composed, but he hesitated before he replied. "I didn't expect it would be easy. People fight when they're cornered."

"And we're not cornered." She saw a glimmer of Jack's head in the surface of his coffee. He was a handsome snake oil salesman/efficiency expert conjured from the Olympia and the Giltmore to deliver the death-blow to the Rex. She felt, without articulating it, that Jack was connected to the darkness that dripped in the backgrounds of her sketches, a vast potential for rot and death. But he seemed vulnerable too. That, oddly, made him more human than she wanted to admit.

She exhaled, turned, and left. She walked stiffly by the window in front. She knew he was staring at her. And that was that. She knew about the other side. She knew about the connection between Lansky in his penthouse and Jack and Jack's link to Don and the goons. It didn't make her feel any better. She made a mental note to tell Frieda.

On Tenth, she turned left and headed towards Astor Place and the subway. She hoped the Rex was still there.

15

The chance meeting with Marcy Benaventura nagged at him like a hangnail. She walked right up and called him Jack the Invader! He'd been scrupulous protecting himself. That was the point of meeting, seeing, and hiring agents in different cafés and bars; that was why he met agents one at a time; that was why he had Don. The project had just started and she—they!—already knew about Don and Lansky.

He called Don. "How does Marcy Benaventura know my name?"

"Jeez, Jack. I try to use 'George' but—"

"Doesn't fucking matter now. What matters is that she knows so much about everything. She knows about you, all the agents, Lansky."

"It's Frieda," said Don. "She's the troublemaker. She tried to start a residents' committee!"

"What? You've got to tell me these things, Don."

"Shit, Jack. It didn't work."

Jack smiled, thinly. "Residents have to know what's going on, but I sure didn't expect they'd organize. And I sure didn't expect they'd know this much this early."

"She told Bert and Jimmy if they hurt anyone, she'd fuck with 'em."

Jack frowned. "What could she do?"

"I told you she works in welfare and I seen people talking to her."

"Right. I'll tell Bert to stay away from her until I know more."

"You got it."

Frieda the gardener, the organizer of the residents' committee. Frieda, social worker. There was the glimmer of a link to Lansky's welfare connections and the program that threw people off welfare. The link was too remote to worry about.

Jack said, "Okay. Tell the agents to keep their traps shut; it's for their own protection."

"You got it."

Talking to Don calmed him, but that run-in nagged him. It nagged him that night.

"Imagine," Jack told Jeanie, "She tried to spook me."

They were in Gringo, a Tex-Mex restaurant on the West Side Highway. They'd had a bottle of Pinot Grigio, eaten tacos and burritos in kamikaze sauce, and watched gulls settle on a splintered wharf, which looked like decayed teeth. One day, that wharf would be developed. People would be charged five bucks to walk on a pier in the Hudson and feel they were part of a cultural history no one remembered. The old and careworn disappeared or became curiosities. He wondered, vaguely, what the next age would do to monuments like the Olympia.

"Tried? Sounds like she did," said Jeanie. "A teenager, huh?" The plates were gone. Jeanie sat across a tablecloth patterned with red, blue, and yellow parrots. Jack had been distracted by the close resemblance between the red of a parrot's neck and Jeanie's lipstick. Her broad, sensual face looked composed, businesslike. Her new job at Carismo's had conferred a dash of class and an underpinning of self-confidence. She was striding away from her past, her alcoholic father, hophead brother, and her rotten childhood upstate. It was odd watching that change up close.

"Maybe twenty. Auburn hair, butch cut, lean, cute ass, green eyes."

"You certainly looked her over," said Jeanie. Jeanie lit a cigarette, and tapped it into a blue glass ashtray. He'd tried to get her to stop, but smoking was de rigueur at Carismo's. Jeanie's eyes crossed slightly, as if she thought she was giving him the third degree.

Cat fights, the male fantasy. "It's part of the job."

"Liking teenagers?"

Jack cracked a smile. "Every straight guy worth his salt has a problem with the young ones. When they hit fifty, men throw out their first wife out and get a younger one. It's not a new trend."

"You wouldn't do that to me, would you?" Weeks ago, Jeanie's face would have drooped. Her eyes would have riveted his own, remorseful and hurt. That night she was composed despite the wine. Jack felt for the first time that he and Jeanie had a secret pact. They would play it out, then spin off in other directions. In a year, someone else would sip coffee with him and make dissenting noises about which video to watch. Suddenly, it made Jack feel empty, as if he had just glimpsed the reality behind the perfumed and polished masks.

"We're not married, and you're young and gorgeous. A trophy gal."

"You might even mean it," Jeanie said, laughing. "Why did this girl get under your skin?"

Harry's name in its glowing box and have Harry blink out in the real world. That would be *too* easy. He supposed the Pentagon was working on something like that, a Rand Corporation-type digital battlefield, which would make American casualties obsolete, or make the most serious battle-field injury repetitive stress from hitting DELETE keys.

The more he got into the project, the more his initial hesitation faded. The Rex was a century old leaking wreck with stained carpets, warped doors, and old residents. He was hitting their weak spots and residents were caving in.

One. Harry Olson would leave. Jack made a note about paying him. Harry leaving would touch Frieda on eight, the desk job, Rudi. Petey, the old guy near the fire escape, was afraid, worried about high blood pressure. Everyone had something to hide, a soft spot, a fear. Jack made another note about a payoff. John McKay, a Vietnam vet on disability, and Imelda, an older Hispanic woman, were wavering. Too many unknowns. He made a note for Tim to keep digging.

Two. Max focused on Sid, the gay black queen, but it was time to tap the rest. Mark and George. Jack felt a frisson of apprehension. His finger froze over the mouse. A few years ago, Jack Kuhl had black and gay friends. John Burrows, black entrepreneur, seller of securities, was a golf buddy. Brian, Geoff, and Mark were fellow Meadows Country Club board members. Could what he was doing be called "situational ethics?" Jack shook his head and clicked up the next diagram.

Three. Blondie and Ace, his most volatile agent, hadn't made much headway. They'd left notes for everyone to leave or suffer the consequences, and, so far, no one had budged. The weak spots were Lester and Millie, both on welfare. Jack wrote: "Lansky's welfare contact?"

Jack tapped his finger on the desk, then glanced outside. The day hadn't changed. It was a move-in-mud, dreary August day. Every now and then one of those pauses would catch him unaware and he'd think about vetting ex-cons or Jeanie asking him how far he'd go. But didn't everyone sacrifice principles? Wasn't that what growing up was about?

Four. Truck had worked hard and two residents were leaving. Of course, four wasn't a pushover. Marcy Benaventura! She was young and foolhardy, but she had her weak spot. She had life, art. A boyfriend? Carly Darling wasn't budging, but Wanda had just moved in. He'd pay her off. Jeb was a soft spot.

Five. Violence fermented behind a few of those doors. Hippies in 506. Ritchie, a heroin addict in 508. Joey, a potential drug dealer. Don had called the cops on Ritchie once. He tapped in a note for Don to target everyone but the hippies and Joey.

Six. He didn't know much about six. Jimmy, his agent on seven, targeted Rose, welfare recipient. That made her *more* obdurate. Bel Benaventura. Where was Lansky's welfare contact???

Seven. Tough floor. Mario, Ivan, Igor, a few other Russians, Brucie, Merri, Raquel. Raquel was the weak spot. But the key might be Mario. Mario had a rocky history, according to Don. He hosted a party a few nights a week. If Mario were out, it could affect those people who partied with him. Jack made a note to check the immigrant status of the Russians.

Eight. Bert Tolen had worked on Meg, Dab, Bill, and Meyer. It looked like Meyer was going. The tough ones were Frieda and Sven. Sven hadn't budged, but Bert knew his route to Sven's Adult Ed class. Following him, a threat outside the Rex, could work. Frieda. A weak spot might be her garden. But he had a bad feeling about Frieda. Residents' association, complaints to the police. Social worker. Jack tapped in a note to have Bert continue holding off.

Basement. He'd plugged the basement into his model last week, when he learned Ben, a troll, lived there. Ben freaked his agents. Too crazy. He'd leave Ben for last.

Finally, Jack looked at the whole. The hotel was old, creaking. It must have a thousand housing violations. Jack laughed. He made a note to ask Lansky about building inspectors. He'd have Lansky stack up violations in his own building!

Jack looked over his list of agents. Some agents worked hard and had results and others were placeholders. Blondie hadn't done much. Don was good with the money, but too soft to intimidate anyone. There was nothing wrong with being a placeholder, of course, until Lansky started "renovating" empty rooms. Jack made notes about bonuses.

After lunch and a nap, Jack decided to take a first hand look at the Rex. He walked through Duane Park. The homeless woman with the brown cap was there. She was scratching her cap furiously, as if she were growing a lice farm in her hair. Jack hailed a cab on Hudson Street and ordered it to the East Side.

Lexington. The Odyssey. He saw Marcy's auburn butch and dark brows rise out of a maze of booths. While they waited for the light, he turned and watched her write an order at the rectangular, silver opening to the kitchen. She thought he was a toad, slime mold. But life changed and the thing that changed it most was money. A few gorounds in a new car, a few restaurants, a few expensive trinkets...

On the other hand, she and other hard-core residents could become too much trouble. What then? Would he call—it was a thought he'd repressed for weeks—Kragen and send him after a kid, a frail woman, a disabled jockey? The thought depressed Jack, but he dismissed it. It was too early for Kragen.

The Rex. The doors to the Rex and the Moat were open. The Moat was an anchor for many residents. He opened his notebook and made a note to call Lansky about getting the Moat closed for code violations, serving minors, or attracting unruly characters. Unruly characters—that was rich. The Moat would go to and, he supposed, the one owner building that housed it. Can't have seedy bars in Gentryville.

Jack wondered what that scene would look like in six months. Would there be a fence, a barrier? Would the rooms of his digital simulacrum and the rooms in the bricks-and-mortar Rex both be empty?

Location, location, location.

Jack Kuhl's job was a riff on that old saw. He'd crawled out of Times Square and the Amsterdam. From one location to another, from down to up. It was a good idea to get the larger picture, to see beginnings and endings. It made those in-between steps seem unimportant.

Jack checked his watch and saw he had two hours before Jeanie would be over. He ordered the cab to Duane Park. He had work to do.

16

It was Thursday afternoon. Frieda had been sitting in her room for an hour. She'd moved what little furniture she had so she could watch the Olympia, especially the penthouse. A fan on her dresser rotated slowly and blew warm air over her face every ten seconds. Her Art Deco blue glass table, which normally held a pack of cigarettes and her man-in-the-moon ashtray, was straining under a wagon load of IMD 209s, photocopies from microfiche files, notes from the library, and notes about which thugs were doing what, and paper-clipped notes with moronic scrawls about getting out or else.

She lit a cigarette, inhaled, and blew a cloud of smoke into the room, which was whipped away by the fan. She stared at her rows of books, as if she hadn't seen them before. Literature, especially the French and Germans, was her solace. It let her escape into other worlds. This one was so frequently difficult and pitiless. But lately this world consumed her thoughts. She was awash in a sea of details, plots and schemes. Plots and Schemes. She told Maritsa, one of her phone buddies, it sounded like an exclusive clothier in Rockefeller Plaza.

But she couldn't joke about what was happening at the Rex or what Michael Lansky was planning in that penthouse.

Plots and Schemes.

The smoke eddied through the room and was swept out the open window. Just like her residents' committee. Frieda laughed, mordantly.

A few days ago, she'd gotten a passel of residents to the roof for a meeting and tried to form a residents' committee. "Tried" was a key word. The roof was an inferno. Several residents brought umbrellas to shade themselves from the sun. Mario, Bel, Rose, Sven, Petey, the Vietnam vet from the first floor, the Farmers, Ivan, Gregor, two other Russians stood between rows and rows of plants and flowers shifting from leg to leg or squirming in chairs around the table.

She explained what was happening from top to bottom, from Lansky to the hoods or goons living on every floor. Most residents knew about the goons from direct contact. They'd heard about why and who, especially Lansky and Jack, from the Rex grapevine, especially Mario and Brucie, their town crier. It didn't take long to see everyone was reading from a different book.

Rose, frowning under black beret, said, "It's a union! It's too political. It avoids the existential meat. It's just a stopgap. Leaving, *real* leaving, is important. And I'll tell you what: I'm not leaving as long as those goons are here. I'll live to be a hundred just to show them!"

Great, she thought. Rose, the resident expert in leaving, charter member of the Hemlock Society, had found a reason to live. "Call it an 'association.' The point is that—"

"The problem," said Melissa Farmer, interrupting, "is that it's top heavy. It doesn't help any one of us. What am I going to do if that pig on four attacks me? Write a letter to you?"

Frieda said, "Not at all, dear. But if we pool all the incidents, if we get enough evidence—"

"You people are something," said Ric. "It's the CIA. A union aint gonna do nothing."

Frieda sighed, ignored Ric. "But—"

"Call it what you want, but we can do without a union," said Brucie, fanning his bald head with his hat. "Unions are about meetings and asking for more money and benes."

Jeb toweled the sweat off his face. He looked at the rest for support. He said, "I don't know about the rest of you, but I don't want to antagonize them. We don't know what they might do."

"What if they attack us *because* of the committee?" said Raquel.

"I've sure had my problems with unions and committees," said Frieda. It looked hopeless, but she asked for a vote anyway. Bel and Mario raised their hands. Two out of twenty.

"Okay, we've had our meeting," she'd said, finally. "Let's go before we die up here."

Raquel, slight, her shoulders sagging, her grizzled head drooping like a wilting flower, turned and walked slowly down the path towards the door. Frieda felt a quick sadness for her and for the rest as they trooped after her fanning themselves or wiping sweat off their faces. Frieda glanced up at the Olympia. She shaded her eyes. Someone stared at them. Lansky? She raised her middle finger in the usual street salutation. She immediately felt how tacky that was and how useless. If the finger was her best shot, they were in deep doo-doo.

It wasn't that she was giving up. Since the meeting, she'd taken a sheaf of harassment notes to the police, called the West Side SRO Law Project, talked to people in the department. The problem was that regardless of what she did, of how many lawyers they found or how many times they sued Lansky, people were scared shitless. It was the difference between the command post and life in the trenches.

And that left her with her own best ammunition: the Triple M. If she could get enough details, if she could start fires in the lusterless cubicles at Central Office, if she could link Lansky with the Triple M. But getting details was impossible that week. Rodriguez, the shit, and the three supes were fixtures at IM66 and everyone at CO was on vacation, including Toby.

Frieda picked up her phone and dialed Toby's apartment for the fifth time that week.

He picked up. She tried to soften her delivery, but it came out too harsh anyway. "Where have you been?"

"Upstate," he said. "Some of us have a life."

She controlled herself. "Did you get my message?"

"About the Rex. Yes."

"What are we going to do? What about the Triple M?"

"Well we can't do anything tonight. Come in tomorrow."

"Right."

Frieda stabbed out her cigarette. She wasn't getting much help from either the department or the residents. Divide and conquer. Pick off the residents one by one. She'd already doped out how Jack—Marcy had told her about her contretemps with Jack, about who he was, and how much he knew—would work it. But knowing the other side, knowing who they were and what they'd do, didn't give her a hint about what their side should do.

That morning, Frieda bundled up photocopies, notes from the library plus a handful of crumpled goon threats. She locked her room and rushed through Sven's gallery. She stopped. Some of Sven's portraits had been slashed from top to bottom. One, a portrait of Glenn Tolliver, a former Rex resident, lay on the ground, its frame crushed, the portrait crumpled. That was part of Jack's plan. Work on the weak ones. Find their soft spots. Every time she thought of the sheer inhumanity of it, it made her blood boil. Once, she thought it was like what the Nazis did to the Jews: Slowly chip away at their rights. Slowly take everything away.

Frieda walked up to Bert's door. She banged on it. "Open up, you miserable little thug."

She didn't hear any movement inside. He couldn't be out *that* early. She glanced down the hall at Sven's door. She'd talk to Sven later.

That morning, the elevator made it to the lobby without stopping. She locked stares, briefly, with Harry at the desk clerk. They were still on the outs. She'd try to make up in a week. Or not. Harry's indifference to what was going on rankled her to her core. Did she really want to sacrifice everything she believed in for a few moments of creature comforts? She snapped off her gaze, turned, and rushed out the open door of the Rex.

On Park Avenue, she turned towards the 34ᵗʰ Street entrance to the subway out of habit. Realizing her error, she did a quarter-turn and faced Park Avenue and Ben, their gaunt hermit. He was wearing his long green army coat, collar up. She could barely see the top of his head.

"How can you wear that?" Frieda said, dabbing at her neck.

An eye emerged, and then Ben's grizzled head. He turned towards her. "Goody Two Shoes. Save anyone today?"

"The day's still young."

"What will that get you?" Ben said. He looked truly puzzled.

They watched another green light come and go. Ben had trapped her before. We all had eyes, ears, warts, feelings, hope. She knew she had to touch something inside of Ben. She knew, equally, she would fail. "You can't go on, you will go on."

"Beckett was too hopeful," Ben croaked. "Truth is death. You choose: death or lies." A scowl grew on the side of his face.

"Prozac."

"Bah."

Ben was right, but you can accept lies gracefully. She took that light and left Ben standing on the corner. She glanced back and saw the crowds eddying around him, as they must have eddied around them both.

She walked slowly in the crushing heat across Midtown to Eighth Avenue, then down Eighth to Fourteenth Street. Despite feeling that she wearing lead boots, that her clothes were sticking to her, that her black curls were mashing flat against her neck, the walk gave her time to contemplate her psychic state. Forget what was happening at the Rex. Forget Harry. The French word was figé, which meant fixed, static. She'd felt like that before, but she felt it more since she'd started uncovering the welfare scheme. Codes and canceled cases. It depressed her, then it led to her own sense of being stopped, canceled in some larger context.

The Central Office building loomed over her. Serious supervisors and administrators rushed hither, frazzled, as if the world depended on their ten o'clock meeting with an assistant to the assistant director. There was a line at the Lego café takeout counter, so she went straight to the elevator. When most of the people in the elevator got out on eleven, she did too. She walked up to twelve. In the big room, a hundred assistants shuffled hundreds of forms on slate gray desks. She was relieved, finally, to escape into the relative sanity of HRA Investigations.

Her empty desk seemed absurd that day. She used it between assignments, but she was always on assignment. It represented a shadow Frieda. That day she would like to be that shadow. She would have long coffee breaks, sigh about the system, go to a birthday party, and forget it was all about death, lies, and coping.

Toby was entrenched like a seedy general behind a hillock of forms, letters, and memos. His brown eyes rotated slowly, lugubriously, from her desk to her.

She sat down, took off her rose-tinted glasses, and dabbed a trickle of sweat from her temple with a white handkerchief embroidered with tiny asters.

Toby said, "I went away, but didn't escape."

She said, "I met a man who wasn't there. He wasn't there again today. I wish that he would go away."

"I wish that he would come to stay. You badger me with Father Brown."

"What didn't you escape?"

Toby snorted. "You. I had a lovely few days near Roscoe. I'm back less than two hours and you call me about end-of-the-world schemes and the Rex."

She shook a cigarette out of the pack, lit it, and inhaled. She exhaled slowly. "If it wasn't me, it would be someone else."

"Okay, what have you got?"

"Loads." She laid out the scheme in logical detail. She showed him everything she'd copied from the library, her notes. She discretely left out her meeting with Sean Borgan.

Toby looked at her notes for a few minutes. Then he shut his eyes and moved his lips silently, as if he were Nero Wolfe. Then his eyes popped open. He pushed her sheaf of papers towards her. "You have to admit, it's an elegant scheme."

"*Elegant!*" said Frieda, voice rising. Her brow tightened.

"Calm down," said Toby, catching signs of volcanic activity.

"I'm not sure of anything anymore," she said, dispiritedly. "I love helping other people, but don't know what to do about myself. And the Rex, the poor Rex. Is it time to go? Is some demiurge telling me it's time?"

Toby shrugged. "I'll help as much as I can. But you have to remember that helping Rex residents isn't what we're here for."

Frieda pursed her lips. "I know. And it seems hopeless. The Rex is a besieged magic mountain and the defenders are shooting blanks."

"Speaking of change," he said. He let the sentence hang for effect. He leaned forward and took out his pipe. He never smoked but liked to chew on it. It looked as if he'd chewed right through the stem. "I think this year will be my last."

She dropped her cigarette on the floor, and ground it down with her heel. "I suppose we were talking about change. Why?"

"I'm tired, but I won't be when I retire."

For the first time—no, not the first time—she saw he *was* tired. His large brown eyes looked almost hurt. "I love it up there." The Catskills. The towns were sleepy and inbred, the country quiet. She remembered Harry and Woodstock. Such a short time ago.

"I'll wake up and do my chores. I'll savor my eggs and potatoes and after breakfast, I'll pet my dog Charlie and read *A Sand County Almanac,* and try to understand the seasons, the subtle changes, and my place in Emerson's nature. In the afternoon I'll fish in my favorite pools in the Beaverkill. Late afternoon I'll sit down and write."

"Your novel?"

"The novel will never be complete; it's just as well. I have a bite-size project. I've been making notes for a book on the legends of the Catskills. That's my retirement project."

"Nine pins, Hudson's men, and shrewish wives. It sounds idyllic.

I'd be bored in a day. I'm doomed to stay here as an agitated witness to the passing folly."

"Even rabble-rousers get tired," Toby said.

"Speaking of which, let's rouse some rabble. I have to do something besides bemoan my fate." Toby seemed annoyed that they finally got down to business, but she wasn't there to savor his regrets or listen to his retirement plans. "If we can't do anything about the Rex directly, what about blowing the Triple M straight to hell?"

"Typical Frieda." Toby leaned back, again, pipe pointed towards the ceiling. He dug himself deep into his chair, as if he was ready to do battle one last time. "Tell me more about the Triple M. When you see a screen with a client 'extracted' from the current system, how much of the case is there."

Frieda thought about what she'd seen. "Name, new case number, address. I don't see a lot of information. But I haven't looked at all the options."

"You may be seeing all there is."

"Which means."

"You think the entire case is going into a digital black hole. The option is called 'extract.' There's likely just a rudimentary case."

"The mechanism doesn't interest me," said Frieda. "Besides restoring cases."

"Restore?" said Toby, frowning.

"There's a Triple M option to restore cases. It works fast. Not that I've been able to touch it for a week."

A frown etched a deep ridge in Toby's forehead. "You see, mechanism is important. Now that I think about it, it makes sense. You didn't tell me?"

"You were upstate reading *Walden*. Besides, look what we've got. Without any records—how they get the real case record is the big question—it takes forever to restore cases. I can do it with a case number and an ENTER key. We'll never have that kind of power to right wrongs."

"You're assuming they are wrongs."

"You know they are," said Frieda. She felt the blood rise in her cheeks. Why was Toby being so difficult?

"I'm splitting hairs. Remember, we don't live in a universe of two." Toby looked ready, earlier, to get down to cases. But now he looked tired, again. She began to feel why he needed to get out. Why bust your balls for thirty years, and then have a stroke a week after you retire?

"Okay," said Frieda, grumpily. "What do we do?"

"I'll take another stab at Special Projects. If this gets hot, we'll have to bring in—"

"Not a committee! We can kiss our asses goodbye."

"Try to be helpful. Find out who's taking the case records. You should have already."

"The workers at IM45 and IM34 have perfected the art of the run-around. I've been too damn nice. I'll go tomorrow."

Toby tapped his pipe on the side of his desk. "I sympathize with your Rex problem. But we have obligations. Let's work on what we can work on."

She got up to leave. "I know you'll do what you can. But if we don't learn a lot fast, the Rex will be history. I hate to see it happening and do nothing but sift papers."

"Danny called me this morning. He said Rodriguez and Shirley submitted a complaint against you. There will likely be a hearing."

"That fuck. Before I'm done, I'm going to send his ass to jail."

Toby shook his head at her, as if he were scolding a child. "For now, you're going to be nice. We need support, not confrontation."

Frieda shook her head. "It's just another thing to worry about."

Toby pulled papers out of the pile. "Find a shack upstate."

"Don't pull a retirement caper in the middle of this."

"Not yet," Toby said, getting up. "Don't close the door. I have to talk to Operations."

She left the door open and found her way down to the elevators. She was about to punch the down button, but stopped. She looked at the door to the stairs. She set her mouth grimly, and walked over and pushed open the door. She walked up to thirteen.

On thirteen, she opened the door slightly and looked around. She'd checked. Morty Bennet's office was in the middle of the hallway, before you got to another big room with piss-yellow walls full of paper-pushers. The hallway was full of people rushing here and there. So typical. She insinuated her body in the human stream. She looked straight ahead and submerged herself in the stream. Opposite Morty's door, she glanced quickly to her left. A man in an open brown coat with a briefcase obscured her view. Then her view cleared. Just seeing Morty's wizened body and permanent scowl made her want to rush in and grab him. She didn't. One reason was that she was outnumbered. Standing on his right, bending down, whispering, was Rodriguez. If she was unsure before, she was positive then. She walked briskly into the big room and took the back stairs down to twelve.

She took the elevator to the lobby, and felt more oppressed than before by the people rushing in and out of the building.

There was an empty booth in the Lego café. She sat down and ordered a latte. She stared morosely out the window at the rush of Eighth Avenue. She wasn't sure why she was down, depressed. It wasn't just HRA, Morty, and Plots and Schemes. It was her entire HRA career. It was a paean to aimless energy and activity. One day she'd have a gold pin, a round of applause, her fights forgotten, thrown on the dustbin, a fading memory for a few.

Frieda looked at the spider web of steamed milk on the long spoon. Plots and Schemes. Frieda felt her eyebrows arch higher, and her jaws tighten.

Screw Frieda Berg's grim personal story. She had a lot more to do.

17

John Moreno, alias Kragen, tilted the mirror of the Toyota Corolla so he could see the doorway better. His target was a man named Manska. He'd watched him for a week. He knew his habits, when his maid would be gone, that he would soon walk down Twelfth Street and Second Avenue, that he would soon be alone in his flat.

Sometimes, they told him more about his targets, sometimes not. In the case of Manska, not. He didn't care. He'd been paid twenty grand to kill him. Period. Why question motives? He found out anyway.

He couldn't follow somebody for a week without knowing a lot about him. He made a few discreet inquiries at the Bordello, where Manska had eaten twice, and he searched online with his new Turbo-charged Gateway with twin processors. There wasn't a lot online, and the World Wide Wait tried his patience as usual.

Correction: *Dr.* Manska. Plastic surgeon, fiftyish, not too athletic, liked the good life. Had a burgundy Rolls Corniche he used once a week, a knockout girlfriend with legs up to her neck draped in simple shifts and pearls. Dr. Manska saw her about the same number of times as he drove the Rolls. Manska was dedicated to making money. It puzzled him. Finally, he made the connection. He guessed it was facial surgery on somebody hot, a Mafia don. Shades of "Dark Passage."

So he knew a lot about his target. It wouldn't change the outcome.

The first few times he had to kill anybody he was a basket case. The Army and a special paratrooper unit trained him well—of course, part of it was his desire. But it was theoretical. They were never in battle, never so much as shot at a deer. Yes the first few times he'd agonized, paced his flat, running the job endlessly over in his head. Then, almost right away, it got easy.

Let's call Kragen. We need him for a job.

Like a plumber, or the cable guy.

Yesterday, he'd tried to explain to Tony that the muscle, the technique, was less important than the psychology, being prepared, planning. He should have known better.

"What da ya mean *planning?*" said Tony. "I'd fuckin' rip his head off. Play with 'em, make 'em hurt. You know cut off some fingers or pull out their nails, one by one."

Maury Rizzo gave him fifteen thousand dollars to take on Tony Gastoni as an "associate" for a few months. Tony was a reform school fuck-up whose father was a top lieutenant in Jersey City. The father wanted to bring Tony into the organization, but he wasn't ready. He needed experience with a pro. Weird deal and he almost said no. But he definitely needed the money. Last year was bad in the stock market and he had expenses. He said yes. He'd show Tony the ropes, give him tips for a few months, and then it was *hasta la vista*.

It didn't take long to see why Tony's father farmed him out.

"Any project is about security and efficiency. It's a contract, not an excuse to go batshit."

"You talk like a fuckin' accountant."

Every dialogue was an exercise in self-restraint. He tried again. "If you see each contract as personal, you're going to right to jail. Don't pass go, don't collect two hundred bucks."

"You sound like a funeral director."

Every time he talked to him, he was that much closer to cutting him loose. It wasn't just that he was impetuous—he was young and they *were* impetuous. But impetuous, violent, mouthy and dumb? It was a lethal combination. He sure wasn't going to take Tony on anything like the Manska job.

What he needed was an easy contract, something like the Amsterdam contract. That was an easy gig. Follow a few people; get 'em scared, rough up the ones who wouldn't leave. It would be perfect way to break in the idiot.

Kragen made a mental note to call Dombry. If Dombry didn't have anything, maybe Lansky did.

There was a flicker in the mirror.

It was Manska. Medium height, good dresser, wore a hat. Crisp walker.

Kragen checked his gun; felt the knife taped to his leg.

He opened the car door, ducked out under the roof. Kragen was six-three. He had long legs and high, thick haunches like a kangaroo. He gave the impression, when people first met his alter ego, John Moreno, of someone easy and inept, someone who tried too hard to please. It was an impression he cultivated.

If his body turned people's heads, his head made them pause. Sometimes, he explained that his head shaped the Kragen persona. When he was young, he was ridiculed, spat at, humiliated. He took it as good-naturedly as he could on the surface, but inside he raged. The paratroopers gave him the tools and, gradually, his Kragen persona emerged. Two perfect embodiments in a single body...and head. His long, awkward body tapered to an almost impossibly small head, sharp nose, and too-large teeth. When he smiled, as he did now, his teeth jutted out elongating his head making him seem like an alien.

Manska started up the front steps to his flat.

Kragen loped towards him.

Time to go to work.

Ace said, "Hey barman, two more."

Larry, the Moat bartender said, "Right away." Larry didn't like them or any of Jack's "agents." He especially didn't like Ace. Ace brooded under his wide forehead and that day his glazed pig eyes showed he was drunk. It was a matter of time before he exploded. But in the weeks since the goons started hassling Rex residents, too many old customers had left. The take was way down. Larry picked out two Buds, keyed the caps, and slid the beers across the bar top.

It was early evening. At that hour a year ago, the Moat would be full, or half-full. It would be outrageous, sometimes tough, but Larry missed those times. It wasn't just the money. That day, with the light dimming on the steps and the Moat darkening slowly, two ex-cons at the bar, and Petey nursing beer in the corner, it was a tomb. A hot fucking tomb. Larry wasn't sure how much longer *he* could hold out. He was getting weird vibes from the owners of his building.

"Hey," said Ace, "isn't it time for a freebie?"

Larry shook his head. "The last round was on the house."

"Fuckin' cheap bastard," said Ace. He crumpled up a five in his hand and threw it at Larry. "Don't keep the fuckin' change."

Larry reached down, picked up the five, and rang it up. He put a dollar in front of Ace.

Ace shook his head at Larry. He wiped his brow with a dirty handkerchief. He stuffed it halfway in his back pocket, where it hung like a wilting rose. Ace turned to Max, smirked. They'd been talking about what they'd done to the residents in the last week. So far, he had the winner. "Did I tell you what I did to Millie?"

Max took a long pull on his beer. He looked at Ace with an air of barely controlled exasperation. "Only ten fuckin' times."

Ace laughed, punched Max on the shoulder. "Breaks me up every time I think of it."

"Hey," Max said, rubbing his shoulder. He flipped the hair off his right eye. It settled back. "A dead rat's not that funny."

"Put it right between the door and the door frame," said Ace. "So when she opens the door, it falls into her room. Stayed in for half an hour, so I could hear the scream."

Max grinned. "I heard it too."

"She's leavin'," said Ace. "Did I tell you?"

Max sighed. "Only ten times."

A droplet of sweat angled down Ace's broad forehead. "When I told him, Don said it was almost time for the crews."

Max looked up at this piece of news. "That's what they're gonna do with all the rooms. Wreck 'em. Like ducks in a shootin' gallery. It's part of the master plan."

Ace growled, "Everybody has a fuckin' *master plan*." Ace's face drooped, his eyes looked hurt, as if he mourned an old friend. "I had a fuckin' master plan. Marie, kids. Can't remember all of it though."

Max watched Larry counting the money in the cash register, and then he took a long, meditative swig of beer. "We all had one of those. Well Jack's master plan must be workin'."

"Those people were easy. The ones left are stickin' like epoxy."

Max said, "The homos'll leave. Other day, I put a clipping about homos gettin' tortured and killed."

"You told me an hour ago. And they aint moved a fuckin' muscle."

"They will," said Max, peeved. "I think everybody's close to caving in. You know what I really want to do?"

Ace shrugged. "I don't remember."

"Fuck up Frieda's garden. You fuck up her garden, you fuck her up. I snuck up there last week. She was workin' like a slave in the heat."

Ace shook his head. He looked at Max as if he were a child. "Fuck

142

psychology. Jack has to do something about that Jewish bitch. He'll have to carry her out in a box. We gotta mix it up sometime, bring in the hard guy. Break some fuckin' heads. You ever see this Kragen?"

Max said, miffed, "Heard about him, never seen him. It's way too soon for him."

Ace scowled. "We're gonna be in this fuckin' hotel for fuckin' ever." Ace took out his handkerchief and wiped his neck. "Don't you sweat?"

"Nope. Must be my metabolism."

"Fuck that."

Voices filtered through the darkness into the Moat. Ace turned and saw Mario and Bel walk in. They looked around and angled towards a table behind the elbow. Mario glanced at them, shook his head, and stuck two fingers up at Larry. Ace lowered his head and glanced surreptitiously at Max. Max stayed calm and took a long sip of beer. The tension was leaden. As Larry made the drinks, he glanced quickly at Ace and Max.

Finally, Mario walked up and paid for the drinks. He walked back to the table, and angled into a seat.

Ace growled in Max's ear. "We fuck him up. *That's* psychology."

Max glanced at Mario and Bel. "What?"

Tink, tink, tink.

Ace tapped his bottle against the ashtray. He watched Mario and Bel. His throat didn't hurt much anymore, but he remembered.

Tink, tink, tink. Ace whispered, "Let's fuck him up."

Max whispered. "Jack's supposed to take care of him. What about last time?"

Tink, tink, tink.

Ace snarled, "Fuckin' lucky punch. I say we fuck him up. That is fuckin' psychology. It'll send a message to the others. It's just like fuckin' up that garden." Ace dropped his head. He shook his head mournfully. "I hate sittin' around leavin' notes and playin' loud music and givin' old ladies the eye. Fuck, the music's gettin' to *me*."

Max rubbed his head. It felt dull, as if his brain was bound in leather. It was the booze. He glanced across the elbow of the bar at Bel and Mario. Bel was giving Mario a hard time. Mario looked drunk. Mario seemed drunk enough to take. "What about stayin' outta jail?"

Ace's eyes grew into slits. "Fuck. We do it right, no problem."

Max frowned, looked at Mario again, then back at Ace. "I heard that before."

"Cake walk," said Ace. Ace rotated half-glazed eyes towards Mario. "Last time, he was sober. Right now, he looks like a baby."

"What about her?"

"Fuckin' bitch. Shit, she looks drunk too."

"I don't know." Max took a swallow of beer. He looked at the label, then checked Mario and Bel's table. "I'd like to fuck him up, too. That is psychology."

"That's what I like to hear," said Ace. "This is perfect. I got my sap with me. We wait until they leave. We follow 'em, then nail him hard. She gets in the way, we nail her. It's not in the Rex and it's not in the Moat. So we're clear. Shit, I'll bet Jack gives us another fuckin' bonus."

Max rubbed his jaw, as if he were judging the odds. "We slip into the Rex. Anybody asks, we were in all night. The barman won't see it and he can't say shit."

Fragments of a fight drifted over the bar top.

"...You don't care about your job...you don't have a fucking job...I don't have a contract. It's always like that...you had too much, as usual...look who's talking...fuck you..."

Mario finished his drink. He shoved his chair back making a loud scraping noise. He looked at Bel, shook his head, and strode to the door. Bel looked after him and grimaced.

Ace dug Max in the ribs. "Look, we don't have to worry about her."

Mario stopped and talked to Petey. Ace felt the leather top of the sap. The adrenalin started surging through his system. He hadn't felt that for a long time.

Mario went to the door and climbed the steps into the night.

Ace nudged Max. They got up and walked to the door. At the door, their shadows closed off the glow from the streetlights. Ace glanced back into the bar, saw no one following them, and nodded to Max.

It was hot and sticky outside. A light in the apartment building across Twenty-eighth Street flicked off. Light from the Rex lobby glowed on the steps of the Rex. A cab roared down Twenty-eighth Street and rocked to a stop at the light on Lexington.

Mario stopped on the sidewalk. He glanced up and down the street as if he was deciding what to do. Ace checked the street. He nodded at

Max, then slipped the sap from his back pocket, and took two steps towards Mario. He planted his foot, drew his arm back.

"Fuck. My head. Arrrggghhh."

Ace hesitated. He glanced over his shoulder. Max was hunched over, his eyes slack. Behind him, Bel grimaced then swung a beer bottle at Max's head. The bottle thudded off the top of Max's head. Max crouched further, his hands held in front of him, as if he were a mantis about to pounce on a fly. Then he crumpled to the pavement.

"Fuckin' bitch." Ace turned, stepped towards Bel, and grabbed her arm. He pulled her to him. Bel eyes were an angry, fearless green. She punched him in the gut with her free hand. Ace didn't feel it. Ace aimed the sap at her face. "You're gonna need some plastic surgery, bitch."

Then Ace's right ear exploded. Bel wrenched away from him.

Ace shook his head dazed. He saw Max curled on the ground. What the fuck was going on?

Mario spun him around. Mario's second punch doubled him over. The next one hit him the face. Blood snaked down his chin and dribbled down his shirt. The last thing Ace remembered was Mario's fist cocked and aimed at his face. Then he was falling back, down. The streetlights made a halo around the night.

He hit his head on something hard. Then it was dark.

18

The Rex. Phase 2. Redux.

Residents left like rats a foundering ship. Six in August. There were no unpleasant surprises from the likes of Marcy Benaventura and Frieda's residents' committee was born dead. When Jack called Lansky the week before Labor Day weekend, Lansky was upbeat and looking forward to a week in his villa in Bermuda.

Jack checked his bank account, then his map of the Rex. The project was humming like a well-tuned car. It was time for a holiday.

Jeanie took days off from Carismo's and on Friday they flew to Miami and spent three days on the beach and four nights in the Fontainebleau. Vacations, interludes, the rupturing of habits always made him horny. Jeanie too. They played sex games in their room—exploring variations they'd thought of, but hadn't tried—ate late champagne brunches, then roasted on the beach. The hot, hot sun, the swarms on the beach, the late afternoon ocean breeze, the isosceles sails dipping in the pigeon-egg blue sea. Jack needed that time-out. No stressful calls from Don. No dark hints from Lansky. No playing god with diagrams of the Rex.

It was a magical time, which reminded Jack more than once of the easy life of KAM, of his wife, moonlit nights watching the Pacific. He'd thought, right after he'd moved into Lansky's condo, that he'd found the first hand hold on his way back. But that holiday made him feel more expansive, as if his return was real. That rarefied feeling lingered and extended itself to the last night in the Fontainebleau nightclub. A hefty Peggy Lee imitator, Pamela Lee, belted out "Is That All There Is," the kind of winsome looking back that put listeners into a different frame of mind, a questioning frame of mind. Was the punch line more than late-night, barfly ruminating? The question was what "that" was. Lost innocence? Lost love? Lost children?

Jack didn't want to think about the big questions, the feints, the missteps, the past, but he couldn't help coming back to the Rex project. He supposed worry was part of the human condition. Years ago, when he should have been enjoying the hundreds of thousands of dollars rolling into Kuhl Assets Management—KAM: he loved to use the acronym when he talked to prospects—he obsessed about the growing deficit, the imbalance between what he was taking in and what he owed.

Jeanie must have guessed his concern. She put her strong-veined hand on his, and stroked it. "What a dynamite time, Jackums. Don't start worrying."

"I'm not," he said, not too convincingly. Pamela Lee talked to the leader of her band. Stage lights shifted from pink to blue. Pamela looked like a glowing statue, her cobalt blue dress shimmered, and her skin shone alabaster, then incandescent. Jack smiled and took Jeanie's hand in his. He traced a vein from the back of her forefinger to the shank of her thumb. "I act cool and unconcerned, but I haven't adjusted to what I'm doing."

Jeanie looked troubled. She turned his hand over. Then she ran a finger down his heart line. Her face looked quizzical, and then she laughed, her dimple tucking in then relaxing. "I guess that's why I still like you. That hint of remorse."

"But I still do it. In two months no one will remember that hotel or who lived there."

A ghost of sadness flickered in Jeanie's eyes. "Given time, you could say that about the condo...or us."

Jeanie's pessimism irritated him. Her dour outlook lay like granite under a gay exterior. She'd have new responsibilities, make money, and buy this and that as reminders of her success. But she'd never escape her rag-tag upbringing, her alkie father, her hophead brother, and dead mother.

And would Jack Kuhl's success always be blighted by KAM's huge failure? The Rex project ebbed back into his thoughts. He wondered if he'd forced himself to take that vacation to prove he wasn't on edge.

"God I hate this heat," said Jeanie.

"Fucking humidity," said Jack. "I'll turn on the air."

"I better get ready. Bobo's expecting me at two," said Jeanie, over her shoulder. "Hey, you got a message."

The black answering message under the Neiman print blinked with a single message. Two messages or three would have been all right. One was bad news. He waited until Jeanie was upstairs, then walked over and punched the Play button. Don's tinny voice leaked out of the machine's speaker.

Agents...trouble...over the weekend.

Jack grabbed the cordless phone out of its cradle. He flicked on the air conditioning on his way upstairs.

"I'm going to the roof for a few minutes," he said.

Jeanie yelled, "What about the air?"

"It's on. Give it a few minutes."

He lowered the stairs. It was deathly hot on the roof. Jack unbuttoned his shirt, sat at the table, and punched out Don's number.

Don said the trouble was about Ace and Max. Ace was in the prison infirmary on Riker's, Max in Bellevue.

"How did it happen?" Jack said. He almost didn't want to know. The sinking feeling when he saw that single blinking light grew. A gull settled on the edge of the roof. The gull stared at him then pushed his yellow bill into the sky and yawked hideously.

"Mario decked Ace a couple weeks ago. I guess it was payback."

Jack gritted his teeth. "Don, Don. Why didn't you tell me?"

"I thought it was over. I told 'em to leave Mario for later. A few days ago, they tried to tap Mario outside the Moat. They didn't do so good."

"Great, just great. It couldn't be down the street or on Park. How does jail fit in?" Jack said. He swiped at a dirt smudge on the table. He got up from the table. He waved his hand at the gull. It yawked once at him, then took off, and became a squashed "M" over the West Side Drive.

"Mario and Bel complained to the cops about them, said they were harassing residents, starting fights. The cops took notes. I know it aint good. Then the cops did checks on Max and Ace. Max was clean, but Ace had a warrant. Burglary."

The traffic mesmerized him, then the river. The heat suffocated him. The reflection off the water blinded him, seared his brain. He forced himself to snap off his gaze. He stumbled back to the table. "How fucking stupid is he, anyway?"

"I don't know, boss. But Truck, Bert, and Tim are planning to get back at Mario."

Calm down. Solve problems. That's what you're good at.

Jack wiped the sweat off his forehead. He modulated his voice. "Call Max and tell him he's fired. Give him a hundred bucks when he gets out of the hospital, and tell him to fuck off. If he has a problem with that tell him he'd better reserve a room at Bellevue. Call me when he leaves his room—it's time to renovate. I'll talk to the other agents before we have a fucking riot."

"You got it."

Jack looked at the phone, as if it had developed a contagion. He climbed down the roof ladder, raised the ladder, and then walked slowly down the stairs. He forced a smile for Jeanie, who waited for him at the door. She gave him a big kiss, as if she didn't see he was about to explode.

After she left, he called his agents. He felt silly saying "George" when everyone knew who he was. He tried to be cool, composed—he *was* dealing with ex-cons. But he was exasperated at their density. Did they understand the words "low profile?" If they didn't, they could suck their thumbs somewhere else.

After he finished with the last one, he was still angry. He printed out diagrams of the Rex, and made a list of vacant rooms. Eight. He called Lansky and left a message that it was time to send in the hardhats. After he hung up, he faxed Lansky a list of rooms. He could have used Max and Ace, but closing their rooms off would work too.

He worked on the diagram of the Rex for another hour. He stopped about two. He'd forgotten to eat. He got up and walked towards the fridge trying to remember what was left.

Bring, bring, bring.

Jack turned and snatched up the phone. It was Lansky. He was still in Bermuda.

"I'm never far from business, Jack. I was waiting for your call. I've called Thompson and Sons and had Moran fax them your list. The hardhats and carpenters are on the way."

That was fast. "Great," said Jack. The Max and Ace fuckup was looking better. He still had six solid agents. Six was enough to harass, slip notes under doors, and do what he needed. And he'd save money. It took time to see the silver lining, but it was there.

"It's good news Jack. Good news. Of course, it could be better."

Every time he had good news, Lansky leaned on him. That morning he was so pissed he leaned back. "It could be a better, a lot better, if those people on welfare had left, or were about to leave. From what I've heard, they're growing roots."

"Are you being difficult again, Jack?"

"I'm being practical, Michael."

The silence weighed on him. Finally Lansky said, "I'll check when I get back. It's hard to do that on the phone. Wait a second, Jack." He heard Lansky say, "Bring me that address book." He heard Lansky flipping through pages. Lansky said, "I'd like you to meet someone, Jack, Moira Maxwell. Her number is 691-2187."

"About what?"

"Your career," said Lansky. Lansky hung up.

A thrill arced through Jack's body. He looked at the phone. His hand trembled as he punched out Moira's number. Moira was there, but she didn't want to talk.

"Let's meet at the Tavern on the Green in Central Park at four-thirty," she said. "I'm short and cute with curly black hair."

"Can you tell me what it's about?"

"That would be indiscreet. See you there."

First Max and Ace, Lansky's pressure, now Moira Maxwell. Who the fuck was she? His career? Jack frowned as he hung up. He timed his holiday all wrong. He needed one right then.

At four, Jack dressed in his best casual outfit. His image reassured him. The mirror showed him the long elegant face, the deep brown eyes, the swept-back, carefully brushed hair. He was the polished, engaging Jack Kuhl. He hailed a cab on Hudson Street. At four-thirty sharp, he stopped at the entrance to the Tavern on the Green, which was the same tacky fantasy outside he remembered from four years ago. Inside, outside. He was struck, again, with the difference between being outside and in. A few dollars, an ounce of chutzpa, a smidgen of luck. Fate could turn again. Jack shelved that thought. The mid-afternoon tea sippers inside never thought of losing or abrupt changes of fortune.

Inside, the Tavern on the Green belied its exterior. It was a vast expanse of white tablecloths, sparkling silver settings, and unctuous waiters. Dominating the middle of the restaurant was a giant floral arrangement of exquisite, but vaguely predatory, South African birds of paradise, bottle-shaped Banksias, and plate-sized Proteas, which looked like shriveled red spiders. A scattering of couples shared intimacies over coffee, teas, and pastries on thin bone-white china.

They had a view of Central Park, of people walking under sycamores on curving sidewalks, roller-bladers, and a self-advertised "Chorus Line" baseball game. Moira Maxwell, real estate agent, was short and animated, with big, dark eyes, a tangle of black curls, and blunt nervous fingers. It wasn't much dialogue at first. Moira had problems with ex-husbands, ex-lovers, her therapists, and her mother. She spilled it out as if she'd forgotten why they were there.

Why were they there?

Finally, she got down to business. She knew the owners of three old hotels in Brooklyn, hotels packed with long-term residents. Could he employ his management methods there? Get out the tenants, renovate, and re-rent for triple the rent or more? It was different from the Amsterdam, although the result was the same—a vacant building. "I'm on a fact-finding mission," she said, giving him an ear-to-ear smile. "Your pay would be handsome, more than you're getting now. Maybe twenty-five K more."

Three buildings at once. Twenty-five K?

They wanted him. He had something to sell. He knew he *could* sell it. He forced himself to calm down. He mentally toted up the money. It would come out to two to three hundred thousand. He would invest, buy real estate. Of course, he'd have to hire more ex-cons and send them into more buildings. There would be more diagrams, more pressure, and the greater chance of a slip-up, police. He felt a thrill, then a letdown.

Moira watched him, a curious expression on her face.

He had to think. "Theoretically," he said, finally. "It's doable."

Moira smiled narrowly. It was a put-off smile, the kind you made when you were about to give someone bad news. "Let's not talk details now. First, I want to see results."

Jack frowned. "How so 'results'?"

"That the Rex is empty or a hole in the ground. I can use that when I talk to the owners of the Brooklyn properties. I say, 'See his track record. Two months at the Amsterdam, a couple months at the Rex.' They nod and say, 'Moira's right. He can do it'."

Moira. The Rex. Jack backed off. "It won't happen tomorrow."

"Michael explained your technique. It's clean, systematic, and effective. What you don't have is time. Time is money, lots of it."

Moira watched him, as if she could tell what he was thinking. He glanced out the window at the baseball game. An overweight guy—what part did he have in "Chorus Line"?—waddled towards third, then slid hard into the base and was put out. He got up slowly, winced, brushed dirt off his sizeable rump, and limped off, head down.

Jack kept to what he knew. "My system is effective and low-profile. That's the point."

"We like what you do, Jack," she continued, quickly. "I know a lot of people who could use your service. But I have to see that hole first."

"Don't worry, everything is on schedule," said Jack. "You'll see that hole."

"That sounds so sexual, I'm almost embarrassed," said Moira, giving him a coquettish smile. She moved the silverware around making crossed spears. "Let's meet again, Jack, say in a week. I'll know more. You can give me an update on your progress."

"Sounds great," said Jack.

A few minutes later, he helped her into a cab. She was going uptown, he down. He watched her cab maneuver out of the Tavern half circle, then accelerate north. Moira could be the next stage, the bigger pot, the means of Jack Kuhl's revival. He didn't trust her.

Jack walked slowly towards Columbus Circle.

What a day. A veritable whirlwind of a day. With Jack Kuhl smack dab in the middle. Not one hotel, or two, but three. That was his game. Jack Kuhl, hotel wrecker. Often lately, especially after he'd called his agents and told them who to target, he felt as if he'd entered a clichéd story about one Jack Kuhl who was slowly becoming estranged from himself, becoming a fictitious George character. That the Jack Kuhl he knew, the polished CEO of KAM, the giver to charities and the supporter of local causes, was starting to reflect the worst around him, was becoming, almost casually, a sum of unethical qualities.

19

Rudi Lopwitz watched the carpenters with their hammers, saws, and leather belts troop into the lobby. He slipped quickly out from behind the desk clerk's partition and challenged them. Who were they? What were they going to do?

They just told him they were going to start renovating eight rooms. They showed him the list. No, it wasn't going to be done room by room; they'd start on all the rooms. They knew exactly what to do.

Rudi argued with them, told them to wait, then called Brendel. Brendel said it was time. Let the renovations proceed. Rudi watched them huddle together in the red elevator. When it slipped up out of sight, his heart fell. His head felt heavy. He shook it slowly from side to side. He knew what they were going to do.

It took them two days. Rudi felt as if a thousand pound weight crushed his chest. He watched, his spirit blank, while they destroyed his hotel. They were wrecking the rooms he worked on seven days a week.

When they left, he walked slowly up to the second floor. It felt different, as if it had been violated. He opened room 204. The "renovated" room had wallpaper hanging in strips, sconces pulled out of sockets, plaster and rubbish in the sinks. He automatically calculated how long it would take him to renovate the room the right way, his way. He walked to the window. On two, you couldn't see much of the Olympia or the sky because of the town house next door. At that moment, he knew Lansky would win. What was so noble about fighting a losing cause? You know what they said, you had to know when to cut your...

Rudi closed the door and walked down to the first floor.

He knew it would get worse. And he knew the residents—the real residents—would accuse him, unjustly, of wrecking their home. Some, like Frieda, Marcy, Mario, and a handful of others knew the real story, but others would think he'd done it. What did they say: It was a lose/lose situation.

He dialed Brendel and told him to come see. But Brendel was busy, had other things on his mind, and was thinking of investing in apartments in Brooklyn. Didn't want to be bothered.

Rudi sat on his stool and flipped the pages of the ledger slowly. He found the eight "renovated" rooms. He drew a line through them. Rooms closed off. Rooms wrecked and unrentable. Residents hustling away in droves. The edge they had was disappearing—fast. It wouldn't take much more.

Marcy Benaventura watched the carpenters in 403. They'd come in early and closed the door. She heard hammering and sawing, the discordant voices of the workers. Frieda told her what they were doing. It was a joke, but a bad joke.

Marcy sighed. She closed the doors to her room and made up her backpack with her drawing supplies. At the last minute, she threw in extra underpants and T-shirts. She was going to see Butch after Pier 17 that evening. What he didn't know was that she was going to spend a few extra days with him. She was sure he'd like that.

The day went by fast. Odyssey. Seaport. Pier 17. Subway. When she got to Butch's, she was tired. Her days exhausted her, but normally she had lots of energy. She wanted to crash, or have a beer and talk. Instead, Butch held up two tickets to the Cul de Sac, his favorite theatre. She liked that existential side of Butch, but he took it too far, made it into a rationale for art. They walked down Avenue B to the Cul de Sac and twenty minutes later, they regarded the bleak set and absurd subject of Ionesco's "The New Tenant." Half an hour later, unseen hands threw a hundred used tires into an empty apartment.

It was almost as if someone up there was tweaking her spirit. Location, apartments, moving in an endless circle. A trip west and back. Living in the Rex. Moving on again.

She wanted to go back and sleep, but Butch had other ideas.

The Zoo. Ten-thirty.

"Okay," she yelled, too abruptly. "What message did that bring you?" Punks with Walkmans cruised the windows. The Putrid Pus screamed hate into the red, black, and yellow oily splatters, which decorated the walls of the Zoo. The only seats were at a ledge in the second room near the Pus. They had to yell to talk.

"Metaphor," Butch said, over the steel guitars, "for absurdity and alienation."

"Alienation sucks," she yelled. "It's a boring, repetitive, pseudo-philo-sophical point about existence. What's happening at the Rex is real. Jack is real. Lansky is real. The goons are real. It's about garbage in your soul." Sometimes their dialogue was replete with monologues punctuated oc-casionally with non sequiturs. When it reached that stage, you couldn't call it dialogue.

"No god, no values. We stand naked in the desert. What's happening at the Rex is a symptom of a hopelessly greedy society. *That's* absurd."

"Absurdist theatre is about nothing, literally," she yelled, angry.

"You can't see everything in terms of a romantic dark side. You've been hung-up on dirt since I've met you. It's Freudian. Maybe you stopped development in the scat stage. Or maybe it's the clichéd menses."

"Fuck you. You don't believe that psycho pabulum."

Butch shrugged and lapsed into silence.

The Rex. Invisible spiritual stains. That night, for a handful of rea-sons, it made her think of the abortion. It was a week before she hit the road. She made it through a line of right-to-lifers holding up pictures of bloody fetuses. She waited for hours in a room with twenty other women and girls all trying to stay calm flipping through two year old "Family Affairs" and "Redbook." When it was over, she felt her brain had been taken out, fried, and dropped back in.

She tried to let the music shake that scene out of her head. No go. The noise accelerated, the guitars were winging higher and higher in an unending Layla-like tune. The punks bunched up outside pressing their nose rings against the glass, captivated by the song. For her, it made an island of silence. She felt another presence in that silence. It was the si-lence of possibility, of another Marcy staring at her. Her baby's hands slid across and down the oily wall. They elongated into the silence. They grasped her stubby head; they pulled luminescent, octopus-like eyes close to her own. She looked in the cold face of possibility. She shud-dered down to her feet.

The song ended. The moment passed. The night leaked away.

Bright light rimmed the shade. As the sun rose, a single slanting bar of light crept down the bags hanging on the door until they were level with Frieda Berg's head. The bar teased her black curls, then her white forehead, and finally her eyes. She blinked once, twice, and stared at the shade. It seemed like a door of perception. She would get up, walk like a somnambulist to the window. The door would open; she would step, possibly forever, into a new alternate reality. Or, how many realities were in that crowded room? All it took was a change in point of view. She supposed she contained an infinite number of points and an infinite number of views. Why then was she committed to this one, the one that felt like a straight jacket?

She grabbed her rose-tinted glasses and stood before the blind. She put on her glasses, held her breath, and let the blind slap the top of the windowsill. The light held her fast, the rat-tat of the blind echoed, then receded in her head. Her mind made connections without volition. The Rex was up, the Rex was down. Lansky, his plot, Jack, Don. The points, the ideas, ordered themselves. Cause, effect. Links in a chain.

She picked up the phone to call Harry, and then put it down. In better days, she would have dug in her garden, but instead, she had to process, make connections, and go to welfare centers. She showered. She dressed in a frilly white blouse, jeans, and espadrilles. She made up her cavernous black bag. She had cow-killing work that day.

She locked her door, sighed, and swept towards the elevator.

Bert—she supposed it was Bert, but she hadn't actually seen him do it—had slashed or trampled half of Sven's small portraits. But Sven didn't quit. As soon as Bert destroyed one, Sven put up another. It looked like a struggle to the death between art and reality. She stopped to regard the room at the end of the hall. Meyer, a chess-player with runny oatmeal eyes, long arms, and spider-like hands, left last week. Bert harassed him constantly and finally Meyer packed. Over the last few days, Lansky's crews tore up eight rooms including Meyer's. Eight rooms closed and locked. Eight nails in the coffin. By her count, Jack had lost two goons—thank you Bel and Mario—but still had six or seven. She wasn't sure about the blond guy on three. In less than two months, a quarter of the residents had left. At that rate, the Rex would be empty by winter.

Her destination that morning was IM 45. Toby was right. She should have gone there already. Phone calls didn't work. The workers were defensive, and then they said, flatly, they didn't have a clue what happened to the case records. Today they were getting the real Frieda Berg.

The elevator was almost too slow, which meant it was back to its old tricks, as if it too was succumbing to the invasion. In the lobby, she glanced in the desk clerk's half-oval and saw Rudi staring at the ledger, as if he were watching his life pass before his eyes.

A half hour later, she stood in front of IM45, which was in the middle of Hell's Kitchen and only a handful of blocks from the Amsterdam. It was a squat, functional abomination in pale gray. Boyfriends and husbands stayed outside and exchanged smokes while the women streamed through the glass and steel doors towards their workers.

She checked the directory and found the center director's office on the third floor. The elevator was packed with nervous women, the hallway on three a cacophony, the center director, Elaine Tibbets, an obdurate ebony statue.

"We didn't lose any cases," said Elaine, stiffly.

"I said they were missing, not that you lost them."

"If there's no record here or in the system, how do you know they were cases?"

She'd traveled that route. "I know it seems contradictory," said Frieda, adopting a mollifying tone. "But here's an IMD 209 closing a case with the wrong code. Why would anyone send it out, if it weren't a case?" Elaine was angry and defensive and not given to helping her, but Frieda saw she was nervous. "The missing cases are not your fault or your workers' fault. This is a high priority problem. If you don't want to help, I'll find someone who will."

Elaine looked at her defiantly, then said, "I don't have time for this. If you have to, talk to Eunice Jones in L & A."

Frieda picked up the form, got up, turned on her heel and left. She understood Elaine's problem, but she didn't have time to make nice.

The L & A office at IM45 was almost identical to the one at IM66 except Frieda knew she was dealing with different people. There were "Sisterhood is Powerful," "ERA Now," and Sierra Club posters of baby fur seals on the wall.

Eunice Jones, Supervisor 2, was a heavy, black woman with huge arms, plum cheeks, and long Rastafarian braids. Eunice talked to her over a wall of photos of kids and grandkids. If Elaine was hostile, Eunice leaned towards total skepticism.

"You say those cases were here?"

Eunice smoked. Frieda lit up. Eunice slid the ashtray so they could share it at the corner of Eunice's desk. "I talked to someone named Fleury a weeks ago, but she was new and didn't know anything."

Eunice shook her head. "Fleury's gone. What makes you think they were here?"

"The clients said so. I think the cases were removed by mistake."

"By mistake?" Eunice said.

"As a test of the new system."

"As a test of the new system?" Rising falsetto inflection, total disbelief. Frieda leaned over the desk and showed Eunice an IMD 209 sent to Floyd McElroy with the code 333. "But there isn't a code 333. This isn't filled out right. There's no issuing center or worker number." Eunice paused and looked at the name again. "I know Floyd. The man's a trip. He carries a long stick with rubber bands, ribbons, and peace medals stuck to it."

She'd recognize a necromancer too. Frieda tapped the IMD 209. "Someone filched his case record before this went out."

"His case worker was Belinda Bates. Hold on." Eunice called Belinda and after a short but animated conversation, put the phone down. "It's peculiar. He called when he got this IMD 209 and Belinda checked the system and couldn't find his case."

"Does she know what happened to the case record?"

"She's one of our best workers," said Eunice, firmly. "She's got over two hundred cases."

"I was a case worker," said Frieda. "I know."

"She finally remembered someone from CO took it."

Frieda's heart fluttered. I could have been anyone, an anonymous functionary, a blank-faced supervisor sent by Morty Bennet. "Does she remember his name or what he looked like?"

"He had other records with him, and she guessed he got those from Record Management, but Floyd's was on her desk. He was a big guy, Hispanic, oily hair, weird tie."

"A Playboy tie?"

"We're progressive here. She thought of filing an harassment."

Frieda felt like doing a jig. She felt like hugging Eunice. Rodriguez had been hoisted—hung—by his fixation. It was divinely poetic. She would nail his ass to the wall. Frieda calmed herself. "It's what he needs."

Eunice shook her head jiggling her braids. "You can't get distracted.

158

Most caseworkers have one hundred and fifty cases. These people are poor or crazy and a check away from the street, if they're not on the street already. If we had thin skins, we'd never get anything done. Of course, you know that."

"You've been a big help, believe me."

"You're an old one, aren't you," said Eunice, stabbing her cigarette into a half-full ashtray. The smoke was an evanescent barrier between them. The barrier floated higher and her view of Eunice cleared.

"Hoary and scarred."

"You're working on something important; what exactly is it?"

Eunice propped her round face on her hands. Despite her healthy cheeks and solid frame, Frieda saw exhaustion. Frieda had been in enough centers and seen enough workers to understand that tiredness. She wasn't sure Eunice could help. She gave Eunice the digest version.

"We fight to keep people alive and someone pushes a button and deletes their cases. They can't do that!"

"If you find anything, call." She gave Eunice her phone number and got out of there. Outside IM45, she heard a rumble towards Forty-second Street, and saw the insane dashing of the cabs, flotillas of cars. It was a hot fall day and she was in the middle of chaos in Manhattan. Another time, she would have felt proud to be part of the chaos. There was New York and the rest of the country. That day, she knew Toby was right. She should be in the Catskills watching catbirds flitting in the underbrush and brook trout jumping out of sunshine-dappled streams.

Frieda hailed a cab and told the driver to take her to First Avenue and Twenty-second Street, the location of IM34, and the Rex cases.

At IM34, she went through the same parry-and-thrust with the center director Mildred Bates, but finally she got Condi, the L & A supe who helped Rose, to help her. It took time, but finally they found someone in Record Management who said that a big guy with a Playboy tie had been there over a month ago and had collected six case records. They checked the files and found that all the cases of the Rex tenants were gone. A link in the chain slipped into place. A Playboy tie, a missing record. Cause, effect. Someone—Morty Bennet? Lansky?—fed Rodriguez a list and Rodriguez filched the cases, dropped them in a garbage can, then used the Convert screen of the Triple M to convert—cancel—the case in the system. QED.

159

She called Toby and left a message about what she'd found. But the next question was what they could do. Of course, they needed more evidence about the Triple M, about its scope, about forging links to charge or convict Rodriguez, Morty Bennet, and whoever else. But the links in her chain didn't reach Lansky, Jack, and the goons in the Rex.

The Rex, the Rex. Magic Mountain and oasis. Target and symbol of resistance to change.

Despite the heat, Frieda decided to walk back to the Rex. As she walked and dabbed the sweat off her neck and forehead, she went through a set of shifting moods, moods she'd felt before a thousand times. First, she felt helpless, then fatalistic, then grimly resolved.

Jack may have found out details about her life, about her clothes and habits and one estranged boyfriend. But he'd never guess that beyond, or in spite of, her own deep ambivalence about people and life, she'd never give up.

Call it a gift for confrontation. Call it obstinacy. Call it compulsion. She'd been like that since she was old enough to yell at the craziness of the Sisters. She wasn't going to change now.

20

Phase 3.

Just thinking about Phase 3 made him jumpy. Jack remembered the Amsterdam, giving a list to Dombry who in turn gave orders to Kragen. He had a vague idea what would happen when he did that. The reality was worse, much worse. People in the hospital, broken bones, ruptured organs. He felt sick to his stomach for days. But then he convinced himself it was like pushing a button. He didn't have to read about the effects. He could push his head deep in the sand. But this time, he'd have to deal with Kragen directly. No getting around what happened when he pushed the button.

He drank too much coffee and stalked between the work nook and the door. Finally, he grabbed his jacket and walked to Duane Park, where he watched the homeless woman with the brown wool cap pile her Starbucks cups, books, bags, coils of wire, and, of course, her broom into a new cart. Across from him, a bum begged nickels off passersby. Life was so much easier when all you wanted was a new cart or a couple of nickels.

The distraction didn't last. Soon the project held his mind in a vice. He recited the many victories of Phase 2. Phase 2 had worked beautifully—residents had packed their bags and left, and they'd closed off a handful of rooms. But they'd sailed into the doldrums. The residents left had adapted to the phone calls, the notes, the loud music, and, likely, treated his agents as troublesome pieces of furniture. Mario's pummeling of Ace and Max meant even less fear and respect. Moira. He knew Lansky sicced her on him. Three buildings. A couple hundred thousand. It was a big fucking carrot. And it meant many big fucking sticks late in Phase 3.

He got up and walked back to the condo. He spent most of the morning worrying, drinking coffee, and putting off Phase 3. He called his agents. They didn't have much to report. A good report was someone leaving, or about to leave. Then he called Jeanie and made small talk about seeing her that night. She was becoming more pointed about what he was doing. He didn't know what to do about that. Finally, he called his father, Leo. Leo was good, off the sauce, sticking to AA, and trying to land a part in a neighborhood production of "Cocoon."

"I'd have the Don Ameche part without the stiffness."

"Sounds great," said Jack, his thoughts a thousand miles away.

"What are you doing again, Jack. Everyone asks."

Leo was playing nice. "Hotel management. It will make money."

"Lot more in life than that Jack. Don't forget soul."

Higher powers. If only he could. It felt good talking to Leo, as if he were tapping into a familiar Jack Kuhl. But after he'd hung up, Jack knew that flurry of phone calls had one purpose.

He held his breath, found Kragen's number, and punched it out.

"Yeah, who's this?"

"My name's George. I worked with you at the Amsterdam."

"Bullshit. Who the fuck is this?"

"I gave Dombry a list for you. You know, the holdouts."

There was a tense pause. "Yeah, I remember. Where's Dombry?"

"I think he went to California," said Jack. That's what Lansky told him. Jack sat down and switched the phone to his left ear. His palms were sweaty. He tried to imagine what Kragen looked like. Big? Muscular? Tall and knobby?

"I heard something like that. What's up?" Kragen's voice was soft, rational, but did he detect a hint of menace? It made him shiver.

Jack hunched forward, his elbows on his knees. "I have a new job."

"That's good news. I could use extra cash."

"Let's meet in this old factory near—"

"No, George. In public. The Hangout at Twenty-sixth and Sixth. At seven. I'll be in front near the window wearing a Yankees T-shirt."

"But—"

"No buts," said Kragen. "I know what I'm doing."

Jack let his breath out. "Fine." Kragen told *him* where to meet.

Jack's hand trembled when he picked the list out of the Rex folder. They were the linch-pins, the hard core. Mario, Bel, Frieda, Marcy, Harry. Jack unclipped and sorted the photos. Don was a lousy photographer. Most of the photos were shot into the light or when the person was moving. Still, you could see Frieda's raven tangle of curls, high cheekbones, and pale, striking face, Mario's large brown eyes, curly brown hair, husky body, and Marcy's whip-like body, trim, almost classical head, and dark brows. It was

162

a rogue's gallery of the Rex.

He carefully wrote down a list of their habits and routines on the backs of the photos.

That afternoon, he roamed up to the roof, then down to the kitchen. He had two martinis, then forced himself not to have a third. He mixed a protein shake. He tried to watch television. NYPD Blue? Street-level extortion, intimidation. There was Jack Kuhl in his split-level. There was Jack tooling through San Diego in his Jaguar. Here was Jack talking to low-life scum. Here was Jack in a bar telling ex-cons to beat on people.

Finally, he gave in. He took a shower, dressed in white shirt and Dockers and a light jacket, grabbed his papers and left. A few leaves skittered across the gray ribbon of Hudson Street. Don had given him a ballpark figure about how much Kragen charged for his services. Jack walked to the bank on Church Street and took out ten thousand dollars.

He never carried that much money. He knew he should take a cab, but decided to walk. He stopped and stared at buildings. He'd started seeing them as moored in time between the past and a future. He wondered, vaguely, how many Lanskys and Jack Kuhls were out there tagging buildings and stringing out schemes to take over, gut, and develop.

He made it into Chelsea without a problem and a few minutes later found the Hangout. This was it. Phase 3. Time to oust the hard core. If he was going to give up the project—an idea he'd toyed with from the start—now was the time to turn around.

Jack took a deep breath and opened the door. He saw right away that the Hangout was an English sports bar. Ten TVs broadcast the same soccer match to every corner of the bar. The mostly male patrons huddled around the televisions and yelled at players who scrambled up and down the field and didn't score points. Jack glanced at the table in front next to a window made of small, square panes. The real-life Kragen *was* a big man with long legs, corded arms and large hands, and a small head with bulbous eyes. He was talking to a smug, young guy with a huge mound of black hair in a "Kiss Me, I'm Italian" T-shirt.

Jack went to the bar, waited too long to get a martini, then walked deliberately to their table. Kragen got up and they shook hands. Kragen introduced Tony as his assistant—Jack didn't know Kragen worked with an assistant, but it made sense. When Jack sat down, Kragen perched his small head close to him, as if he were inspecting every word for potential double-crosses.

Jack took a sip of his drink, glanced at Tony to include him in what he was going to say, then told Kragen about the Rex project, where they were, what he thought Kragen could do. As he talked, Chelsea yuppies, couples, and gays, who had strayed from the Village, flickered in the square windowpanes. The images were separate, but bound by the season. Everyone was in summery shorts, sandals, and loose printed shirts.

"You want us to kill people," Tony said, running his hand through his hair as if he were thinking. "For a hotel? Cool."

"He told us we have to rough up a few residents," said Kragen, shaking his head. His head was bald and matte in front rimmed by a quarter-moon of closed-trimmed iron-gray hair. "Does that sound like he said kill them?"

"Listen." Tony crouched over his chair as if he were going to get all over Kragen.

Jack's chest felt like a feather. In one windowpane, he saw a policeman stop a man in the street. The man shrugged then dug in his pants for his wallet. He saw a policeman stopping Jack Kuhl, interrogating him. *How long have you worked on the Rex? How many people have you hurt, maimed, thrown out in the street? You're the one. You can come quietly or...*

"Jesus, Tony. I told you to listen, not play tough guy. Let the man talk." Kragen put his hand on Tony's shoulder and pushed him down. Tony brushed his shoulder and sulked. "You want us to lean on a few people," said Kragen. "Just like the Amsterdam."

It was hard to look at Kragen. His big floppy body, pinched head, and jutting teeth made him look like a huge piranha with a butch. But Kragen was responsible. Kragen was getting it. Tony, a typical Italian Benzedrine jack-in-the-box, acted as if he someone was pulling a gag he didn't get.

Jack cleared his throat. "Same deal as at the Amsterdam. Follow the people I tell you to follow. Lean on the people I tell you to lean on. Mostly this is going to be psychological. I don't want anybody seriously hurt. And don't do anything in the hotel."

"So we're the professionals," said Tony, smugly.

Mother of Christ. Jack glanced at Kragen. Kragen shrugged, as if to say, "I have to put up with him all the time." Jack smiled, turned to

Tony. "You're the professionals."

Kragen lifted a shot glass and took a sip of whatever he was drinking. He put the shot glass down empty. Kragen said, "Who? What? When?"

"I want you to work on three people. The guy's tough, an ex-marine. He's knocked two of my agents out of the project. Muss him up. We want to send a message. Here's a photo." Jack held up a photo of Mario, then flipped it over. There were four lines on the back. "I've listed where he goes and when he goes out. He's usually with Bel Benaventura. Here's a photo of her."

"A woman!" said Tony. "I don't do women."

Kragen shook his small head and leaned across the table towards Tony. "Women have been emancipated, Tony. Women are kick-boxers, cops, marines, and truck drivers. Remember that movie with Demi Moore? If they want to play with the big boys, they have to take their lumps. I'll take the woman, if it bothers you."

"I didn't say anything about *taking* the woman," said Jack.

"It's just that women are too easy," said Tony.

"If we have to take the woman, you can tie a hand behind your back," said Kragen. "Okay, we leave the woman alone. What else?"

Jack threw out pictures of Frieda and Marcy. The pictures formed a little mound in the center of the table hemmed in by Kragen's shot glass and water, his martini, and Tony's Bud. He picked up Frieda's picture. "This one's a prime target. She tried to organize a resident's committee. On the back, I've written where she works, eats, drinks, and anything important."

Kragen smirked. "Cut off the head, the body dies."

"We got to cut off her head?" said Tony.

Kragen shook his head. "It's a manner of speaking, Tony."

Tony brightened. "She's the ringleader."

Kragen said, "Bravo."

Jack pointed to Marcy. "I know it's hard to believe, but she's part of the hard core, too. Make sure they know you're following them. Don't rough them up. Strong-arm stuff will work with Mario, but hidden threats work better. Gives them more to imagine."

"I know exactly what you mean," said Kragen. An ugly grin took up most of Kragen's small head. Jack masked his inward frown with a smile.

"We could scare more than these two."

"The word will get out," said Jack. "Everyone will think *they're* being followed. On the other hand, if—"

"Targets of opportunity," said Kragen. "Just like bombing runs in World War II."

"Where's the money," said Tony, glancing at Jack.

"What do you care about the money," said Kragen, annoyed.

"How much?" said Jack.

Kragen said, "For Mario, I get three thousand bucks. If you want more than that, we'll have to talk privately. Following people is time-intensive, but a lot less risky. I usually get two thousand. I'll throw in a few freebies. Right now that's seven thousand. You got it today?"

"What about me?" said Tony. "I thought we were partners."

Kragen said, "Are you fucking crazy? Finish your beer." To him: "Got it?"

"Yes." Kragen made him feel better about the Kragen and Tony act. Jack looked around the bar. Everyone watched the soccer game. The square windows were empty. He took out an envelope and flipped quickly through the bills. He took three thousand and folded the money into his jacket pocket. He slipped the envelope with seven thousand dollars to Kragen.

"Cool," said Kragen. "See ya."

Kragen and Tony got up and left. Jack watched Tony's big head of hair and Kragen's small gray one duck through the entrance, appear in a line of square windows, and disappear.

Jack swallowed the rest of his drink in one gulp and realized his hand was shaking.

Fuck, fuck, fuck.

Kragen! Mr. Piranha and his Italian Stallion were crude, dangerous, x-factor. If they screwed up...*You have the right to remain silent. You have the right to one phone call. It is the verdict of this court.* Arrested, convicted, sent upstate. Jack hurried towards the bar. He needed another drink fast.

Kragen parked his Corolla on the east side of Third Avenue at nine o'clock. From that position he saw the door to the Olympia opening and closing, and in the distance on the other side of Lexington, light coating the Rex steps. The same guy in a Yankees hat and a Walkman leaned against the pillar, his head tracking the women on the street or cabs zipping down Twenty-Eighth Street. He was always there; it was his spot.

Earlier, there was a steady stream of people from the Moat to the Rex and vice versa, but people were starting to stay in either one place or the other. Half an hour ago, a small woman in a beret hurried down the steps and up Twenty-eighth towards Park. Five minutes later, one of his targets—her name was Frieda, a leading member of the anti-Jack, anti-Lansky opposition—came and stood on the steps. She scanned the street before hustling up to Park. She was spooked. That was a good sign. He'd had Tony follow her, as his first real assignment. Frieda walked back fifteen minutes later with a paper bag. A lot of residents ate take-out. So did his target.

He'd followed Mario for three days. Jack's notes were accurate, as far as they went. What they didn't include was timing. That's what he added. Mario ate a lot of take-out. He supposed it was because he worked as a cook and hated to cook for himself. Or, it could be because you couldn't cook much on a hot plate or in a microwave.

Mario stayed in the Moat until seven, then went up to his room. According to what Jack had written, he drank there with a couple residents in what Mario called Mario's Circle. That was pretentious. Once in the last week, Bel Benaventura walked with him to get take-out. The rest of the time he went alone. He usually left between nine and ten the last few nights and took the same route down Twenty-eighth to Second, then down Second to Twenty-sixth. There were a swarm of restaurants and take-out places between Twenty-sixth and Twenty-fifth. Paglia's Pizza and Pasta, Nippon Sushi, Torrid Tex-Mex.

Kragen liked Second Avenue for nailing Mario. In that area at that time, it didn't have the crowds, which welled up periodically on Lex and Third. Kragen felt upbeat. If Bel stayed away, he would nail Mario that night. Even if he didn't, it didn't matter. He wouldn't miss him forever.

"I hate this fuckin' waitin'. Why don't we just march up to his room and waste him?"

Kragen stared at Tony. He'd done his best with Tony. Met with him in bars and restaurants. Explained patiently about how to approach targets. Told him how and when to follow Frieda. He gave Tony the benefit of all his experience. What Tony needed was a double dose of Ritalin, not OJT. "How are you still running around loose?"

Tony frowned, shook his head. "I want action. That's the whole point of this gig. Tailin' somebody is kid stuff. It's fuckin' boring. And fuck, you spend ninety percent of your time starin' outta a fuckin' windshield."

"This guy is big and tough. If you do exactly as I say, it'll be okay."

"Fuck—"

Mario edged into Kragen's peripheral vision. "Shut up."

Mario walked past the Olympia. He stopped at the light, and then continued towards Second Avenue. Kragen touched his sap, the fold-up ball peen hammer, the gun. All there. All ready.

When Mario was in the middle of the block, Kragen said, "Let's go."

They followed Mario down Twenty-eighth and watched him turn on Second. They followed him down two blocks. They stopped when Mario went into Paglia's Pizza and Pasta.

"Pizza tonight," said Kragen. "Good choice. See that alley three buildings on the left?"

"Yeah."

"You stay in the alley. If we can do it without being seen, I'll get him in; if not, we wait for another night."

"More starin' at windshields," said Tony, grumpily.

"*If* it's okay, you can work him over for thirty seconds, no more. Then I'll take care of him. Then we're out. Can you remember that?"

"When do I get to do it on my own?"

Maybe never, Kragen thought. "We'll see."

"Fuck."

"You're like a fucking kid," said Kragen. "Let's go."

They walked quickly to the corner. They waited for the light to change and crossed. They walked towards Paglia's Pizza and Pasta. When they were opposite the alley, Tony hunched over like a whipped dog and walked into the alley. He kicked a can on his way in, and disappeared in the shadows.

Kragen leaned against a streetlight pole and watched the entrance to Paglia's. He couldn't see Mario's face, but through the window, he saw an arm gesturing. A pizza guy checked the pizza in the oven, inserted the peel under the pizza, and brought it out.

It looked like Mario was getting the Paglia's Special.

A few minutes later, Paglia's door opened and Mario came out holding the pizza with one hand. The few people on the street walked downtown away from Paglia's. Two cabs passed.

Mario was close now.

Kragen decided it looked good. He took a deep breath. After all those years, he still felt the adrenalin rush. He reached inside his three-quarter-length coat with the extra pockets and palmed the snub-nose Colt Detective's Special he'd picked for the job.

Mario glanced quickly at Kragen as he approached. He shifted the pizza to the other hand and kept walking. As Mario walked past him, Kragen stepped towards him. Mario stopped, sensing something wrong. Kragen jabbed the gun into Mario's neck.

"Walk into the alley." Mario glanced at Kragen, then the alley. "Now."

Mario hesitated and Kragen pushed the gun hard into his neck. "It will take off half your head," said Kragen. Mario glanced at him, turned, and walked stiffly into the alley. Kragen was right behind him with the gun buried in Mario's neck.

Tony stepped in front of Mario. He grinned. "This the scumbag?"

Kragen whispered, "You've been too much trouble, Mario. Right now, we're going to teach you a lesson. If it doesn't stick, you're going to get hurt again."

Mario turned his head slightly. "Fuck off," said Mario. "You and your Keystone Cops don't scare anyone."

"We will now," said Kragen. Kragen started to slip the sap out of his pocket with his right hand, when Tony threw a roundhouse left.

Mario ducked right. Tony's swing caught Kragen on his arm and the gun flew out of his hand. Kragen, stunned, watched the snub-nose tumble end-over-end and land on the ground. It skipped once, twice, then lay on the ground like a dead animal.

Kragen lurched down and back to get the gun.

Mario dropped the pizza, turned, and hammered Tony in the face. As Tony crumpled to the pavement, Mario pivoted, turned, and kicked at Kragen. His foot whistled by Kragen's face. Kragen grabbed Mario's foot with his left hand and accelerated the arc of Mario's foot. Mario crashed to the cement.

Kragen's right hand closed on the gun. He turned and whipped the butt end of the snub-nose down on Mario's forehead in one movement. Mario seemed stunned, but as he tried to roll away, Kragen hit him again in the middle of his head. Mario sunk to the pavement.

Mario and Tony's bodies lay head to toe, as if they were positioned for a sixty-nine.

Tony groaned, then moved. Mario was out.

Kragen took a long breath. It could have been bad, very bad. Fucking Tony. He got up and checked the entrance to the alley. A cab streaked past going uptown. Kragen came back, kneeled, holstered the gun, and took out his folding ball peen hammer. He unhooked it and snapped it out to its full length. He hit Mario on his nose breaking it. Then he felt for the nub of the radial bone near Mario's elbow. He raised the hammer and hit it once, twice. The second time he felt it give. Tough fracture. Kragen folded the hammer up and put it back in his pocket. Clean, fast, efficient. Mario was going to be fucked up for awhile.

He reached over and shook Tony. "Come on, idiot."

"What?"

"Let's go!"

Tony got up on one knee, and then stood up and shook his head. Tony saw Mario and his face twisted in hate. "Fucker." He kicked Mario in the side. He looked at Kragen. "Give me the fuckin' gun. I'll shoot his fuckin' head off."

"We've got to go, dumbbell." He pushed Tony away. Tony looked at him as if he didn't understand and kicked Mario again. Mario moaned. "Goddamn it, let's go!"

"Wait." He walked over and picked up the pizza, a white smear in the darkness.

"You idiot," said Kragen.

"Makes it seem more natural. Besides I'm hungry."

They walked out of the alley and started uptown.

Kragen glanced at Tony. "Put your collar up. You look like shit."

"If he hurt my face, I'm going to kill him, slow."

Kragen snapped, "Like shit you are. You've got to learn to take orders, or you're going to end up in jail or dead."

Tony pulled up his collar with his free hand. "At least I have the fuckin' pizza." He popped the lid. "Fuck! Anchovies!"

The afternoon sun blazed around the drawn drapes making laser-like bars across the sofa, the blond floor, the kitchen island, and cut the microwave in two.

Jack stood in the middle of the condo. The light gave him a headache and he wanted to crawl in bed, but instead he reached up and scratched behind his ear. He did that years ago when he was nervous. He couldn't stop himself. It felt just right.

Scratch, scratch, scratch.

He pulled the scab off and scratched again. He took a deep breath. His heart bobbed near his throat. "Fuck me. I have to do it sometime."

He sat at the table and his hand found the cordless phone in the half-dark. He called Kragen. He picked up a pencil, twirled it, and tapped on the table. He distracted himself with the sprinters in the Neiman print. Streaking towards infinity.

"Yeah?"

"This is George."

"Yeah, sure. Calling about Mario. We got him. Last night."

"Got him?"

"In an alley, near Third. Piece of cake." Kragen laughed. It was a brutal, cutting laugh. "No, slice of pizza."

What was that about? "Sure."

"I was being funny. Mario just picked up a Paglia's pizza."

Jack dropped the pencil. He got up and walked towards the drapes. The slash of light pierced his head like an ice pick. "Was he hurt bad?"

"Depends what you mean by 'bad.' Beaten up, broken nose, broken arm, maybe a couple broken ribs—no more."

"Good, good." *Good?*

"Listen, I worked over people at the Amsterdam. Tony may be an idiot, but I know what to do. It sends a message."

"That's what we want. Good work."

"We've already started on the others. They're getting the message."

"Good. I'll call you, if I need anything else."

"Don't be a stranger."

When Jack hung up, he saw his hand was shaking. He threw the phone on the sofa. He started scratching.

Kragen, Mario. Stalking. He didn't want to do it, but did. Oddly, Jack started feeling better about Mr. Kragen. He was a piece of the project, necessary. It was time to capitalize on him. Late Thursday afternoon, he called Don and arranged to meet him at the Boathouse Café in Central Park.

It was a hot September day. Rollerbladers swung down the paths around the lake, couples walked slowly arm-in-arm, and teenagers in boats shouted and made ragged Vs over the glassy surface of the lake. The café was on the east end of the lake next to the boathouse. They had a view of the Dakota, a dark, pointy Gothic monstrosity that shot out of the collar of trees at the far end of the lake. The café was crowded with tourists, some circling the frozen yogurt machine at the entrance, others eating the snack food the café dished up. The deck was open and the tourists out there huddled over fries, sandwiches, and beer.

"Hey, Jack. What's up? You hurt your ear?"

It was hard to scratch with a bandage over it. "It's just a boil. Tell me about Mario."

Don belched. "I aint seen him, but everybody's talkin' about it. They're freaked."

Jack nodded. "Good. Tell the agents to change their notes to point to Mario."

"Huh?"

"Don't mention him by name. Have them say something like 'It could happen to you' or 'You're next.' We did the same thing at the Amsterdam."

"I remember," said Don, laughing.

"It's all part of the plan," Jack said.

Jack swirled the coffee in his cup. Don took a long swig of beer, then belched. Jack frowned. He wondered how long he'd have to deal with people like Don. If he did those three hotels in Brooklyn, he could work with them a long time. He drummed his fingers on the table. "What about problems? Tell me everything."

"Quit being paranoid. It's a good crew. We got it under control."

Don launched into a laundry list of what the agents had done and who was close to bolting from the Rex. He'd thought Phase 2 was in the doldrums, but he guessed not. After a few minutes, Jack took out his notebook and took notes. He felt almost cheery when he closed his notebook and slipped it back in his jacket pocket.

"What about Frieda or Marcy," said Jack.

"Don't know, Jack. I haven't heard a thing."

"Tell me if you hear anything. What about the welfare cases? Let's see there's Jeb, Rose, and Raquel, Millie. Their welfare was supposed to dry up."

Don squinted at his beer, as if it helped him think. "Know what," he said, finally. "Frieda. She might've helped them. Got a bad feelin' about her. Guys don't like her, or are afraid of her." Don peered into his plastic glass of beer, saw there was an inch of foam on the bottom, and upended the cup. Don put the glass down with a contented sigh.

Jack's hand reached behind his ear. He touched the band-aid. He laid his hand in his lap. "Christ. Her name's popping up everywhere. Welfare cases. Shit, I'll find out about them myself. How's Blondie?"

Don scratched his pelt. "I don't know. Oh, right. He called, asked about Mario."

Jack took out his notebook. "*He* called *you?*"

"Yep."

Jack frowned. The same feeling he had when he interviewed Blondie boomeranged back. "I'll talk to him."

"Maybe you should," said Don.

They talked about the project some more, but when Don left, Jack stayed, thinking about the project, what they'd talked about. Finally, he got up, put fifty cents in the pay phone, and punched out the number of his answering machine. There was a message from Jeanie about not making it that night. He should have expected that.

Jack stared at his reflection in the window, then the landscape beyond. A ripple disturbed the lake. The Dakota shimmered and flickered, then clarified into a somber, hulking body and pointy gables. Don reassured him but there were gaps, potential problems. His reservations about Blondie had been smoothed over, but they were back. If one of his agents began to talk, or worse...

21

It was a cool, beautiful morning. When Rudi walked down Park Avenue, his spirits were up. There was a gleam in the eyes of people on the street; the intense, clear sun made the windows on the western side of Park glow like heated metal. Even when he saw the Rex and ideas of what was happening at the Rex, of what had happened to Mario, of what might happen, tumbled through his head, he had hope.

That hope vanished an hour later when Bel and Mario's shadows inched across the floor of the lobby. Bel looked glum. Mario limped. Somewhere in the back of Rudi's mind he knew—hoped—that his salvation, the saving of the Rex was bound up in the residents. If they held out long enough, he might have a chance. If Lansky saw it was hopeless, if Brendel would open his eyes to see, if, if. Too many ifs. Too many.

But Mario.

His arm was in a cast. He limped. His face was swollen black and yellow; his nose was bundled in surgical gauze. It looked as if it had been beaten with clubs.

Mario was down, horrible, broken. But he didn't seem down. It puzzled Rudi.

"I'm so sorry," Rudi said. He took off his glasses and let them rest on the ledger. He stuffed his hand in his salt-and-pepper hair and rested his head on it.

Mario managed a grin, which became a grimace. "We've been over this in the hospital. Not your fault. I ignored the warning signs."

Bel said, "I should have gone with him. Ever since we knew—"

"We've been over *that* too. It's too late for regrets," said Mario. "And it's not over."

Rudi cocked his head, frowned. "What?"

"I'm not leaving on a bet. I filed a report with the police. They have fifty notes, a score of complaints. They'll do something when they have enough."

"You're talking too much," said Bel. "Let's get upstairs. I'll make you some soup."

"Oh boy," said Mario.

"Don't sass me," said Bel, tiredly. "You can't eat anything solid."

Mario looked at Bel, shrugged.

Rudi watched Bel take Mario's arm and help him to the elevator. Rudi's heart felt like a stone. As Bel held the door to the elevator, the basement door opened. Ben walked into the lobby. He watched Mario struggle into the elevator. Then he watched the door close.

Ben turned and shook his head. Ben said, "Heating up, I suppose."

Rudi glanced at Ben, shook his head. He had a special connection with Ben. Ben was an alien—Frieda had that right—but in some hidden place they shared the same despair. "I don't know what to do."

"Nothing. Accept it. Truth is death. Choose: Death or lies."

Rudi shook his head, mournfully. "Today you might be right."

Ben stared at Rudi, shrugged, and walked through the open door.

Mario sat on the chair near the window. The window was cracked and the breeze felt cool on his neck. His left hand trembled as he brought the cup of soup to his lips. He took a sip.

"Still rocky," he said. His hand shook as he leaned over and put the cup on the floor.

Bel sat on the bed, legs crossed. She was wearing Capri pants and a white shirt open at the collar. Her face, drained of color, was a bland counterpoint to Mario's. Her striking green eyes, normally penetrating, were red-rimmed and tired. She almost never sat on the bed. From that angle the Olympia dominated the view. It made her think about the connection between the Olympia and the thugs in the Rex. She and Mario ran into those connections first in the Moat. Ace and Max, career fuck-ups.

That morning, she didn't care. She'd spent the last few days running between her room and the hospital and she was tired. And she felt for Mario, but he was starting—no, it had been going on for too long—to seriously piss her off.

She said, "Did you mean that downstairs?"

"What?"

"About 'we have not yet begun to fight'."

Mario scratched his head with his good hand, winced when he hit the lump above his ear. "I guess we didn't talk about this in the hospital."

"It was in the background—all the time."

"Don't we have this conversation every night?"

"It's more than academic now."

A toilet flushed. They both listened to the light beat of feet on the carpet. A door opened, then closed.

Mario adjusted his seat and rested his broken arm on the edge of the table. "Did we ever decide anything?"

She found Mario a year after Ray died, before Marcy left. She liked him. He was tough, friendly, intelligent, didn't put up with her bullshit, and drank too much. Talk, drink, fight, fuck. It felt so comfortable. It felt like a dead end. She knew it. He knew it.

And now the crisis. She knew it would happen some day, she just didn't know when or how. Mario had already called Luigi's and told them he'd be out a month.

Bel said, "No. We never decided anything. What are the options?"

"We're staying because we can't move?"

Bel uncrossed her legs. "You keep saying 'we'," said Bel, angrily. "*We* haven't decided that. *We're* staying because we can't do anything else." From that angle the room looked like the St. Paul's Thrift Store. Mess of a closet, messy floor. "Fucking place is a mess. My life is a mess."

"*We're* a mess," said Mario, struggling to his feet.

He limped to the door. He opened it and turned back to Bel.

They stared at each other.

Bel got off the bed and went to the door. She was lithe and small next to Mario. She'd always liked that. She still liked it. She reached up and kissed him on the cheek.

Mario grinned, touched her shoulder with his good hand, turned, and limped towards the fire doors. Bel watched him. She felt sad, dislocated. Finally, worry etching lines in her forehead, she closed the door.

At six, Brucie walked down the seventh floor hallway. It was dirtier than he remembered. Their floor was a rock against the goons, but lately it had started crumbling. It looked like Petrov was leaving, maybe Raquel. That meant their rooms would be shut, locked, then Lansky's crews would move in. Brucie felt suddenly empty, as if what was happening to the Rex was as inevitable as the next baseball season.

Then there was Mario.

Brucie opened up his room. He turned and stared across the hall at Mario's door. He shrugged, then walked across the dark carpet, and knocked.

Mario opened a few seconds later.

It was hard to look at Mario. Brucie talked to a spot near Mario's belt. "Heard you were back. How you feeling?"

"'Bout the same. Glad to get out of that fucking hospital."

Brucie looked up past Mario. The room was a mess. He usually kept it pin-perfect neat. He looked at Mario. He winced. "I guess the Circle's been suspended."

"I know how I look," said Mario. "As for the Circle, I don't see why." Mario limped to his chair, sat. Mario reached for the phone with his good hand, put the phone on his lap, and punched out the number. "Bel, we're open. What? You sure. Right." Mario hung up the phone. He looked miffed.

"Bel?'

"Bummed out. I don't blame her," said Mario. He stared into the hall. "Want to mix?"

"My pleasure." Brucie walked to where the bottles were stacked at the end of the bed. He mixed two drinks. He handed Mario his glass. They toasted each other with whisky and sodas.

Brucie said, "Petrov is moving. Maybe Raquel. Two more down."

"Still a lot of us."

Brucie shook his head slowly. "Think they'll win?"

"Don't know," said Mario. "It looks bad, but there are almost forty of us left. And we're the ones who want to stay."

"You're sure about that."

"How can we be sure of anything?" Mario took a long pull on his drink and put it down. "What's your contingency plan?"

"I'm not sure. I've thought of a few. None too exciting."

"You'd miss your spot."

Brucie took a long pull on his drink. "That's true enough." He thought about that for a few beats, then said, "I lost my job while I lived here, got an inheritance from an uncle, and found my spot just like Don Juan. Know what?"

Mario shifted in his chair. "I've probably heard it before."

Brucie took off his hat and rubbed his bald head. He put the hat back on and squared it in front. "You've probably heard it a hundred times."

"You're happy."

"That's the fucking truth. Call it the slow lane or a no lane. I'm happy right here. Don't want to leave; don't want to think of where I might go."

Mario rubbed his beard and took another pull on his drink. "What are we going to do? Before long the Rex will be an infirmary. You know the one thing I never thought of before those two goons got me in that alley was that they could get to me. I mean inside."

"Did they?" said Brucie, curious.

Mario looked solemn. "I don't know. I'm worried. I think I might be afraid."

22

Butch pulled in with a truckload of scrap metal, iron pipe, and re-bar. When he cranked up the garage door, Marcy took her coffee out to watch him. He'd gotten up at five and gone on a scavenger hunt through the backyards and salvage yards of Brooklyn. Marcy always wondered exactly what he was thinking when he picked up a particular piece of metal. She knew sometimes it was just because he liked the feel of a piece, other times he saw the piece fitting in a larger piece already mapped out in his head.

"What's this pile going to be?" she said, trying to modulate a sarcastic accent that had edged into her voice too often lately.

"Don't know. I've been thinking of a piece called 'Village Angst,'" Butch said, frowning.

"Who would want to see what they see every day?"

Butch shook his head at her. "It's an expression. It's not for *them*."

Maybe not, but he'd sold enough to *them* to keep the Butch Show afloat. Maybe she objected to his conceit. He threw a bunch of scrap in a pile and called it "world view" as if it meant something. Maybe it did. She admired the way his muscles rippled as he piled the re-bar. He looked—and sometimes acted—more like a construction worker than a sculptor.

She went back into the studio, grabbed a pair of gloves, and went back to help him. It took them half an hour to move the scrap from the truck to the garage.

When they were done, they stood staring at each other, sweating.

"What's on your agenda for this marvelous day, sugar thighs?"

She saw his look, grinned. "Shower and Pier 17. It's my big day. You know that."

"All this aimless activity. What ever happened to havin' fun."

"It's the only reason I keep you around, muscle head."

Butch grinned. "Sex, sex, sex." Butch wiped his face with his shirt and waved his hand at the junk. "It's about piling metal to make cocks or digging Henry Moore holes. Obsession comes from sex. Look at those TV preachers. What's the one thing that always does them in? Sex. Any kind. Doggy style especially."

He was big and he was hers, when she wanted him, which she decided she did that Sunday.

"Too much talk, not enough action," said Marcy.

She grabbed his hand and they went to the waterbed. They were already hot, sweaty, and dirty. Her hands were dirty, her feet. It acted like an aphrodisiac, as if he were a kind of Minotaur, she a rutting, horny, mud virgin. They peeled and it got dirtier and hotter. She played her games with him, teasing and then getting his cock ready with a lip lock.

She finally slid his cock inside and they went into the Butch-and-Marcy death grip. It was all near-rape and power struggle. She bunched, he rammed. His back was slippery, her legs too. They rolled over the bed like monkeys. Twenty minutes later, they decided doggy-style *was* best.

Wet and hot, hot and wet. He always came in big wads of cum which would leak out at the most delicate times. And that's what happened that day. She felt it oozing while she tried to nap. She left him spread-eagled on his waterbed, rebar forgotten, and washed off the dirt and cum in the make-shift shower with the plastic curtain, where she could see the cantilevered roofs of the warehouse next door and anybody up there could see in, if they wanted.

She put on her jeans, black sweatshirt, tennis shoes, and cheap peace earrings. She flung her pack over her shoulder and gave him a parting kiss. It was like putting her mark on him. The lips of guilt. He couldn't play around. Wouldn't. Guilt. Guilt. Guilt. She was probably hoping for too much there. But she did it by instinct, as if that was what gals did to keep their men in tow.

"Leaving?"

"For now, lover. Remember how good it was. Remember I'm the one. Remember."

"Is that a spell?"

"Put a spell on you."

"You off to the Pier."

He lay there, cock lolling like a cow's tongue, head lolling like a black bowling ball, half-asleep, half-not. It felt so comfortable, but she knew she had to leave. "Yep."

"You coming back?" Butch raised himself on his muscled forearm.

"It's easier to get to work, if I stay at the Rex. Besides, I have to make sure it's still there."

Butch talked about Heidegger, about eliminating distractions. Talk about distractions. The Rex was at the top of her distraction list. Goons, Jack Kuhl, Lansky, the Rex. Destroyed rooms, broken windows, frightened residents. The Rex was starting to look like a hotel in the Bronx.

Mario.

When she first heard Mario got beat up, she was furious. After she saw him in the hospital, she decided she was going to grab a goon and slice his head off. She wanted Jack. Then she flipped. She saw *her* arm in a sling. She saw her face black and blue and bandaged. When was she going to get real and leave?

Butch shook his head, concerned. He said, "I worry about what those assholes could do. If someone takes out after you—"

"I can take care of myself."

Butch grunted. "Bullshit. You think you can. You have a problem, call me."

Butch lay back on the bed. He was right. "Nothing will happen."

When she was away from the Rex, she tried not to think about it. She wasn't always successful. That day, she thought she would. Nooner sex. A glorious September day. As she walked through Thompkins Square, she tried to lose herself in the day, the crowds, joggers, and dog walkers. She caught the bus and got off on Chambers Street.

She walked past the Louise Nevelson sculpture, a huge rectangular slab of metal with alternating textures, then down towards the Seaport. When she got to Pier 17, she bought an extra large coffee from the Starbucks on the first floor and walked over to the gang of street artists.

Mindy, eagle-nosed ace artist was already there and so were Tim, Jimmy, and Ron. She propped her coffee on wood planks, got her stuff from the maintenance room, and set up. She laid out three caricatures her subjects didn't want. She definitely had her hooks into the dark side. When she was nice, her caricatures looked like a funny Gahan Wilson; when she was trippy, more Scarfe. It put the burden of selection on her subjects. Mindy, Tim, and Jimmy did the same thing with a range of stars from Elizabeth Taylor to Madonna to Tom Cruise.

They usually split evenly, although she attracted a very different type. It was hard because with so many street artists the prices were down— but they all had business. An esprit de artiste kept them a tight group. When it was slow, they did each other. Of course, she didn't exactly go along with Ron's take on Marcy. He made her look like a cross between Tilda Swinton and Sinead O'Connor, a butch nun with attitude. Ron had too many stars on the brain. Of course they didn't exactly go along with her take on them.

That day, she drew in a wild head space. She wondered whether it wasn't because of that nooner or that she was getting better at figuring people out. Her caricatures had more reality to them, but a quirky reality, which had a hint of something abstract as well. Was she finally getting at the person behind the cucumber schnozzes, corkscrew eyes, and basset ears? Was she finally in a David Levine space where she was less projecting her own black background and more corralling her subject's soul? Looked like it.

She ate a quick lunch at four. Then went back to it.

It was a long day, but a good one. Then, when she was packing up, she felt something wrong. Pier 17 loomed behind her. She heard the yelling of the kids, the screeching of parents, the general bustle, the lone tugboat horn on the East River. She scanned the second floor deck. People leaned over the railing looking out towards the bay. He was on the second floor deck. He was floppy looking in his big coat, but his face was small and lean. He stared towards the bay and the Statue of Liberty, but she knew he'd watched her.

She'd seen him when she arrived, but didn't think anything of him, except that he was fence-post ugly. Fuck, he'd spent the entire afternoon at the Seaport! That freaked her out. Other people had followed her. Other people had tried to pick her up.

She wasn't about to get into a one-on-one with that guy.

She stored her sketch board in the utility room. When she walked back to her pack, she tried to figure out what he was doing. The question of why came up right away. Mario. There were two thugs, a greaser, and a tall ugly guy with a small head and short hair. She just got the tall guy.

She looked around. Her friends had left. The Lexington local was too far—she'd have to walk through the deserted streets of Wall Street. The closest was the Broadway local. She could hike along the bay, and backtrack towards the subway. That was the best she could do.

She made up her pack, as if she hadn't decided one way or another.

Then, without a glance at Pier 17, she cinched up her pack, hoisted it, and took off. She raced along the boardwalk, which at that hour was still full of tourists and gulls. In the bay, boats drew ragged lines through the water.

After a couple blocks, she couldn't help glancing back. A thrill arced through her body. He was there like flypaper. He was big and he didn't seem to hurry, but his long legs ate the distance. His globular eyes followed her. His head was like the prow of a ship angling forward out of a secret momentum. She was being chased by one of her caricatures.

She hitched her pack higher on her shoulder and cut back towards the subway. Five minutes later, she was out-of-breath when she hurried into the almost deserted subway. She dropped in her token and a few seconds later slung her pack on the floor of the Broadway local.

She scanned the next car through the small square window. She didn't see him. She tried to figure out the best route back to the Rex. She decided to get off in the Village. She didn't want to end up stuck on the West Side.

When she got off the subway, he emerged from the last car. Then he smiled. Her heart beat against her rib cage. His face looked like a Halloween mask.

She felt in her bag for her Mace and couldn't find it. She ran up the subway steps. Above ground, she scanned Seventh Avenue for a cop. For the first time in decades, she didn't see one.

Fuck, fuck, fuck.

Later, she realized she'd panicked. She could have gone into the Cave, Frieda's bar. She could have waited at Christopher Street and Seventh Avenue. The asshole wouldn't do anything to her there. But that was all after-thought. When the light changed, she ran across Seventh Avenue.

She almost ran into him coming out of the other subway entrance. She turned and bolted down Seventh, then button-hooked back towards Hudson Street and the piers. Her breath was ragged. Her backpack felt like a boulder. She saw she'd made another mistake. She thought she could lose him in the crossword puzzle of streets of the old Village. But that was stupid. There were fewer people, fewer cops.

She made it to Hudson and cut back towards Christopher. Time to get into crowds. She scanned the streets in every direction. Then convinced she'd lost him, she started back towards Seventh. That's when he popped around the corner of Bleeker and Christopher, two blocks away.

He smiled at her. He had a pursed mouth with too-large teeth, which looked like they could eat through steel. He started towards her. His stride ate up the blocks. She hesitated a second. He was bigger than she thought, but he had that small head. He looked like one of the heavies from Super Mario Brothers.

She shook herself out of a strange feeling that she wanted to give up, then turned and took off. He stayed a block behind her.

She shifted her backpack to her other shoulder. She zigzagged south, then north of Christopher Street, trying to lose him in the warren of Village streets that fronted the Hudson. She passed the huge old Post Office building, recently converted to condos, and then ran towards the piers. She found herself in a battlefield landscape of vacant lots and broken glass. She saw the Jane Bar under the Jane Hotel. She hurried to the hotel and circled it. She saw him two blocks away. He was looking in an alley. She ducked into the bar.

She panted. Perspiration ran off her head. She forced herself to calm down. The Jane Bar was a small, ratty bar with a few heavies at the counter, a few streetwalkers acting out. She walked to the far side of the bar, and dropped her backpack on the floor. Then staying as close to the back as possible, she ordered a beer. When she got the beer, she dug herself deeper into the corner.

She watched the door with her heart thumping against her chest. When she didn't see the fish-faced goon, she thought of Butch. She dug in her jeans for change, then sidled up to the phone, which was, fortunately, on the wall behind her. Butch was in one of his moods, which meant he wasn't answering the phone or had turned off the ringer. He said he did it so he could concentrate, but it pissed her off that night. Why tell her to call if she needed help, then turn off the fucking phone?

She slunk back to her beer. She noticed the big window in the front of the bar. He could have been watching her. She scanned the concrete, then the West Side Highway, and beyond, the bombed out piers and the Hudson.

"Lose your boyfriend, darling?" said a six-foot black transvestite in pink chiffon, who had sidled up to the curve of the bar. "I'm Chiffon and I want to hear your story. Go on, you can tell me. People tell me their stories because I'm like Oprah, sympathetic and kind to a fault."

"Not now," Marcy said, brusquely.

"You sure are in a holy state," Chiffon said. She brought a large black hand up to her chin.

Marcy looked Chiffon over, then shrugged. "I was having a dynamite day, when this guy started following me."

"Is he here?" Chiffon glanced at the bar, then out the window.

"I think I lost him. But I can't be sure."

"That's been happening a lot around here," Chiffon said, shaking her head.

"It's a no-man's land."

"It's not just the street. You know this hotel was in Bakshi's 'Heavy Traffic.' It was a lovely piece."

"Never saw it," said Marcy. She looked past Chiffon. It was dark outside with a rim of luminance hugging the West Side Highway. Suddenly, she felt at ease, protected. It was a ratty bar full of transvestites, street people, and voyeurs, but it felt safe. Out there were empty streets and fish-faced perverts.

"It's not the johns that are the problem. It's the heavies, the bad guys, the ones with evil in their hearts and eyes."

"What's the difference?" Marcy said. She realized she had a full beer. She took a long drink, felt the lift, then set it down.

"Mean folks who want to get rid of the Jane."

Marcy frowned. "Why?"

"No one knows exactly. Rumor is they want to build a high-rise."

"Here?"

"They've put in two new restaurants down the highway, a Tex-Mex and a Jamaican. I like the Jamaican. It's full of tropical plants from floor to ceiling. It's hot and muggy. It's like eating in a jungle."

"Why is it more dangerous?" said Marcy, although she'd guessed.

"Punks, thugs, and low-life. They pound on doors, play music, threaten. I like the music—it makes the place seem like a carnival. But then I think I'm going to end up in the river."

She sure didn't think Lansky-types would want the Jane. "Cops?"

"They don't like us and they all live in Jersey or Long Island. What's he look like?"

"Tall, small head, a pinched steel-trap mouth with lots of teeth, like a piranha."

"I shiver just thinking about him. Stay here sugar."

185

Chiffon sauntered—to the whistles of several patrons—out into the night. Marcy watched her disappear around the corner. She reappeared a few minutes, later. "I didn't see anyone. I think you shook that fish face."

"I sure hope so."

"Here's my card. Give me a ring the next time you're down here. I'll buy you a drink."

"I don't have a card, but I'll give you my address and phone." And she did, but she wasn't sure why. She and Chiffon didn't look as if they had much in common.

The scheme to turn the Rex into a high-rise seemed more real that night. Who was the ugly guy? Why was he following—stalking—her? The only thing that made sense, as she watched the cars swerve and dance in rhythm to streetlights, was that Jack sent him.

Jack had hiked the invasion of the Rex up to another level. It looked like she was on that level whether she wanted to be or not.

Marcy took a cab from the Jane. Her head pivoted at every street corner. Every guy with a small head was Fishface. But it looked like he'd slunk back to wherever he slunk to. When she got off at the Rex, she scanned the crowds in both directions. Then, seriously freaked, she bolted up the Rex's steps. Into the lobby. Safe. She never thought she'd be that happy to be back.

Mario was framed in the desk clerk's half-oval. Rudi had made him part of the desk clerk rotation, until he got well enough to go back to work. Mario looked bad. His eyes were fading from blackish blue to a sickening yellow. The plaster cast on his broken arm had "get wells" all over it and it looked smudged and soft.

She dropped her pack and leaned into half-oval. She noticed there were fewer letters in the boxes over Mario's shoulder. She'd never thought of it before. Fewer residents, less mail. It was a symptom, another symptom, of the decline and fall. "Somebody followed me tonight."

"Fuck me," said Mario, frowning. "What'd he look like?"

"Might have been one of the guys who got you. The big one. He was big and tall with a small head and a face from hell. He looked like a piranha."

"That's him," said Mario. "The other looked Italian, acted like a moron. Gives us a bad name." He scratched his beard with his good left hand. "I'd like a rematch."

Marcy had an image of an Mario taking on two Fishfaces. He might do it, if he were whole, but not with a broken nose, busted arm and a couple of cracked ribs. She hung in the half-oval, her worry switching from Mario to herself.

One day soon, perhaps in the next hour, she would walk out of the Rex and Fishface would follow her. She'd been in some dicey places last year, but she always felt immortal, that nothing human, divine, or alien could touch her. But Marcy Benaventura's photo was tucked in someone's pocket, her name and habits on a list. She shivered.

Mario looked at her seriously, then reached under the counter. He brought out a plastic stick. It was a foot-and-half long, green, and looked like it had been hewn out of plastic tree branch for a storybook ogre. When he dropped it on the shelf, it gave out a loud thud.

She hefted it; it was a lot heavier than she expected. "It has lead inside," said Mario. "Bartenders use it to whack drunks. It's yours, if you want it."

She felt the knobs. They felt like boils. "What am I supposed to do with it?"

"Protection," said Mario.

"I'd probably end up whacking myself." She shrugged, hefted it again, and then stuck it in the back of her pack. "I'm starting to feel like a Samurai with all this junk."

"Yell first, attack second, and never give in. They never expect you to fight back."

"I don't mind fighting back. It's winning I worry about. Later."

She dropped her pack in her room. She was about to go to the Moat, or anywhere where there were people, when she stopped. She heard showers turned on, rap with its hypnotic rhythm and senselessly violent lyrics, a police siren, which grew louder, then faded, and was clipped off.

She thought of seeing Bel, then decided no. Bel never made her feel better and since the attack on Mario, she was seriously depressed. She shut her door and walked across the corridor.

She knocked on Carly's door.

She felt relieved when she saw Carly's full face in the cracked door. They exchanged glances, and then Carly smiled and let her in. For the first time in two hours, Marcy felt safe.

Carly fingered her rattail. "What's up," said Carly.

"Somebody followed me," said Marcy. "He looks like a piranha."

"Shit. Tell me over a drink?"

"That's what I need."

Carly opened her fridge and pulled out a bottle of Chardonnay, then two sparkling, clean glasses. Marcy was always amazed at Carly's room. It was clean, but full. Marcy understood the clean part, but she hadn't managed the fullness. Odd, it made her think of her abortion. Her life would have been full with a diminutive Marcy, but over. She wondered how Carly had managed the fullness without the baby trap.

Carly handed her a glass and they sat on the bed, back against the wall. Carly's curtain was open and you could see lights blinking on and off in the west towards mid-town. They both heard soft, quick steps in the hallway, then a pause, then the steps hurried on.

Carly took her hand. "Is it time to leave," Carly said.

"It's all I can think about after seeing that guy. What about you?"

"Remember Mac, the bartender?"

"Sure."

"He's either nicer than I thought, or I'm about to start another irritating cycle of hope and despair. Anyway, I told him what was happening here and he asked me to move in with him."

Marcy wasn't sure that was what she wanted to hear. "Are you?"

"Not yet. I'm going to consult my runes, toss a coin, and spend a weekend by myself. I'm tired of seeing the thugs. They're like weasels creeping under the radar."

"I guess that's Jack's strategy. At least they're not following you."

Marcy trembled. She pressed her head against the wall. She knew she was going to see Fishface again. She had a feeling about him. It wasn't a good feeling.

Carly stroked her head. "You'll be okay. You're strong."

"Strong! Every time I think of that guy, I get sick to my stomach."

"What about your boyfriend?"

Marcy shrugged. "I spend more time there. But I can't see living around him 24/7. We'd end up strangling each other. It will be tough with you gone. You know that."

"I'm not moving to Montana," said Carly, laughing.

"Sometimes next door seems a thousand miles away," said Marcy.

"Let's forget separation anxiety for tonight. I have another bottle."

A shower was turned off; then they heard fast, light steps grow louder then fade. Marcy moved back further into the wall, held her glass up to Carly's and tapped it. "Maybe it will help to talk about it. Let me tell you about the guy who followed me, the Jane bar, and a transvestite named Chiffon."

"This is going to take awhile."

23

Tap, tap, tap.
   Tap, tap, tap.

Frieda opened her eyes. Her hand fumbled over the end table dislodging change, which tumbled to the floor and fired tacks into her brain. She found the clock.

Eight o'clock.

She thought: Hemlock Rose started this. I know gang. It's early. Let's go pound on Frieda's door! What fun!

Tap, tap, tap.

"Stop that!"

Frieda got out of bed and put on her robe. Then she shuffled to the window and lifted the shade up a foot. The light seared her brain. Too much. Too soon. She shuffled back to the door, stopped at her nightstand, flicked out her rose-tinted glasses, and put them on.

She took a deep breath and cracked the door.

Sidney Jackson—in sepia—stood there looking awkward. Sid was a tall, old, gay black man, HIV positive, who was obsessed with Vita Sackville-West and white gardens. He'd decorated his room with photos of white flowers mostly dahlias. She thought it odd that a black man liked *only* white flowers. But Sid was soft and kind. He looked beaten. Frieda felt guilty for being angry. Of course, it was eight o'clock.

Frieda frowned. "What's up Sid?"

"Sorry to wake you, but I got another one of these forms."

"Shit. That asshole. I'll take care of it. Just—"

"It's more than that," Sid said, shaking his head. "Trying to get money out of the city's like pulling teeth, but it's the rest that getting to me. Been thinking it's time. Best go where I don't get these notes. Anyway, I want to thank—"

"Oh shit. C'mon Sid."

Sid shook his head. "Every day I get a note about nigger queen, or Tim or Bert sneer at me. It's like living in some cracker burg in the South." Sid paused. "Then there's Mario."

She could see the fright in his eyes. "I know."

"Brucie said he might never get full use of his arm."

"I know, darling. And don't listen to the Rex grapevine. Mario will be all right." Frieda sighed. "I'd hate to convince you to stay, then have you get hurt. But try to hold on a little longer. I'll take care of the welfare side although probably not today. The rest will take longer."

"Okay. I guess I just wanted to tell someone how I felt. Sorry to wake you again."

"Not a problem."

She watched Sid walk down the hallway, then turned and closed her door.

She got orange juice, sat in her chair, picked up her pack of cigarettes, plucked one out of the pack, lit it, and threw the pack on the bed. She'd promised herself she was going to quit, but there was too much going on.

She'd quit after it was over.

Over?

Frieda chuckled to herself. Was reality ever over?

Frieda knew she had to go to IM66. She didn't want to. She wasn't sure she could control herself if Rodriguez was there. And she felt tense, a trembling in her heart, she hadn't felt since Libby, the last of the sisters, died.

Soon the assault on the Rex was going to get nasty. Something bad had to happen. Two thugs, one a dork in a black bouffant, the other a kangaroo with a small head, the same ones who got Mario, followed a handful of residents, including her.

Soon.

She showered, dressed, made a pot of coffee, sat at down in her chair, and drew out her address book.

She called Johnny at IM66.

"Johnny. Is Rodriguez there today?"

"Yep."

"Shit."

"And he doesn't look too happy."

Frieda frowned. "Why is that?"

"I'm not sure. A few days ago, I heard him talking to Adrian about

191

getting rid of you, some hearing. He muttered something about you to-day. Maybe it's been canceled."

"Fat chance. I suppose I should start taking it seriously."

"Are you coming in today?"

"Don't think so. If anyone asks, I have a bad case of ennui."

Johnny laughed. "Okay."

After she hung up, she decided it was time to take the disciplinary hearing seriously. The hearing was sheer farce. But HRA and IM weren't known for being rational. And she'd left bodies in her wake.

She called Personnel and asked to speak to the head. She used to know who it was, but George Kelso replaced the last one. She found the new head was Marion Gordon.

Frieda put on her best voice. "Marion, this is Frieda Berg. I'd like to talk about—"

"The hearing?"

Frieda frowned. "Yes, dear. Can we delay it?"

"I'm afraid not, Ms. Berg."

Frieda began to get a bad feeling about the hearing. It was farce, but people had been railroaded before. "Why, dear? You've delayed hearings before. Just—"

"It takes a wheelbarrow to cart your file around the office. You've had more hearings—"

"But—"

"I'm sorry. There's nothing I can do," she said, hanging up.

Frieda scowled at the phone. She dialed Toby, again.

"What about this hearing," she said. "Personnel won't touch it."

"I know. I've talked to them."

"What about George?"

"He doesn't want to interfere."

"Who's going to be there? Rodriguez, Morty, and the KKK?"

"Jamie Waite. You know him?" Toby said, concerned.

Jamie Waite? Frieda tried to modulate the concern in *her* voice. "Once, he tried to fire me for insubordination. He wasn't feeling well. It was really more a joke. It wasn't—"

"How do you antagonize so many people?" Toby said, exasperated.

"It was easy in the old days. Age has softened me."

"Pooh. It looks like you're going to have to go through it."

Frieda sighed. "What about the Triple M? What about Morty?"

"I'm sniffing after him and Special Projects. I've got Legal to help."

"I know," she said. "Everything is 'under investigation.' I've been there before."

She felt disgusted when she hung up. She couldn't do anything about the goons in the Rex and it looked like she couldn't do anything about the Triple M scheme.

The hearing. She needed reinforcements. Should she call on the powerful HRA union and Labor Relations? Did she want to rattle those chains? She hesitated a moment before dialing Dugan Peters, a force in Labor Relations and former lover. She realized her voice was strange when she finally got him. There was a long pause. They both read their history into that pause, the furtive meetings, the declarations, the final disaster. Frieda thought he'd hung up, but he finally came back on the line. After a few forced pleasantries, he agreed to meet her at the Dugout after work.

At least she had one chance. But when she thought about seeing Dugan again, she wondered whether it was worth it.

At five-thirty, Frieda took a cab to the Dugout.

Just as she was getting in the cab, she saw her stalker. The wavy-haired dorkface who had followed her for the last week was on point leaning against the stoplight on Twenty-eighth and Lexington. When she first saw him, she was afraid. But he didn't intimidate her anymore. That day, he wore a raincoat with the collar up. No, no one thinks you look strange. No, you look perfectly normal on one of the hottest days in the city wearing a black raincoat leaning against a stoplight. Jack's requirements must have slipped a notch with that one.

She took the cab to Canal Street and got out in front of the Dugout. The Dugout was an old hangout of caseworkers and supervisors. She supposed the Dugout was still a place for supervisors trained at the old Central Office off Canal Street. She didn't recognize anyone. Most of those fresh faces were at the bar, whose tilted, gilt-edged mirror showed Canal Street and dots scrambling in and out of the subway or toy cars crawling through the steam of shish kebab vendors.

Her last meeting with Dugan was a cold summit. Dugan's wife had finally figured out that Dugan and Frieda were exchanging valences at Frieda's old apartment on the West Side, the one she had to give up when the divorce was final. She felt vulnerable and clung to Dugan while Dugan feeling exposed—or so she thought—started clinging to his wife and kids. Why did she think it would be any different? Her head was floating on waves of caffeine, anti-depressants, Valium, and vodka martinis. She had acted out. She remembered threats, a scene in the Cave, and then anonymous letters to the Dugans, wayward hubby and wife.

It was terminally embarrassing. And what was truly embarrassing was that she couldn't forget it! Why didn't she have the luxury of repressed memories like everyone else? Frieda took a long swallow of her drink, lit a cigarette, and posed it in the ashtray. She dug in her bag, her fingers touching objects she should have recognized, but didn't.

When she looked up, she saw Dugan in the doorway. She might have known that he would look like two Dugans, overweight, pattern balding, de-fanged and de-valenced.

Frieda gulped, smiled. "Duggie," she said, getting up.

They kissed ritually. "How long has it been?" he said.

"A couple of lifetimes. How are Betty and the kids?"

"Betty fusses around the house, or throws pots. Karen's at MIT, Jerry's at NYU."

"I'm happy for you." She would have hung on. She would have done anything for a little security. And there were a score of reasons not to screw up Dugan's life starting with the kids.

"I guessed you wanted to see me because of a problem, so I checked. It look's like you've made more enemies than usual—a Supe 2 named Rodriguez, a center director, Morty Bennet. I'd forgotten your capacity for pissing people off. "

"It's a stupid diversion. I don't worry about it, then I do."

"It was always a setup," said Dugan, smiling.

She shook her head, gave Dugan a lopsided smile, and then forgave him his doubt. "Toby can't seem to squash it. I decided, probably too late, that I needed more allies."

"And you thought of Labor Relations. It's a stretch after what you've put us through," said Dugan, sourly. "Let me get a drink."

She watched Dugan get his drink and size up the place as if he hadn't been there for ten years, which was probably true. Dugan came back, sat down, and frowned at his drink as if it were a stranger in a ho-hum life. He took a sip.

Frieda said, "You've lost hair, gained weight, and have ironclad habits. Don't worry, Duggie, it happens to all of us. Despite the surface, I sense the old Duggie is still alive and well."

"Compliments were always your forte. It's odd they're trying so hard to get you out. The charges are disrupting business, wild goose chases about non-existent cases, etc." Dugan set his drink down and folded his arms over chest. "None of it makes much sense."

"You know, Duggie, I'm not sure I care anymore. Maybe I'll let them send me away."

Dugan unfolded his arms and went for his drink. He took another sip and made a wry face. "Always fishing for sympathy. You haven't changed. Now tell me about the Triple M."

"I'll feel hurt about that later," said Frieda. "What do you know about the Triple M?" She always thought she was the only one who knew anything. The Dugout was filling with more after-work workers. Everyone was young, bushy-tailed, and optimistic. She would love to do a census in twenty years. What did you think of your twenty-year trial-by-fire? Do you have any ideals left worth talking about? She was sure most of them would leave the department, if they could. Odd, she thought, the department was like the Rex, a refuge. Her carapace extended in every direction, from the Rex to the department, from morning light to the thin darkness of the Cave.

"The old computer system is a monster. We supported the idea of the new one even when they didn't use HRA programmers. Every now and then John brings it up, then we forget about it. We still believe in a new system where clients get their check on time and eighty-year-old grandmothers don't have their heat turned off in January."

"Right now, the Triple M is a digital twist on the big lie," Frieda said.

"We've heard things." He patted the remaining strands of hair, realized what he was doing, and stopped. "We'd like to know more."

Frieda tried to see what her infatuation was about. They were both needy then. Dugan was from a working class background, his father a garbage man, his mother a secretary. He'd worked his way up. At City College he'd met and married Betty, an arts major whose father was a surgeon. Betty liked playing with her pots and the society scene, Dugan the trenches. When Frieda Berg met him, he was bored with Betty and his life. At the time, she was going through men like jellybeans, and wondering what happened to her marriage. It was a lot of history, too many memories. But, then, Dugan lived, Betty lived, Frieda survived. It was life after all.

"I won't go into details, but essentially, someone gives this Rodriguez a list of clients in a target building—there have been two that I know of, the Cardiff and the Amsterdam—then he goes to the issuing center, pulls the case records and throws them away. Then he uses a live Triple M terminal to convert the cases from the old system to the new. I uncovered it when IMD 209s started popping up with a non-existent code 333. Here's an IMD 209, a printout showing the client's not in the system, and a printout of the restored case."

She dug in her bag, found the papers, and threw on the table.

Duggie glanced at all three documents. "How was it restored?"

"It's my favorite Triple M option."

"And what was the point? Why those buildings?"

"A landlord wanted to develop the property. Same landlord in both cases. Michael Lansky. I'm sure you've heard of him."

"That exposé on slumlords in the Times." Dugan sat back and put his fingers together and stared at the mirror. "My first impulse these days is to see everything as mechanical. It's like a theorem or lemma. All I have to do is find the right slot and fill in the numbers."

"Are we getting too old for these battles?" Frieda said. She dug out a cigarette, lit it, and then blew the smoke towards the window on Canal Street.

"After awhile, you want peace, which means not making waves."

"Like Toby. I'm getting old too. What about John?" John Clark was Dugan's boss, a Harvard graduate, lawyer, and exceptional negotiator.

"He's been around too long, like all of us. There was a move last year to oust him."

Frieda rested her hand on his arm. "You'll do what you can."

Dugan hesitated, then moved his arm away. "I'll try, but I've given up promising."

"What a line. It was a shitty job, but we had fun. Remember that party with John—"

Dugan shook his head. "You've used that one, remember?"

"I was reminiscing, not blackmailing."

It was a year after the divorce. On a whim, she flew to Paris to find Frenchie's spore. She'd taken off without leave and without mentioning it to anyone in the department.

It was fun sitting in the Tuileries in Paris imagining her father decades before sniffing his Pernod and rubbing his ash into a cone happily unaware of the future, of the seed he would plant in a Russian Harpy, Frieda, and, sigh, his own premature death. But she could never truly appreciate that fantasy. She'd gazed at the ancient dirt of the Tuileries, which wound its way to the Impressionist Museum, and knew deep in her guilty heart she'd have to trek back to HRA and face the music. And the music was cacophonous. Fortunately, she'd had a few cards left, one thanks to that Labor Relations party. That black ace had been played long ago.

"This whole scheme is too weird. Then there's the final insult."

"There's more?" said Dugan, frowning.

"They've targeted the Rex, my Rex, an old hotel on the edge of Kip's Bay surrounded by high-rises. It's happening just like the Amsterdam and the Cardiff. Some residents have gotten cancellation notices. I alternate between seeing life as riffs on Raymond Chandler or the Keystone Kops."

"It's all coming back: the whirlwind, the infatuation, the guilt, the terminal ambivalence."

"The secret is charm, Duggie. And what is charm? Just one-liners with looks."

"Now I feel sorry for you. I've been here for twenty minutes and I haven't done enough."

Frieda smiled and arched her eyebrows. "I know you'll help. You're already interested."

"I said I would. But I'm not sure about the hearing."

"Don't worry about the hearing. If they kick me out, it might be the best thing that happened. No, that's not true. I have to go on. I have to expose the plot. I'm not sure why."

"We all have those moments. I think you'll get help on this one."

"I loved you, Duggie. But you knew that."

"Did, past tense," said Dugan. They were trading memories. Dugan seemed to get another faraway look, and she was there with him in a spiritual space, holding hands, knowing they were doomed to go back to their separate lives. "I'll see what I can do."

"Thanks, baby. I've got to go."

Frieda got out of there fast. She was trembling when she reached the street. She had to do it, she reminded herself, as she hailed a cab. But seeing Dugan brought up too many memories. And, she realized, it wasn't just their doomed affair. No, it was more that they were both fresh, both eager and ready to hurl themselves into battle against anything. It made her pine for that time. It was all about nostalgia, a useless emotion, but lately, when it swept over her, and it had swept over her often in the last few weeks, there wasn't a thing she could do about it.

Frieda was glad that Labor Relations and Dugan were on her side, but they were too used to HRA time, in which investigations were in a constant state of delay.

The problem of time came up soon enough the next morning, when she opened her door to find Sally, Raquel, and Merri all with code 333s canceling their benefits. Sid was the tip of the iceberg. It looked like Rodriguez had canceled all their benefits, again. She told them that she would take care of it and put them in her handbag knowing that she might not be able to do a damn thing.

After they left, reluctantly and sour, she trudged up to the roof. That day, the invasion stayed with her when she worked in her garden. That man in the penthouse was pulling strings on a marionette who pulled strings on sub-marionettes who entered a number in terminal who turned off people's benefits, or slashed a painting, or slipped a note under a door. There was no question of truth or justice or goals or anything that made life good. Sometimes, she thought most modern life was like that, that the people around her were burnished marionettes, regardless of how high up they were or how well they tugged the strings.

Around eleven, she realized she'd put off going into IM66 long enough. But she had a real dilemma about Sid and the others. If she restored their benefits, Rodriguez would cancel them again and he would know she was doing it. She couldn't help Rose, Sally, Raquel, and Jeb right away. She needed more evidence, names, and case numbers for the hearing.

When she walked through the doorway into IM66's L & A, she felt the tension in the air. The door to Rodriguez's office was open. He stared at her. She held herself back. It was going to be a long day.

That day, they watched each other like two animals prowling around the same kill. She ignored Rodriguez, or at least tried to, and helped John and Adrian with a batch of tough Fair Hearing cases most of that morning and afternoon. Late in the afternoon, she took the list of Rex residents to a terminal on the far side of intake. She plugged the names on her list into the old HRA database. Sally, Jeb, Raquel, and Rose, plus two others at the Rex, had, truly, been sent into the digital black hole. She called Toby and told him about the new turn. Rodriguez pretended to be busy but once, when she'd glanced at the clock on the far wall, she caught him watching her. The undisguised hatred in that look shook her.

At four-thirty, Shirley, the center director, called Rodriguez into a conference. The door to his office was open and she heard him make excuses. In the end, he got up, irritated. When he walked stiffly out of the office, he crossed to her desk as if he had to say something. Instead, he gave her a withering look, a look that said, "I will kill you if you touch that terminal."

She shrugged and picked up the phone and started dialing Toby. She watched Rodriguez leave, then hung up the phone, and walked to Adrian's desk. "Darling, could I see that case I helped you with this morning?"

"I'm not sure where it is now. I'll have to look for it."

"Could you please? I think I made a mistake."

"Not likely, but I'll get it anyway." Adrian shrugged, got up, and went to wander around intake, where she was sure he would be for at least an hour.

As soon as he was outside, she hurried to the Triple M terminal. She signed on. She almost clicked on the Restore option, but she stopped herself, then, reluctantly, clicked on the Search option. She started with the "A's" and started writing down an alphabetic listing of the clients and case numbers. After half-an-hour, she felt, rather than heard Rodriguez outside. She logged off and was back at her desk when Rodriguez stalked into the room. He glanced quickly at her, the Triple M terminal, and then stormed into his office, slamming the door.

She had been up to "L" when she stopped. She had fifty names. That meant there were roughly one hundred clients who had been cashiered by the Triple M. She carefully folded the paper and slipped it into her bag. It was more evidence, a lot more. But she needed another strategy to restore benefits, and she needed it soon.

That evening, Dugan called and said that Labor Relations would support her in the hearing. He also said John, his boss, was mounting an investigation of his own. Excellent, Frieda thought, she had powerful support. But why did she have to go through a hearing at all?

She heard a slow tread on the carpet, which she recognized as Sven. She walked to her door, opened it.

Sven heard her, his hand on his doorknob.

"How goes the battle," she said.

Sven shrugged. "This man follows me. Black hair, trench coat. A movie extra."

"Believe me, he's not with the CIA. Be careful."

"You can only tolerate it so long," Sven said. He opened the door revealing an artist's stand with a tiny painting in the middle. He closed it carefully behind him.

She made herself another drink, smoked, and thought. She had to marshal her forces for the hearing. She had evidence, but it could be interpreted in different ways. New system, testing. It was all bullshit. She was about to stab out her cigarette, when she remembered something Sean Borgan said. She snatched up the phone.

If she was right, it was going to be an interesting hearing.

24

Jeanie tap-tapped down the stairs. A few seconds later she curled up on the sofa with a mug. She took a sip of coffee. "You seemed worried last night," she said. "Distracted."

He'd finally had a good night with Jeanie; at least he thought it was a good night. Distracted? Of course, he'd been distracted for weeks. Driven Lansky, ditzy Moira, the Brooklyn real estate maven with a wagon load of emotional baggage, Don, his "agents," Kragen. They were a rogue's gallery in his spirit. When Mario limped back to the Rex, Petrov, a Russian on Mario's floor, packed up and left and Mildred, a bookkeeper on four, did the same. Cause A renders effect B. The logic of intimidation was too strict not to admire, but it made him chip away at the larger picture like a frustrated sculptor.

Jack shrugged. "Not particularly."

"I know it's the project," she said, curling her white legs on the blond leather couch.

Rim of curls, wide face, lipstick removed. Jeanie's satin robe draped over breasts and hung fashionably like curtains in a theatre. Her legs were pulled up and tucked on the side. Her strong legs and sensuous ankles looked like carved alabaster, her toenails a deep burgundy. Jeanie's top half seemed washed out, half-ready, the bottom curled, polished, and armed.

When he thought about it, *she* had seemed distant last night. Jack said, warily, "Almost finished. Another month, maybe two."

Jeanie shifted a few inches, which hiked up her robe. "I don't know everything you do, but you know I don't like it. I work hard. I dance every weekend. In between, I worry about my brother, you, and what you're doing. I don't want to come home to a message that you're dead. Or have the police grill me about what you're doing."

Jack settled his arms on his legs. "I said it would be over in a month. Two, tops."

"I don't know if that's enough. Maybe we shouldn't see each other for awhile."

Jack felt leaden. Jeanie had always felt edgy about the project. It was coming to a head at the wrong time. He couldn't deal with that too. "There's a lot of money. It means Jack Kuhl's renaissance. I can't just stop."

"You could get—"

"No, I can't," he said angrily. His eyes narrowed. They'd been over it before; why did she start on him that morning? He reached up his hand to scratch behind his ear, but stopped.

Jeanie frowned, then smiled. Her smile said "bad news." He'd seen it on Moira. Lansky's smile was like a wolf's. Couldn't he get a regular old twenty-five cent smile anymore? "I like you Jack, but I mean what I said. I don't want you to be a statistic. Let's take a few days off. Meet for dinner. Get a little air."

"If that's what you want."

"That's what I want."

Jeanie got up and stretched. The satin bunched around her arms, then slipped back when she picked up her coffee. She came over to Jack leaned down and kissed him on the nose. Her right breast brushed against his robe.

Jack held her for a moment, and then inserted his hand in her robe. He felt her soft, doughy flesh, and her nipple. She smiled. "Later, Jack."

A wave of longing rushed over him, and then left him empty. "Okay, baby."

Jeanie tucked in the folds of her robe and walked slowly upstairs, head bowed, as if she were thinking of every step.

Outside it was graying into blue. New Jersey wavered, then clarified into points of quartz embedded in square dim buildings. Jack watched the crystals glow brighter until Jeanie appeared at the door and left.

Pressure from all sides. The apartment felt like a trap. Upstairs, the mirror showed him the band-aid behind his ear had worked its way loose. He tore it off and put on another one. Then he dressed quickly in jeans, sweatshirt, boot socks, brown Mephisto light hiking boots, and a leather jacket. Twenty minutes later, he set up in the small triangle of Duane Park with the crazy woman, her cart full of toys and Starbucks containers, a snoring bum, and a flock of pigeons.

It was a nice day, cooler. Maybe it was September after all. The traffic from West Broadway, Hudson, and Church Streets formed a barrier around their little island. When he thought about it, it was less island than prison.

A Devil's Island in the middle of Manhattan. *Distracted*? He couldn't stop working the project because of Jeanie.

Jack walked over to the pay phone at the Church Street point of the park triangle and called Kragen. Kragen said he and Tony were stalking Frieda, Marcy, and Bel, and for variety Sven and Petey.

Jack grimaced. *Stalking*? Kragen could have used any other word.

His second call was to Blondie, agent/programmer. He worried about Blondie when he hired him. So far he'd been okay, but he didn't like hearing he'd called Don about Mario.

Blondie worried about Mario, about what had happened.

"But it wasn't you," Jack said. He shifted the phone to the other ear. He tried to sound sincere. "I hate it as much as you do. But after a certain point, we have to show we have teeth. If not, they're going to thumb their noses at us."

"Notes and harassment are one thing, hurting people another. Beating people up attracts the wrong attention. You should know that."

The bum in the park was up. He blinked his red eyes, scratched his gray hair, and looked stunned. He pawed through his pack, and then looked around as if he'd lost breakfast. "You've done a great job. Forget about Mario. It was an isolated case. Everyone is worried that they're next. Work on Mike Dibbick. You know who he is."

"305. Salesman."

"Ace thought he was about to bolt. Offer him two grand to move. If he says yes, call me."

"Okay."

Maybe okay, maybe not. "After you talk to Mike, take it easy. Work on your game. By the way, you're getting a bonus. Two hundred bucks. Keep up the good work."

"Okay, Jack."

Jack scowled at the phone. His other agents had to be corralled into doing less. Jack called Don and told him to give Blondie a bonus.

"And watch him. I have a feeling about him."

"You got it," said Don.

The rest of the morning, he called other agents, told them who to work on. But the project had hit the doldrums. He needed something to get it going again. Plus, there was the nagging problem of the welfare cases.

Around noon he got up and walked to the Front Café on the Hudson.

Lots of people in the street, cars crawled along the Hudson like rats, a few tall smokestacks poked through the New Jersey smog. He had a sandwich, followed it with strong coffee, and got back to work.

He was going to find out about those welfare cases himself. He dialed the Rex and asked for Rose Tutwiler. Jack knew there were buzzers in the rooms and house phones in the hall for those residents who couldn't afford their own. Rose was one of those residents. He knew about her—thin, diminutive, on SSI and welfare for five years, bad poetess, and death-tripper. He could almost imagine the room buzzer shocking her out of writing yet another line of pessimistic drivel.

"Miss Tutweiler," Jack said, formally.

"Who is this?"

"I'm a case worker. We've been looking over your file and—"

"I know. You've been sending out the wrong forms, again. Why does welfare hire such idiots? I suppose it's the only thing you know how to do."

She must be a tough nut for her caseworker. "Wrong forms, Miss Tutweiler?"

"That form 200 with its idiot code. I don't remember, I just know it was wrong."

"We're still trying to run down the error. If you could—"

"How should I know—you sent it! Talk to Frieda!"

Rose banged the phone down. Frieda? Welfare. Rose. He'd told Lansky there was a connection. He dialed the Rex, again, and that time asked for Jeb, another welfare recipient.

It took him a few minutes to get to the phone. "Yep."

"I'm with the welfare department. And we're checking—"

"Code 333? It's some sort of welfare conspiracy to kick us out of the Rex. Higher-ups in the department. Some developer. Frieda Berg knows. Room 806. Talk to her."

"Right."

Code 333? Fuck. They knew more about Lansky's welfare connection than he did! It had always irked him. He couldn't control it, dice it, put it in his master plan. He called Lansky. Lansky was out. Where the fuck was he?

Rose said to talk to Frieda. Jeb said talk to Frieda. Frieda had done this, Frieda had done that. Kragen and Tony hadn't scared her. He'd have to do something about her soon, but he didn't know what.

Jack checked his watch. Time for another go round with Moira Maxwell. He still hadn't decided about the gig in Brooklyn. He supposed if he went for it, Jeanie would wave bye-bye. His life had become complicated in ways he couldn't imagine.

Jack Kuhl met Moira Maxwell, ditz and real estate agent, at Rosen's Deli at Broadway and Eighty-sixth. While he ate a salad and she demolished a pastrami sandwich, she talked about her projects, about how she was going to be one of the top agents in New York City, and, of course, about her therapist, her psychotic mother, her high blood pressure father, and an ex-boyfriend named "Ike," whom she'd slept with, again, and who hadn't called back.

"These buildings in Brooklyn won't wait much longer, Jack," she said. Did she always lay down a personal smokescreen to hide her real purpose? Her smile said it was time for more bad news. What this time? They wanted to start last year?

Jack put his fork down and paid attention. He chose his words carefully. "You can't rush these things. It's about timing *and* security. That's how I work. It worked at the Amsterdam, and it will work at the Rex. You don't want to have a victory party in jail."

Moira grimaced. "I understand. But other people have priorities, schedules, deadlines. You make money if you hit the deadlines, you lose if you don't. These landlords in Brooklyn have people who want to move in next year. They have to start December 1, no later."

Jack felt light-headed, then nauseous. It was too fast, way too fast. There was the carrot, then the stick. "Listen," he said, seriously. "Find someone else. I can't finish by December. We'd planned on spring—at the earliest."

Moira didn't give up. "You have people there. Put pressure on the residents, make better offers to leave. You know what to do." Moira's hands and fingers were in constant motion. If she wasn't digging in her bag, she was prodding and poking her plate and silverware.

"What do you think I have been doing?" Jack said, testily. "I've gotten rid of twenty residents in less than two months. There are still forty left and they're the hard core, the ones anchored to their rooms. I'm working on them, but it takes time. If I use more pressure, I attract the police, which is exactly what Michael doesn't want. You don't want that in Brooklyn, either."

Moira frowned. "Of course, I wouldn't want you to do anything illegal."

Jack stifled a laugh. What a fucking comedy! She knew about the Amsterdam and the Rex. Lansky's reputation for ruthlessness was common knowledge and plastered all over the Internet. He played her game. "No, nothing illegal."

"I know you're doing what you can and that you're good. But if the Rex isn't finished by December, I'm afraid the Brooklyn deals are off."

He was tired of bandying words. "I'm tired of people pressuring me. Find somebody else."

"C'mon Jack, work with me. I'll talk to the Brooklyn people. Try to get an extension."

Jack shrugged. "Sure. But the Rex isn't going to waver and disappear overnight."

Then Moira went into her frenzied mode. She'd forgotten an appointment. She gathered her bag, left the check for him, then gave him a peck on the cheek, and dashed for the door edging between people stacked up at the deli.

Jack watched her leave. He knew Lansky sicced Moira onto him. It was Lansky's idea of pressuring him. It was the middle of the afternoon. Something about the deli—it was subterranean, dark, and noisy—made him afraid. Lansky, Kragen, Moira. The word was "implicating." Jack reached behind his other ear. That time he scratched.

Lansky called back at eight that night.

Jack told him he'd call back in a few minutes. The apartment without Jeanie felt like a desert. He poured his martini into a scotch glass, put on his leather coat, and went to the roof. It was chilly and black that night. He punched out Lansky's number.

Lansky came on right away. He said, "What's up, Jack."

"Everything except the welfare evictions," said Jack. "I talked to two residents on welfare. They talked about some welfare conspiracy, code 333. They knew more than I fucking did."

"Normally, they'd be guessing. Not this time. I talked to Morty."

Morty? "And?"

"Frieda Berg landed in Rodriguez' welfare office. He's never seen her use the new system, but the cases he canceled have been restored."

"What the fuck are the odds of that happening?" Jack realized his neck was cold and zipped up the leather jacket to his neck. He took a long pull on his drink. Fucking welfare scheme. There were too many people, too easy for someone digging up a paper or digital trail.

"Million to one. It gets worse," said Lansky, angrily. "Frieda is an IM investigator."

The gnawing, nauseous sensation he'd had with Moira washed over Jack. "A welfare cop?"

"Something like that. I don't know exactly. It's a fucking bureaucracy. Everybody has a weird fucking title."

"Can this Rodriguez do anything about her?"

"She has a habit of pissing people off. Rodriguez lodged a complaint about her and our people made it serious, but he's not sure it will do any good."

Jack digested this news. It was bad, but not hopeless. *Reason it out. Solve the problem. It's what you're good at.* "Frieda's boyfriend is a defrocked doc. He's trying to leave. You could offer him money to leave."

"You mean you could offer my money to leave," said Lansky, irritated.

Jack hid his own irritation. "Of course that's what I meant."

There was a pause. Jack felt cold. He hunched his shoulders, put the drink down, and put his free hand in the jacket pocket. "Fine," said Lansky. "Tell me when and I'll send the money over. Listen, Jack, you're doing a great job. Forget your reservations. Think big picture."

Jack noticed, for the first time, that there were stars. It was black when he came up, but now there was a glow over the side of the roof, an umbrella of light. Stars. Jack felt tied down by their subject. "So far, it hasn't been a problem."

There was another, longer pause. Why was Lansky pressuring him? "I've lined up two big developers for that space, Jack. Right now, they're outbidding each other. But that won't last. If this slow approach starts taking too long, we might have to do something dramatic."

Jack frowned into the phone. "Which means?"

"Not yet, not yet. Step up the pressure. More notes, more threats. Use

Kragen. Let's see where we are in two weeks. If we're not making good progress, we'll have to go with Wing Attack, Plan R...or F."

Jack thought of Kragen, of Mario. He didn't want to use him again. "Of course."

"You have to be tough in this business, Jack. Moira likes you and wants you to get the Brooklyn business. She's working for you."

Not for the first time, Jack felt a fleeting sense of subterfuge about Lansky. Jack reminded himself daily he had to be careful with Lansky, then, deep in the project, he forgot.

"I'm just getting started."

After Lansky hung up, Jack decided it was time to do more than wonder about Frieda or have Kragen or Tony stalk her. He made a mental note to call Bert. It was time to launch a preemptive strike on the Rex's number one social worker/welfare cop.

25

HRA, the Triple M, Rodriguez. Frieda Berg realized she'd called too many people for something not to happen. Dugan talked to John. John talked to Toby. Toby talked to Computer Operations and Accounting, and finally George Kelso, the head of IM. George despised her and said she'd gone off the deep end. It would have ended there, except George found that John—antagonists on the scorched plain of labor relations—had started his own investigation. After waxing apoplectic, George had—extremely reluctantly, according to Toby—started his own inquiry. If it weren't so serious, she would have admired her handiwork. She hadn't created so much chaos in ages.

Of course, she told Toby, it wasn't her; it was what *they* were doing. She couldn't have invented the Triple M or Lansky's scheme, if she'd tried. Reality won that round hands down.

She didn't have time to gloat. A handful of Rex residents had been knocked off welfare—that was a big item on her plate—but they were a small part of Lansky's scheme. As she told Marcy, her real worry was about the front line in the Rex, Jack's resident goons, and outside the Rex, Mr. Fishface and the dorky Italian with the black bouffant.

But the HRA leviathan lumbered on, which meant it was time for the hearing about the Rodriguez complaint—at least it wasn't a committee. And that's why a week after Rodriguez canceled the Rex's HR cases again, Frieda found herself standing in front of an old door of rippled glass and wire and faded gold lettering. From where she stood, she saw a perfect reflection of the scene behind her.

The reflection took in an institutional corridor, a barren and worn industrial strength window frame, and the trunk of a blotchy-patterned sycamore which swayed slightly and which had mesmerized her the way a cobra was mesmerized by the music of the fakir.

What was it about that image that riveted her to the spot? Was it the barrenness of it, the total bleakness? Was that post-apocalyptic mirrorscape what her life was becoming? The bridges were burning, the die cast. She would lose her place, her garden, and Harry. The Rex would be razed; a new Olympia would shoot up. The leaves would drop and clutter the blasted heath.

She snapped off her gaze and zeroed in on her image, which was slightly under the sign, which announced "HRA conference room, Room 101." She surprised herself by looking imperious, cheekbones high, eyebrows raised in "attack" mode.

She ground her cigarette into the gray floor, grabbed the doorknob, and swung the door open. The knob slipped out of her hand and the door crashed against the wall. Four people at the long table flinched. She saw their heads, and then focused on their shocked faces. The first person she recognized was the director of IM, George Kelso, who had put a reprimand in her record himself.

Well.

Besides George, there was Toby, John, Dugan, and a skinny woman with a dictation pad sitting behind the table. Where were Jaime Waite and Rodriguez?

George was a brusque former Army colonel with close-cropped silver hair, and a hooked, belligerent nose. His open mouth clamped shut.

As the faces around her relaxed, she had time to get a feel for the room. Was it a feeling of apprehension? She tried to read Toby's face. He anchored the table on her left. He looked seedy with his drooping mustache, booming belly, and brown suspenders. The surprise generated by her entrance had faded into an avuncular, meditative pose, which told her nothing.

When she turned to Dugan, he turned to John and a strand of Dugan's wispy hair sprang into the air like a newly risen shoot of bamboo. John looked at her, eyebrows raised as if he were probing her. She stared at John an extra beat. He was drop-dead handsome with an aquiline nose, a thin perpendicular forehead line matched by parted, carefully combed brown hair, which was graying around the edges. She was never sure how people got into HRA and John was one of the oddest. Harvard Law School. Family connections. He could have been a hotshot investment banker on Wall Street or top tier Park Avenue lawyer. And he'd given that up to fight his way up the ladder of HRA's Labor Relations. He was one of the good ones. He made you think that idealism wasn't dead and truly meant something.

A secretary sat behind George and to his right. She was a thin vinegary woman with a horse face faintly resembling Lily Tomlin. She tossed her head, as if unnerved by the intrusion, and then occupied herself with her notepad. She never looked directly at anyone for the rest of the session, almost as if she were avoiding a curse.

Light from Canal Street streamed into the conference room, but stopped short of their table. Dust motes rose. Frieda retrieved the door, and then closed it.

Her entrance had shocked everyone into silence for a few seconds. She sat, acknowledged everyone with a raised eyebrow, then said, "This Rodriguez complaint is a setup."

"Do you always enter a room like that," said George.

"Only in the department," she said.

George shook his head at her. "As for the complaint, we'll decide its merits later," said George. "I've postponed the hearing."

Frieda felt her stomach churn, her heart skip. She gave Dugan and John a crooked smile. She felt elated, then curious. She looked at Toby. "You didn't tell me?"

"It just happened," said Toby. "I didn't have time."

"Why am I here?"

George looked squarely at her. "Toby and John think we have a problem with the Triple M. I'm here to be convinced. And I don't want conjecture or talk of wild schemes."

"There *is* a mess," said Frieda. "Call it what you want."

"Which has to be proved," said George. "To my satisfaction. Convince me. If this is another one of your shitass crusades, we'll have more than a hearing. Linda."

Linda began jabbing lines in a gray notebook.

Frieda's heartbeat settled into a regular pattern. George didn't intimidate her. She drew her coat around her, thought of smoking, but thought better of it.

"I don't trust your judgment, George. But I think you're fair."

George waved his hand at her. "I don't care what you think of me. Get on with it."

She sorted out what she knew and laid it for them. She detailed what she had dug up on the mystery code 333s and how she was led to the new system, the Triple M. Finally she told them about Rodriguez' lists and that he was the one who threw away old case records, then used the Triple M to erase the case from the old system. She hesitated, knowing she was about to let the cat out of the bag, then told them about the Restore option.

She had George's attention, but he was skeptical. "What's important is motive," she continued. "Some of the cases I've run down seem to be people picked at random. But most of the cases involve clients at old hotels. Two of the hotels where clients had their benefits stopped and were evicted have closed. One, the Cardiff, has the shell of a high-rise going up right now. The other, the Amsterdam, is a hole in the ground. By sheer luck—bad luck—I live in a hotel that has been targeted by the landlord who owned the other two hotels."

"How did you end up living in a hotel?" George said, frowning.

"It's a long story full of melodrama and divorces. It was supposed to be temporary."

"I was supposed to be in Labor Relations temporarily," said John, fingering his watch.

"And I should be teaching romanticism at Columbia," said Toby.

"Please," said George. "Sort the problems of time and existence later. What evidence do you have to back up this fantasy?"

"I would have brought more evidence, if I'd known," said Frieda.

Toby glanced at her apprehensively. She hesitated, and then calmly picked up her bag. She looked concerned, frowned into the bag, shook it, then dug deep into it. They watched her as if she were a magician who had misplaced a rabbit. Finally, she extracted the folder, dropped her bag on a chair, and then dropped the folder in the middle of the table. George looked at her, then the folder. She waited a beat before opening the folder and sorting through the forms.

She picked up one packet, glanced at it, and then slid it across the table to George. "Those are IMD 209s for every client in the Rex. They have been canceled with a code 333, which is not in our current system." She picked out two more packets. "Here are printouts showing the clients are not in the current system, and printouts showing their cases after I restored them using the Triple M." She picked out a last paper and shoved it across the table. "Here is a statement from Jennifer Morales saying that a tall, dark man with a Playboy tie, who said he was working on a special project, collected the Rex cases from IM33 a week before their cases were closed. Mr. Rodriguez wears those ties. This is a list of cases I've copied from the Triple M. It has about fifty names on it."

Yes, she had her five minutes in the sun. Yes, they were paying attention. But she was too cynical to believe George was convinced. George had, after all, been convinced that glad-handing, anti-client PR man Morty Bennet was God's gift to the department. The atmosphere in the room was heavy. She glanced at John and Dugan, and realized, for the first time, that she'd slept with half of the men in the room. It made her feel peculiar, as if she'd been another person when that happened. She *had* been another person.

George ran the papers between his fingers for five minutes then carefully put everything back in the folder. George looked at her then the others. "I don't see a convincing case," he said, finally. "You don't know if Rodriguez threw the cases away. That's a supposition. I see a special project designed to convert cases for the new system. It might have been used prematurely. I'll talk to Morty. I should have talked to him in the first place."

Toby looked at her and shook his head, as if to say, "Be quiet." John looked at Dugan, Dugan at her. She zeroed in on George. "George, you're the only person in this room who doesn't think that Morty Bennet is an asshole, a ratfink, and likely a criminal. Rodriguez works for Morty. Theo Dryseck works for Morty. Morty had to know about this. Shit he might have designed it. If you alert him, he'll close it down, or move it so we'll never find it."

"Morty has made enemies," George said, looking at her, then around the table. "I hadn't realized how serious it was until now."

"Go ahead," said Frieda, leaning across the table. "Protect Morty when Health and Human Services finds out his special project closes AFDC, SSI, and Food Stamp cases without authorization. You'll have a hundred federal task forces to help you."

"It's a wicked scheme," said John.

"We wouldn't be here, if we didn't believe it," said Dugan.

George buried his silvery blond butch in his hands. "I still don't buy this fantasy. How could someone design a system this sophisticated with one purpose? You need battalions of programmers, testers, and parallel studies. Someone has to find out."

Toby cleared his throat and hunched over the table. "I'd like to clarify what's going on. The outside vendors, Oracle and IBM, are not in on a welfare conspiracy. I'm sure they followed the specs we gave them. A few well-placed individuals—I think it's too early to name names—are using this conversion program for their own purposes. And either by design or inadvertence it's easy to do. The mainframe is in Computer Operations. But none of the Triple M terminals at CO are hooked up—too many people would wonder about it. The only live terminal is at IM66."

"I'm beginning to see the how," said George. "What else?"

"This program removes most of the indexes, keys, or the directory structure in the old system and creates a skeleton case in the new. I don't understand a lot of it myself, but it's devastatingly thorough and well-designed."

"Why 'most'?" said Frieda. "The case aint in the old system."

"You can restore cases," said Toby. "It has a way to find them."

"So it's in there, we just can't see it," said Frieda.

"We have several problems," said John. John always looked too handsome to be smart. It caught people off-balance. He talked over the top of his pyramided fingers. "The first involves the clients at the Rex, or, for that matter, any clients who have had their benefits stopped. We'll have to set up a task force to make sure that when their benefits are canceled, they are restored."

"I'll do it," Frieda said.

George shook his head. "We need a more official protocol than you pressing a button."

"I can't press a button anymore," said Frieda. "Rodriguez knows I know. I'll set up a task force at IM33—that's where the Rex residents have their cases."

"I don't want you to do it," said George.

Frieda felt the blood rush to her face, her eyes narrow. "Listen—"

"I've been working with the IM33 center director," said Toby. "It will be ready Monday."

Frieda relaxed. The meeting was going badly; then it turned around. She supposed it was the threat of the feds getting involved that did it. But she was still bothered. The power to restore with a button was about to run into a bureaucracy that lived on paper, forms, more forms, and delay. "As long as a committee doesn't decide our clients' fate."

"We try to play by the rules and the rules are spelled out everywhere," George said.

"Morty and his gang are breaking the rules."

"Guilt, guilt, guilt," George said. George took the folder back and looked at it for a few seconds; then he threw it across to Frieda. "I'll grant we have a problem. Let's see if we can solve it without prematurely assigning guilt or responsibility."

John said, "Let's talk about scope. If the conversion program can wipe out the indexes for a select group of clients, it could wipe out the indexes for a larger group, possibly every client. You would, of course, have the case records, but without restoring them using the Triple M, recreating the electronic versions would cause havoc and would take months."

Dugan said, "And the problem with that last scenario is millions of pieces of litigation from the Legal Defense Fund, ACLU, and welfare lawyers. That would add to the chaos. It seems to me that we have to identify who is doing this—we can leave Morty out of this for now, although this Rodriguez has to work for somebody—and see what we can do about shutting them down without exploding the old system. We need a task force for the computer side and we need a task force which includes the fraud division of the NYPD."

"What about an exposé," Frieda said. She knew George wouldn't go for it, but she didn't expect all the faces at the table to swivel towards her at once. It looked like she'd stepped on their toes with lead boots.

"No Frieda," said Toby.

"You do that, and I'll fire you without a hearing," said George.

And that might have been a good thing. "Right, 'go slow.' There are still investigations plodding along from when I started twenty years ago. HRA suffers from self-perpetuating task forces and investigations. And while you're investigating, this slumlord is trashing rooms and hounding residents. If your investigation lasts into next year, the Rex won't be standing."

"The Rex per se is not our problem. As John said, it's an NYPD matter," said George.

"Precisely," Frieda said. "And because everything is so compartmentalized, and because the evidence is so sketchy, this landlord will get off. The cops aren't going to make the connection between Mario getting beaten up and Rodriguez pressing a button in IM66."

Toby said, "If you go to the papers, Frieda, we won't catch anyone— if that's what we're doing." Toby paused, stared at the wall behind her, then at George. "I talked to Jerry Marguiles in Computer Operations.

Operations programmers are talking to Oracle. If needed, we could disable the terminal at IM66 in seconds."

"I'll talk to him," said George.

"Sure," said Frieda. "Great. But the conversion program is just one tool. If we exposed the entire scheme, the thugs, the beatings, the—"

"Can't you hear," said George, angrily. "No, no, no."

George was getting purple. Fuck him. She wasn't going to start backing down now. "It's hard to believe we're on the same side, George."

"Frieda," said Toby.

"I think we're done, for now," said George, ignoring her and looking around the table. "I hadn't realized how seriously you were taking this. Now I see why. Keep me informed."

The tension in the room was palpable, and everybody got up to go. She wasn't done. She supposed it was Frenchie's flare for drama.

"One last thing, George."

"What," he said, angrily, his eyes cold blue stones.

She felt everyone pause. She had their attention, again. She dipped into her bag and pulled out a Xeroxed sheet. She shook her head slowly back and forth. "I'd be the last person to assign guilt prematurely, but here's a copy of the newspaper article on the owners of the Cardiff, the hotel I mentioned earlier. Seems one of the co-owners was one Morty Bennet. Geez, I wonder where he got the idea of using the welfare system to gut clients in his buildings."

She flipped the paper over the table, got up, and marched out.

Toby caught up with her in the hall. "Why didn't you tell me?"

She measured Toby with her eyes. Sean Borgan was her ace in the hole. "Sorry Toby. I just dug it up yesterday. Didn't have time."

Toby said, "That seals it, doesn't."

Frieda shrugged. "Plots and Schemes. Fuck it. C'mon, let's get drunk."

Toby smiled ruefully. "Can't. I'm going upstate in an hour. I'll talk to you Monday."

"I wish I were up there, myself."

Frieda watched Toby lumber to the door, and then disappear.

John and Dugan walked up to her. Dugan shook his head. "You haven't lost your flair."

"Just a lucky snag. Up for a beer?"

"Nope. Got a concert. I wouldn't ask George."

Frieda laughed. "John?"

"Let's grab a cab."

She left with John on her arm. Hearing. Trial. Fuck George. She felt a thousand times better that other people were paying attention. She didn't want to think of how long it would take or if they'd accomplish diddly.

They hailed a cab, and soon were hurtling up Sixth Avenue towards Greenwich Village and the Cave. At seven, they were sitting in a half-full Cave, rolling their glasses between their fingers.

"I don't know how you're still here," said John. He took a large swallow, and then set his drink down on a coaster from Joe's, a bar across the street. "Or why."

Frieda took a healthy sip of gin and tonic. "*That* is the question."

"I knew something was happening," said John. John grabbed his glass, rotated it with his hand, and watched the tiny whirlpool. His nails were cut short, manicured. Their lovemaking of over ten years ago was brief, intense, and technically perfect despite being loaded to the gills. She'd wondered about John. He'd never married and there were hints that he was bisexual. "George is sticking by Morty because he promoted him, but George isn't a fool."

"Poor Toby. All the man wants to do is go fishing."

"We all think of some perfect spot," said John.

"I haven't, until recently."

"I'm amazed at schemes like this, but after twenty years of Food Stamp kick-backs and welfare rip-offs, I shouldn't be," said John.

"Sometimes I feel I'm in the fight of my life, other times I feel it's another empty gesture."

"No matter what was happening, you always gave us hope," John said. He smiled, and then put his hand over hers. "I mean that."

"I used to love the fight, now I'm not sure it's worth it."

John kept his hand over hers, and she didn't remove it. She thought of another go-round with John. It would be tacky. It would be sad. It would bring the Harry connection—as wobbly as it was—to a fast close.

The night in the Cave was winding down and so were they. They got sloppy sentimental and watched the feet of the passers-by in the small window in front. Lenny, terminal HRA drunk, came over and, for a change, was almost sober and they made faces in the bar mirror, which was decorated with fallen leaves, twigs, and gourds. It was the Cave's take on fall. For some of the regulars that was as close as they would get to the season.

At midnight, she kissed John and got in a cab. As she rode back to the Rex, she wondered whether she should have stayed with John. Harry was too cynical and hurrying back to the middle class. John was a mensch and her kind of people.

But right away she was back obsessing about what had happened in that conference room. She'd made them believers, but it was too easy. It made her think that the Fates had given her that victory as a feint, and they were just getting her softened for the kill.

26

Fishface showed up outside the Odyssey his nose inches from the front window, his eyes bulbous and staring, as if he were going to punch through the glass. He was gone when she quit. Marcy saw him again, once outside the Rex—he'd followed her for two blocks, but couldn't do anything on Park Avenue—and once more at Pier 17. That time was during the week. When she got off the subway, ready to bob-and-weave through Astor Place, he was gone.

He didn't have to follow her. She saw him if he was there or not.

That wasn't all. A dickhead with a black bouffant followed Frieda and for variety switched off on Bel and Sven. Oddly, she worried about Bel. And she dreaded going back to—or living at—the Rex. She and Butch were going to see Sartre's "The Flies" at eight at his favorite little theatre, the Cul de Sac. But the Rex with its closed off rooms and with the constant presence of Truck, four's personal thug, made her duck out early. She made sure she had Mace, pepper spray, and Mario's club, hitched up her pack and skipped down the four flights of stairs. Outside, it was cool and clear. She checked west and east and headed to the Lexington local.

She arrived at Butch's at noon. She pushed open the door on the side of the garage, which he always left open when he was there. She didn't see Butch. She did hear sounds coming from the direction of the waterbed. It sounded like a low grade pneumatic drill; then panting; then a moan. She frowned, and then walked through Butch's junk/art with a flutter in her heart. She crept around "Village Angst" and stopped at "Soft Cock." The waterbed was shaking and rocking. She thought at first that Butch had grown into two Butchs because his cock seemed at the right height for where his cock should be, except it wasn't his cock. When she looked closer, she saw that Butch was fucking Mark Thompson, a graphics designer she'd met at a party, in the ass.

"Jesus Christ."

Butch turned, his jaw open, his eyes wide. "Shit."

She stared at him for a few seconds, not sure exactly what to think. It was a moment when everything drops into place. The dripping phalluses, Butch's light, almost feminine touch, the stretches of time she didn't see him. She saw that some kind of sexual ambiguity stoked his art. He was right: it was all about sex. But sex was more than Adam and Eve. The moment was hopeless, but she wanted to hold onto it. It was perverse. She even thought it was funny. When you see everything for the first time, when the light flashes on...

Butch pulled out. She swore, later, she heard a distinct "pop," as if he'd uncorked a champagne bottle.

Butch may have said something, but she didn't hear it. She was already threading her way through the rusted rebar, dented fenders, and chains coiled around I-beams. Halfway to the garage door, she started pushing over stacks of metal. Hubcaps, balanced stacks of rebar crashed to the floor. Just before she got to the door, she tried to push over a batch of iron, but it was too heavy. It made her madder.

"Marcy!"

She kicked open the door.

Butch caught her and twirled her around. She shook off his hand.

Butch zipped up a pair of jeans he must of put on in record time. He wore a skinny T-shirt, his pecs were prominent and sensual; a trace of sweat shone above his dark eyebrows. He was framed in the garage door like a photo.

"So what do you have to say, shit for brains?" she said. Tiny squares of glass in the garage door trooped out from his shoulders. Mark's face appeared in one.

She could tell Butch was worried. He scratched his head sheepishly. "It was an experiment. It's just different. You have to see that."

A pane reflected her image. Her hair was two inches long. She could see a rattail. Her brows were dark as Bel's, her boobs sharp and jutting, her mouth a pencil thin line scratched across her face. She seemed confrontational; but they were having a confrontation. "Lover? AIDS? You ever think of that?"

"C'mon," he said. "Sex is not death."

"Fuck you. And fuck your miserable art. It's a bunch of bullshit. Butch and his bullshit art. Fuckin' rebar, fuckin' asshole metal. You're a fuckin' construction worker, not an artist."

"You don't have to be nasty," said Butch, stunned.

She could tell she'd gotten to him. She could tell she'd opened that black pit of self-doubt. She'd seen it before and for a split second she regretted what she'd said. It was about them, not about what he did. But she couldn't help herself. It was a fuck second.

Butch sighed, then seemed anxious, as if he were torn between wanting to talk about it and thinking he didn't have to. "I wanted to talk about it, but—"

"What's complicated about sticking your dick in every hole in the East Village?"

"Shit no. How do you know what I do?"

"We never know, do we?"

Talking was an afterthought. Words were balm, an ointment, and a barrier. The "eureka" moment inside staring at Butch and Mark masked her own hurt. She wasn't a bystander. Her world had shifted; the ground split open and then grew into a chasm. And she was pissed. She couldn't think when she was pissed.

"Mark's waiting for you, asshole. I mixed that up. He's the asshole, you're the moron."

She left him standing there, framed in the garage door, angry, but with a hint of regret clouding the anger. She stomped down that familiar street, feeling his eyes on her back. She hesitated at the corner, almost turned to see if he was still there, but didn't. The street was an inverted V racing to a point. A lone car turned, a solitary man poked his pale hand into the top of a garbage can.

She kicked a can halfway across the street. As she walked, she tried to feel out her hurt. She wasn't a Pollyanna. She knew about sexual identity confusion, bisexuals, transgenders, transvestites, and, of course, there was Carly. But Carly was different, although she couldn't explain exactly how. She liked Butch, maybe even loved him and his rebar and his pretensions.

She walked aimlessly down one street and up another. She seemed to know where she was walking, but if anyone had asked, she would have been stumped. The last place she wanted to be was at the Rex, but she went back, her mood hovering somewhere between rage and depression.

Marcy pushed through the fire doors on the fourth floor of the Rex. Truck's door was open. She frowned, and then walked carefully around the elevator housing. She stopped when she saw Truck stop at her door then lean over—with difficulty; he was grossly overweight—and start to tuck a new love note under her door.

She dropped her pack and rushed him. Halfway down the hall, she started screaming. Six feet away, she launched herself. She caught a look of horror on Truck's face just before she kicked him as hard as she could with all of her hundred and ten pounds in his rear. Truck lurched forward and his head bounced off her doorjamb. He dropped to the worn Rex carpet. His fingers still clutched the note; his head leaned against her door; his big ass stuck up, as if it were positioned for a spanking.

She picked herself up off the floor ready to yell at him or kick, when she saw he wasn't moving. She walked up to him and stared, curiously, at the dent on his head. Dead? She saw his chest rise, then fall.

Doors opened behind her. In a few seconds, Carly and Donna Wilson joined her.

"What happened," said Carly.

Marcy felt a sudden sense of release. "I rushed him. It was a reflex."

"We bagged one," said Donna. "Now what?"

Marcy looked at her. "I hadn't thought that far ahead."

Carly looked at both of them, then Truck. "They say women make the best torturers."

"Yuck," said Marcy.

The door next to Truck's cracked open. A few seconds later, Jenny, a quiet, intense woman, joined the group standing around the fallen agent.

Jenny looked at Truck. She accepted what happened. Jenny said, "Let's castrate him."

Marcy and Carly grimaced.

"Let's just lop his balls off," said Donna.

Marcy said, "That's what 'castrating' means. And no, we're not. He's a thug, not a bull."

"He's made my life hell," said Jenny, her lips pressed close together. "Every time I leave, he opens his door and leers at me. And those horrible notes, that awful music. He knew when I was trying to sleep or just wanted to be alone."

They nodded together. They knew.

"We can't stand here all day," said Carly. "Let's get him back to his room and figure something on the way. At least we can take his boom box."

Jenny raised her foot and kicked Truck's large rump. Truck's body seemed frozen for a second, then it tumbled over. His large belly flopped out of his dirty Daffy Duck T-shirt. Truck's thick-featured face was slack, his bulging eyes closed as if he were taking a nap. "What a gross person," Jenny said. "How could a mother love that?"

"If he had one," said Carly. "Marcy and I will grab his legs. You two take his arms."

Marcy snatched the note out of his hand. It was cold in its threat. "It could be you." It pointed right at Mario. She stuffed it in her jeans, bent, and picked up a leg. "Fuck," said Marcy, straining. "He must weigh three hundred pounds."

"Two fifty at least," said Carly.

They half-dragged, half-carried Truck to his open door. Five minutes later, they rolled him onto his bed.

Carly left. A few minutes later she came back with an armload of supplies. They included a bra, a pair of high heels, lipstick, and rouge. "I saw this in a Three Stooges, or was it the Marx Brothers, or Rodney Dangerfield? We'd better make this quick. He's not going stay out forever. Take his clothes off."

Donna frowned, then shrugged. "I'll take his shirt."

"I'll take his shoes," said Jenny.

"Dive in," said Marcy. "There's plenty for everyone."

Five minutes later, Truck was revealed. He lay naked on his bed, his head lolling to one side, his small cock bent towards the other. "He's not exactly Adonis," said Carly. She handed her accessories to Marcy, her high heels and bra to Jenny. "Get him ready. I'll get the camera."

When Carly came back, Truck sported bright red lipstick, rouged cheeks, a bra that lay across his chest, a wedge of worn black panties, and a high heels jammed onto the first three toes of his enormous feet.

Truck stirred.

The four looked at each other and started out the door. Jenny stopped on her way and snatched the boom box. "I'll take care of this."

"What about your stuff?" said Marcy to Carly.

"All old. I was going to throw them away. You guys ready?"

Marcy stayed in the doorway with one hand on the door.

Carly stepped to the foot of Truck's bed and said, "Say fromage."

The flash filled the room. Truck groaned. Carly shot another from the side, then skipped to the door. Marcy shut it. The four glanced at each other. Donna went back to her room.

Jenny locked her door, held the boom-box high, and said, "Bye, bye." She walked towards the fire doors. A few seconds later, the elevator clicked into life.

Marcy was furious when she walked into the Rex, but suddenly she felt giddy. Somehow her rage at Butch and his undercover work with Mark, Jack's "agents," and life in general had disappeared.

In Carly's room, the only thing they could do was laugh, and wait.

One down, five to go. It was almost a counterattack. It was odd about Truck. It was as if he did his thugging or gooning against his better judgment. Marcy had thought that about Tim as well and Blondie. If nothing else, Truck stayed quiet the rest of that day. Just to be sure, she teamed up with Carly. They ate a late lunch and then shopped most of the afternoon. Carly was a clotheshorse, but knew what she was doing. They took a long walk down Twenty-eighth to the East River and she tried to talk about what had happened that morning with Butch. She didn't do a very good job. She couldn't tell whether the people in her life were flaky, or whether it was her, that she expected too much of them, or that she wanted to control them.

Later, Carly left to see Mac, her boyfriend.

Marcy felt at loose ends. Butch's was out. She didn't want to stay in her room. She couldn't predict what Truck would do. She put on a warmer sweater, socks, tucked her money in her back pocket, put her Mace in the other, and went to the Moat. The thugs used to drink there, but not after Mario and Bel's fight with Max and Ace. The rumor was that they drank in Paddy's on Second.

The Moat was dark and deserted. She almost turned around and left, but through the gloom, she saw Frieda's cascade of black curls. Frieda hunched over a drink at the end of the bar.

Marcy walked over, sat, and tapped Frieda on the wrist.

Frieda looked up. Her dark eyes looked sad; her black checkmark eyebrows drooped. She said, slowly, "You never drink in here."

"You either."

"You tell me your story; I'll tell you mine." Frieda fished a cigarette out of a huge burgundy bag.

Marcy shrugged. She pointed to an empty Big Apple Ale on the bar top and made a sign to Larry to bring her one. "It started as a miserable day, but there were compensations. You?"

"I won a victory, but not the war. Residents disappear, Brendel is close to selling, and Rudi will too. The Rex is tottering, about to fall in the black hole. Then there's Harry."

"Harry?"

"Now we're together, now we're apart. It's been like that for almost a year, but I feel it's time for Harry to go. I thought secretly he'd stay, but we're all on different trips. Harry's trip never included being Dr. Desk Clerk. It all comes back to seasons and gardens, life springing up, then falling back withered and dead." Frieda tapped her cigarette into a glass ashtray and swirled an ice cube around her drink. "You should leave."

Marcy shrugged. "I think about it. I thought about moving in with Butch. Today I found him with a guy, a boyfriend, whatever."

Frieda frowned and shook her head. "Mercy."

"It was a lousy week and a horrible day until we had a little talk with Truck."

Frieda's eyebrows arched high towards the Moat's dark ceiling. "Tell me." She did. When Frieda stopped laughing, she said, "We don't win many."

"And I have Fishface, the asshole, you the dork with the bouffant."

"We're all confused about what to do. As for Butch, be friends, have white wine at openings and wax nostalgic about the old days." Frieda inclined her head towards the juke and Edith Piaf's "La Vie en Rose." "Goons, illiterate notes, dark alleys, and fading footsteps in a black night. It's farce, then Grand Guignol."

"I'm surprised they haven't gone after you," said Marcy.

Frieda rapped on the table three times. "I have my personal wraith." Frieda shook her head, then lifted her glass and looked through it. The side of Frieda's face wrapped around the glass and stayed there ballooned until Frieda put the glass down.

"It doesn't bother you?"

"Sometimes it leaves me trembling with fear; other times I'm too neurotic to care."

"Is Harry leaving or is that a guess?" said Marcy.

Frieda shook herself out of a trance. "A prophecy. I'll be okay, if I make it to spring."

Spring seemed far off that night and Frieda didn't want to make it a real night. A few minutes later, Frieda finished her drink and left Marcy in an empty Moat.

Marcy was about to leave, when Blondie came in.

Blondie hunkered at the bar. She'd seen him in the lobby and once in Madison Square Park tapping furiously on a laptop. It was funny to see him bent over the keyboard. It looked as if he were drumming a message to his cock.

She didn't necessarily want to stay, but inertia took over. She motioned to Larry for another beer. It was around nine. Through the open door, she saw cars speeding down Twenty-eighth. After a few minutes, Blondie raised his head, and recognized her. Then he looked in the mirror behind the bar, as if he'd lost something. He looked at her again. "I'm sorry," he said, as if she knew what he was talking about.

"You mean about fucking with people," she said, angrily.

"I just needed a job," he said. He took a long pull at his beer. He held the bottle in his pudgy hand, and turned it as if he trying to find the right angle. "It's hard when you're an ex-con, sometimes impossible."

At that time, she felt sorry for him. "Are most of you ex-cons?"

Blondie snorted. "Doesn't take genius to see that."

"If it's any consolation, you don't look like a goon. What were you in for?"

Blondie shook his head, as if he didn't want to talk about it. Finally he said, "I was a crackhead for years. Got caught. Got caught again. Spent time in Riker's. A couple years ago, I knew I was going to make it. As soon as I got out, I scored some crack and got into a weird head space. Stole something and got caught. Then it was back inside. It's a long story. I try not to think about it, but then I think about it all day."

"It's not a good life. You know I'm on the other side."

Blondie laughed. "Not anymore. I quit."

Marcy cocked her head at him, not understanding. "You mean

226

you're leaving?"

"Not right away. It's odd, but with what's happening and what could happen to me, I feel safer here than any place else. Maybe because it kinda feels like a prison."

"Jesus."

He rubbed his hand through his fine blond hair and it settled over his face like yellow dust falling slowly through a shaft of light. "I didn't mean it that way."

Marcy laughed. Frieda said "Magic Mountain" and "ship of fools." The Rex as prison? She thought of Bel, Frieda, Mario. She guessed that was true too. "Now you're a faux resident, now you're a real one. You're flickering in and out of reality like a firefly."

He had an ironic grin, which she appreciated grudgingly. "Leaving nasty notes for retirees wasn't on my résumé. I specialize in self-destruction."

"I'll bet Jack wasn't too happy."

"You know about Jack?" Blondie said, surprised.

"We're not stupid." She took a sip of beer, and then realized what she said and how it sounded. "It seems odd to talk about them and us. You guys talk too much. I saw Don talking with someone who fit Jack's description. I told him he was a jerk. It made me feel better."

Blondie grinned, then shook his head. "That was gutsy."

"I'm impulsive," Marcy said, thinking about Truck. "Has Jack done anything yet?"

"I just told Don today."

"I hope you know what you're doing." She was starting to like Blondie, but he seemed fatalistic, as if he knew his trip had to end badly. "Know a big guy with a small head, big teeth?"

Blondie looked puzzled. "Should I?"

"He's been following me. I know Jack sent him."

Blondie shook his head, wearily. "Fuck. It might be a guy called Kragen. The other guys talked about him. He's the enforcer type, probably one of the guys who did Mario. Mario was one of the reasons I quit. It starts with a little thing, then leads to a second. I could see the implications. I didn't want a thing to do with it." Blondie looked at her with an expression half-concerned, half-afraid. "I went to one of their afternoon beer bashes. They think you're one of the tough ones. They talked about you and Frieda."

Marcy took a long pull on her beer. "That's funny."

"It's not funny when you get beat up. What are you going to do?"

Marcy shrugged. "Not sure. I'm pissed, but I'm not a fool." Marcy thought of the time she'd seen him in Madison Square Park. "What's with the laptop?"

"I've always been a programmer. I program games. Except—"

"What kind of games?"

"Video-type games like Myst."

"I played it once. Like the graphics. Except what, then?"

"Fuck, the game's a mess. It's like my life, chaotic. I don't think I'll finish it, but I can't stop working on it. I put in clues, hints, and gizmos. When I find them the next day, I wonder what they are. I'm trying to dig out my own secrets."

"Too much head, no reality," Marcy said, oddly worried about Blondie. He was just a guy trying to make it, after all. "Jack may seem a yuppie, but look what he's done. Look at Mario. When you're a *real* resident, you go on their list."

"I know. Thanks for listening. Can I buy you one?"

Marcy shrugged, then, feeling peculiarly attached to Blondie, put her hand on his arm. It felt strong, but when she looked in his eyes, she saw fear and hesitation. "Another time, Mr. Blondie. I've had a long, weird day."

She took a last swig of beer, set it on the bar top, and headed towards the open door.

Butch, Truck, and Blondie. Weird men. Controlled by radiation from the Mars, the planet of testosterone oceans. But it wasn't just the men. That year was an epochal year in the life of Marcy Benaventura. Her trip led to spiritual garbage, sexual confusion, and a citadel balancing on the edge of a cliff. If she'd learned anything, it was to err on the side of paranoia.

27

Said he was quitting," said Don Breem. "I told him to split and he slammed the door in my face."

"What?"

Jack Kuhl paced the space between the condo's work nook and the elephant fern at the front door. He started the day in an alcoholic haze, fragments of the night balancing on the edge of his mind, and then falling in the pit. He hadn't seen Jeanie in days and he was going batshit. His only companion was relentless violence, senseless sitcoms, and staged reality shows on TV. And, of course, booze. Booze won that round hands down. Jack glanced in the mirror next to the door and saw his long, handsome face set in a grim clown-like mask. The edges of band-aids poked past his ear lobes looking like misplaced earrings.

He knew something would happen with Blondie. He'd always gone on his intuitions. And there it was. Blondie, disaster. Being right in hindsight never made him feel better.

Lots of good news lately.

According to Don, something happened on four—Marcy Benaventura likely!—and Truck was thinking of leaving.

"Fuck. We lost two agents and gained a resident in a spin of the dial."

Don said, "We start breaking heads?"

"No!" Jack yelled. He caught himself, backed up. What was he going to do? Pressure from above, pressure from below. He had to let things simmer. He knew he couldn't. "More notes, more harassment, louder music. You work on the Freak Brothers. Tell them Mario's just the beginning. Tell Blondie he's got a week to get out, if not...Leave that part blank. Let it work on his imagination."

"Sure, Jack, sure." There was a pause on the line, a long pause. "You're going to tell me if anything big goes down?"

What was that about? Jack, worry lines distorting his forehead, sought meaning in Don's expression. "Make sense. What big?"

"You know big."

Lansky said "dramatic." Don said "big." Through a scotch haze, he

229

remembered the last few days of the Amsterdam. When he came back from talking to Lansky—his first visit to the Olympia penthouse—there was a fire in the basement. Lansky hadn't told him, so he thought it was an accident. Old hotels were firetraps.

"What do you mean 'big,'" Jack said.

Don's voice dropped to a whisper. "I can't say over the phone. But you know." Don hung up. Jack stared at the phone.

Dramatic? Big?

Jack threw the phone on the sofa, went upstairs, and took a fifteen-minute shower. That helped his hangover, not the project. He dressed, put on fresh band-aids, came down, and called Truck. What exactly happened? Truck wouldn't say; said it was personal.

"Personal? What the fuck is that?"

"They kinda ganged up on me. I didn't see it coming."

"You can't let *them* intimidate *you*! You're the tough guy! Write notes to all of them. You're getting a two hundred buck bonus—hazard pay."

"I don't know Jack. I'm starting to get a—"

"C'mon Truck. Help me out here."

"Sure. I'll do what I can. Don't forget the bonus."

Who could have ganged up on him—a couple of seventy-year olds and bunch of women? Fucking Christ.

Jack booted up the laptop and jabbed open the Rex project. He scanned the floors, looked at his notes. He typed in suggestions about which residents to target. He called Bert, then Jimmy. He felt better when he worked from the Rex model. It was clear, clean, the Rex bits and bytes. But those vague words—what the crap did "dramatic" and "big" mean?—scratched at his brain.

At noon, he was at the door about to go to the Front Café for lunch—he could only stand the apartment so long—when he stopped, stared at the laptop, and walked back. He plugged his modem into the phone jack and logged on. He surfed the Internet. It was agonizingly slow, but in the end, he found websites on Lansky. They repeated what he'd found at the Chelsea library. Social workers or lawyers set up most of the sites, an ex-resident of the Cardiff another. Lansky's name appeared and disappeared like an incantation. There were quotes from the New York Times. What made him stop was a photo. It took him three minutes to download. It showed fire trucks, flames licking the outside of an old building. It was the Cardiff.

"Mysterious fire guts SRO hotel. Two dead, five injured."

Two dead, five injured.

The words slid off his consciousness. What did that mean for the Rex? Fire in the basement. It could be put out, but what if it wasn't? Tongues of flame slipped up the elevator shaft, snaking up the stairs, slipping under doors. Frieda's garden vaporized, hot tar washed down from the roof. The Rex became an inferno, the stairs clogged with smoke. Rose screamed, hammered on her door, coughed, fell. Twenty dead; ten in burn units. Arson suspected.

Jack was pinioned to his tubular steel chair.

Yes, yes, that's our *dramatic* option, Jack. Quite *dramatic*. Can't say exactly what it is, but, well, you know, *dramatic*. Big, said Don. You know, *big.*

"Fuck, fuck, fuck. What the fuck."

He had to get the residents out. By hook, by crook, but not be fire. He wasn't a mass murderer. The Rex project hung in the balance. It was his life, his future. Jack checked the map of the Rex. Each floor looked like a treasure map with X's on the closed-off rooms. The rubbery, red button moved the cursor through the rooms aimlessly, as if it were looking for clues.

He got the Rex folder.

He was in a race with Lansky. He knew that was what Lansky wanted. Blondie. He'd make an example of Blondie. It would send a message to his agents *and* it would send a real message to the residents. Blondie, fucked up, would get his clothes and trudge out of the Rex. Everyone would see. He'd have his agents deal out another round of notes pointing to Blondie. And maybe, just maybe, he'd go after Frieda and Marcy. One strategic blow to the hard core. Then he'd flood the other residents with notes, offer more money to leave.

He called Kragen. Kragen could meet him later that afternoon. Good. Jack dug through the folder and finally snatched up a photo of Blondie. He copied notes on the back. At four-thirty, Jack walked to the bank on Church. An hour later, he walked into the Hangout. The Hangout had the same interminable soccer game broadcast to all the corners.

Kragen and Tony were already there. Kragen looked up at him. He had a half-full shot glass in front of him and a glass of water. Tony stared at his reflection in one of the windowpanes. He cocked his head from side to side and seemed to examine a bruise, which took up half his face. Jack didn't want to know about that bruise.

Jack was at a loss for words. He said, finally, "How are things?"

"Fine," said Kragen. Kragen looked at him suspiciously. "You don't look so good."

Jack shrugged. "It's the job, you know. Hard to keep guys in line."

Kragen nodded sympathetically. "You reach a point," said Kragen, "where you have to up the pressure. Same thing at the Amsterdam. You know that. But when you do it, it can get dicey."

He was getting sympathy from Kragen. "I know."

"Good," said Kragen, smiling. The shot glass disappeared in Kragen's hand. Kragen took a sip, savored it, and swallowed.

"Yeah," said Tony. Tony turned and condescended to look at him. Tony cocked his head at him. "What happened to your ears?"

"Nothing. Boils."

"Two identical boils?" laughed Tony. "Biblical."

Jack shrugged. He took out the envelope. He sorted through the papers and photos. He threw out the picture of Blondie. "The guy's name is Blondie. He was an agent. But he got cold feet."

"I hate finks," said Tony, frowning. "We rub this one out?"

Rubbing out? Did people say that anymore? "No," said Jack, quickly. "No rubbing out."

"We'll take extra special care," said Kragen.

Kragen's smile made Jack queasy. He hated to do that to Blondie, but Blondie had become a key. "He stays in room 301 most of the time diddling his computer, but goes out to lunch. Tell him he's got to get out, if he doesn't it will be worse next time."

"What about the girls?" said Kragen.

Jack gulped. His throat was dry. He took a long pull on his drink. He had to sic Kragen on them. They were in his way, at the center of the hard core, linchpins. First Blondie, then the girls. One-two punch. "Yeah. Marcy and Frieda. Stagger it over a week."

Jack hesitated, and then grabbed the envelope in his pocket. This was it. When he handed over that envelope, anything could happen. He was targeting Blondie, Marcy, and Frieda, people he hardly knew.

Playing god. His hand trembled as he handed the envelope to Kragen. "Nine thousand."

Kragen smiled and yellow teeth protruded from his small head like miniature tusks. "We'll both take the guy and I'll take the women," said Kragen.

"Yeah, women are too easy," said Tony, sulking.

Kragen, women. Kragen was grotesque, but better than anything *dramatic*. Still, Jack felt like snatching the photos back. "Remember: Rough them up. Nothing else."

"You telling us our job," Tony said. He leaned over, sneering.

Kragen looked surprised, then angry. He reached over, covered Tony's face with his large hand, and pushed him back in his chair. Tony flipped his chair back and got up. Kragen said, "Sit down you miserable little wop."

Tony stared at Kragen for a split second, then Jack, then the rest of the bar. Tony smiled, picked up the chair, and then sat down. "I don't like amateurs telling us what to do."

Kragen put his hand on Jack's shoulder. "Don't worry. We'll do things right." Kragen's smile showed yellow outsized incisors. To Tony: "Drink up. We're going."

Kragen took his hand off Jack's shoulder. Kragen and Tony got up and left.

Jack waited a few minutes. The incident with Tony had lasted a few beats, but Jack saw how little control he had over either of them. He pointed at Blondie; he pointed at Frieda and Marcy. Attacks, beatings, hospitals, broken bones.

He got up and checked the window. When he saw Kragen and Tony were out of sight, he left. Outside, he zipped his leather jacket up and stuck his hands deep in the pockets. He turned right and walked to Fourteenth Street, then on an impulse, he walked towards the Hudson River.

The light was fading. It was a time of day he'd always liked, the transition between light and dark, a soft in-between time. A short time ago, in early summer, he stood on a dock near Forty-second Street in that light and wondered what he was doing, where he was going. He'd just talked to Lansky about his idea of shooing residents out of the Amsterdam efficiently. It was a question of psychology, he said. Knowing who to push and how. And here he was. He ordered people beaten up. He chased people out of hotels. Point A to Point B. The geometry of life. He was rushing—lurching? stumbling?—from San Diego and Lompoc, from the Amsterdam and Kragen, towards a dim, distant goal.

The nausea started in his stomach and became a thick knot in his throat.

Early evening, the phone rang. Jack looked at it and let it ring. Jack made a face and picked it up. Lansky wanted to see him.

Jack glanced at the laptop. Dramatic? Did Lansky want him to start a fire? That was the end. No can do, Michael. Even if Lansky didn't want that, Jack felt that momentum—momentum he didn't control—was creeping over the project like an evil fungus. Kragen, Tony, beatings. At the Amsterdam, that all happened very late in the project. There were a handful of residents left. There were upwards of forty people at the Rex. It would take at least six months or more to get everyone out. He could kiss Brooklyn goodbye.

Could he get out? He had enough money to leave. He could go to La Guardia and wait standby. Port Authority. Grand Central. Many ways to leave. But if Kragen did his thing and his agents theirs, if this new pressure made residents leave in droves...

Jack called a cab. In the cab, he took a deep breath and ticked off what had happened last week. Lansky had "renovated" four more units. The third owner, Brendel, steamed after seeing Lansky's renovations, saw the hopelessness of his position and told Lansky he'd consider selling. When he ticked off the items, it looked good. The Rex was being attacked from within and without, from above and below. Jack brightened: It *was* going to work.

The cab let him off in front of the Olympia. He walked quickly down into the garage, and took the elevator to the penthouse.

Lansky was on the patio near the pool.

"Get yourself a drink, Jack," Lansky shouted.

Jack mixed a scotch and water at the bar near the big fireplace. A few people talked in a group at the far end of the room. Jack nodded to Bill, one of Lansky's guards, and then walked out on the deck.

Lansky was talking to a short, wizened man who was ill at ease in an expensive suit, which looked two sizes too big. When Jack walked

234

up, Lansky shook the man's hand and told him he'd call. The short man stared at him intently, then left.

Jack watched the man disappear with a tingle of apprehension.

Lansky turned to him, but Jack could see he was preoccupied. "It's good to see you, Jack." Lansky was dressed in a sweater, blazer, and deck shoes with Argyle socks. With his V hairline, he looked like vintage Edward G. Robinson. Night was creeping over the city canceling block after block. Three women—precious, beautiful, in long designer coats—played cards on the far side of the pool. Every few minutes one would throw a card down and laugh like a hyena. Their reflections danced over the surface of the water like wraiths.

Lansky walked to the side of patio and Jack followed him. Frieda's garden stood out like an Easter bonnet on a scarecrow. It looked like Bert was sleeping on the job. He'd told him to mess up Frieda's garden. He made a mental note to prod Bert tomorrow.

He expected Lansky to start talking, but he didn't. Jack took a sip of scotch and water and felt the burning then a slight lift. "Anything new about the program?" Jack said, trying to jump-start the conversation.

Lansky shook his head. "I watched that woman prune her petunias every day, and later she pruned us. It's enough to make you believe in synchronicity."

Synchronicity. "How so?"

"We're sure she used our program against us."

"Chuck it," Jack said, quickly. "Fast."

Lansky shrugged. "I told them to quit using it, but it may be too late. They're trying to cover their tracks. Too bad, too bad. We could have used it." Lansky seemed contemplative. "I feel a fondness for Frieda's obsessions. I have an aunt like her, a cousin. In another world and time, that would have been me."

Jack smiled ruefully. He didn't expect Lansky's sentiment. He felt a quick empathy with him. They were both doing something they wouldn't have done in another time, another era. Jack thought of Miami, Peggy Lee, and "Is that all there is?" "Makes you wonder what it's all about."

"But it's not another world and time," Lansky said sharply. Jack looked up, surprised at Lansky's shift from maudlin to icy. "I worked Brendel, but he's stubborn. He'll come around. So will Rudi." Lansky paused, glanced at the level of his drink, and then took a slow sip. His black eyes reached Jack's, then his eyelids lowered slowly. "I want those fucking people out of there!"

The violence in Lansky's voice stunned him. He stuttered, "We're ahead of schedule. Residents leave every week. Four more rooms—"

Lansky grabbed his lapel and shook it. "I don't want excuses!" Lansky shouted up into his face. "I...don't...want...fucking...*excuses*."

The three women glanced at them. It was a long, knowing glance, then they looked at one another and one—she wore a big, floppy black hat, a black dress with padded shoulders, red lipstick, lacy black gloves—slapped a card down and laughed. The other joined in.

Lansky's face was inches away. It was livid, red, his eyes slits. A thread of ice snaked up Jack's spine. Jack tried to back away, but Lansky held onto his coat. "It's a thousand times better than we hoped."

Lansky released his jacket, but stayed right in his face. "The man who just left is the head of Canadian Ventures. They're looking at two locations for a new high-rise. One of them is right on that fucking gold mine corner. If they take the other place, I lose a million bucks."

"You can wait for another buyer. You can take—"

"No I can't wait. Every time I talk to you, I hear delay, waiting, stepping back. I want Rudi squeezed. Use Kragen. Get Frieda out of there. Attack the others—you know who they are. I don't care what you do or how you do it."

Jack spoke past the lump in his throat. "What about cops?"

Lansky stared at him; then he flicked his hand at him, as if he were dismissing a stupid idea. Lansky backed up and puffed out his chest making his blazer draw tight around him. Reflections of card players shimmered in the water and formed a third card game on the sliding doors of a bedroom. Three hands raised. Three cards smacked down.

Jack's chest was empty, his throat dry. He could feel the ground slipping away, as if he were sliding off a cliff. He tried again. "I control who my agents target, how much pressure to bring, how to use force selectively. That's why you hired me...and it's working."

"I know it's tough. But think about other hotels. Think about Brooklyn. Think about your future. Speaking of money, here's a bonus." Lansky dug into his blazer pocket, found an envelope, and then slapped it in Jack's hand. "It's an extra five thousand dollars. Get this done fast, Jack. There's a lot more where that came from."

Jack paused, looked at the white envelope, then, trembling, slipped it into his jacket pocket. "I'm counting on you, Jack. And I want this over. And that means you can start with Moira. She's working on the Brooklyn deals, but these landlords in Brooklyn are tough. They want to make money too."

"Of course," said Jack, listlessly. Lansky hadn't used the word "dramatic" but he implied it. It brought up everything else. Jack felt oppressed by the night air, the blackness, Lansky.

Lansky took a step towards him, then took his elbow. His voice was soft, confidential. He whispered, "Listen Jack, this is a make-or-break project. You do this right, you please the right people, and your future is golden. You'll live in a penthouse suite; eat at the Palace, vacation on the Riviera. Don't let a few brainless scruples stop you. I know we're on the same wavelength. I remember San Diego. Okay?"

"Okay."

"Good. Deal me in," Lansky yelled at the card players. They looked up as if they'd just noticed Lansky for the first time.

A few minutes later, Jack walked out of the Olympia. He gave Don and his agents bonuses; Lansky gave him a bonus. They were bribing each other, keeping each other in line. Jack felt manipulated, but then he felt he was manipulating himself. The cab ride back to Duane Park was too fast. Minutes later, he was on the roof.

Kragen was out there stalking Blondie, Marcy, and Frieda. If that didn't work...

Jack watched the Hudson River, shuddering, alone.

28

Bert waited until he was sure Frieda was gone. He didn't tell the guys, but he was afraid of her. She was the witch, the evil one. The other residents thought she could stop the invasion by herself. She was Jewish, of course; they had a psychic control over reality.

To fortify himself, Bert got stoned. He inhaled deeply, coughed, and blew dope smoke out the window, towards the Olympia. He thought: The guys. The hotel. They were going to take over the hotel! He'd done a lot. Meyer and Meg. Down for the count. Sven was next—he wasn't sure how he'd held out. The big guy—Mr. Big—would give him a bonus himself. He would shake his hand, and look proudly into his eye. He'd say: "Bert, we couldn't have done it without ya."

Bert smiled, and then frowned when he thought about Frieda's garden. He wanted to stay stoned. He wanted to shake Mr. Big's hand all morning. Bert got up from his chair and regarded the room. He wouldn't live there for long, not after Mr. Big found out what he'd done.

Bert took a long breath, checked his keys, opened and shut the door to 802. He pushed open the fire doors. He walked slowly up the stairs past Frieda's fertilizers, gloves, pruning shears, and pots. The door was locked. That was good, perfect.

He flipped open the lock and opened the door. The sun made him rear back. It was like being hit with a fist. Bert shielded his eyes with an arm that looked white. He saw the roses opposite the door and smiled. It would be the first thing she'd see when she came up.

Bert stepped forward, grabbed the first yellow rose, and ripped it off the trellis.

"Fuck me! Shit!"

Bert stared at the three gashes in his hand. A drop of blood snaked past a thick blue vein and dropped on the roof. A thorn stuck out of his palm. He picked the thorn out and stomped on it. "Fuckin' thorns! Goddamn you!"

Bert felt hot. He could feel the sweat on his forehead, collecting on his neck. He kicked at the trellis and broke off one of the slats. He kicked at it again and bent one of the slats. Not so good. It would take him forever if he *kicked* everything. Bert remembered what he'd seen on the stairs. He turned and padded back down. When he came back, he had a pair of gloves and hedge clippers. He wiped the sweat off his forehead, put on the gloves, and unhooked the clippers.

He smiled at the roses. "Got the anecdote, boys."

Twenty minutes later, Bert wiped the sweat off his face with the back of his right glove. He surveyed the garden. He'd clipped all of the roses and trashed most of the trellis. It hung near the entrance, bent over like a wounded animal. He'd turned over pots, he'd cut flowers, he'd uprooted tomato plants, and pulled vines climbing up the water tower.

Not a bad piece of work.

He realized the sunflowers had bugged him the entire time. Their heads drooped over and watched him as if they were prison guards. Bert put the clippers around the green stem under dark brown head fringed with yellow petals. Snap. The head fell and bounced on the tar.

"Hey. What are you doing?"

Bert froze. He turned and saw Sven, the guy at the end of the hall. He was old and skinny. He'd left a bunch of notes for him, but he hadn't budged. It was time to be a little more direct. "Come here. I'll show you what I'm doing."

"You idiot. I'm calling the police."

Police? The word had the usual effect. He was clean, but on parole. Any little thing, any smudge. He sure didn't want to stop because of grandpa. "Fuck you. Get outta here, before I—"

"Tell it to the police."

Sven disappeared.

"Shit. Goddamn it."

Bert threw the clippers down. He hustled towards the roof door. He flipped one glove off as he hit the first step. He threw the other one at a bag of potting soil. When he got down to the eighth floor, Sven had disappeared. Bert tried to think. He couldn't break down Sven's door—that was a no-no. Parole status. Dope in his room. Bert pushed through the fire doors and punched the elevator button. Hurry. Hurry. He paced the small space. He didn't want to talk to the cops, at all. He didn't know *how* to talk to them.

He opened the elevator door, the accordion gate, then pushed it closed. He punched one.

The cables groaned. The elevator jerked. *Hurry! Hurry!*

It ground to a stop on one. He opened the gate and door and hopped through the lobby.

He did the steps in one bound, then hurried towards Park. A squad car turned off Park and sped down Twenty-eighth. Bert forced himself to walk slowly, one foot in front of the other. He felt like he was walking on his knees.

The squad car passed. He glanced over his shoulder and saw it stop in front of the Rex. He let out a long breath. He'd deny everything. It would be Sven's word against his. Besides, wasn't that garden illegal?

Bert smiled to himself, whistled, and turned towards McDonald's. He had a few things to tell the boys. They gathered most mornings at McDonald's. Bert shook his head, sorrowfully. He liked talking to Max. But he went bye-bye with Ace. There was still Truck and Tim and Don, sometimes Jimmy. He'd have an Egg McMuffin and tell 'em what he'd done.

The gig had been okay for over a month. And it wasn't over yet. Not by a long shot.

Don Breem tucked his head closer to his plate and scooped a handful of fries into his mouth. He chewed for a few seconds, then gulped the wad of potatoes, grease, salt. He belched.

Outside, Park Avenue was full of people rushing uptown and down. And cabs. Flotillas of cabs. Don had driven a cab for six years. He liked talking to people, pointing out sights for tourists, seeing different parts of town. Gave you a feeling you were part of Manhattan, part of the scene. Yes, I was a cab driver in New York. New York was a helluva town. My town. Knew it like the back of my hand. Killed your back and kidneys.

Don wiped his hand on his extra-wide fit jeans. He looked at Bert Toland, who sat across the table, and said, "Frieda do anything when she saw it?" Bert told him he'd wrecked Frieda's garden yesterday. He was glad Bert did it, not him. His agents were a tough crew, but something about Frieda made them tremble in their boots.

Bert shook his head. "Thought she'd try knockin' my door down. But she didn't. Maybe she's finally gettin' the message."

Don scowled. "Not her. I don't like it when they lie low like that."

"Got to sometime. We're the guys, el numero unos. Nobody can stop us."

The agents left, except Blondie—the fink—and Jimmy, were a close bunch. They drank together, ate together, and talked over strategy. He didn't like it at first—Jack fretted about conspiracy—except the Rex job was different than the others. He needed somebody to talk to besides his mother. The boys were okay and he found out a lot more about what they were doing. "Exceptin' that little thing with Truck."

Bert grinned. "They pulled one on him, didn't they?"

He thought of that photo. Truck was out cold, red circles on his cheeks, and shoes stuck on his feet like elf caps. It caught all of them the same way. They laughed; then they saw what it meant. Don chuckled, then frowned. "It was that girl. She's fuckin' fearless."

"You got that right. Aside from that, we're right on target."

Don shook his head. It was time to try to set Bert straight. "The problem is it aint fast enough. Somebody's puttin' pressure on Jack and he's puttin' pressure on me. Which means I put pressure on you. Like dominoes."

Bert stirred his coffee. His hand was bony, pale, the palm scarred from his attack on Frieda's roses, his long face puzzled. He took a sip of coffee. "Whatya mean?"

"Felt the same thing at the Cardiff and the Amsterdam. You get to a certain point, you have to do something big in order to get the squatters out."

"But we just started," said Bert, a whine inflecting his voice. "You said it took a lot longer at the Amsterdam."

"It did. But I still have this feeling. Once the pressure starts..."

"What could happen? You mean Kragen? Shit, he's already messed up Mario."

"Something bigger."

"What does that mean?"

"Fire. Had one at the Amsterdam and the Cardiff. The one at the Amsterdam was a little one. But it scared the last residents into leavin'."

Bert held the cup up to his mouth, but didn't drink. "Fuck. What about the Cardiff?"

"A couple people died, couple people in the hospital."

Bert frowned. "Fuck, Don. That's not so good. What about us?"

"It was different at the Amsterdam. There weren't any of us left. They knew though. I don't know about the Rex. Can't get anything out of Jack."

"Fuck, he should know."

"Dombry was tough. Jack is different. I get the feelin' the boys on top aren't tellin' him everything. You never know what the big guy is going to do."

"Sure like to meet the big guy. Mr. Big."

"I know who he is. I'm not tellin', cuz it's best you not know."

Bert frowned. "Gettin' fried aint part of deal. Fuck, I'm on eight. I'd never get down."

"I'll try to find out. It aint gonna be too soon."

Bert shook his head slowly. "I'd leave tonight, if it weren't for the money."

"Good money. Good gig. Can't leave before you have to."

Don lifted his Big Mac and took a bite. He munched slowly, meditatively. Bert looked troubled. He held his cup balanced on the side of the saucer and watched cabs on Park.

It was close to ten o'clock on a soft fall night. Earlier, Twelfth Street was crowded with couples and people queuing up for "The Grifters" at the Film Forum. Now the few couples on the block strolled slowly towards either Fifth Avenue or Sixth. Next to the Film Forum, the Forum Café—burgundy walls papered with headshots of film stars, a long counter of brownies, cookies, and biscotti—was closing. A man with a pad of paper sat near the window of the café. Every few minutes, he scowled at the pad and wrote a few clipped sentences.

Kragen and Tony sat in Kragen's Corolla. Tony chewed a wad of gum; then he blew a bubble. The bubble was big, six inches wide, seven. Then it popped. It collapsed on Tony's face. "Fummm. Dummmit."

Kragen switched his attention from the entrance of the Film Forum to Tony. Kragen shook his head. Tony was a prime candidate for the Darwin Awards given to those people who through their stupidity eliminate themselves from the gene pool. There was the genius who put a rocket on his car, the hunter shot by his own trophy deer, the eight people who drowned trying to rescue a rooster in a well. Most of them were urban legends. Still. If Tony didn't kill himself, Kragen decided he would.

Tony pulled gum off his face getting it over his hands. He worked it off his hands for a few minutes, then balled it up, and threw it on the floor.

"Pick it up," snarled Kragen. "I don't want it in my car."

"Sheesh," said Tony. "It's just a little ball. He leaned over, picked through the dirt in the carpet, and finally touched it with his fingers. "Got it. He rolled down the window and tried to flick it out. It stuck to his fingers. He flicked it once, twice, three times. "Dammit." Finally it arced out of the car and landed on the sidewalk. He rolled up the window.

Kragen shook his head. He turned and watched the Film Forum.

Tony said, "I hate waitin'. Maybe he went out another way."

"I know the place," said Kragen. "All the exits lead to the front."

"We gonna do it here?"

Fucking Tony. "Can't you remember anything? We're going to follow him back. He'll probably take the same route past Madison Square Park. Lot's of alleys, lots of construction."

"Let me do it," said Tony. "I'm ready."

Kragen looked at Tony and shook his head. "Remember Mario. You didn't do too good until I knocked him out."

"I fuckin' slipped."

"You threw a stupid punch and almost took both of us out. No more of this shit. This time, it's by the book. We take him out, do our job, and split. That's the plan. It sends a message. Got it?"

"That's easy. I got that," said Tony, scowling.

"I doubt it," said Kragen.

The doors of the Film Forum opened and patrons began walking out onto the sidewalk. A few looked confused that they were back in the real world. They looked up and down the block then started confidently either towards Sixth Avenue or Fifth. Ten, twenty, thirty people walked out.

Blondie came out after five minutes. He looked suspiciously in both directions, and then started towards Fifth Avenue.

"There he is," said Tony, pointing.

"Quit pointing. I can see," said Kragen. He started the car, but waited until Blondie was close to Fifth Avenue, before putting the car in gear.

He sped up as Blondie turned the corner north on Fifth.

Kragen followed him from a distance up Fifth Avenue, then down Twenty-third to Madison Square Park. While Blondie walked through the park, Kragen maneuvered the car onto Madison in front of the Metropolitan Life Building. He parked and waited until Blondie walked through the park. Then he got out and walked quickly towards the end of the park. Tony was a few feet behind him.

When they got to the end of the park, Blondie had disappeared.

"Christ," Tony said, distracted. "Where'd he go?"

"Wait," said Kragen. Kragen saw a movement half a block away. Blondie emerged from a small grocery. He tore the wrapper off a candy bar and took a bite of it.

Blondie hadn't seen them. That was good.

Blondie walked into the next block. They gained on him, fast. They were twenty feet behind him. Blondie was in front of a church that was being renovated. Cement blocks, piles of wood, scaffolding, an alley. Perfect, Kragen thought, as he picked up the pace.

Tony rushed past him. Kragen stared at Tony.

Blondie hesitated, cocked his head, and saw Tony. He spun around and crushed his candy bar in Tony's face.

"Mothaaa fuuucckk."

Tony shook his head, stunned. Blondie set his foot and hit Tony with a hard right. The blow backed Tony up and set him sprawling on a stack of two-by-fours. Kragen thought: If he hadn't been paid to do a job on Blondie, he would have bought him dinner.

When Blondie turned to run, Kragen stepped forward and tripped him. Kragen checked out the street, then brought out his sap. When Blondie struggled to his feet, Kragen tapped him, hard. Blondie collapsed on the sidewalk. Kragen reached down, grabbed Blondie's collar, tested the weight, then dragged Blondie past the scaffolding into the alley. Then he went out and dragged Tony underneath the scaffolding. He propped him up against the wall of the church.

"What the fuck," said Tony, dazed. He wiped his face and looked at his hand. It was a mix of blood, chocolate, and peanuts. "What the fuck."

"Don't move," Kragen growled. He went back into the alley. He bent down over Blondie, and hit him with the sap in the face once, twice. He laid the sap down, took out his leather case, and chose a scalpel. He inserted it in Blondie's right nostril and slit it.

Blondie's eyes opened. He screamed.

His hands grabbed Kragen's jacket. Kragen held him down with his left hand, picked up the sap, and hit Blondie hard above his ear.

Blondie spread out on the floor of the alley. He was starting to look pretty beaten up. Kragen wiped the scalpel on Blondie's jacket and put it away. He took out the folded ball peen hammer and flicked it out to its full length. He felt for the tip of the exposed ulnar bone in the elbow. He aimed, hit the spot hard, and then hit it again. The second time, he felt the bone give. Olecranon fractures meant surgery. Blondie would be out for a while.

Kragen got up, folded up the hammer, turned, and started to walk out of the alley.

Tony rushed past him holding a crowbar. "Hey."

"He fucked with me," Tony shrieked.

"Get the fuck back here."

Kragen reached for Tony, but missed. Tony skidded to a stop in front of Blondie. He raised the crowbar and brought it down hard on Blondie's head. There was a sickening thud. Blondie's head rolled an inch. Blood streamed out Blondie's ear.

Kragen covered the distance in two steps. He stared down at Blondie. He bent over. It looked bad. The side of Blondie's skull was crushed. Hemorrhaging. He wouldn't last. He got up. "You fucking moron." Kragen wrenched the crowbar away from Tony and hit him hard in the stomach. Tony bent over. Kragen grabbed him by the collar and dragged him to the side of the alley.

Tony whispered. "You didn't have to hit me."

"I should fucking kill you. Stay here."

Kragen checked the street. He took out his handkerchief, wiped the crowbar, and let it clatter to the concrete. "Let's go, asshole. You fucking killed him."

Tony looked into Kragen's face and straightened up. He smoothed his long hair back. He left bits of chocolate in it like debris in a polluted river. "You think," said Tony, brightening.

"We were supposed to beat him up."

Tony grinned, "I fuckin' killed somebody. Jesus Christ."

"I know," Kragen said, "you can't wait to tell all your friends."

"Fuck yes."

They walked out of the alley and hurried back to the Corolla. When he got to the Corolla, Kragen said, "Get in." Tony frowned, got in, and sat. Kragen grabbed Tony's throat. "If you don't stay right fucking here, I'll cut your head off. Got it?"

Tony nodded vigorously.

Kragen released his grip, reached in, and took a pad of paper out of the glove compartment. He wrote "Payback" on the pad and tore it off. He flipped the pad onto Tony's lap. He hurried back to where they left Blondie's body.

A car passed; a few seconds later, it turned towards Park Avenue. Kragen checked the block, and then slipped into the alley. The crowbar had taken out a small section of Blondie's fine hair. The blood had started to congeal out of Blondie's ear. Kragen felt for a pulse. Gone.

"Tough luck pal." Kragen bent over, rifled Blondie's pockets, and finally came up with his wallet and ids. If he hadn't cut his nose and broken his arm so precisely, the cops would think it was a mugging.

He flipped the note on Blondie's lifeless form.

He checked the street before he left the alley, then hurried back to his car. Tony's face was white against the curve of the windshield. If he didn't get rid of stupid little wop, he was going to get both of them killed.

29

When she saw her garden, she almost cried. Her roses, Gerber daisies, sweet alyssum, morning glories, tomatoes. Her babies. Cut down, mowed down. Thrown willy-nilly over the roof.

She sat down at the table and stared at the devastation as if she were in a trance. After ten minutes, she realized she was calculating how to clean it up. There. There. And there. Plants still grew. There were a few holdout flowers. It was fall anyway. She went down and called IM66 and told them she wouldn't be in. Then she called Toby. The investigation into the Triple M, the code 333s, and Morty Bennet's connection to Michael Lansky was "in progress." In progress! She'd been there before, too often. She told Toby she was taking the day off.

She came back to the roof, put on her gloves, and went to work.

It took her most of the day. When she flipped her gloves on the stairs at five o'clock, she decided it didn't look bad. Bruised, but not on the canvas. Like the residents and the Rex itself. She might have been optimistic about that last. When, finally, she relaxed and had a glass of wine, her mind switched to the residents' esprit. It didn't look good.

The list of those about to cave in was long, longer because of Mario. Once they realized that Lansky or Jack or the goons meant it, it tore hope right out of their hearts. And it continued, and they knew it continued. A smug, but bruised, Italian followed her, Sven and Petey. Fishface followed Marcy and Bel. It looked like they were losing. Had to. There was the occasional bright spot. Marcy, impetuous, the invasion amplifying an inherited violent streak, knocked out one of the goons, painted him up, and left him for ridicule and humiliation. Photos were distributed. That end of the fourth floor was quiet.

A mixed bag, Frieda thought. Pluses and minuses. She expected it would get worse.

Tap, tap, tap.

Frieda looked at the door. Rose? Another resident beaten up?

She shrugged, as if to say whoever it was or whatever happened wasn't going away.

She opened the door. It was Dr. Harry Olson.

She smiled. Time for another détente? "Harry."

He looked squeamish. What was that about? "I've found a position."

"That's great. They couldn't keep you down for long. Where?"

"Boulder, Colorado."

Her heart fell right down to her shoes. "Right. Colorado."

"I have a friend there, Quentin Tobes, an opening in his practice. University, counter-culture, writer's workshop, skiing."

At that instant, she felt remorse and release. Same thing when her mother and Libby died. A deep sense of loss followed by a feeling that the bonds had snapped. "Thanks for letting me know."

"We should go someplace. Dinner," Harry said.

"It was what we did best," she said, not quite meaning it.

She realized, suddenly, that her bed was a mess, a tangle of covers; books and papers covered the blue glass end table; butts overflowed her man-in-the-moon ashtray.

Harry ignored her demur. "A drink in the Cave, dinner at Sam's Grotto."

"When are you leaving?"

Harry looked sheepish. "Tomorrow."

The Cave. Harry wore a false ear-to-ear have-a-nice-day smile. He was trying in his dull, hearty way to prime the pump of leaving. He fantasized about craggy mountains and slopes with long mantles of snow. She tried to imagine Harry in the middle of a ski resort surrounded by obnoxiously happy skiers with big worries about skis, poles, Dead Man Runs, parties, and the latest yuppie tank from Detroit. It irritated her that she *could* imagine it. Harry would reclaim his status in the slick, competent, contemporary madness. He'd had his fling helping poor folks in the King's County ER. One day that residual Midwestern altruism would be snipped off his CV like a gangrenous toe. It made her think about her worker ethics and dynamo unionism, which time had made as anachronistic as the Rex.

Sam's Grotto. "You're primed for success, Harry." She took a bite of her marinated sole, then stopped. She was thinking of their first date and food. Food was such a leitmotif. There was the kitchen table, the eating, and the decisions. It was like that with the Korsokoff sisters. They plotted over the matzo balls. And here she was again, drawing trails and charting the future over sole, steak, and baked potatoes.

"A doctor who hasn't worked for a year. It'll be easy," Harry said. He cut a large piece of steak and shoveled it through his thick lips.

She didn't like red meat and Harry knew it. It was another sign of the times. He was leaving the world of the Rex and Frieda and assuming his natural place in the society of meat eaters, ham-handed CEOs, and NFL TV. "Easier than most."

"I know that's true. I was lucky to get a second act."

"I didn't mean it to sound critical. I am happy for you."

They had a view of the street, but the light inside made the window impenetrable. A week ago outside the HRA conference room, it was a blotched sycamore in a blasted world, now it was black, inscrutable. Harry was going to walk out the door of the Rex and disappear. She couldn't blame him. He hated being desk clerk, the tiny problems of the residents, the merciless drafts, and the scheme to turn the Rex into another Olympia. She knew he thought she was a mixed bag.

Suddenly, Max's Grotto was too cold, too public. She needed her books, her man-in-the-moon ashtray. She needed her tar beach and her dahlias, as ravaged as they were.

"You're tough, smart, an experience. I'll miss you," he said.

She'd miss the little things. Harry mopping up her plate, a drooping ear lobe or gumdrop belly button or his blond straight-back hair, tokens which time would take care of too slowly. "Someone has to keep local traditions alive."

Harry paused, and laid his fork down, although he hadn't finished. "I will miss you," he said, as though he didn't mean it the first time.

"People come and go. Some you're close to, others live in our peripheral vision and disappear one day. Yesterday, smelling of sushi and plastered on sake we had all that fun. And now it's time to disappear. I knew it from the beginning, but that never stopped me. Let's go back and make one last memory."

Rex sex. Harry was energetic with fast-track energy, she passive, almost too passive.

They came. They went.

She stayed.

How did they get in bed that first time? Sake? Harry blocked out her books. The ceiling had turned; they'd broken a wine glass. So exciting, yet so very normal. That night, even though she didn't care a whit, it felt better fastening her arms around Harry. It beat trying to block out the black and airless void on the other side of that body.

It was a gray September day. The Olympia was a piece of granite shot up from the earth, Kip's Bay a foreign landscape. Frieda glanced at the brown vines and dead morning glories. The garden was worse. Wrecked, dead, dying. She cinched her burgundy-colored robe and tucked in the collar. When she turned from the window, she saw the note. She picked it up thinking it was a note from Bert, the wrecker of her garden and personal harpy.

She left the note on the table, poured a glass of OJ, plopped in her chair, and lit a cigarette. She flipped the note back and forth with her fingers.

She read: "Jack paid me to leave. It only made sense. Harry."

She stared at the lines. Then she tore it up slowly, as if she were torturing the paper. She let them flutter to the floor like giant snowflakes.

She lit another cigarette and realized she hadn't finished the first one. She had a vision of an envelope, greasy bills, Harry and Jack shaking hands, chatting about small-cap mutual funds. No, that wasn't the scene. That was a feint. The question, the real question, was why he left the note. It had to be that he wanted to get back at her. Frieda Berg, pariah, black widow, emasculator. She didn't quite get that vision of herself. Maybe it was guilt after all, that he was slinking away from New York, licking his wounds, blaming her.

Frieda stubbed out the cigarette. She dressed and left.

She hurried down the eighth floor hallway, but stopped at one of Sven's tiny paintings. Sven had done Harry, a Harry with tiny blue eyes stuffed in a huge face in a tiny frame. Put up in the last few days, too new for Bert to ruin with his knife. She'd walk past it every time she walked down the hallway. She toyed with the idea of tearing it down. Sven would think Bert did it. She shrugged and hurried towards the elevators.

It was the day of the long walk. She'd done the same thing when her mother died and her aunts. It eased the pain before; she was sure it would work again. She walked down to Twenty-third, then over to the East River Park. The park was almost deserted and Frieda thought, vaguely, she shouldn't be there, that her personal wraith was stalking her. A car followed her, yesterday. She couldn't see if it was Mr. Bouffant.

She stared across the East River at Queens. Under the dull gray sky, a morning mist obscured the piers, but dissipated as she watched. All those people, all those buildings. Everyone had a different life, but the same problems. She wondered at which point she decided to go into the department, marry Ron, divorce him. That day it seemed as if she couldn't have done anything else. She wondered why people felt comforted by religion telling them their lives were predestined.

Stuyvesant Town. East Side. Lunch in a diner. More walking. She went back to the Rex, changed into warmer clothes, and went to the Cave. She walked down Fifth. People huddled by, isolated in the fall chill. A few leaves drifted down and were swept through the tunnels around the Flatiron building.

Washington Square. People rocked on benches trying to stay warm. She gave a handful of quarters to a man in a rag-tag Punchinello suit. She dropped them in his cup. When they hit bottom, they gave out metallic clinks: a cup, a giver, a receiver. The end of the world.

She walked down the steps into the Cave, set up at the end of the bar, ordered a vodka martini—vodka martinis were her downfall in her bar hopping days—and watched shoes in the small grated window. She tore her coaster into small pieces. At some point, she decided the problem was practical. It was about emptiness. It was figuring out what to do with the things around her, her books, her scarves, her hats, her boots, her man-in-the-moon ashtray, and whether she should animate them with a new Harry, or rope off the whole mess and call it a museum.

She was about to leave when she saw Terry, leprechaun, poet, and owner of a greeting card company. She did an about-face, and had a second vodka martini. She had a wild time that night and got in a space she hadn't been in for months for which, at the time, she blamed Harry. She flirted, got drunk, and felt a rare sense of freedom when they left. They took a taxi to Terry's loft in Chelsea.

It sounded offbeat when he talked about his "loft." The loft was cavernous and dark, had little running water, and no shower. The kitchen was a couple of drapes, which closed off a makeshift sink and portable gas stove. The walls were covered in bookcases stuffed with gray boxes of unsold greeting cards. Terry pulled them down and showed her cards done by his gang of artists who had their own peculiar take on birthdays, holidays, sickness, and travel.

She listened as the hyper-tongued Terry told her about Ireland, the movement, the IRA, the problems he had with kooky artists who worked in orangutan costumes, and the huge problem of selling greeting cards in a market dominated by the big bland one and a gang of wannabes. His company, Terratone, was struggling to be a wannabe, a state that didn't look too good for Terry.

But even at Terry's she couldn't escape the problem that haunted that summer and fall.

"The landlord hired someone to watch me when I leave," said Terry. "And I just got a letter saying that I'm not really a tenant."

"Been there, done that. I rate a personal shadow."

"Soon we'll all be living in Queens."

After awhile he talked about bed and she said yes. Then they did a woozy hand-over-hand up a ladder to a loft high over the floor.

She'd been in many strange spaces in her life, but that was one of the oddest. While Terry worked away, first with the prelims, then with the centerpiece, she watched car lights bloom and fade on the molded copper ceiling and thought of cycles of light and dark, hot and cold.

The night was strange and amusing, Terry a kind of catalyst. She couldn't sleep. She listened to Terry's ragged breathing and stared at the ceiling wondering about Harry, then the Rex. After an hour, she crawled down the ladder. She spent ten minutes rounding up her cigarettes, lighter, and accessories. Finally, she exited into the desert of three-in-the-morning Manhattan.

She walked slowly up to Thirty-fourth. She wasn't quite sure what she was doing. She walked one foot in front of the other, on an imaginary line. Break Frenchie's back; break her mother's heart. She walked past the Empire State towards Third Avenue feeling she was in her own Diaspora.

She supposed she was so preoccupied with being depressed that she didn't see the car. She remembered, vaguely, that it crept up behind her. It made her look up. The face was a white smear across the windshield. The car wasn't behaving right because it turned sharply to its right and came at her. It was over two hundred feet away, when she turned to watch it.

When the car jumped the curb, she turned and ran. Fifty feet ahead was a bus shelter. As she ran, she sifted options. Thirty-fourth Street sidewalks were broad. Too late for a doorway. A second before she got to the shelter, she'd feint left, then jump right. The car would hit the shelter, or turn left to avoid it. Twenty-five feet. Fifteen. She did a short feint left, then jumped right.

She heard a roar and felt a hot lash on her face. Then she was lifted. In that instant, she thought of Rose Tutweiler and her plans for death with dignity. "Leaving time," Rose called it.

Leaving time, Frieda thought.

She hit the bus shelter, then the pavement. She stared at the scratched rim of the shelter. Streetlights pressed down on her forcing her to the pavement, forcing her further, pressing.

Then she closed her eyes and felt nothing.

30

The fourth floor was quieter, much quieter, since Marcy, Carly, Donna, and Jenny had done a makeover on Truck. They had slipped photos of him—he looked like a warthog in drag—under the goons' doors and since, Truck seemed to slink from spot to spot. He was still there, of course, but quiet. Then Carly left and it was even quieter.

That was okay, Marcy thought, but then it was *too* quiet.

No notes. No loud music. You don't plan to take over an old hotel, install goons, and harass people, then stop cold. Something was wrong, very wrong. And she was right—in spades. When she walked into the Rex that day, she got a Mario who was tired, anxious, and angry.

"What?" she said, her heart fluttering in her throat. Bel? Frieda?

Mario shook his head. "A hit-and-run driver clipped Frieda. She's in Bellevue."

She felt hollow. "Fuck me. How is she?"

"I haven't seen her," said Mario. "Rudi said she has a lot of bruises, but she'll be okay."

"There's something else?"

Mario looked down, his face grimmer than she'd seen. His face told her it was going to be bad. "Blondie was murdered a few nights ago near Madison Square Park. Skull crushed. His papers were gone; that's why it took time to identify him."

Her heart felt hollow. She leaned against the wall. "Jesus."

"The police have been here this morning and afternoon. Rudi told them what was happening at the Rex and identified who was behind it. They talked to the thugs, but they thought Blondie's murder was about something else, payback. He was pretty messed up."

"The police have never done a thing. Assholes." She had to do something. She lifted her pack and put it in the half-oval. "Watch my pack. I'm going to Bellevue."

"You gotta be careful," said Mario.

"I sleep with Mace under my pillow." She flipped open the pack pocket where she kept the Mace and pepper spray, took out the Mace, and slipped it in her back pocket.

Marcy hiked over to Bellevue. She felt isolated from the crowds, who seemed obnoxiously happy that clear fall day. Isolated and scared. She must have looked frantic the way she swiveled her head at intersections. Loud noises made her flinch.

It took awhile to find Frieda. When she did, she saw purple bruises on her arms and face and a laceration, which followed her right cheekbones as if she were a living drawing.

"I had them break the mirrors," said Frieda.

"Was it that guy who follows you? The dip with the hair?"

"I don't think so. I'd had a long night. It looked like Rodriguez, that guy at work, but I'm not sure. He's wanted to do something like that for weeks. He must have followed me all night." Frieda looked past her, as if she were regarding a distant object. "Jack paid Harry to leave."

Harry always looked sad. Frieda knew he wanted to leave. Somehow she couldn't blame him. "I'm sorry," she said. She didn't know what else to say. "You heard about Blondie?"

Frieda nodded, then shook her head, grimly. "I don't know what to do anymore."

"You're just down because you're hurt and in here. I'll visit tomorrow."

"I could be out by then. Water for me."

"Tell me how."

"It'll be easy. Bert didn't leave much."

Marcy felt as low and depressed as Frieda and she wasn't up to another walk. She took a cab back to the Rex and watered the garden. She hadn't been up there in a week and she finally understood what Frieda meant. Bert had done a job on Frieda's garden.

After she finished, she went back to her room. She stared at the contours of her canvas. Beyond her room she saw the edge of the Olympia and that made her alternately scared and angry.

She had known for weeks about the two sharks circling the Rex residents, biding their time, attacking Mario, following her and Bel and Frieda. Blondie. She remembered the Moat, talking to Blondie, the concern, which seemed a permanent part of his face. He *knew* something bad was going to happen. And he stayed anyway.

In the next few days, Marcy went to work, visited Frieda in her room—they released her the next day—and stayed in her own room and brooded. She'd clipped out the Times article about Blondie and put it on the small dresser in the corner. Every time she saw it, she shivered. Beaten up, stabbed, broken arm bones, crushed skull. Finally, she balled it up and threw it away.

Late one afternoon, after she had finished work and was staring at her last painting, the phone rang. It was Bel. She wanted to see her.

She shrugged, grabbed her Mace, and walked up to six.

On six, Bel shouted for her to come in.

Bel had a drink, but it was full, cradled in her right hand. She looked morose. "What's up?"

Bel looked puzzled as if she didn't know why she'd called. "I'm tired of this rut. And I'm tired of what's happening. Count me out. I thought you should know."

Marcy trembled; her chest was hollow. "When?"

Bel shook her head. "I'm not sure. Brenda called. I talked to her. I told her what was happening here. She's worried, wants to help me get out."

Marcy frowned. The hollowness spread through her body. "That's great. How is she?"

Bel picked up her drink and took a long swallow. "I'm becoming a boor. I fantasized she was living a life of leisure, of bonbons and nail polish."

"Why did you say that?"

Bel shrugged. "She's separated, filing for divorce. She wanted to talk to me about that and I gave her my problems."

"I never liked Jerry, but at least he was stable."

"Are we all so worried about stability? It won't be so bad for Eric and Sam. They're just a couple years younger than you."

She remembered Eric was fun, Sam troubled. Sam stayed in his room, had therapists, and the last she'd heard, would be with Brenda forever.

Photos over the dresser, empty cigarette packs on the floor, two black sweatshirts on the floor near the closet, a whiskey bottle, dirty glasses in the alcove. Ray's self-portrait. Wave after wave of smoke pulsed into the room. The smoke made Bel and her books seem unearthly. Bel took a sip of her drink, and then she rested the glass on the corner of her chair.

"What about Mario?"

Bel shook her head. "I don't fucking know. I didn't want to leave because of him and I don't want to leave because he's hurt. But it's the rut, the goddamn rut. It was a rut before Lansky and the thugs."

She didn't know what to say. She gazed past Bel. The Olympia dominated the window.

The Olympia mesmerized her. The windows were dark stains against the sterile, white stone. "I hate that building."

Bel glanced out the window. "When I shut the shade, it makes me feel I'm hiding."

"When I look at it, it brings up the rest, why everybody's leaving."

Bel watched her. She seemed contemplative. "What about you?"

"You mean about leaving?"

"What else?"

She thought about it all the time, about how, about when. She said, "I'm not."

"There are other places besides the Rex, other hotels, apartments, people you could live with. What about this sculptor?"

"A fight—I told you. I've talked to him. It's too early to think of getting back together."

"We do fight well." Bel crushed her cigarette into a full glass ashtray. "Brenda wants to meet. I don't know; it will bring up all the old shit."

"You won't know, if you don't try. Say hello for me."

The phone rang just as she closed the door to her room
It was Butch.

"Hey." She sat on her futon and tucked her legs underneath her.

"What about coming back."

He'd said as much last time. And she missed him. It could have been the right time. Frieda. Blondie. "I'm not sure. I feel weird."

"About me?"

"There's certainly a lot there to feel weird about. But no. The Rex. The people here. I don't think I can leave."

"What is that about?"

Marcy thought about it, but came up empty. That was standard, lately. "Frieda was hit by a car and this guy Blondie was murdered."

"Fuck. You've got to do something!"

Butch sounded exasperated. She couldn't help that. "I've felt weird since I found about them. Blondie was an ex-con, but nice. They beat him up, crushed his skull."

"Jesus! Fuck! This is real! Come on. It's safe here."

She thought of Butch's studio/living space with a deep sense of regret. She wanted to go, but knew she couldn't. "I told you last time. You've got to stay out of it for now."

There was a long pause. "You could live here. We could try."

Marcy frowned. She'd thought about it. But that was before she found Butch with Mark. But that wasn't it. She'd talked herself around that. She'd be abandoning the Rex, the other residents. She couldn't do that. "Not now. Let's talk about something else. Anything."

And they did. And it felt better. There was another world out there. The Zoo. Plays at the Cul de Sac. It was a world where people made art, made love, made life.

When she hung up, she started feeling weird again. It was almost the same feeling she had after the abortion. She felt as if the bottom had dropped out of her world and she felt angry at the same time. That time, over a year ago, she could only be angry with Mickey, the prick, and herself. This time, she had plenty of people she could be angry at starting with Jack and Lansky.

The night she talked to Blondie haunted her. She saw Larry setting a beer in front of her, Blondie turning, his explanations, and the hopelessness in his eyes. He knew something bad was going to happen and he stayed. It had a fateful feel to it, a giving in to destiny, or accepting it.

She wasn't going to leave either. But she was not going to wait for Fishface—Kragen—and the idiot with wavy black hair to hurt her.

Paddy's Bar was the poorest tenant on that block of Third Avenue. The Fortuna, a new bar adjacent to Paddy's on the north, was empty at that time of day. Lombardi, a new Italian restaurant on the south had a line for lunch. Two couples outside talked animatedly, then glanced at their watches.

Paddy's had two heavy tables with heavy, lacquered chairs in front, a small bar top shaped in an L, a lumpy dartboard wedged into the corner across from the bar. A light in the doorway to the toilets made the back sepulchral. Noon sun touched brown cracked linoleum tiles inside the front door, but didn't light up much more. A heavy, bored bartender in shirtsleeves glanced at the four men sitting at one of the tables, and went back to turning pages of the Daily News.

Bert, Don, Tim, and Jimmy looked at each other and stared at the shot glasses and bottles of beer stacked on the table. They never drank that early. They never drank boilermakers, either. A thick air of depression hung over their table.

Bert, stoned, broke the silence. "Everything was goin' so good."

Don knew things were going good. His agents had shifted into high gear last week. They'd left more messages, worked the toilets, broken windows, and had a few pointed conversations with some of the weaker residents. Three more residents were about to scoot. He was about to call Jack with the news when the first wave of cops showed up. They talked to Mario, Rudi, some of the other residents, and then they talked to every one of the agents. They kept trying to tie Frieda's hit-and-run with the threatening notes the residents had given the cops.

They were recovering from the first wave, when the second hit. Blondie's murder.

They went over the whole thing again from top to bottom. The cops were suspicious, but Jimmy said he thought they were convinced Blondie's murder was prison payback. Still, they got too interested in why so many ex-cons were living in the Rex. It was bad fucking karma.

The official attention freaked the guys out. What happened to Blondie was worse.

Tim, who normally sat straight up to add a few more inches, slumped, his head barely above the back of his chair. "Fuck," Tim said, breaking the silence. "He knew."

"No he didn't," said Don. "They used this guy before. He never killed anyone."

"I didn't like him," said Tim. "Kept to himself. Guys like that..."

Jimmy wiped his bald head with his hand, and then touched the top of his scar. Jimmy said, "He was okay. He was tryin' to stay straight. You know how fuckin' hard that is."

"Fuck," said Tim. "He knew about the gig. He knew shit would happen."

Don scratched his double chin, slowly. "Problem is the cops. Problem is they got their eyes on us. First Frieda, then Blondie. It's like a fuckin' one-two punch. They know we're all ex-cons. Who knows what they'll find if they start diggin'."

Bert said, "I fuckin' do not know how to talk to them."

Tim said, "Who fuckin' does."

"Let's disappear for awhile," said Bert. "If we aint there—"

"What about our job?" said Don.

Jimmy said, "Fuck, Don. This is a perfect time to let things ride. You have to know that."

"Gotta talk to George," said Don.

"You mean Jack," said Tim. "Everybody knows who he is."

Don scratched a second day's growth on his chin, took a long pull of his longneck, and then belched. "Okay. I'll talk to him. You guys are right. We have to let things sit."

Bert looked at Don suspiciously. "What about something big?"

Don looked at Tim then Jimmy. He saw that he hadn't reacted. "Not now. I'll talk to you about it, later."

"Big?" said Tim.

"It's nothing," said Don. Don picked up a half-full shot glass. "Here's to Blondie."

The others raised their shot glasses. They downed the whiskey in one movement and set the glasses down on the dark table empty.

31

"John Moreno" was on the letter box in the marbled lobby of Coho Apartments. He adopted the name "Kragen," when he started his sideline. He liked the name. It connoted mountains, craggy peaks, deep crevices, and hard guys. It gave him a cachet that "John Moreno" never could. John Moreno had a life too. John was the respectable owner of houses in Colorado and Florida, a well-liked landlord who liked to sail into the ocean off the Florida Keys in his power boat, "The Other."

Little jokes everywhere. Hidden lives. It was more than Jekyll and Hyde. It had to do with the modern era, with an existential barrenness, with the excitement of a real other life. Moreno/Kragen understood that aspect of his own double existence. It never stopped him from leading—why not say "enjoying"—both.

Moreno was kind, friendly, and affable when dealing with renters, neighbors, grocery clerks, tradesmen, and even the homeless. He talked about computers—he had two—cars, boats, and had a fund of topics and attitudes about everything from politics—he was a fiscal conservative, a social progressive—to the stock market. People saw him as a guy trying to make up for his lack of physical attractiveness. When he tried to explain his Kragen shadow, sometimes he pointed to a bent for subterranean violence inherited from his father, Flint, a drunk and all-round asshole. Or his stint in the paratroopers. Or discovering the thrill and, later, the competence. People in the business, Maghot, Maury, and others knew he was a pro. That counted for a lot.

The apartment, rent-controlled and taken over from his mother when she died six years ago, had five tall rooms with a gleaming new kitchen in the back and four rooms which flanked a long hallway filled with paintings—New York artists, the Hudson Valley school, mostly landscapes, the one Moreno/Kragen liked the most, a woman in a room, a lonely accent on her drawn face. Moreno/Kragen spent most of his time in the front room, which overlooked Central Park, among books and bookcases, Persian throw rugs, a few paintings, a liquor cabinet in the corner, and a huge oak desk. John Moreno managed his properties, clipped coupons, cheated on his taxes, and otherwise kept his nose clean at that desk.

Kragen occasionally managed his affairs at that desk.

That day was a Kragen day.

Kragen poured three ounces of Laphroig unblended scotch whisky into a special small scotch mug, which held five ounces. Then he poured a small glass of water. He took both over to the desk. Outside in the park, trails snaked around a small pond like veins. Rollerbladers, Frisbee players, a small family picnic on a checkered red-and-white tablecloth, couples walking arm-in-arm through the first drop of leaves. Couples. Sometimes it bothered him that he couldn't have that kind of normal. It never bothered him for long.

Kragen sat down with his scotch and water. He took a sip of Laphroig and savored its smoky flavor. Some people didn't like that brand because of the smoky flavor. It warmed his face. He smiled, which thrust his outsized front teeth over his lips. Kragen's tongue flicked out and over his teeth and licked a drop hanging from his lower lip. He took a sip of water.

He settled in at the desk, opened a desk drawer, and pulled out the cordless phone unit for his unlisted number. The cord to the AC adapter and the phone line snaked out of a hole in the drawer and was plugged into outlets under the desk. He retrieved an address book from the same drawer and flipped to the last page, where there were ten numbers without names. Kragen knew the order of names. Maury Rizzo's number was second from the top. He punched out the number on the speakerphone base.

"Maury, Kragen."

"Hey. How's that kid working out?"

"Just what I was calling you about. He isn't."

Maury said, "What do you mean? I told you it's important, for a friend in Jersey."

Kragen switched the speakerphone over to the cordless. He picked up the phone, leaned back in his leather upholstered chair, and swiveled towards the window. He watched a pigeon land on a telephone wire on the park side. "Let me try to talk about this rationally, Maury. The fucking moron is going to get me killed. He doesn't know how to take orders and he's dumb as a post. I have to think of my survival here."

"Now, now. Let's think about this. Tell you what. You keep the kid on for another two weeks while I work out something else."

"I can't, Maury. I'm on a project. The kid almost fucked the entire deal."

"What if I sweetened the deal? Gave you an education stipend."

What the fuck is that? A little bit of knowledge was dangerous with some of his friends. He was surprised Maury knew how to pronounce "stipend." He knew Tony couldn't. "What kind of 'stipend' are we talking about?"

"Five grand to keep him for another two weeks."

"This friend must be really important to you."

"He helped me stay out of jail a couple years ago. It's important. Payback."

Payback. He'd heard that before, and not exactly in that context. "I don't know—"

"Ten."

Kragen mulled it over. He thought of that GPS system for his boat. He was sucker for tech toys. "Okay. I'll meet you at the Hangout at five tomorrow. I keep him for another two weeks, then you take him back."

"I appreciate it, a lot"

What could happen in two weeks? He'd have him follow ambulances or dig out gophers in Central Park.

As soon as he switched off the phone, it rang.

Kragen jumped. He shook his head and hit the "Talk" button.

"It's George."

It was Jack Kuhl. He'd talked to Lansky about "George." Lansky told him his real name, that he was a fallen investment counselor from San Diego. He liked to know who he was dealing with, who was giving him projects.

"Howdy." Kragen got up and stood at the window. He stared out at the cars, a couple in windbreakers kicking at the few leaves covering the sidewalk, walking downhill towards the underpass on the other side of the pond.

"Listen," said Jack. "I don't know what's happening, but things seem to be—"

"Just tell me what's happened," said Kragen, calmly.

"Frieda, hit-and-run. She's in the hospital. Shit, you could have killed her."

Kragen frowned. "When?"

"Two nights ago. Don heard three in the morning."

Kragen thought about that. Tony? Three in the morning? "We didn't do it."

There was a longer pause on the line. "Not Tony?"

"He would have wrapped himself around a street light," said Kragen. "If he'd managed to miss the light and hit your girl, he'd have taken out an ad in the paper. I think he was in Jersey two nights ago."

"Jesus, I wonder who did."

"Mysteries make life interesting, n'est-ce pas?"

"Life is getting too interesting. If you didn't do Frieda, then what have you been doing?" said Jack. "I'm under a lot of pressure here."

Pressure. He knew where that pressure was coming from. Lansky wanted everything done two years ago. "Oh we've been at work," said Kragen. He thought of Tony burying a crowbar in Blondie's head. Ever since, the fucking moron had been pimp walking like he had hundred whores flatbacking for him. "I have what you might call bad news."

Jack didn't reply right away. Then he said, "Well."

"Wayne Reynolds, Blondie, met an untimely end."

"What? Well, Jesus."

"Listen, it's okay. I'm a professional. I took care of it."

"If you were a professional, you wouldn't have killed him."

"Wait a fucking minute," Kragen growled. "It was a mistake. Tony got a little impetuous. I told you I took care of it. Nobody will connect his murder with the Rex."

"Still. Fuck. It's all about planning, psychology. I didn't want—"

Kragen's voice was cool, calm. "I told you it was all right. Forget about him. He was an ex-con who made too many enemies. No one is going to look at his case more than five minutes. Still, you want to be careful. Tell your agents to cool it for a few days."

Kragen heard a tired sigh on the phone. "What about the girl?"

"Ah yes, the girl. I like looking at her. Wait a second." Kragen opened a desk drawer, pulled out an envelope, and took out a handful of photos. He sifted through them until he found Marcy Benaventura's photo. Kragen did like looking at her. She was spunky. Led him on a couple wild chases, where he didn't want to catch her anyway. "I'll wait a few days until everything dies down, then I'll go after the kid. And don't worry. It'll be clean, neat."

"I wonder if you should go after the kid."

Kragen looked at the photo. It was shot into the light. Whoever took it couldn't take a photo worth a shit. He could still make out Marcy's dark eyebrows, butch-short hair, lean body, sharp, jutting boobs, thin, pursed mouth. She didn't look like much, but from what Jack said, she was a terror. Said she'd yelled at him in diner. Kragen wouldn't mind a little extra with the spitfire, but the bottom line was important. If Jack wanted results, he had to lean on the tough ones. "This is exactly the kind of pressure you need. You're digging out the roots. In a few weeks no one will remember the girl, Frieda, or Blondie."

"I suppose," said Jack. "I still don't know about her."

"I'll be extra special nice. I'll scare her. Slap her a couple times. Nothing too rough."

"Okay," Jack said, tiredly.

Kragen punched the phone off.

Kragen looked at the phone for a few seconds. Someone nailed Frieda. He knew Tony didn't. Who could have? Lansky would have contingency plans, backups. Kragen understood it, but he didn't like it. Too many question marks. Too many.

Kragen grabbed the little mug and sipped the scotch. He liked looking at the photo of Marcy Benaventura. He wondered what it would be like to do more than slap her around. Tie her up for awhile, play around. He'd have to be extra special careful. Make sure he didn't leave any DNA lying around.

Kragen slipped the photo back into the envelope. He killed the scotch.

The cordless phone rang. Kragen frowned, then picked up. "Yeah?"

"Hey big boy, my main man. It's your proto jay. Tony, himself."

Kragen grimaced. Two more weeks. He wasn't sure it was worth ten grand.

Jeanie stayed away for a few nights, then they decided to see each other and hash it out. Then, at the last minute, she called it off. Jack half-expected it. She wanted him out of the hotel management business. If he'd had a functioning brain cell, he would have gotten out before last week. Just when he needed her, she was slipping away. The great sex had drifted away. The pleasant, quasi-domestic evenings too.

Jack grabbed his keys, money, threw on his leather jacket, and walked to Wall Street. He found a bar, the Brass Ring—pseudo Nineties black and red, fake gaslights, big beveled mirror, subdued lighting. A few couples huddled together and talked about their day. He joined the ragged group of suits at the bar. He ordered a double scotch and water. He realized his mood was down, black. He thought living in the Amsterdam was the worst time of his life, but it was nothing compared to that day.

Someone clipped Frieda at three in the morning. What the fuck was she doing on Thirty-fourth Street at three in the morning? Then the mystery. Who the fuck did it? Tony was an idiot, but he trusted Kragen. That was a laugh. He trusted a professional killer. What if Lansky thought he was expendable? That lay in the back of his mind like the proverbial monster in the closet. Lansky—oily, devious, tiny black eyes staring at him as if he were dinner—would sacrifice his mother, aunts, uncles, wife, and girlfriends for the Rex.

Jack finished his first drink. He waved his hand at the bartender for another.

He could have dealt with Frieda's hit-and-run—shit she was alive—but then Kragen announced his bad news. It hit him like a sledgehammer. Tony—that asshole—killed, murdered, Blondie. Kragen said "impetuous" as if Tony had ordered too many entrees for dinner. It was fucking murder.

Then Lansky called about upping the pressure!

Then Don called, worry gnawing at him like a pit bull a neck.

Don babbled at him for five minutes about the cops swarming the Rex. His agents, who a few days before went on a rip through the Rex trashing windows, breaking toilets, leaving notes, and staring down old ladies, were freaking out. Cops, background checks, Blondie, Frieda. He told Don to lay low for a few days. But if anyone found out; if he was ever implicated. At first, his mind refused to stretch out the consequences, then started a litany. Accessory to murder. Conspiracy. Accessory, conspiracy. Accessory, conspiracy.

The Brass Ring was half-full when he came in, but it had emptied. The couples had gone on to dinner. There were still a few after work investment bankers, stockbrokers, or traders nursing drinks at the bar, trying to figure out what to do with the night. He shook his head. He could have been one of those traders. Clean, well-paid job. Money in the bank. Clear conscience.

Two drinks later, a small, pinched-looking kid in a double-breasted suit, started talking to him. Greg was twenty-five, a stockbroker, knew the insiders, was going to be a millionaire by thirty. Was well on his way. Greg slowed down his one-way, one-man tribute to Greg. "What'd you say you were in?"

Jack tried to focus. He realized he was drunk. "Didn't. Hotel management."

Greg frowned. "There's money in *that?*"

Jack shrugged. "Depends what you manage. I turn old hotels into high-class places." Jack thought about what he said. It was almost fucking true!

"Problem with those old places are the fucking tenants. They stick like glue."

"I work on their psychology. Give them money to move."

"Should be able to throw 'em in the street," said Greg. "Or burn 'em out. I hear they do that in Texas. Shit, they've done it enough times. Tulsa. Tulsans had the right idea. Burned down a whole section of town. Same with Philly. Country's too fucking soft."

Fire!

"Right," said Jack. He gulped his double scotch; the booze hit him. Greg was an idiot. Pseudo-Naughty Nineties, pseudo-conversation. What was he doing in this place?

"Anything you do is all right with me. Who gives a shit about them?" Greg chuckled. "Now, when it comes to my apartment..."

Jack stared at him uncomprehending. "Your apartment?"

"Landlord raised the rent, again. I'll see that fucker in court."

Jack shrugged, then killed his drink. Hypocrisy. Me-first. Were they all stone-blind? He got up, staggered to the door.

Greg toasted him. "Gotta think of numero uno, bucko."

Bellevue. A confusing collage of Terry, greeting cards, a painted coppery ceiling, a car tracking her on Thirty-fourth Street, a hideous face painted on the window, a whip across her face, the crunch of her body

267

against the pavement. Visits. Many visits. Calls. Toby called. Others. She called Borgan. It cheered her up for a few fleeting minutes when he said he'd started an exposé about Lansky and the Rex. She sneaked into the Rex late on a balmy September afternoon. Of course, she couldn't avoid Rudi and the stares of a few residents in the lobby. Rudi looked guilty and tired, as if he were ready to throw his hands up and admit defeat. She hesitated, almost talked to him, but then put her hand on his arm, squeezed it, and told him they'd talk later.

On the way to her room, she figured she was sneaking back because she had lost her sense of balance. She walked through Sven's gallery. The tiny eyes and faces of what was left of his gallery seemed as sad as she felt. She stopped at Harry's painting. His eyes seemed stolid, heavy, as if they'd fall right out of the oil onto the eighth floor carpet.

Her apartment was a strange place, which, in a few seconds, started seeming familiar. She threw her bag down and limped to her refrigerator. She pulled out the carton of orange juice, smelled it to see if it was still good, and then poured herself a glass. She took it back to her sitting room. She shucked off her shoes and sat down.

She felt better right away. She took spiritual stock. It was bad. Harry, paid off by the powers of darkness, was already pumping Kristi Laptop who made loud post-coital deals via wireless phone. Her interlude with Terry was fun but had already been consigned to the dustbin and the punch line was a hit-and-run and Bellevue. If she believed in sin and damnation, she would have thought her personal black angel was working overtime.

She smoked. She called Maritsa and babbled for ten minutes. It felt good. She called Meryl and listened to a liturgy of diseases and ailments. She picked up the notepad she'd started keeping near her phone of things to do about the invasion. She scribbled a note to call Toby, tomorrow, then, instead, called him right away.

Toby told her they were working hard on the Triple M. Then he told her to hang up and get a life. She decided that was a good idea.

She took a couple days off. The Rex was a mess, people leaving—Bel Benaventura?—rooms shuttered and locked, but those days were grand. It was starting to be fall, finally. The air was crisper, the light brilliant.

She put on her gardening clothes and coddled her garden, which was just as bruised as she was. She propped up damaged plants. She watered, although they needed less water, not more. It *was* fall and many of the holdout flowers were folding their petals and dropping. The leaves on her miniature Japanese maple were falling, and practically everything else.

Her interlude, her slow time in the garden, let her think about the hiatus, the long hiatus, in Frieda Berg's life. A week after being bounced off a bus shelter on Thirty-fourth Street, she examined herself in the mirror. She looked bruised. A laceration on her cheek gave her a rakish air.

She knew she had to go to IM66 and face Rodriguez. She knew she had to find out more about the Triple M. But, but, but. For the first time, she realized what she'd been thinking. If she had her druthers, she'd never walk into another welfare center.

32

It was a cool day in September. There was good light in Marcy's room, but marred, as usual, by the Olympia. It wasn't simply its "thereness" that bothered her. Lansky lived there. Lansky sent his goons, his Trucks and Berts, into the Rex. He'd sent Kragen. He'd murdered Blondie. He had become a symbol of everything wrong with the world. He was the hot, stinking garbage, the black-edged corruption in the background of her sketches and paintings. He was right there, all the fucking time.

She made up her pack, but, impulsively, she decided to see Frieda before she left for work. She locked her door, walked swiftly down the hallway, and pushed open the fire doors. She almost stabbed at the button on the elevator, but decided to walk up.

On five, she pushed the fire doors open, walked around the shaft housing. She stared at the doors. She did the same on six and seven. Most floors seemed calm enough. That was because of the closed rooms, the intimidation. Residents didn't talk loudly anymore; their voice had been taken away. The few residents she saw walking either to the elevator or bathrooms were nervous. Were they next? Would they be taken into alleys and beaten, or left crumpled on deserted street. A disease worked on them, a disease of space and spirit, and the disease was spreading through the corridors, bathrooms, and pipes, through the routines, habits, and moods.

Frieda wasn't in her room, but she was on the roof.

The roses had been butchered, trellises broken, a weather vane. Vines snarled around the cock's legs, but head, comb, and beak bent down, as if it were crying. She couldn't remember whether it was like that before Bert—Frieda assumed it was Bert—had trashed the garden. Most of the flowers were gone too. Still, it felt like Frieda's place, had Frieda's touch. Frieda was hunched over some pots on the far side of the table. Marcy walked down the central dark path towards the chairs and tables. Beyond the table, right of the fire escape, the brown vines of dead morning glories straggled up the water tower.

She moved a chair so she could see Frieda and sat. "Shouldn't you be in bed?"

Frieda looked up, her face shadowed by her broad brimmed straw hat. She was wearing jeans, a work shirt, and had tied her black hair up with a red handkerchief, which peeked out from under the hat. Frieda was a week away from her hit-and-run and bruises had bloomed on her face, on her arms. She looked like a mutilated flower.

"Can't. Have to do something constructive."

The morning was calm, the city not yet in its rush-rush mode. It felt peaceful with Frieda moving slowly through her pots, touching plants, touching dirt. Frieda had quick, practiced hands. Her nails had thin lines of dirt under them and two were broken. "What if this shit goes on for a year, or two? Leaving would make my life—all our lives—easier."

Frieda frowned and laid her trowel in a plastic pail full of dirt. She shielded her eyes against the sun. "We've all thought that. You don't believe it."

Marcy looked at her closely to see if she was kidding. Frieda was right. She didn't. "I've been thinking of Blondie. I talked to him. I can't shake the hopelessness in his eyes. He knew something bad would happen, felt it, but stayed. It was almost like a suicide."

Frieda thought about what she'd said. "Maybe. I've known ex-cons through the department. Lousy parents. Lousy neighborhoods. Can't get jobs. Addicted to drugs. Their friends are inside. It's a recipe for fatalism."

"The others aren't like that."

"Maybe they are. You just can't see it."

"Are you planning anything?"

Frieda looked at her closely. "I've been toying with a few ideas. HRA, especially IM, needs a kick in the ass. And I'm ready to do that—soon. You remember that reporter, Borgan."

Marcy touched the edge of the table, and then rubbed the plastic. "Why wait?"

"He's started on a story, but he needs the bigger picture, more evidence than unsolved murders or hit-and-runs at three in the morning. I'm not sure what he needs." Frieda seemed more distracted. She talked as if she were reciting what another Frieda would have said.

"I'm going to do something."

Frieda cocked her head at her. "What?"

"We've been waiting, just like Blondie. I'm not going to wait. I know that Fishface—Blondie said his real name is Kragen—will come back. I know he'll come after me. It's all part of the plan."

Frieda sat down on the wooden runner and watched her. "Go to Butch's."

Marcy shook her head. "Not yet."

"Then what are you going to do?"

"Make him pay."

"Listen, darling. Slow down. We have spirit on our side. We're not giving in. That's one thing. They have the muscle, the fists, and the knives. You're not going to—"

"I'm going to try." Marcy hadn't articulated it until that moment.

Frieda shook her head. "You don't know what it's like to get hurt."

"Yes, I do. I've been hurt my entire life. Bel, my Dad. They're all fucking phantoms, sometimes real, sometimes not."

Frieda put down her trowel. "You're angry. Let's talk this out."

"I have to work."

"Come up afterwards. Please."

"I'll see."

Frieda picked up her trowel. "Just be careful."

She left Frieda and walked back towards the roof door. It was odd how that came out. *She* was going to make them pay. It wasn't a macho statement. It was more a statement of fact. She stopped at the roof door and glanced back at Frieda. Frieda was already digging, the floppy hat hiding her head. No, she wasn't coming back after work. She was going to Pier 17. She knew he'd be there. She knew it.

Back in her room, she made sure she had the Mace, the pepper spray, and Mario's club. She put on a thicker sweater, warm boots, and a black leather jacket.

Outside, the yuppies were up and jogging. Dogs were walked; cars zipped up and down Twenty-eighth. She took the corner on Lexington and watched the traffic in the Giltmore lobby, catty-corner. Everyone seemed bubbly happy. She supposed she would be too, if she could afford three thousand bucks a month for a place to sleep.

At the Odyssey, she threw herself into the day, as if she had to prove something. It was busy and as the day wore on, she tried to forget Kragen and his friend. Once, she stood stock still when she thought they were in a booth in the Maze. Once, she was startled to see a smear of teeth in the window. But it was just a reflection of orders sitting on the silver pass-through slot.

At six, she changed into her street clothes, but as she put on her jeans and sweater, she wondered if she really wanted to leave. Nikos was at the register. Sandy, the waitress coming on, was a friend. She could hang out with the cooks.

She gritted her teeth, put on her jacket, hitched up her pack, and headed for the Seaport.

It was a beautiful fall day. The sun was sharp, the air cool. The Nevelson sculpture with its harsh metallic patterns seemed softer. It reminded her right away of the first day Kragen followed her. She kept walking but that image of Kragen staring at her from Pier 17 stayed with her. She knew it would happen again. What would she do? Run? Hide?

Pier 17 was calm that day, fewer tourists, and fewer subjects for everyone. She set up, almost as if her board was a prop. It was funny, because three tourists liked her caricatures, that hint of mystery, that barren tree hanging over their shoulder, their skewed faces. She'd just finished the third, when she felt a mystery over her own shoulder. She shook off the feeling. A large woman sat down.

The woman wore a billowing blue dress and had a round face and a small nose with prominent nostrils. She didn't have to skew that face. After five minutes, Marcy turned and regarded the three levels of Pier 17's shops and restaurants. Beyond the frigate-like building the sky was darkening. Tourists hung over the railing of the open deck area in back. They ate and yelled at their kids, or watched boats in the East River. You could almost miss him leaning over the side railing on the walkway and staring at the other artists on the rough planks in the courtyard. His globular eyes rotated towards her.

She tore her eyes away from him. Her fingers fumbled with the charcoal. It fell to the ground. She apologized to the woman she was drawing.

The woman squinted at Marcy's sketch. "I look like a pig. And what is that in the background? It looks like drops of blood."

Marcy ripped it out of her sketchbook. "You can have it for free."

"I don't want it." She got up and grimaced at her husband.

273

Marcy balled up the sketch and threw it over her shoulder. "Caricatures mean something, lady. You leave bodies in your wake."

"I may have to report you," the woman said, angrily.

"Go ahead," said Marcy. "It won't change who you are."

The women strode to her abashed husband, grabbed him by the arm, and led him away.

"You're not making money insulting your customers," said Tod. Tod was a quiet, skinny twenty-five year old who did airbrushed portraits. He would have made Miss Piggy look like Doris Day.

"She wasn't going to pay anyway," said Marcy. "Fuck her."

"Are you okay?"

"No I'm not okay. There's lot's of stuff going down at the hotel," said Marcy. She scanned all levels of Pier 17. Kragen had disappeared. She looked for him at the first floor entrance. It was time. "Watch my coat and pack. I'm going to fuck somebody up."

She zipped open a side pocket on her pack where she kept Mace and pepper spray. The Mace was closer, so she grabbed that. She slipped it in her back pocket and, ignoring the stares of her friends, headed for the Pier 17 entrance. She pushed the doors open, scanned the first few shops, and then walked down the short corridor into the atrium. She checked the balconies, which rimmed the atrium, but all she saw were tourists peering over the side. She circled around the stairway in the open space and checked the shops on the other side.

Nothing.

Her hands were sweaty. She tried to control herself as she scanned the crowds, but she couldn't. Not that day. She was pushing herself towards some dim, bloody fight.

She took the escalator up to two, got off, and hurried down the row of shops. She went up to three, to the fast food floor. Fast Chinese, fast Mexican, fast heroes. Hamburgers, fries, ice cream. She walked through the tables and seats at the river end of the food floor. A hundred people salted fries and gobbled dinner.

She crisscrossed that dining area twice. He wasn't there. She went outside. There were a few families bending over the railing, but he wasn't there. It was brisk. The wind chilled her. Gulls circled high up, ships navigated the East River. She walked over to the walkway around the building, where she'd seen him. Empty. She leaned over the railing. The other walkways were empty too.

She shook her head, and then realized she was trembling. What the fuck was she doing?

She took a deep breath and hiked down the outer stairs to the deck. She walked slowly over to the hardy band of sketchers.

"Thanks Tod."

They stared at her. Tod looked serious. "What about the Rex?" They knew about the Rex, but most days she didn't talk about it. That day, she wanted to tell them about the predator in Pier 17, about what he'd done, and who he was. She wasn't sure why she didn't. She could have found a cop, but she knew Kragen would disappear, and then reappear later. She was scared and in a rage at the same time. She knew one thing: She had a date with Kragen that night.

"Fucking morons following me. People getting beat up. They killed somebody."

"Jesus Christ, Marcy." Tod started getting his stuff together. "We'll share a cab. I'll drop you at your hotel—"

"We can all leave together," said Mindy.

"Thanks guys. Nope. Enough people have been hurt."

Tod said, "What are you going to do?"

She felt her lip hitch up in a sneer. "If I knew, I'd probably stop myself."

Poor Tod. The guy had a thing for her. She'd probably rip him in two inside of a week. She needed someone big and strong and occasionally flaky like Butch. The asshole.

She packed up. She said goodbye to everyone, to Tod.

Tod said, "I wish you'd—"

"Sorry Tod. I'll see you tomorrow."

She took a deep breath, slung her pack over her shoulder, glanced at the building, and left. She headed to the Village. She used the same route she had the first time he'd followed her. Along the waterfront, sharp right up towards the Broadway local, up into the Village. She didn't see him, until she got off the subway. Fine.

It was a crisp September evening and the Village streets were crowded. Sycamore leaves dotted the pavement. She picked her way through the crowds and headed towards the river. She knew she could get hurt, very hurt. People would visit her in the hospital and write on her cast.

She shrugged that thought away.

She walked down Christopher Street. She thought of turning on a score of side streets. She knew a café on Bleeker Street. She could slip into any of the gay bars. She could wait for a cop. She kept walking. Finally, she came to the West Side Highway. The Hudson molded itself around the decayed piers like dark taffy. The Jane Hotel stabbed the night. She was repeating the first night Kragen followed her: Chiffon in the bar, Kragen sucked into the night.

She speeded up, rounded a corner, and then ducked into an alley two blocks from the West Side Highway. Her breath came in gulps. She felt faint. She took the Mace out, took the cap off, and palmed it. She took the cap off the pepper spray and put it in the back pocket of her jeans. She felt the rubbery surface of Mario's club and made sure she could slide it out easily.

She pushed herself hard against the wall. She waited what seemed like a day, before she heard soft footsteps. A shadow knifed into the alley then vanished.

She took a last look at the alley. It was dark, safe. She crept along the wall, feeling the thick bricks with her fingers. The light was like a line daring her to cross it. She counted to three, took a breath, and then let it out. She walked woodenly out of the alley.

Kragen had disappeared. She looked frantically towards the Jane, then over her shoulder. She heard the scrape of shoes against pavement. Kragen walked around the corner.

He stopped, sniffed the air, hesitated, and then turned towards her. He grinned maliciously. His buckteeth settled in front of his face like fangs. "Almost missed you."

She should have been thinking of other things, of what she would do, of what he would do, but she was caught for a split second, by the uncanny scene. The deep black Hudson, the Jane, another doomed hotel, the straggle of lights racing to infinity, the hopelessness of it all. She was in the background of one of her sketches.

She shook herself and paid attention. "I've been waiting."

His eyes narrowed. "Really. Now what were you waiting for?'

"I've seen you watching me, following me. I'm ready."

Kragen shook his head and laughed. "I can't believe this. You think I'm actually going to fall for—"

He was smarter than she thought. He wasn't just a killer. But she could tell he was interested. She'd seen it in his eyes. *That* gave her an edge. "Violence gets me off. Mario. Blondie. It did something to me. Got me hot. I've been dreaming about it, your big cock."

Kragen looked puzzled. A hooker disappeared into the Jane. The streets were empty. He licked his lips. He cocked his head at her. "You're either crazy or—"

"Or I want it. I want it bad. So I am crazy. Don't you want any?"

Kragen walked casually towards her. He stopped six feet away. She could almost smell his breath. He watched her suspiciously; then he grinned hideously and sidled the last few feet towards her. Her hand twitched. The Mace weighed a thousand pounds. She forced herself to pull it up and aim it.

Kragen stepped forward fast and put his hand over hers. She sprayed into his hand. She jerked away. He had the Mace. He tossed it over his shoulder. He rubbed his hand on his coat. "That was close. That stuff really hurts. Let's start this over. Listen. You're spunky. I like that. So here's the deal. I'll slap you a couple of times. It won't be hard. You'll have a couple of bruises. You go back to the Rex and tell everybody you can't take it. Pack up and leave."

She stopped trembling. If she wasn't cold and ready, she was going to get hurt. "Why would I let you do that?"

"Because it could be a lot worse. I can't believe I'm having this conversation."

"You want to make a deal," Marcy said. Her hand brushed the top of the pepper spray in her pocket. Too early. "Here's my offer. You and Jack and Lansky and your idiot with the black bouffant take off and never come back. Why? Because we're not leaving."

"Jesus, where did you get your balls? I guess it has to be rough."

Fishface grabbed her jacket, pulled her close to him. This was it. She'd put herself here, for a reason. She wasn't going to give up, now. Before she realized what he was going to do, he raised his hand and slapped her hard. It hurt, a lot. She let her head snap back with the blow and her hand had the pepper spray. He raised his hand again. She guessed when his hand was at the top of its arc. Both of his hands were busy. She jerked the pepper spray out of her pocket and held it in front of his eyes.

She guessed he knew what it was. But he guessed late.

She hit him right above his buckteeth with a full blast, then wrenched away from him.

Fishface backed up. He clawed at his eyes. "Fuck."

She moved in, and sprayed again, then a third time.

He gasped for air, staggered back. He tore at his eyes. He reached for her, but she stepped back, dropped the pepper spray, and grabbed the club letting the backpack slide off her shoulder. Her heart hammered her rib cage. Kragen stepped, swung. She ducked under his swing and cracked him hard on his knee. He cried out and bent over.

Through the pepper spray dribbling out of his eyes, she saw a vein of hatred. Large hands, a hollow under his throat, grizzle around his face like a smear of charcoal, tiny head, barracuda teeth. They'd made fun of him his entire life. She almost felt sorry for him.

Mario. Blondie.

She'd always been fast and she was fast that night. She stepped forward, planted her right leg, and swung as hard as she could at his forehead. He seemed to stop, as if he'd hit a wall. She drew the club back and swung again. That time, it caught him on the bridge of his nose. His body swung back as if it were on a rope, and then it flopped down and lay splayed on the pavement. The butt of a gun protruded from his jacket pocket. Pepper spray dribbled towards his cup of an ear; a crease of blood widened from his nose to his protruding teeth.

He beat up Mario, followed her, killed Blondie.

She found the pepper spray where she'd dropped it. She stared down at him. "You asshole. You fuckface. Try this on." She emptied it in his face. Some of the pepper spray mixed with the blood dripping from his nose; the rest coated his face like the glaze a ham.

She shook herself, almost as if she'd been daydreaming. She started trembling. Then her whole body shook. She looked down at Kragen as if she didn't know how he'd gotten there. She forced herself to breathe. One breath, two. It felt as if she'd held her breath since she walked out of the alley.

Blocks and blocks of streetlights coned the sides of warehouses. She was in one of her backgrounds. She was in Marcy World. And what was there? Two people, alone on a vast plain, crouched and tore at each other. In the middle of cleanliness, grotesqueness. She felt a tired agony that people were not all right, that she was not all right.

She walked over to where he'd thrown the Mace and picked it up. She capped the pepper spray and Mace and put them back. She tucked the club in her pack, shouldered it, and turned back towards the distant lights of the Village.

She saw a pay phone on Hudson Street and ran towards it. She was surprised it worked. She called 911 and told the operator where to find Kragen, told them he was armed, and that he was implicated in a series of attacks on residents of the Rex. She didn't care if they believed her. He was bound to have a warrant of some kind lying around in his past.

After she hung up, she waved at a cab, and in a few minutes, she was on her way to the Rex. She crouched in a corner of the cab, pulled her leather jacket around her, and held her pack to her as if it were pillow. She wasn't sure what she'd done. She was in a trance. Park Avenue, Twenty-eighth Street. The Rex.

At the Rex, Ivan was asleep and she left him like that. She took the elevator to eight and walked like a somnambulist to Frieda's door.

Frieda opened after the first knock.

She just looked at Frieda. She thought later, she must have looked like a wild dog.

Frieda took her hand, brought her inside, and shut the door.

She dropped her pack and went into Frieda's arms. She started sobbing, long racking sobs. Then she felt Frieda. Frieda was solid, a pillar. She realized Frieda was stroking her hair. "Stay here," she said. Frieda came back with a wet towel and a bottle of wine—she wasn't sure what kind. "Here, hold this on that bruise."

"I'd forgotten it was there."

Frieda poured a glass for both of them. "Now tell me."

They sat on the edge of Frieda's bed and she did. As she talked, she started wondering about herself, why she did what she did. How she ended up in one of her backgrounds. It was likely something she'd never be able to explain.

"I thought I was bad," said Frieda, finally.

"Now what?" said Marcy.

Frieda looked at the ceiling, then at her books, then outside. The noises of Kip's Bay anchored them to reality. Frieda took a long sip of wine and said, "Now we attack. Fuck 'em. We deliver *our* notes. We tell them what you've done tonight leaving out your name. Special note to

279

Don. Special note for Jack. Letter to Lansky, which you will deliver to-night. It's time to take back the Rex."

Marcy realized that her breathing was normal. She sifted what Frieda had said, then smiled. "Let's start."

Frieda killed her wine. She got up, limped to her desk, and pulled out writing paper. "Here's what I think we should say."

The notes to the goons read, "Tonight we hit back. Kragen is going to jail. We know about Jack and Don and Lansky. You're going back to jail. This isn't just a threat. Ask Don."

The note to Don had much the same lines, except she detailed who he was, that he was the second in command, and told him to give the letter to Jack.

Frieda's letters to Lansky and Jack were more to the point. She told them they were responsible for Blondie's death. Then she named all the ex-cons in the Rex and that Jack was orchestrating Lansky's scheme. She also said Jack wasn't doing a good job, because the residents who were left were staying.

Frieda paused over the letter to Lansky, frowned.

"What," said Marcy. Writing notes to the goons made her forget what she'd done earlier. Whenever she stalled, she felt Kragen's hand on her jacket, saw the hatred in his face.

"Just wondering whether I should mention the Triple M. If I do, it'll be a red flag to Lansky's people in the department. What the fuck." Frieda muttered, "Triple M…investigation…articles in the Times." Frieda regarded her letters. Then she got out two envelopes and wrote "Mr. Jack Kuhl" on one and "Mr. Michael Lansky" on the other.

They split up the notes. Frieda did the goons from five to eight. Marcy took four to one. Don got his own and the letter to Jack. Marcy walked past Ivan and out the door. She walked slowly across Lexington to the Olympia and handed Lansky's letter to the doorman. The doorman looked suspiciously at the letter, but finally he shrugged and took it.

When she got back to the Rex, she threw off her clothes, double-locked the door, and shut the shade tight. As she pulled the shade down, the Olympia disappeared. At that moment, it seemed like an omen. The Olympia—and Lansky—followed her wherever she went. She couldn't ignore it, or what it meant forever, but she did that night.

33

Raul Vasquez, his nose big and now crooked, mugged for the camera, winked conspiratorially, then turned and thrust his face at a black lesbian hooker from Atlanta, and started sputtering.

Who do you think you are, homo?

Fuck you, Raul.

You're disgusting. People like you...

Black? Lesbian? Hooker? Atlanta? Didn't they kill black lesbians in the south? Don shook his head, picked the remote off his stomach, and hit the power button. Raul's face lingered for a split second, then flashed off. "Face Off" hadn't had a good fight for weeks. It was the bunny fight. Fuckin' queer dog.

He'd turned on "Face Off" hoping he could forget. He'd started feeling rattled, as if any minute the cops were going to break down his door. Nothing but bad news. Blondie dead. Frieda. He wasn't sure who nailed Frieda, but fuck. Hit-and-run. She could be dead too! The cops had talked to him—twice. How could he pat his agents on the back and tell them everything was all right, when his heart skipped a beat every time the elevator ground to a stop? He told the cops he got money from his mother, had a small stake in the bank. He sure couldn't tell them his job was to terrorize the residents of the Rex.

They cooled it for a few days. Everything seemed better. They were gearing up to start again, when they got the note.

Don fumbled for a cigar under the nightstand. He found one, found his Bic, and lit up. Smoke enveloped his head and drifted away. Don picked up the note from the end table. He read it again, then balled it up and threw it at the waste can. The fucking note was the last straw. Said we fucked up Kragen. Named him, Don, by his full name. Named Lansky. Named Jack. Said a note was going to the cops. He'd checked: every agent got one. Sure he'd fucked up a couple of times, but he was religious keeping Lansky's name from the agents.

What about Kragen? He was supposed to be a stone killer. Who could have nailed him? It couldn't be Frieda. Mario? He was still beat up, couldn't use his left arm. The Russians? Joey, the drug dealer? Naw.

The Freak Brothers in 506? They'd told him to fuck off the other day, but he saw they were worried. Don ground his teeth, then nodded grimly. He wasn't sure *how* she did it, but he knew it was that skinny bitch Benaventura. He knew she'd fucked up Truck. Truck never said. Sure like to see her on "Face Off." She'd feed Raul his balls.

Don felt a lump grow in his throat. Nothing was workin' out. He had to tell Jack. He didn't want to. He supposed it was because he felt—it was a feeling he'd had when the project started—that the project was shit. Was it time to bail?

Bring, bring, bring.

Don looked at the phone as if it were a scorpion.

Don picked up the handset gingerly. "Yeah."

"It's Truck."

"Hey man, how they hangin'?" From what he saw in the photo—Marcy, he was sure she did it—they weren't hangin' very low.

"Listen Don. The guys and I were talkin'."

"Yeah. What about?"

"Shit Don, what else? What the fuck's happening? What's with these fuckin' notes. What the fuck is this?"

"I got a note too. I'm not freakin' out," Don lied.

"Maybe it's time to *start* freakin' out."

Don scratched his head. Everybody wanted him to do something. "What can I do?"

"I think we should meet, talk about what we're gonna do, then you talk to Jack."

Don knew he had to. It looked like a losing battle anyway. "Okay. Say an hour in Paddy's? That okay?"

"Sure. We aint got nothin' else to do."

Don thought about Jimmy. Jimmy rarely drank with the others and, if he had to rate agents, was the worst. But he still had a room and Jack didn't want to get rid of him. "Be sure Jimmy gets the message. He's never fuckin' around."

"You got it."

It was a crisp fall day, early evening. Second Avenue was full of yuppies, dog walkers, Mercedes, BMWs, and cabs. There was a crowd of suits,

282

dresses, and drinks in the Fortuna's octagonal window; three couples waited outside Lombardi's. Paddy's looked like a starving cousin come to beg money off rich relatives.

Don and four agents slunk through Paddy's doorway. Paddy's was half-full with an assortment of regulars holding down the bar top. A couple had empty longnecks in front of them. The bartender glanced up from his paper. He came to the end of the bar.

A few minutes later, they took over one of the tables in front.

Tim glanced at the two guys at the next table, then said, softly, "What I'm sayin' is that it was a good gig. I think for the first time in years, I got something done."

Bert picked at the scab on his hand. Then he looked up and said, "Feeling of accomplishment, Don. I don't know if you felt it."

Don took a cigar out of the pocket inside his Knicks windbreaker and clamped it in his mouth. "I'm more worried about the next gig. I done two before this. It took longer, but there was always another gig. Shit, there are lots of old hotels. But if this one..."

Truck looked at Don and said, seriously, "Sounds like you know this one aint turnin' out right. Shit, somebody gets killed in the joint, they might or might not care who did it. Mario, Blondie, hit-and-run, this fuckin' note—the cops aint stupid."

Tim said, "Not to mention that photo of you dressing up. Get you on a morals charge."

Bert said, "I almost died of fright when I saw it."

Truck winced. "Caught me with my guard down."

"And pants," said Don, shaking his head. "I thought you looked kinda cute, specially those shoes. You gotta tell me where you got 'em."

Truck shrugged away the laughter. "Like I said earlier, it's time to cut and run."

Jimmy looked up from his beer. He'd been feeling his scar, but he stopped and rubbed his bald head. "Yeah."

Don got pissed. "What do you care," he said to Jimmy. "You never do nothin' anyway."

Jimmy smiled. Don remembered that smile and looked away. Jimmy leaned towards him. "Fuck you, Don. I done stuff, but look at six and seven. Benaventura, Rose, Mario, the Russians. You do something with that shit."

Don backed up in his chair. "Sure, sure. Okay, I go along with that. So why do you—"

"Because it aint workin' out Don," said Jimmy, in a voice heavy with sarcasm. "And I don't want cops pokin' around about what I'm doin' here and I don't fuckin' want to go back to Riker's. Aint that why we're here?"

"Wait a minute, wait a minute," Don said, irritated. "It aint over till it's over. I'll talk to Jack. We gotta lay low for a while. We don't want the money to dry up, do we?"

They were silent for a few seconds, then Bert said, "What about something big, Don. We gotta talk about it sometime."

Don frowned. He looked at Truck, Tim, and Jimmy then made a decision. He leaned across the table. The other agents leaned in. "There might be something big happening," said Don. "Some way we get the hotel without doin' too much. I don't know when and if it might happen. All I can say is that I'll find out. Before it happens, we'll get out."

Truck said, "By 'big' you mean somebody's gonna torch the Rex?"

"Fuck," said Jimmy.

"Dying aint worth a few extra bucks," said Tim.

Don shook his head and put his finger to his mouth. "We aint gonna die. Cool it 'till I find out what's goin' on."

And that was the best he could do. Don knew they'd go along with it. It was the easiest gig of their lives. They got paid for stayin' in their rooms, playin' music, and watchin' TV. Life couldn't get much better.

34

Jack stumbled down the stairs into a darkened kitchen. Glasses everywhere. Empty bottles. The darkness felt good. He put on water for coffee, stared at the bottles, then started gathering them up. He opened the garbage can under the sink and dropped them in. He made coffee.

He took the coffee to his worktable. Then he walked over to the curtains and jerked them open. The thin light hit him hard. He backed up and tried to focus. It was a cold gray day. People huddled by in jackets and coats. The river, shimmering gray, streamed by impenetrable. Any vision for the day, some goal, slipped past his eyes and dropped in a black hole.

Jack walked slowly back to the work table. The slashing reds and yellows of the Neiman print stabbed into his brain. He angled the laptop away from it. He waited. He knew that as soon as he fired up the laptop, the whole mess would rush into his head.

Finally, he booted the laptop. The Rex diagram. The Rex project *appeared* as if it were firing on all cylinders. Kragen and Tony had intimidated then scattered victims in their wake. Mario. They stalked Frieda, Marcy, Bel, and a handful of residents. He paid Harry to leave and Harry's room was "renovated" along with a handful of others.

That's when Lansky went ballistic. That's when he upped the pressure. That's when the shit hit the fan.

Frieda had always been a problem, a real problem. But her hit-and-run drove him batty. Kragen said he didn't do it, neither did Tony. Who the fuck did? He was trying to figure that out, when Kragen told him about Blondie. Blondie. Jesus Christ. Jack tried not to think about Blondie, but thought about him anyway. He knew Blondie was going to be trouble, but he didn't know how. His programmer/agent lay on a slab in the morgue.

Jack leaned over and dropped his head to the table in front of the open laptop. It felt nice there, unmoving.

The metallic ring of the cordless phone crashed through his skull. He raised his head and watched it, uncomprehending. He reached across the table and snatched it up.

It was Lansky. Jack sighed, moved his chair, and straightened up. And what was this about? "When I got back to town, this letter was waiting for me. Handwritten, no stamp. It lists everything we're doing. It named you, me, your agents. Fuck, I can't remember everything it said. Somebody murdered, said they took out Kragen, Times' exposés. What the fuck is this?"

Jack scratched behind his left ear furiously. It took him a second to realize he was scratching a band-aid. He resisted tearing it off. He lowered his hand. "Jesus Christ. I don't know about any letter. I'll call Kragen, Don."

"What about the rest of this shit?"

"Well, first Frieda Berg, the gardener, got nailed by a car. Hit-and-run. Then your man Kragen and his idiot partner killed one of my agents. I thought you told me Kragen was the man. The stone cold killer. The professional."

"Jesus. Why didn't you fucking tell me?"

"I just found out a couple days ago. I'm still trying to see what that means to the project."

"Right, right. Might be okay. How do they fucking know about the welfare program?"

The murder didn't bother Lansky. "The program is your baby," Jack said, angrily. "If Frieda knows about it, everyone fucking does." Jack felt light-headed. What the fuck happened to Kragen? He got up and walked slowly to the sofa feeling like a puppet. He sat down and leaned back into the pillows. "Let me find out what's happening and I'll call you back. We'll let everything calm down and figure out our next move."

"I'm not letting a welfare worker and woolly residents stop me," Lansky said, angrily. "I'm meeting Brendel tomorrow. You step up the pressure."

Lansky was losing it. "We stepped up the pressure and we got a hit-and-run, a murder, police, and you got a fucking letter. Do you see any connection?"

"Don't play around with me, Jack."

"I'm trying to get your building *and* keep you out of jail. You're pissed about the letter. Let me find out what it's about. You need strategy, not sputtering."

Jack thought he heard a sigh on the line. Lansky was always a hair away from blowing up about something. "Find out, call me back. But listen Jack."

Here it comes, thought Jack. Every time he talked to Lansky, Lansky had to throw in a threat, make some stupid argument, which would put him in jail. The Rex. He knew it was a bad idea when Lansky proposed it. It was too exposed, too many residents. "What?"

Lansky's voice was soothing, insinuating. "It may be time for another tack."

He was sure that Lansky was outside. Last time, three witches played cards by the pool. Jack felt tired; his chest felt alternately empty and as if there was a thousand-pound weight on it. He whispered out the words. "A 'dramatic' tack?"

"Yes."

Jack hesitated. He wasn't going to cave in about a fire. "Let's talk about it. What is it, exactly?"

"You'll see."

He tried again. It was like whispering in a gale. "Listen, Michael. Somebody's been killed. The cops are swarming over the Rex. Maybe they did take out Kragen. It's adding up to too much fucking attention—just what you didn't want." Jack breathed deeply. He'd never talked to Lansky like that, but he had to do something. "Just because some developer is going to give you a few extra bucks, is no reason to jeopardize the entire project or your life." The only way he could salvage the project was with time. If Lansky couldn't see that, they were both fucked.

There was a pause, another pause, too many pauses. "Okay, find out what's happening. But I'm not going to be stopped by your hesitations. You reach a point where you play or fold. Maybe you forgot that in Lompoc." Lansky hung up.

Jack stared at the phone. Lansky's words bit deep. Jack's past imprinted itself on the cold sky above the Hudson. The trial, the divorce, the sentencing, the disgrace.

Jack let the sky oppress him for a few minutes. Then he dialed Don. "What the fuck is happening over there."

He heard a sigh—too many sighs that morning. Don said, "Yesterday, we got these fucking notes."

"Fuck Don, why didn't you tell me? How many fucking times—"

"I wasn't sure, Jack. I thought it was a joke, until the other guys—"

"Okay, okay. What did the note say?"

"They all said the same thing. They said they got to Kragen. Half the guys are scared shitless. I got a letter for you. It said a letter went to Lansky."

Jack laughed, but he detected an accent of shrillness in his laugh. Was he losing it? "A mass mailing; that's almost funny."

"There's something else, Jack. Maybe we should meet."

He wanted to go to bed. He should grab a plane, go to Florida, sit in a bar for a year, and make boozy talk about Manhattan and the housing wars. Hotel management. What a fucking crock.

"Right, I'll see you in an hour at the Boathouse. Bring the letter. Maybe there's something I can do."

It was brightening in the apartment, glaring. It hurt his eyes, his brain. His headache rushed back. Kragen. Notes. An investigation; Lansky's "dramatic" option. Jack had a premonition: He knew it wasn't going to work. He also knew he was going to play it out as long as he could.

Jack picked up the phone and dialed Kragen. He let it ring ten times and hung up. Maybe something did happen to him.

Jack dressed, put on his leather jacket, walked past Duane Park, and hailed a cab on Church Street. He got off in the Seventies. He walked to the park and followed one of the trails around the lake to the Boathouse. It was as cold outside as it looked earlier. The branches of the trees rimming the lagoons were becoming bare. The lake, which normally had a few boats on it, was empty and reflected a gray, brooding sky.

The Boathouse itself, a bustling place in summer full of tourists, fast food, and cheap beer, was doing a bad business that fall day. The deck was empty. There was a tired counter guy with a ponytail staring at the clock. Tourists at a corner table talked in German and dabbed their fries in slicks of ketchup.

Don was already there a heavy, solitary figure nursing a beer at eleven in the morning. Jack paid for a weak coffee from the bored ponytail at the counter and sat across from Don. The window showed Don's short, round silhouette balanced by his tall one.

Don had on a frayed, gray cotton jacket, a huge pair of jeans, and worn work boots. His scarf wrapped around his neck like bunting a maypole.

Don looked grim. His eyebrows were furled over his eyes and his gaze switched between the center of the table and the beer. Don took a gulp of beer and belched.

"You still got those boils?"

Jack stopped himself from touching his band-aid. He shrugged, annoyed. "It's hereditary. Okay, what's up?"

Don's gaze shifted from the table to the lake. There wasn't much to see out there—grays and whites, a dime-colored sun, green and gray boats stacked like falling dominoes. Don shook his head wearily. "You done a good job, Jack, better than I thought. And everything seemed okay. In the last few weeks, everything got fucked."

Jack watched a sparrow alight near the stacked boats, then hop between two of them. Survival, purpose, threaded itself through the natural world. Don and their reflections seemed foreign and unnatural. He didn't feel like talking yet. "Looks like it. Where's the letter?"

Don dug in his coat pocket and brought out a fistful of transfers, toothpicks, what looked like a phone bill, and a dirty crumpled envelope. He threw the envelope on the table.

Jack tore open the envelope. He laid the letter flat on the table and read it. Kragen, Lansky, his agents, the welfare scheme, Blondie, exposé in the Times. It was all there scribbled in long hand. He knew what was in it before he saw it, but seeing it laid out so neatly, made him feel nauseous. "Must be Frieda's work."

Don shrugged. "My guess. What the fuck happened to Kragen?"

Jack thought of Kragen's assignment. Marcy Benaventura. "Jesus Christ. I don't know. His assignment was Marcy Benaventura. What about Joey, that drug dealer, or Crazy Ritchie."

"Naw. We aint fucked with them. That girl aint big, but she's fuckin' fearless. If she—"

"It doesn't matter who. I'll try Kragen again. Anything else?"

"Lots," said Don "The guys called me up and wanted to meet."

Jack's stomach knotted. Revolution? Strike? He thought he'd heard all the bad news, but it kept coming on like the thing that couldn't be killed. He reached up to scratch, but stopped. He touched the band-aid, and then dropped his hand. "About what?"

"You know. Mario, Blondie, Frieda. That fuckin' note."

The dearth of people around the Boathouse, the stacked boats, the unremitting sky tormented him. Locations. He was running out of any location that felt safe. "What do they want to do?"

"They think it's time to hold off. If we don't, they're afraid of the cops. Too much has happened. The guys are trying to go straight. They don't want to go back to Riker's or upstate. They're startin' to like bein' out."

"The Rex, Rehab Central," said Jack.

Don looked at him, gave him an ingratiating smile. "See Jack, we don't want the project to end, we just think we ought to cool it...for maybe a couple weeks. Is that okay? I mean, you're not planning anything big, are you?"

Big, big, big. Dramatic. "Fuck, Don," Jack said, agitated. He looked at the other tables. The Germans had finished and were trailing out the door. Jack lowered his voice. "I know we have to stop for a few weeks. But Lansky wants it now. I don't know what he plans to do. I'm trying to find out."

Don nodded. "You'll tell us—"

"When I find out," Jack said, exasperated. He looked at Don. Don was at the Cardiff, the Amsterdam. "You have any idea who's going to do it?"

Don frowned, looked around. He hunched over and whispered, "There was this guy Casey. You know that fire."

The name on the inside of the résumé folder next to Kragen's. "Who contacted him?"

"At the Amsterdam, I'm pretty sure Dombry did. Dombry invited us all to dinner the day it happened. When we get back, the fire trucks were there. It didn't take long—"

"I remember," Jack said. "I had a meeting with Lansky. I see now."

"We all had alibis...if we needed one. Here's the deal about the Rex. There are five of us left. We're scattered through the Rex. Bert's on eight, Jimmy six, me five. If it was a big fire—"

Jack saw it very clearly. The inferno. He closed his eyes.

Don moved in his seat as if he were looking for the right spot. He finally settled down, but brought his hand out and held onto the edge of the table as if it were a last grip on reality.

"I had this feelin' about the Rex—"

"Tell everybody to sit tight. I'll work it out."

"Remember about tellin' us."

He watched Don tip up his glass and put it down empty. Don got up and shuffled out of the Boathouse.

Jack glanced at his reflection, then beyond, at the lake. He was running out of ideas. He was reaching the point he and Jeanie had talked about, the point where he would have to choose between losing, that very un-American concept, and doing something unnatural, something that exceeded his grasp, something dramatic.

Rudi Lopwitz sat in the small office. He used to feel secure behind that desk with all its papers, notes, addresses, and ledgers, and his tools in the small tool chest on his left. Used to. So many things happening. Fights. Beatings. Murder. Now, Frieda told him they'd counterattacked. *Counterattack?* What was that? Yes, the residents were fighting back. Of course, the residents didn't know the real story.

Since his last talk with Brendel, Lansky had "renovated" ten rooms. It meant he couldn't rent them. He couldn't rent vacant rooms.

A few weeks ago after the first renovations, he'd showed Brendel one of the rooms, the hanging plaster, the ripped-up floor, and the ripped-out sconces. Brendel was puzzled and said he'd call Lansky. Brendel had called him a few days. It was just the first pass. No problems. The construction crews had other apartments to attend to. It was all done on a system.

Through the potlatch of explanations, Rudi saw that Brendel was getting anxious, very anxious. They were both used to a stream of income from the Rex, he more than Brendel. But that had dried up. All they had was hope and Lansky, which meant they had no hope. It was time, he realized, to look closely at the writing on the wall. Lansky meant to have the Rex. He would get it one way or another. If he sold now, he'd get more money for it. If he waited until it was almost empty, he'd get less. What was the expression in that song? *There was a time to hold 'em, and I time to fold 'em.*

Rudi heard the front door open, then close, then the door to the outside door to the office. Seconds later, Brendel stood in the doorway.

"More good news," said Rudi.

Brendel sighed, entered, and dragged a chair from the wall. He sat and looked at Rudi. "We've had our disagreements, yes?"

"Very yes," said Rudi. "What's the message from Lansky?"

Brendel looked sorrowful. He seemed to make up his mind. "Lansky offered to buy me out. He said that his crew worked here and there, that they only had time to start the initial renovations, that it might be a long time before they got back."

"You said that already. I told you—"

Brendel waved his hand at Rudi. "I made a mistake. I can see what he wants now."

Rudi frowned. At least Brendel knew. "Is it too late."

Brendel scratched his head furiously with his thick fingers. He looked at Rudi puzzled, as if he were deciding something. "I don't think so."

A smidgen of hope rose like a bubble in Rudi's breast. He thought of what Frieda had said. *Counterattack*. Maybe it was. Once you started anything, it developed its own momentum. Rudi dug into his store of sayings and aphorisms and came up empty.

"And..."

Brendel leaned forward and propped his arms on the desk. "This is what we should do."

35

Frieda didn't know what Lansky and Jack were planning, but suddenly everything was quiet. No more notes, no more stopped toilets. The thugs had become invisible. When she was optimistic, she ticked off that quietness to Blondie's murder, her own hit-and-run, the notes to the thugs, the letters to Jack and Lansky, and her next-day detailed letter to Borgan. The residents, most of the residents, soon knew what happened and she felt a hike in their esprit.

Still. At the top of her worry list stood the fierce, unmoving form of Marcy Benaventura. Dark side. Taking on a murderer. There was too much going on there for Frieda to do much. Some days, when she woke out of a nightmare of a car veering towards her, of the sickening thump of metal against her body, of spinning lights and the cold feel of pavement against her skin, she thought they were both lurching towards disaster. And for what? A holding pattern in an old hotel.

Marcy was sure Kragen would be arrested, convicted, and sent upstate forever. It was a naïve hope. When Marcy couldn't find out what happened to him, Frieda started calling. She got Borgan to check. She called Lou Meredith, caseworker and former cop. She called John. She begged Toby to do something. They all came back with nothing.

Early Friday morning, Frieda went down to talk to her.

The Rex was quiet that morning. Marcy's floor, especially. Two rooms had been shut and renovated, but it was early. There was movement inside a room, a stray voice. She knocked on Marcy's door. Marcy cracked the door, her head appearing above that chain lock she'd just installed.

Marcy unlocked the door and let it swing wide open. "Leave the door open," she said. "I'm starting to feel like Ben in his burrow."

"It can't be that bad."

Marcy's room was spartan. The sketches on the wall were harrowing landscapes with black clouds roiling in the background. The painting on the easel near the window was a cityscape featuring the Giltmore and Olympia full of van Gogh swirls in reds and blacks. Frieda had a vision of Marcy dying young, or in a staged, violent way. Frieda shook that vision away.

Marcy's pack was on the chair in the corner.

"And today's news?" said Marcy. She hopped on her futon, arranged herself yoga-style, back against the wall, and stared at her with steady, green eyes.

"Not good, I'm afraid." Frieda glanced at Marcy's pack. "What are you doing?"

Marcy shrugged. "Going to work like a good girl."

"Stay here. I'll exhume more contacts. Someone will help us."

Marcy shrugged. "You've done your best." Marcy adopted a meditative pose. Even in that pose, Frieda saw the unbending quality, Marcy's stiffness. Her green eyes could be alluring, but could change in a beat to a jade-like hardness. "I just started doing stuff, getting ready to fight him. If anybody had asked me what I was doing, I couldn't have said."

Frieda sat on the edge of the futon. She found a spot that didn't hurt her hip. "You can't think about it. It's done. We forge on."

"But it means something for me. Why? Will I always be like that?" Marcy bit her lower lip, and released it. "They have been quiet for the last few days."

"I think Lansky over-extended himself. Most of the thugs are older ex-cons. They aren't going to stay out of jail by messing with the cops," said Frieda. "The momentum is on our side."

Marcy shook her head. "Eye of the storm."

Frieda felt the bump on her head, adjusted her leg so it didn't hurt. When she looked up, Marcy's print was right in front of her. Sturm und drang. The violent slashes of the East Village. Turmoil. She felt again Marcy's quirky power. "Stay here. Lock the door. I'll—"

Two lines dug themselves in Marcy's high forehead. Her lips pursed until they were a single hard line. "Que sera sera. Fuck him. I can't roll into a ball like a pill bug."

Frieda reached over and took Marcy's hand. "It may look bleak. But we'll find this guy."

Marcy squeezed her hand back, then shrugged. "Okay."

Frieda got up, opened, and closed the door. She paused outside. Marcy shouldn't go to work. But she understood. She couldn't live in fear. It was what the entire invasion was about.

She took the elevator to eight. Bert's door opened when she passed. She shot him a dirty look and he closed the door. Good. Let's intimidate them for a few months. Inside her room, she was about to call Toby again, when her phone rang. It was Johnny from IM66.

Johnny said, "When you didn't come in, I got worried. I called your boss. He told me what happened."

"That's sweet Johnny. I'm okay." She fingered her scar and fought an impulse to check it in her mirror. "What's going on over there?"

"That's the other reason I called. I thought you'd want to know. Rodriguez unhooked the Triple M terminal and left. I heard he was reassigned."

Darkness descended over her spirit. "Shit. Thanks Johnny."

She dialed Toby. Either the scheme had blown up or was about to, or it was going to be hidden where they couldn't do squat about it. Something important had happened when she was recuperating.

Toby told her she had to wait.

Saturday. Frieda Berg tried to quit worrying. It was impossible. It was what she did best. She called Marcy and told *her* not to worry. She called Toby and left a message. What was next? And what about the Triple M and Rodriguez? She was in a fury of waiting for Toby to call. She tried to work in her garden, but at ten she stacked her tools on the stairs.

She took a shower and changed into jeans, ruffled white blouse, high-topped burgundy boots, and a three-quarters brown leather coat. She wore big gold hoops, a touch of rouge, and a hint of lipstick. Her dark curls tumbled over her shoulders. Except for a slight bruise on her neck and a slow healing scar, which tracked her cheekbone, she looked ready for a night of flamenco.

It was time to reaffirm life, although while she was dressing, she felt dislocated. It was more than the season. In her garden, she found herself pausing, staring at the plant in her hands. Later, she stared at the titles of her books, but didn't read them. Something was percolating inside her spirit. It was about the Bronx, her trajectory, the department, and stasis.

She took the elevator to the lobby. The light spilling in the front door of the Rex looked warm and friendly. Frieda felt her spirits lift for the first time in days. Rudi was at the desk. His head was bent at a forty-five degree angle over the big ledger.

She walked over and stood in front of him. Rudi looked up. He propped his glasses on his forehead making him look, literally, as if he had four eyes.

"The counterattack is working," she said. "But I feel something is wrong."

Rudi waved his hand, and harrumphed, "Counterattack, smouter-attack."

Frieda rested her arms on the ledge and focused on Rudi. "What?"

"There might be something."

Frieda frowned. "What something?"

Rudi looked at her for a long second and then motioned her closer. She wondered what that was about. Rudi looked left then right. "You've got to keep this quiet."

"What?"

"I talked with Brendel. He finally saw what Lansky was doing."

Frieda snorted. "Fat good it does now."

Rudi shook his head. "You just live here. You don't know or care about our problems."

"Your problem is Lansky."

Rudi shook his head. "No. Look at the Rex. Old building, small rooms, long-term residents who pay less than a hundred bucks a week. With the few SRO residents, our hands are tied. Our problem is paper-thin profits. Lansky just made it worse. But Lansky started us thinking— started Brendel thinking. *We* are going to renovate. We'll advertise better rooms and try to attract tourists. It's going to be a boutique hotel."

Frieda couldn't stifle a laugh. "Boutique hotel! After all we've—"

"You can't live in the past forever," Rudi said.

Frieda frowned. "What about us?"

"Whoever wants to stay stays. We renovate when somebody leaves."

Frieda's frown deepened. "Lansky?"

"We have a majority stake in the Rex. As you say, screw him."

Frieda wasn't sure what to think. It looked like they were winning the war of the goons, winning the war against Lansky, but losing another. "Boutique hotel. Funny. Doesn't anything stay the same? I still worry about Lansky. Lansky-types don't give up."

"You'll always worry about something."

"Thanks. I'd better get out before something else changes."

"You'll be here. You'll see the changes."

Frieda looked at Rudi a long second. "I suppose I will."

She walked slowly out of the lobby, but despite what Rudi said that sense of unease followed her as she kicked sycamore leaves on Park Avenue. Gradually that feeling ebbed away. It was a beautiful September, crisp, mellow-lighted, and fair. New York was full of tragic heroines at the Met, Mahler at the symphony, the harvest from upstate and Long Island, and life stirred under half-denuded trees. The clear air, the reflected light off windows, the laughing, the cabs honking like metallic geese. She felt a Manhattan Rush. She crossed Madison Square Park with its dog walkers and babies bundled up in bunny costumes, and then walked down Twenty-third to Broadway, and down Broadway to Union Square.

At the Farmer's Market, she bought a hot apple cider and scooped the loop. It was crowded, but the market was brimming with mounds of nuts and fruits, gourds and squash, honeys, and preserves. Demeter and Persephone had laid out an urban cornucopia before descending into the underworld. It gave her a sense of possibility, that on the far side of that summer and fall, on the far side of personal tragedies, there was a larger, seasonal hope.

Later, back in her apartment, she piled her goodies on the bed, took off her coat, and sorted through it all. Wreaths on the door, leaves scattered on the table in the other room, gourds on the window, which blocked out her dead morning glories, cider in the fridge, a pyramid of apples on the table, maize on her Art Deco end table.

She made a new pot of coffee. When she had a mug in hand, she settled into her big chair, and stared at the bookcase. Still too quiet. Her mother, the saint, said Frieda needed everything in an uproar to feel alive. That may have been true once, but she wasn't inventing Lansky and Jack or their welfare scheme. She called Toby at home. He didn't answer.

She called John. John picked up after five rings. "It's too quiet," she said. "I'm nervous."

"Something happened to the system yesterday," said John. "I'm trying to find out what."

Something wrong with the system—wasn't that a truism? Frieda thought of the Triple M terminal, Rodriguez. "I know I've put you through the ringer a few times John. But could you call me when you find out?"

"For old times' sake," said John.

When she hung up, Frieda got up and stared out her window. The Triple M terminal had been disconnected. No more code 333s.

What happened to the system? She was not a conspiracy nut. She believed the Trilateral Commission, Watergate, Irangate, alien abductions, and Commission J were distractions from creep. Creep happened. The general direction mattered, not the local conspiracy. Except that year it looked like she had to deal with the conspiracy first and refine the philosophical points later.

She tried to read, but her attention wandered. She marched up to the roof and walked the tar paths of her garden. West, the afternoon sun made Midtown into an Emerald City; south, on Twenty-third Street, the gilded spire of the New York Life building blazed gold. All at once, she felt an enormous sense of nostalgia, of pining for what she'd lost forty years ago, thirty years ago. All that time fused into an inescapable feeling of regret. Regret, that useless emotion.

Frieda walked down the path towards the door, then meditatively down the stairs and through Sven's gallery. Halfway to her room, she heard her phone. Why did they call when she wasn't there? She fumbled with the key, opened the door, and snatched up her phone.

It was John.

They'd talked about the remote possibility of Morty Bennet or Rodriguez using the Triple M to cancel all the welfare cases in the city. But that was what happened. Last night, late working caseworkers had called CO and said their cases had disappeared from the system.

"It's chaos at CO. Morty Bennet resigned. He said there were too many problems with the new system, that he was mentally exhausted."

"Like anyone believes that."

"They might. It will be hard to pin anything on him. Our fraud work group convinced the police it was time to talk to Rodriguez. He's disappeared."

"Still. If every welfare case in the city is canceled, they could simply point to a conversion program gone wrong."

"The prosecution could take years," said John.

"Rodriguez and Bennet are the least of our worries. What happens Monday when the screens are blank? What happens to the checks?"

"There's a meeting," John said.

"Where?" she demanded.

She could feel his hesitation. "If you behave."

"You have my promise."

"As if I believe that. Same room, same place, five-thirty."

As soon as she hung up, she tried Toby again. Then she called him at work. Toby should be at that meeting. Her composure had been shattered. Her personal problems, or regrets, or pining had been edged out by a city of out-of-luck welfare recipients. She was going to that meeting. She wondered whether she should change and decided not to. There was too much going on to be a clotheshorse. She looked presentable, if too Carmen.

At five, she locked her door, and walked quickly through Sven's gallery, and took the elevator to the lobby. She strode through the lobby and started waving for a cab while she was still in the Rex's doorway.

The cab dropped her on Canal and she walked over to the old HRA building. The corridors were immense, the sycamore outside bare, except it was growing dark, the late afternoon light, reflecting off a score of windows, soft. Her reflection in the meeting door, oddly imperious a few weeks ago, was clearer. The leather collar, hoops, and curls formed a ragged rhombus. She looked geometrical. The sense of apprehension she'd had before their last meeting had been replaced by a sense of doom.

She rapped on the door then barged in. Light streamed into the room with her and gave it a false sense of joy. Dust danced. Smoke eddied.

Four people stared at her, some shocked, and others surprised.

Most were in their casual Saturday clothes, but they didn't look casual. She threw her bag on the table, and plopped down in the nearest chair. She landed on the bruise on her left hip. She grimaced, and shifted her weight to her right hip. She scanned the group. John, with whom she'd downed gin and tonics and gotten maudlin with a few weeks ago, was standing near the window on her right. He wore jeans, black tennis shoes, and a burgundy Harvard sweatshirt. He looked distant and grave, his long straight nose and gray eyes troubled.

Toby was sitting on her left and wore a plaid shirt, suspenders, and boots. He shifted in his chair and it creaked. Toby looked almost wise with a grace note of concern.

Across from her, Dugan was unbuttoning a black tie. He was in full

299

evening dress, black suit, and white shirt. "Where were you," she said, trying to cut the dense atmosphere.

"The Opera, Don Giovanni," said Dugan. "Betty is still there."

"We may all be pulled into hell on this one," said Toby.

Frieda turned to Toby, "You didn't tell me."

"I was told, pointedly, not to tell you," said Toby, shrugging.

George Kelso stared at her. He wore a black turtleneck, black slacks, and a blacker expression. "What happened to you," said George.

"Hit-and-run. I told you what was happening at the Rex."

"She's been out for a week," said Toby.

He frowned at her for a second. "Sorry," said George. "Truly."

"Now that the amenities are over," said Frieda. "What are we going to do?"

"I'll run the meeting, Frieda," said George, giving her a stony glance. "First, you weren't invited. Second, this is our problem, not yours."

"Fine, great. But what are we going to do? We should have blown that Triple M terminal straight to hell while we had the chance."

"We should have planned for it," said Dugan.

"Twenty-twenty hindsight is standard HRA vision," said John.

John sat down and shifted in his chair so he could watch everyone. John looked tired, exhausted. She hoped she didn't look that bad. Toby, John, Dugan. They'd all been through the ringer. She felt that pause again. That time it was an intimation of people wearing out. At some point in the future, none of the problems they quarreled about would matter. Toby would watch fish jump and pen Catskill legends. She would prune roses and grow involute dahlias. The conspiracies and schemes, the down-and-out homeless, the welfare recipients, would inhabit another world, a world of hope and hopeless, unsolvable problems and half-baked solutions.

"All right, we've kicked the horse," said George. The dark hollows under George's eyes looked larger. "I don't want to think of trying to cut millions of emergency checks manually. But that seems to be our only option."

The phone next to George's elbow rang. He picked it up. "This is George Kelso. What?" He propped his elbows on the table and listened for almost two minutes. Then he said, "All right." He put the phone back in its cradle. To them: "Our programmers and the Oracle programmers are looking at the connection between the Triple M and the current system. So far, they don't know how it works. Two different databases."

John said, "Last week's backup tape?"

George shook his head. "Somebody scrapped them. The most recent backup is three weeks ago. They don't know if they can mount it."

"It's never been tested?" said Frieda.

"Of course it's been tested," said George. "Three weeks is so out-of-date, it's useless. Even if we could mount it, it would take a week."

John looked at George, then Dugan. "Cutting checks by hand means thousands of hours of overtime, stressed workers, exceptional checking and rechecking."

"Use the Triple M to restore them," said Frieda, interrupting. "It that taketh away, can giveth back."

John looked at her, then Dugan. Toby brought out his pipe and popped it in his mouth.

George looked at Toby. "Didn't you say the cable was pulled?"

"Big deal," said Frieda. "That doesn't mean it's not live. I'll bet that asshole Rodriguez used it before he disappeared. Hook it back up. If it doesn't work, it doesn't work."

Dugan looked at John, then her. "Even if it was live, it would take forever."

"Rodriguez had a way of doing all cases at once," said Frieda. "He couldn't type in thousands of case numbers. He used ranges."

George put his head in his hands and ran them through the bristles on his head. Crisis meetings made everyone want to hide in a burrow. And George had more than that crisis to worry about. She was sure the feds would want to talk about Morty Bennet, and Morty was George's mistake. "We can't be sure that we're restoring only those that Rodriguez, or whomever, canceled."

"Of course it won't be absolutely the same," said Frieda. "But after we restore the system, we'll have time to figure out the Triple M. What I'll never understand is how Special Projects was able to do this for over a year."

Toby looked at her, then around the table. "That's another investigation. Back to business."

"Use the Triple M," said Frieda. "People first, accuracy later."

"John?" said George.

John stubbed out his cigarette, then looked at the butt. He glanced at Frieda. "Why not? We can weed out the real canceled cases later."

"Toby?" said George.

Toby spun his pipe in his thick fingers. "It's attractive, but it's not a job for Frieda, or whomever, and a rogue program. We're not cowboys anymore."

George looked around and shook his head. "I agree. Before we do anything, our programmers have to look at it. If they can't figure it out, we'll have to meet again."

Frieda looked at the dusty floor, then out the window. Light was fading; caramel-colored rays stepped across the floor and stopped behind John's chair. She tapped her fingers in the dust on the table making what looked like shots on a target. She supposed she was trying to calm herself. She came back to George. "We should have had a plan and didn't. It shouldn't have happened and did. We're not going to sit here and wait for labor relations and IM management to form a committee."

George's jaw hardened, his back straightened. He dismissed her with a wave of his hand. "We have no choice. We have to play by the rules we've made for ourselves. We've already broken a few when you used that Restore option."

It was hard to believe they were on the same side. And Toby had just sandbagged her. "So what's the plan?" said Frieda, angrily. "To form another committee, which forms another oversight committee, which decides to meet next month?"

"We have to do something soon, we know that," said George, seriously. "If our programmers can't come up with something better, we'll start sorting through the paper records Monday. We'll cut checks for active cases. It might take a few weeks."

Frieda stared at Toby, then George. "I don't see why I try."

Frieda got up, grabbed her bag, kicked her chair back, and stormed out of the room. If she'd stayed, she would have thrown a fit.

Frieda arrived back at the Rex at seven. Dusk had quickened to darkness. Noise from the Moat floated out onto Twenty-eighth Street. She picked out Brucie's voice. Lights burned inside the lobby. She walked slowly up the steps. Ivan was at the desk. She took the elevator to eight, her thoughts on the meeting, the canceled cases, and what would happen Monday.

She started to take off her clothes, but stopped and sat. Surely Bennet and Rodriguez knew what she and Toby and the committee knew. That was why they blew up the system. The question—a minor question considering what had happened and what Rudi had told her—was whether that meant that Lansky had given up on the Rex.

Part of her wanted to curl up for a week and let the fallout begin. The other part, the part that was growing tired of the whole mess but couldn't give up, told her it was time for Frieda the Bad Seed. She pulled out her cigarettes. She made a stiff G and T. She angled her chair so she could watch the Olympia. She saw figures moving.

She gazed at the Olympia, smoking and drinking. Then she called Borgan.

She was surprised he was home. "It's time," she said.

"Tell me," Borgan said.

She gave him the digest version of what had happened in the last two days. Borgan was skeptical until she told him Morty Bennet had resigned, Rodriguez disappeared. Borgan had done his research on Lansky and Bennet. He'd also interviewed Mario, a circumstance Mario had omitted telling her. Borgan had the police reports of the beatings of Mario, Blondie's murder, and her hit-and-run. He had her letter of last week. Borgan had already started the story and would add to what she'd told him. He could file it Monday.

She didn't tell him about the welfare Armageddon. He'd know soon enough, if they didn't do something. That is if *she* didn't do something. She propped her bag on her lap and dug through it. Finally, she came up with her keys to IM66. She called a cab. Then she locked her door, and walked through Sven's gallery. On the stairs to the roof, she picked up the flashlight she used at night and stuffed it in her bag. A few minutes later she breezed through the Rex lobby. The yellow cab screeched to a halt in front of her.

Half an hour later, she stood in front of IM66. Livingston Street was deserted, the Metro Tech development padlocked and quiet, the bodegas closed. IM66 was empty and dark. Her reflection in the glass of the door startled her. She shook off that shock, unlocked the front door, stopped, and listened. At first, it didn't sound like a real building. It was a mausoleum. Gradually she heard water gurgling in pipes, ticking clocks, the distant hum of a motor.

The door clicked shut behind her. Streetlight cast her shadow inside a shadow of mesh from the reinforced door. She walked to the stairs and switched on the flashlight.

She stopped on the second floor landing and listened. Creaks, the soft scurrying of rats; the hushed sounds of an aged building groaning under neglect and gravity. She walked carefully up to the third floor. She wasn't in good shape. Her hip ached. She limped across the big room, angling between the desks. She flicked off the flashlight and opened the door to the L & A office.

After a few seconds, she recognized the three desks on her left, her desk near the window, and Rodriguez's office door. She crossed to her desk, touched her "Tree of Life" stick, and glanced at her terrarium. Her terrarium had been turned over, the moss thrown across her desk; Venus flytraps lay on their sides, as if they were small, green fish.

Rodriguez must have done it after everyone left Friday. She steadied herself on the side of the desk for a moment, then walked slowly to the window and lowered the shade. She retraced her steps through the room, but veered left towards the Triple M terminal.

A tremor arced through her body. The terminal was plugged in and the cable hooked up. She sifted through the reasons why. Rodriguez could have been disturbed and left before he could unhook it. Why would he assume they would try to restore all the cases?

She flicked the flashlight on and balanced it on the side of the desk. It made a huge shadow of the terminal on the wall. Frieda held her breath and booted the terminal. The Triple M burst to life and flooded half the room with a bluish nuclear glow. It asked for her password. She rapped three times on the table and stuck in X'. It worked.

She entered the Search function. There was an option for a numerical sort. She used it and lines of case numbers starting with 000000101 stared at her. She brought up the Restore option and put in a range from 000000101 to 000000103 and pressed the ENTER key. The progress bar was so fast that she barely saw the blip on the screen.

She knew the program was fast. If Toby was right, all it did was reestablish a bunch of keys. The only thing she didn't know was whether the old system was up. She picked up the flashlight and hurried to John's desk, and flicked on the terminal. She let out a sigh, logged on, and plugged in 000000101. The case record of Moses Aberdeen blossomed on the screen.

Frieda felt a mischievous smile grow and stretch.

A few minutes later, she typed in a range of 100,000 case numbers. The progress bar took over a minute. After it vanished from the screen, she walked to John's desk and checked five numbers at random. They were back, all of them.

She found the last case number, 001431450. It represented almost a million and a half cases. There was no way to sift out the closed cases or the people who had died or the ones living in Tucson. At worst, a few might get an extra check. She typed in the case number after the last one she'd restored then the last case number. She hit the ENTER key.

That's when she heard a door close.

Frieda froze. She stopped breathing. She heard the tap tapping of footsteps. She fumbled for the flashlight and flicked it off. She hurried quickly to the door. She shut it leaving a two-inch crack. She watched the top of the stairs.

A shape appeared. It stopped at the top of the stairs and held itself rigidly. HRA had always been sloppy. That room should have been cordoned off, the Triple M terminal boxed and shipped to Computer Operations. There should have been guards at the door and the locks changed.

She should never have gotten in. Neither should have Rodriguez.

She recognized the square head and wide shoulders.

Rodriguez started across the floor.

Could he see the light from the terminal? For a second, a suspended second, Frieda didn't know what she was going to do. She had an impulse to run across the floor. She wasn't fast and her legs and hip hurt.

Rodriguez's figure grew bigger as he angled through the desks. There was no way to be subtle. She slammed the door shut. It sounded like an explosion in the empty building. She hoped she'd given the asshole a heart attack. She flipped the lock and raced back to the Triple M terminal. The status bar inched slowly towards the right.

The door shuddered.

The glow from the terminal spread through the room like an alluvial plain touching the three desks in front of her and her own. Frieda limped to her desk. Upended terrarium, pale dislocated fingers of Venus flytraps, postcard of Kafka, a spread of forms, cases stacked in her in-basket. She was so preoccupied with labeling and identifying that lunar landscape that she forgot why she was there. The Makonde "Tree of Life" sculpture with its intertwined faces and bodies was the only thing that looked vaguely like a weapon. She grabbed it.

The status bar inched right. A million cases, a million five.

The door splintered.

Frieda limped to the Triple M terminal. She put the fertility stick down and grabbed the iron-gray metal-framed chair. She watched the status bar, urging it on. It seemed stopped, as if it had run out of energy, then it filled in the last few millimeters and blinked off the screen.

The door splintered, the noise booming off the walls of the room. She grabbed the back of the chair with both hands, stepped back from the screen, then gritting her teeth, she lifted it as high as she could, and swung it at the terminal. The screen blinked, but it stayed on. "Fuck." She dropped the chair, felt her way around the terminal, propped her back against the wall, and kicked at the square shape. It hesitated then toppled from the table. When it crashed to the floor, she saw a flash of light, heard a sputtering. It lay there like a shot animal.

The door crashed behind her. She fumbled for the Makonde stick. Her fingers found it and she gripped it tightly. She backed slowly into the center of the room.

The door crashed open. The room lighted up with moonlight from the far windows in the big room. Rodriguez was a hulk in the doorway.

He rushed into the room, but stopped when he saw the terminal on the floor. His face twitched. She could see he was struggling with himself, as if he were trying to contain his rage. Frieda recognized that distorted face as the face in the car, the one that tracked her down, the one that tried to kill her. The barely imagined possibility that she and Rodriguez would fight to the death had become too real.

Frieda whirled around her desk. A thrill went through her as Rodriguez calmly walked towards her. They stood three feet apart.

She held the Makonde stick like the lance of a deadly insect. Before she could get out of range, Rodriguez reached across the desk and grabbed her blouse. She swung the stick and hit him on the arm, then wrenched away from him. She heard her blouse tear. She veered right and before she could put the desk between them, he was on her. He threw her to the ground on her sore hip.

"Fuck." She felt the pain, and then it went away. She saw his face, his leer. One hand grabbed her throat. She reached up and dug her fingernails in his face.

"Jesus, you bitch."

Rodriguez hit her hard. The room spun crazily. She couldn't pass out. It would be over. Leaving time.

Rodriguez ripped at her blouse, then pawed at her jeans. "This will be so much fun," he said, gasping. "Then I'll have to get rid of you."

She forced herself to stay awake. She felt her Makonde stick under her body. Rodriguez grabbed both sides of her jeans to rip them off. She kicked at him and missed. When he rocked her to his left, she rolled further and got a hand on her stick. She wrenched it loose.

Rodriguez was so intent that he didn't see what she was doing. She rammed it blindly upward towards his throat.

She heard a gurgle, then a strangled cry. Rodriguez sat down hard holding his throat. She rolled right. She got up, hitched up her jeans. Rodriguez' gagging filled the room. She grabbed her bag and turned towards the door, when she felt his hand close on her boot. She wrenched away then stumbled towards the splintered door. She limped through the doorway, then through the first row of desks. Go left, go right. Around that chair, around that desk. It was like skiing downhill. At the top of the stairs, she glanced over her shoulder. Rodriguez appeared in the doorway.

She hobbled down the stairs.

At the second floor landing, he was halfway between second and third floor. She saw the dim light coming from the front door and speeded up. Halfway down, she fell. She bounced on the steps, lost her bag, but caught herself on the railing, wrenching her arm.

Rodriguez was almost on her. She turned, ready to fight.

He stumbled over her bag, which had opened letting its contents of lipsticks, purse, Post-its, cigarettes, and matches spill over the stairs. Rodriguez caught at the railing and his feet splayed out in front of him. His thin mustache and white face bobbed up. She swung at that face with the Makonde stick and caught Rodriguez on his moustache. He shook his head, dazed. She used her last ounce of energy and brought the stick down on his crotch. She must have connected, because he screamed. He clutched at his pants. She swung a second time at his head and connected. Rodriguez leaned to his right, then rolled down the stairs and sprawled in the mesh shadows near the door.

Frieda limped back up to her bag. She stuffed handfuls of things inside. Then she stumbled down the last few stairs and edged around Rodriguez. She opened the door and glanced back at Rodriguez. It looked like he was out cold, but maybe not. Outside, she wedged the Makonde stick in the door and ran to the dwarf-like pay phone. She punched out 911, but hit a 2 on the last digit. She punched it out again and got it that time. She reported a break-in at IM66.

Then she shouldered her bag and limped into the cold Brooklyn night.

36

Kragen sat in his apartment. It was clear outside with fall sun throwing shadows through the oaks and sycamores and reflections off the small lake. It was dim and gloomy in the apartment. He'd told his doctor, Fred Palmer, that he'd been mugged. Palmer had set his broken nose and given him prescriptions for an anti-irritant for his sinuses and Tylenol with codeine for the pain. The Tylenol gave him a fierce headache, but took his mind off his knee and head and sinuses. Then he shuffled between his bed and the kitchen in the dark. For two days.

And for two days, he'd obsessed about Marcy Benaventura.

When he saw her he felt something was wrong. No, he *knew* something was wrong. None of his targets came right up to him knowing what would happen. Her sheer audacity threw him off. Even when he knew he had her, when she was inches away, his hand wound around her jacket, his hand raised, he hesitated. And she had seen it or known it subconsciously. He saw it in her eyes. In that split second before she'd sprayed him, they'd changed from a soft, arresting green to a fierce stabbing color. It made him flinch to think about it.

Kragen shook his head, as if to get rid of a bad dream. He stood up and limped slowly over to his desk. It was time to find out what was happening out there. He wasn't ready, but he couldn't hide forever. He pulled out his cordless phone and reattached the phone jack.

He pulled out his address book and flipped to the last page. He could barely make out the number in the half-light. He punched out the number.

"I'd like to talk to Michael Lansky."

"Who's calling?"

"Tell him it's Kragen."

A minute later, Lansky came on. "Kragen?"

"Yeah."

"What happened? I got this fucking letter. Jack is acting weird."

"Little problem. Don't worry."

"I do worry. The project is attracting too much attention. If we don't act soon, I'm going to lose it. I got things for you to do."

Kragen frowned. The frown made him wince. He felt his cracked tooth with a large forefinger. He'd met Lansky, but he always got his contracts from Dombry, then George, that is Jack Kuhl. He cleared his throat. "Back up. What letter? And how is Jack acting weird?"

"It was left two nights ago. Listed everything we've been doing at the Rex. They know about you—your name was in it—and they knew about my welfare contacts. It must have been the work of this Frieda. But what did they mean about you?"

"A little slip. Believe me, it was nothing."

"It's not nothing, if it screws up my getting the Rex."

"Believe me, it won't. Now what about Jack?"

"Cold feet maybe. Wants me to hold off."

"Fuck, *I* told him it was a good idea. You don't harass people, kill them, hit them with cars, thumb your nose at the police, and then say I've got to fucking forge on."

"Right, right, right. We won't do anything for a couple days, maybe a week. But I've got a developer with his checkbook out and I want this to end. Now."

Kragen frowned. He wondered where Lansky came from, what demons played inside his skull. It was, likely, growing up poor. There was never enough insulation. "Wait at least a week, or get somebody else. So what is so urgent?"

There was a sigh on the line. "I suppose a week isn't that long. I want you to follow Jack, find out what he does, who he talks to."

"I've got other things to do."

"Don't you have anyone who could do it? I'll pay."

Tony? He shook his head. "I'm breaking in a guy. But—"

"Use him. This is important. Give him my number. Have him call me, if he finds anything suspicious."

"I don't know if you really want to talk to Tony."

"That his name? Give him my number. I have a bad feeling about Jack."

Kragen shook his head. The money better be good. "Okay. What else?"

"Item number 2. It's time for something dramatic."

Dramatic. He'd met Lansky twice. Both times they seemed to be on the same wavelength. They were both—how did you say it—realists.

Pragmatists. You didn't stay on top if you played patty-cake with people in your way. But if you watched Lansky closely, if you watched his glittering black eyes, his restless pudgy fingers, you could see he liked it too. He liked sticking it to his competitors. He wanted people to know he was the one who screwed them. Kragen could appreciate that. And they had their little joke. Whenever things got dicey, Lansky said it was time for something dramatic.

Lansky sure wanted that building. He appreciated Lansky's ruthlessness. But the Rex. Too many people. There'd be an investigation. Arson. Of course, Lansky always got off.

He'd given Casey's name to Dombry. If Lansky wanted him to set it up, it was going to cost him. "You want me to call Casey?"

"Do I have to spell everything out?"

"It'll take time to set up."

Lansky laughed. "You must think I'm crazy," said Lansky. "Timing, timing." Lansky said to himself. Finally, he said, "Okay, wait a week, but no longer. I can buy the Rex and sell that corner the next day. You handle it, not Jack. Double your rate."

He liked that. "I get paid directly from you?"

"Yes."

"Send enough for Casey."

Lansky said, "I'll send a guard, probably Rod. Where?"

"I'll tell you how much, when, and where in a few days."

"Okay."

Kragen hung up. He had two phone calls to make. He felt like crawling back into bed, but didn't. He dialed Tony.

"Hey man. You all right? I tried callin'—"

"Don't worry about it. I want you to follow Jack, the guy we've been talking to."

"You mean George."

Jesus. "Yes, George."

"Asshole. He never fuckin' respected me. I could tell. But why?"

His throat felt like hot cinders. He'd inhaled enough pepper spray to give him emphysema. He coughed once, twice. His voice sounded like it'd been broken in two. "Because the big guy wants him followed." That should quiet Tony. Whenever he heard it was a big deal or the big man, he started wetting his pants.

311

"Fuck. Shit yes. Imagine, Mr. Big. I'll bet he's tough. Christ."

Mr. Big! Fuckin' Tony. What a low-life asshole.

"Now listen carefully. Just watch him. For god's sake, don't do anything."

"What if he like runs for it? Do I clip him?"

Kragen felt his nose with his fingertips. It was stuffed with cotton batting. And it still hurt. Where the fuck was Jack going to run? "I'll tell you more later. Just watch him for now and report tomorrow. If it seems important, call 893-5798 and ask for Michael."

"He the big guy?"

"One of them. And use your head for once."

Kragen hung up. He grimaced. If he had anyone else...

He tapped his fingers on the phone before picking it up.

Casey had worked on both the Cardiff and the Amsterdam. Those hotels were almost empty, when he torched them. The Rex was full of people. Kragen sat back and thought of the implications of torching the Rex. Too many people. Too soon.

Kragen shrugged. It wasn't his problem. He picked up his address book and flipped to the back. The one on the bottom was Casey. He dialed the number.

"Casey, Kragen."

Charles "Casey" Connors was raw-boned, red-haired, and Irish. Maghot had introduced them two years ago. Casey was a pro at his specialty, but was a stereotypic Irish drunk. Kragen didn't like that. You had to be careful.

Casey said, "How're you doin'?"

"Fine, fine. I want you to do something for me, a hotel. It'll take a few days to get the money. We'll meet somewhere in Midtown. I'll tell you where."

"This like the last two?"

"We'll talk about it in a few days." Kragen thought of his schedule. He wasn't born a beauty. But now. Black eyes, nose puffed up like a sausage, cracked tooth. "Make it Wednesday, five o'clock, O'Reilly's on Broadway and Seventy-second."

"See you there."

Kragen replaced the phone. He hadn't thought of when to do it. Lansky didn't care as long as it was soon. Casey would have to get in and out without anyone seeing him. From Jack's notes, talking to him, and tracking the movements of Mario, Marcy, and the others, he knew almost as much about the Rex as Jack did. Date? He was starting to see it. It would be on Saturday, September 21, midnight. He'd call Jack's goons early in the week and tell them to get out. They'd be out when it went off.

And he'd settle his score with Marcy Benaventura.

Twenty-first. Midnight. The solstice. Who said people didn't believe in ritual? Naked screaming virgins, a fire.

He was positive Marcy Benaventura wasn't a virgin.

As for the rest...

37

He finally talked to Kragen.

Kragen said, "What's up George."

George? As if everyone didn't know he was Jack. "I've been trying to get you."

There was a deep cough. It sounded like Kragen had marbles in his throat. "Right. I know. I've been in...*cough*...*cough*...communicado. Recovering."

"What happened? My agents got notes. I got a letter. Lansky—"

"Lansky. I know. I talked to him."

Jack blinked. Kragen talked to Lansky! "What's going on?"

Kragen croaked, "Talk to Lansky."

"I've called him a dozen times. He doesn't call back."

Kragen coughed, swallowed. "You're talking to the wrong person."

"But what happened to you? Was it that girl?"

There was a long, sinister silence. Finally Kragen said, "I had an accident. Gotta go."

Jack looked at the phone. What was that about? Don and his agents were in limbo. Kragen incommunicado—what the fuck did that mean? Control over the project, which he worried about slipping away in the last few weeks, seemed to have evaporated.

He tried Lansky again.

That time, he got him. Jack took a long breath and sat down. "Jack, Jack. How's my favorite hotel management consultant."

"What's going on, Michael?"

"Nothing Jack, nothing. I decided to take your advice. Let things sit. Right now, I'm negotiating with Brendel."

"That's great, Michael. Believe me, it's important for your protection."

"Exactly, Jack. I'll call you when I need you."

Lansky hung up. Jack looked at the phone. That was surreal. Lansky had never been nice and accommodating before.

Jack knew something was going on, but for the next few days, he had an edgy respite. It was like a tough final exam being called off. It was what he needed—a timeout. He quit scratching behind his ears. He took that as a good sign. He called Don and his agents each day and made sure they were behaving. He and Jeanie were still on the outs and at night he hit Tribeca bars trying to forget the letter, the notes to his agents, and the project.

Finally, he knew something was going on. He tried Lansky again. Whoever answered told him Lansky was out of town.

That day, he called Carismo's. He pleaded with Jeanie to see him. He needed someone to talk to besides drunken stockbrokers, traders, and tired secretaries. He missed Jeanie's touch. She listened to him; finally, she agreed to see him. Jack had an idea it might be their last chance. Last attack, last note, last try. Everything had *last* stamped on it in bright red colors.

At eight, Jack heard the door open. He looked and smiled, hopefully, at Jeanie.

Jeanie was wearing a short, blue dress, which showed off her muscular legs and pushed her breasts up. "Evening, Jack." She watched him for a second. "I really need a drink," she said. "Trying to make nice with bad customers. It takes it out of you. You want something?"

She was acting casual, as if she belonged there. Good. "A martini, please." He watched her slip into the kitchen. He felt an itch he hadn't felt for weeks.

"The project is hitting the skids," he said. It slipped out before he could edit it.

"Good!" said Jeanie. She started making noises in the kitchen.

"Good?" he said, angrily.

"Come on, Jack. I never liked what you were doing. It's not a secret."

"It's the only thing that keeps this going." His window arm gestured at the apartment.

Jeanie stopped making noises. Her reflection stared at the back of his head. "What's with the band-aids?"

Jack shook his head. "Nerves."

Jeanie's reflection nodded. "You look like you're wearing hearing aids. You don't look good, Jack. Don't wait until it's too late."

It was time to get out. He knew he couldn't. At that point and not for the first time, he saw Lansky was playing him. Jack Kuhl was in the middle. Jack was the organizer, the instigator, and the launcher of Kragen and Tony. "It's time to let everything sit, back off," Jack said, tiredly.

"But the guy that hired me wanted to up the pressure, then he backed off. It doesn't feel right."

He heard ice, pouring, and a few minutes later, Jeanie handed him his drink. The martini felt cold, and a shiver arced through his body. He sipped it and put the drink down on the glass table. Jeanie took a sip of her drink, rested on the arm of the sofa, and crossed her legs.

"You mean Lansky?" Jack stared at her. She shrugged. "It's not a secret. I heard you talking about this hotel, the Rex. There have been articles in the paper. A mugging, a murder. One article mentioned Lansky. It doesn't take a genius to put it together."

Jack laughed sardonically. "I tried so fucking hard to be anonymous."

"I don't think that's possible anymore." She laughed, her dimple tucking up, then falling back. He missed her laugh, her body. He even missed the irritation of mornings. "Those people who want to be left out, aren't. Those that want their names in lights live lives of quiet desperation."

Jack shook his head. He even missed that pessimistic undercurrent. It was better than listening to hypocrites like Greg brag about how brilliant they were. Jeanie was real, Greg not. Carismo's was real, the Rex project not. And where on that rubber continuum was he? "At least you're out of it. Anybody asks, you don't know a fucking thing."

"You want to talk about it, Jack."

Jack thought about that and decided no. "It's my hole. I'll figure it out."

"Think it out, Jack. That's what you do best. Just because he's pushing you, doesn't mean you have to do anything." Jeanie took a sip of her martini. The setting sun broke through the dead, gray day. It made Jeanie's body glow, almost as if he was looking at a film that was too bright.

Jack ran his hand through his hair. "I know."

"You okay, Jack?"

He shook his head. "No, I'm not okay." He looked at Jeanie. She was watching him closely. "Listen, I like you here. It makes me see things better. You always have."

Jeanie looked at him curiously. She put her drink on the table. She reached over, put her hand on his, and squeezed. "I still like you, Jack. It could be different."

"A few more days, then I'll try something else."

Jeanie shook her head, "We'll see. I'd better go."

Jack sighed. "You can't stay?"

Jeanie looked at him, tucked her dimple into a smile. "Okay, Jack."

Jeanie stayed. It was like a month ago. Then she left. Then she called and told him, she wouldn't come back as long as he worked on the Rex.

And it looked more and more as if he couldn't work on the Rex. The project was in ashes, Lansky playing some cat-and-mouse game. He'd quit scratching behind his ear, but since Jeanie left, he couldn't find the energy to shower or shave. He lived on coffee and vodka. The only place that made him feel half-sane was the roof deck. That day, stubble growing on his face, his leather jacket open, he sat on a deck chair on the roof. He propped his right leg on another chair. He moved his silver coffee mug in circles.

Dramatic. Big. Fire.

Across town at the Rex, the residents who were left were going about their business, possibly casting a hard glance at the agent on their floor, possibly wondering why his agents were ignoring them. Lansky, watching Frieda move through pallets and drooping dead sunflowers, gritted his teeth and plotted his next move.

Jack grimaced at the tinny sound of the phone. He punched the "Talk" button on the phone.

It was Lansky. "We have a crisis, Jack. I'd like to see you."

"What crisis?" Jack said, frowning.

"I can't talk about it on the phone," said Lansky, brusquely.

Jack shrugged. "All right. I'll come over."

Jack looked at the phone. It wasn't good. He didn't know what the crisis was, but he didn't like it, at all. But he had to go.

Half an hour later, Jack was in the Olympia service elevator. Incipient depression about the project was replaced, not for the first time, by claustrophobia.

Jack shrugged off that feeling. Besides the two guards in the lobby, Lansky's penthouse looked deserted. He couldn't see anyone on the deck. Rod looked at him suspiciously and told him to go out on the deck.

Jack hesitated. He felt Rod staring at him. Finally, stiffly, he walked

317

through the living room. The bar was closed, the liquor case locked. It was cool out there. The deck chairs were empty, the pool blue, quiet, and cold. Jack zipped up his leather jacket and sat at a table.

A few minutes later, Lansky walked out. He was dressed in a blue suit, black shiny shoes. He looked prosperous, secure, supported by a rock-solid inner vision of himself. "You don't look so good, Jack."

Jack shrugged. "It's been a rough couple days."

"I suppose so. Come here." Lansky motioned him over to the side, the side where they watched the Rex and schemed about old properties and new high-rises.

Jack shrugged, got up, and followed Lansky. He glanced down at the Rex for what was likely the last time. He saw people sitting at the white table. He recognized Bel and Mario. Mario's arm was in a cast. He hadn't seen Mario after Kragen nailed him. He felt a twinge of guilt.

"What's up?" Jack said, turning to Lansky. He realized he was tired of the whole mess. It was a bad idea to come up here. "Did you buy out Brendel?"

Lansky rested his elbows on the ledge. He watched the Rex for a few seconds, and then turned to Jack. Lansky's thinning greasy hair gleamed in the sun. Lansky exuded confidence; his manner was too friendly. "There's not a crisis, Jack. I wanted to clarify a few things."

"I'm game. What does 'clarify' mean?"

"I suppose you could call that a crisis," said Lansky, irritated. He gestured towards a New York Times on the nearest table.

Jack stepped towards the table and leaned over the paper. He scanned the headlines. One of the lead articles was "Landlord Uses Strong-arm Tactics." He read the first paragraph.

"That looks bad," Jack said, straightening up. The article seemed like the official notice of the project's demise. "Just what we wanted to avoid."

"My contacts in HRA are on the run."

"We shouldn't have used the program," said Jack, shaking his head. "It was the one thing I couldn't control." Even then it didn't add up to Blondie's death, Frieda's notes, or a score of details. Of course, moving one grain of sand could have moved a second and a third...

"It's not over," said Lansky, grinning.

For the first time, he knew it was over. "If it's over, it's over."

Lansky's rings flashed as he waved his hand in dismissal. "You see that's the problem with movies, stories. Everyone thinks that once the bad guy is vanquished and the wedding bells ring that it's over. It's never over, Jack."

At that moment, Jack realized how stupid Lansky was. Lansky knew brute force, intimidation. Jack Kuhl—George—was becoming a Lansky, had almost become a Lansky. "Your 'dramatic' option? That's insane. Didn't you read that article? The dumbest detective, the stupidest prosecutor could make a case against you in his or her sleep."

Lansky shook his head, as if he were a parent scolding a petulant child. "You see, Jack, that's why you'll always be a has-been."

It was over. He didn't have to play nice anymore. "You're insane."

Lansky frowned, motioned towards the other room. Lansky's guards hustled through the living room. Lansky put up his hand. "Stay there," Lansky said. "I just want to make a few things clear to my good friend Jack Kuhl." Lansky smiled devilishly. "That brings us to that word, 'clarify.'" Lansky's gaze held him. "I've made a dossier of your activities. Of your meetings with ex-cons, of your conspiracy to harass and assault residents of the Rex."

Jack saw it was bad. He juggled the implications behind Lansky's words. "So?"

"Now, I'm not going to do anything with this dossier, but if you should try to stop me or make any trouble, it is going to friends of mine. I have friends on the police force and I have Kragen. Sometimes it takes Kragen a long time to kill someone. You understand, Jack."

Jack shuddered. He didn't know what to say. "Anyone can make up a dossier."

Lansky chortled. "But you don't have the guns, Jack. You don't have the guns. If I turn over this file to the police, you'll certainly go to jail. If you accuse me, my lawyers will certainly get me off. By the way, I'll give you a week to pack up, but you can't live in that condo anymore. You're going to be on your own in the New York housing wars."

"You may be forgetting a few things."

Fake puzzlement spread over Lansky's face. "What would they be?"

"Anything dramatic. Attempted arson could put your roly-poly body upstate for some time."

Lansky sneered, then laughed. "With my file, any confession on your part would be scoffed at. You would have a second strike and sent upstate. You're not the only one who is well organized and clever. I'm

319

afraid there's not much help for you, Jack."

He'd lost. He knew he couldn't trust Lansky. But then there was the money, the common goal, sharing a bottle of Chateau Neuf de Pape. He'd been seduced, again, by the money, by his vision of Jack Kuhl on top.

Jack felt used, tired, and beat.

Lansky motioned with his hand. Lansky's bodyguards appeared behind him.

"Bye Jack."

He hesitated a second, then turned and walked towards the elevators. Lansky's guards hemmed him in. When he got to the elevator, Rod whirled him around and hit him in the stomach doubling him up. He saw the punch coming from the other guard, but he turned too late. His face exploded with pain. He fell into the elevator.

Rod reached in and pressed the button for the basement. "Just a sample, Jack. Do anything, it will be a lot worse."

The doors swished shut. Jack struggled to get up. His stomach felt like lead; he was dizzy. He slumped against the side of elevator.

By the time the elevator stopped in the garage, he'd straightened his clothes. He wasn't bleeding, but he felt like he'd been in a car wreck. Two women in tennis shorts stared at him as he limped out of the Olympia. Outside, he stared at the Rex. It was only a fucking building, but at that moment he felt the Rex had defeated him, not Lansky. He wondered whether the Rex could take on a fire.

Jack got a cab. The ride to Duane Park was too long. He felt small and shriveled. He stumbled into the apartment. He made up a compress for his face and collapsed on the sofa. The dirty crease of New Jersey barely relieved the unrelenting darkness.

The phone rang. He looked at it, wondering. Finally, he picked it up.

It was Jeanie. "I got a call at Carismo's. Someone told me you wouldn't live there anymore and not to come back," Jeanie said. "He didn't sound like a nice man."

"Shit. Listen—"

"I told you something like this would happen. I don't care how you explain it." Jeanie sounded less angry, more sorrowful. "I'm thinking of getting a bigger place. You could stay there."

Jeanie was still there. It was the only thing left. "I need a few days to think. I'll call you."

"This is not a time to get hurt."

"I don't intend to, but I have to think."

Jack hung up and looked at the phone, then around the apartment.

That day rivaled the last day of his sentencing. KAM was dead, the divorce final, his money, property, cars, and checking accounts gone. The parallel, the continuity, crept like a phantom into his brain. Two downfalls, two spirals. Jack Kuhl and his own personal boom-and-bust cycle. He would ascend, reach for more, graze the ring, then he would slip, his hand fall, the merry-go-round recede into the carnival.

38

Three taxis sped by Frieda Berg before one stopped. She must have looked like she'd risen from the grave. Her blouse was torn, she had a new bruise on her arm, and her fingers were sticky with blood. She couldn't tell whether it was hers or Rodriguez'. Through the open window, the driver asked her if she had any money. She dug through her bag, hoping she'd picked up her purse on the stairs. Before she could find it, the driver told her to get in.

She eased herself into the back seat and rested a second before digging deeper into her bag. She found her purse, but no money. A lipstick, Post Its, protein bars, matches. While she dug, she felt calm, as if that banal activity grounded her and let her forget what happened. She found two wadded-up twenties. She unfolded them and displayed the two twenties, as if she'd found a gold nugget. As the cab pulled away, the first police cars, sirens on, sped past them.

"That wasn't you, was it?" said the cab driver.

"I just fell down. Amblyopia," Frieda said.

"I thought that was wandering eye."

"Same thing. You can't see to walk. Bellevue, please."

She was acting brave, but once the staunch girders of the Brooklyn Bridge flipped by and Manhattan hovered on the horizon, her spirit puddled. The empty office, the smoking terminal, Rodriguez, the hate in his eye, tearing at her. She shook her head, grimly.

"You got a cigarette," she said.

"It's a no smoking cab."

"I won't tell," said Frieda.

The cabby—tall and lanky, with large, splayed hands—shrugged, reached into the glove compartment, and took out two cigarettes. He steered with one hand, lit both of them noir style, and then handed one to her.

She reached for the cigarette, took a drag. "You may have saved my life tonight."

"I'm looking for a big tip outta this, lady."

When they got to Bellevue, she asked him to help her to the emergency room, which he did. They stared at each other. He was a mensch, a gangly mensch. She couldn't help it; she embraced him and cried.

After a second, she backed up, then found the two twenties and gave it to him.

"Too much," he said.

"Not enough," she said. "Take it and thanks."

He looked suspicious, as if he'd been tricked in a new reality show. But then he shrugged and took the twenties. Frieda watched him leave. There were the big deals, the megawatt money, fancy schmancy limousines, the Lanskys. But the human touch made the difference.

Bellevue hadn't changed much since her last visit. She waited hours before someone looked at her. She looked so beat up that they admitted her. Nothing was broken and after everyone scurried out she was left in a room with an AIDS patient. She almost called Toby, but instead she stared at the ceiling. She felt soothed by its barrenness, its coolness. She felt protected for a brief while from out there and neuroses, psychoses, greed, and deadly location struggles.

Early the next day, she signed herself out. She called the dispatcher and asked for Ric. She waited at the Bellevue entrance until Ric picked her up half-an-hour later. When his cab pulled up, he stared at her. She told him she'd talk later, that her mouth hurt, which was true. A few minutes later, they were at the Rex. There were no police in the lobby, although she half-expected them. Rodriguez could have told them anything; that she had broken in, that *she* was trying to damage the system. She had powerful friends on her side, but, obviously, Rodriguez did too.

No police. Ivan, the desk clerk, looked up and opened his mouth. She just shook her head and kept going. The eighth floor was calm, her door reassuring. She dropped her bag on the bed, took off her clothes, put on her robe, and took a shower. Freshly scrubbed, she put on her pink slip, knee-hugging socks with individual toes patterned after piano keys, cinched her burgundy terry-cloth robe, and settled in her chair.

She called Toby.

"Where have you been," said Toby. She could tell he was tired.

"I've been beaten black-and-blue, almost raped, but I'm still here," said Frieda, stolidly. "It hasn't hit me yet. When it does, I'll need a team of therapists to piece me back together."

"What happened?" His voice sounded harried.

323

"Frieda the Bad Seed paid a visit. I restored all the cancelled cases. Go ahead, fire me."

"Just tell me what happened."

She gave him the short version of what happened, of another night in Bellevue. As she talked she realized how close she'd come to getting raped or dying. Why did she do it? Was she ever going to grow up?

"So that's what happened," said Toby. "George told me the cases were restored."

While she listened to Toby, she began to feel suffocated. She got up, opened the door, and left it open. As she turned, she glanced out the window. It was a beautiful, sunny day. Sunday. She hadn't noticed in the ride from Bellevue or walking up the steps of the Rex.

A slip of breeze from the window ruffled her hair. "Could you find out about Rodriguez?"

"I'll call the police, when we hang up."

"What will they do to me?"

Toby was silent, as if he were sifting the right words. "I don't know. John and Dugan are on your side of course. George might try to fire you, but he has more to think about than getting at you. And, although it was reckless and illegal, I won't hold out for a public lynching."

"Wow, thanks. When I think about it, I might have done George a favor." She rummaged in her bag and plucked out her rose-tinted glasses. The fracas with Rodriguez had bent the frames. She dropped them back in the bag and walked to the window. On the street, people bought Sunday papers, lit cigarettes, and waited at lights. She broke the silence. "If you're not going to fire me, I quit."

There was a long pause. Frieda could feel Toby cogitating over the wires, feel his hesitation, feel his stringing out what that meant for him. "Before me?"

"It's been creeping up on me. I pause, I wonder what it's been about."

"Take a few days off and come in. We'll work something out."

"I'll think about it today, but it won't do any good."

Monday, she went in. Toby had checked about Rodriguez. The police arrested him and charged him with a shopping list of crimes including fraud, break-and-entering, and destruction of property. She was surprised her name hadn't appeared in any deposition. She sure wasn't going offer it. Lansky and Bennet and Rodriguez wouldn't use the Triple M again. And from what she saw at the Rex, the invasion had stopped. Stopping Rodriguez helped but events over which she had little control tipped the scales. Blondie's murder. Marcy's foolhardy attack on Kragen. The notes. The other side had called a unilateral cease-fire. The irritating acts of sabotage stopped; fingers dialed the radio and TV volume knobs down; the daily notes that "your next" or "it could happen to you" stopped. Peace settled over the Rex.

Of course, she knew Lansky wouldn't give up.

She dressed in jeans, an op art blouse of Escher black-and-white birds dovetailing into each other, burgundy high-top boots, matching bag, and burgundy coat with belt. When she looked in the mirror and saw her shimmering reflection, she looked better than she expected. Her bruises were fading and were disguised by a new pair of sunglasses. She'd retired the rose-tinted ones. She'd strung out that cliché long enough. Her scar was fading too.

She walked to CO down Park Avenue, through Madison Square Park, and through Union Square. That walk was epochal. She was leaving the department. It wasn't the bureaucracy, the committees, but the last gasp of her own tired idealism. She kept hitting her head against injustice, when she should have been thinking more of herself, of what she wanted for Frieda. Welfare, the department, had become a way of dodging life.

CO looked as busy as ever. She stood in line and noticed, as she must have noticed before, the patchwork attire of the standees. The department attracted people who wanted an oasis, people unsure of the strife of the business world, people who were smart, afraid, ambivalent, and wore the wrong clothes. She got her latte at the Lego Café and as the slim young man with the dorky hat was making it, she began to feel that she wouldn't go into the Lego Café again.

"Sorry," she said. He glanced at her, inquisitively. "Could you make it a double."

"No problem, lady. Say, haven't I seen you on TV?"

"What, a horror show?"

"An old movie, a western."

She smiled, paid, and dropped a healthy tip into his tip jar. "Compliments will get you everywhere, but I'm not that old."

She capped her latte and went into the lobby. The lobby, a place she knew well—a soaring marble space with Art Deco capitals and chevrons in gold leaf, metal-and-glass mail drops, and crowds—felt foreign that day, as if it were part of a dream. The intense activity, the running, the crescendo of voices, the sheltered people who acted as if the world hung on what they would say or who they would say it to. She could add the results of all those voices and find a zero sum. It was phatic speech, recognition without content, an elaborate social exercise.

In IM Investigations, she threw her bag on the desk of the phantom Frieda and walked over to stand with Toby at the window. They watched Eighth Avenue. She followed the street towards the Village. Whenever she looked out that window, she extrapolated into the night, the Cave, and a wanton Frieda ten years younger. She rested her head on Toby's shoulder. He was surprised; then he put his arm around her. They stood like that for a few more seconds, before looking at each other. She saw resignation in his eyes; it was a hopeless quality they both knew would go away.

She walked slowly to her desk, picked up her bag, and dropped it in front of Toby's desk. Toby settled in and she did too. It was going to be one of their last acts. She felt sad, then amused. She knew the next few weeks were going to be like that.

"You're beating me to the punch," he said.

It looked as if Toby Minus had come to his own accommodation with her leaving. She wondered what he'd do. They'd propped each other up for the last few years. "If you don't resign in the next few minutes."

"I think about resigning, but of course I always do." Toby leaned back in his chair and bit on pipe. She lit her cigarette and blew the smoke away. Behind her, cubicles were entered and exited. Shoptalk reached her about forms, clients, and new regulations. "George wanted to fire you, but John talked to him. We said it might be best considering your flair for publicity, to concentrate on the mess with the Triple M and the feds. He came around."

"Thank you, Tobius Minus. I appreciate it. I didn't expect anything from George, although I did get him out of a bind. We both know I didn't do it for him or the department."

"Don't be so testy," said Minus. "We're working it out."

They were in their old roles, one last time. It made her feel better. "What does that mean?"

"We find you an office. You twiddle your thumbs for a couple years, do something like quality control, and retire with a bigger pension."

The din behind her acted as an ironic accent. Over Toby's shoulder, she saw a cloud pass slowly by. For some reason she glanced down at her blouse. What was true: the white birds on black, or the black birds on white? Escher was about Janus, the god of entrances, of going in and coming out, of arriving and leaving.

She laughed out loud.

"I guess that's not an option," said Toby. Toby looked over his rat's nest of a desk. "Buried somewhere in here are the forms that sum up your HRA life. Start date, raises, disciplinary hearings, reprimands, grade."

"Everything but who I am, what I cared about."

Toby waved at the mess. "I'll find it later."

"How much would I get?"

Toby shrugged. "Almost $3000 a month."

"More than I thought."

"I want you to think about it," Toby said, seriously.

"I won't think about it long."

She didn't remember much of what they talked about after that, nor the cab ride back to the Rex. That cab ride started near Fourteenth Street, and she could see the CO building out of the corner of her eye, then in the rear-view mirror. Frieda was leaving, embarking on a cab ride to a new life. It would be less interesting, if she knew where she was going.

She gave Toby the benefit of the doubt and thought it over. She spent that night in the Cave watching Lenny. She hadn't been able to talk to Lenny for years. The drink glued to his hand, his big brain, which housed dislocated memories, and a quirky panache. If she stayed in the department, she would become Lenny. One day she'd throw up her hands and stay drunk for the duration.

She sipped her drink and watched the shoes in the street-level window. Some hurried, some didn't. Others were tentative. She was mesmerized. She almost didn't see Terry come in. He tried to talk to her, but she demurred. Later, when she was about to leave, she declined his invitation to his "loft." She told him he'd entered the league of ex-lovers.

Take a card, your turn may come again.

Tuesday, she called Toby and told him yes. The amazingly complex severance forms from the department and the union pension fund started arriving a few days later. It was a big step. It made her pause not a few times to wonder exactly what she was doing.

Soon, she would be out. Either life was ahead of her, or it was over.

39

The water was black, putrid. Garbage bobbed on the surface. Hidden things made swirls in dark water. A vee cut towards her. Straight at her. The vee got bigger, huge. Open mouth, teeth. A long tooth protruded. It touched her on the cheek like a butterfly kiss.

Marcy kept her eyes shut. She remembered.

She opened her eyes and got out of bed, trembling. She left the blind down. No reason to see the Olympia. No reason at all.

Note. Notes. Frieda. They were going to take back the Rex. She had no idea whether it would do any good. She had to find out about Fishface—Kragen.

She knew he'd be arrested, tried, sent away. She knew it.

But she wasn't sure.

When she didn't find anything in the paper, she had Frieda try.

Frieda said she called friends in the police, the reporter Borgan, and a few people in the department. They reported absolutely nothing. No arrests. No bodies lying around the West Village near the West Side Highway. Nada.

There was a chance, possibly a good chance, Kragen had died or had gone away. If he hadn't, she knew he'd come after her. Would be after her. Wouldn't stop until he found her and then...

She had the nightmare every night. Same water, same nameless swirls, same sharp vee in the water, same jagged tooth. Sometimes she saw blood. She knew it was hers.

After staying in for two days, she decided she had to go to work. She went Friday and Saturday. Yes, she was paranoid. No, she wasn't going stay in her room like a hermit. Sunday, she stayed in the Rex, talked to Bel, went to the roof, and drove herself crazy until Mario called and said that Frieda had just come out of the hospital—again.

What was that about?

She hiked up to Frieda's room. Frieda—haggard, bruised—sat back in her chair, shook her head, as if she were trying to shake off a curse, and told her of a welfare Armageddon averted. Marcy held her breath while Frieda told of her night in a dead welfare center, IM66, the Triple M, and Rodri-

329

guez. It sounded scarier than being face to face with her nightmare.

"It's almost as if we're in a contest to see who dies first," Marcy said.

Frieda rapped three times on her shimmering blue glass table. "You know, I don't believe in luck or superstition, but I find myself doing the same things my aunts did. Rapping on tables, throwing salt over the shoulder. Demons and devils, imps and spirits. Life would be so much easier if they did exist. What about you?"

Frieda's rooms were packed, the opposite of her own. Tons of books in three languages, embroidered bags, shoes with Arabic tracery, blue glass tables, fantasy Art Nouveau mirrors. Frieda was like an exotic flower. Much more resilient than one, of course. "No Kragen. Nada. Nothing. Zero. How long will I have to wait?"

"If we knew that..."

"I'm just talking. Talking makes it sound reasonable as if I'm waiting to hear about a job interview or medical exam."

"Kragen may be a pseudonym or an alias. No one knows who he is. The one good thing to come out of this is that the counterattack is working. I'm all right and so are you." Frieda lit a cigarette. "With these new revelations and this exposé, maybe Lansky gave up."

"Ha."

"We're trading pessimisms. But I think you're right. I don't think it will be over until Lansky gives up his ownership of the Rex."

Marcy scowled. "We can't force him to do that."

"That doesn't mean there's not a way."

She left Frieda to ponder that and drifted down to her room thinking about what Frieda had done, how intrepid *she* was.

Late Sunday, she spent an hour talking to Butch. That made her feel better, but she wanted to be with him, not babble on the phone. After she hung up, Bel called. She wanted to see her.

She shrugged, put on a warmer sweatshirt, and walked up to six. She stopped in front of Bel's room. She heard the radio, the rasp of a blind, Bel's voice, the click of a phone. She looked at the weathered door, the stained number 604, the sliver of gap between frame and door.

She rapped. Bel cracked the door open; she saw who it was and waved her in.

The room looked clean, almost picked up, the ashtray emptied. Bel's clothes, usually in heaps, had by unseen hands, been washed, dried, and hung. The photos, the rogue's gallery of another era of the Benaventu-ras, were gone. So was Ray's self-portrait. Bel walked to the window and stared out. Brenda and Bel had met several times. Marcy thought it was because of Brenda's divorce from Bill, her philandering husband. She wondered if there was more.

Bel turned to her. "How are you holding up?"

"Going bonkers. Worried about Kragen."

"I don't know why, or how, you did it. Just working out the Benaventura curse, I suppose. You want a soda?" said Bel, turning towards her. Her eyes were dark and hesitant, as if she'd crawled out of a car crash.

"Naw. Too much sugar and caffeine." Marcy leaned against the door-frame. She saw a microcosm from that perspective. Bel framed against the window, the Olympia rising out of her shoulder. "You seem different."

"You want the gossip?"

"Sure," Marcy said. There were the days Bel and Ray hid their early afternoon drinks, the tension with Bel when Ray showed Marcy how to paint, Ray's last days when Bel sent her away. There would always be an edgy distance between them.

"It won't be a mystery long," said Bel. "Brenda has a cottage, a house really, on Long Island, in Montauk. She's going to let me stay there."

"What will you do there?"

"Brenda knows people in real estate. I could get a license."

They'd just fought a war against a slumlord and Bel was going into real estate. Marcy shrugged inwardly and imagined, briefly, Bel and Lan-sky at a real estate convention talking over strategies for taking over parts of the city, Long Island, wherever. "What about Mario?"

Bel shook her head, grimaced, and looked away. "He doesn't want to live out there and, especially, he doesn't want to change. This might be a break for me, to clean up my act. Mario wants to stay the same."

Bel and Mario were like knives and forks, eggs and bacon. She couldn't imagine seeing one without the other. But she'd never imagined them together in the first place. At least Mario was staying. "That's too bad."

"Listen, you could hide out there for a month or two," said Bel.

"It would make it easier for him."

"I knew you'd say that. But I had to ask."

She'd tried to crack Bel's masks. There was the harried wife, the stut-tering of concern for her daughter, a rare glimpse of feeling. A tiny crack opened, and then was soldered shut. She'd heard alcoholics were like that, closed, angry, and erratic. She'd thought it of Bel before, and then forgot. "I'll visit," said Marcy. "Eat seafood and walk on the beach."

"Anytime. I mean it."

"When are you leaving?"

"A week from tomorrow."

Marcy realized she couldn't move without feeling awkward. She ground herself deeper into the door frame. She wasn't sure what to do with her hands. "If you need any help."

"I'll ask."

Marcy pushed herself away from the frame and turned to leave. She paused for a second in the open door. She was going to say something, but forgot what it was. She closed the door.

She pushed through the fire doors and walked slowly down to four. She felt the same when she found Butch with Randy. She'd felt it with Bel and Ray. Her placeholders shifted, evaporated, and then edged back, as if their flakiness was a big joke. *Big fucking joke.*

She had made another memory, another incident, and another piece of her own personal waste. Maybe that was what life was about. The dark spots on the canvas got larger until it reversed. Out of the darkest despair, the enfolding ugliness, white dabs of hope rise in the background.

Marcy sat down in her room and regarded the Giltmore. What was going to happen to her? What would Kragen do? What, what, what?

The days started running together. She worked, talked to Butch, talked to Frieda, helped Bel pack, commiserated with Mario. Despite all that attention, she felt trapped. Wednesday night, she felt like going out to spite herself. Instead, she went to the washroom in the basement. She was out of clean clothes. There was no way she was going to the laundromat on Third Avenue.

The washer was finicky, but she got all of her clothes washed in one load. The dryer was next. She remembered it didn't like to start no matter how large the bribe. And it didn't.

"Fucker." She braced herself on the pipe a foot over her head and kicked the rusty coin mechanism with a sharp jab of her old tennis shoe. The dryer clicked, its tired motor groaned, then her clothes heaved from the left and fell right.

Marcy dropped into a chrome chair with torn white plastic cushions, which clung to her bare legs. From where she sat, she saw, out the open laundry room door, most of the basement. It was a Stygian cave of broken furniture, boilers, shadows, and tangle of rusty pipes. She hated the basement, but that day the basement felt safe, like a burrow deep in the earth.

She brought her sketch pad with her, although she wasn't in the mood. She opened it to the last sketch. The sketch had started huge and formless, grew a huge cock which she'd erected then drooped, then skewed, then dragged through the erasures. All which made the bearer of the mighty member look like a cross between Butch and the knobby-kneed Rodin she'd seen years ago at the Brooklyn Museum. It looked like Porno the Frog.

She regarded the figure, ripped off the sheet, balled up all those tumescent possibilities and bounced it off the wall near the washer into a wastebasket of Tide boxes, socks, and lint.

Marcy hitched her legs up on the chair and propped her sketch pad on them. She couldn't think of a thing to draw. She heard grumbling from the elevator housing. Bare light bulbs made conical oases through the basement and highlighted Frieda's bags of peat and dirt, pipes, chairs, and a broken refrigerator. Ben's door, on the edge of one of those cones of light, cracked open. When an eye wedged itself in the gap, her heart beat wildly. That eye, that face.

Kragen!

A few seconds later, she relaxed as Ben emerged, a grizzled head stuck on a gray overcoat.

"God damn cold. Why is it so cold down here? Do you think they'd turn up the heat? Fuck, I know better. What are you doing? The wash, I'll bet." Ben scratched his head, almost disappeared in a shadow, and reemerged in the open door.

"Sit down, Ben. I'll talk to anyone, even you."

Ben dropped in the other plastic white chair and splayed out his long legs. "It's easy for you to say. Talk, talk—who needs it? Truth is death. Fucker, Celine. He knew and—what the fuck was his name, the one they put in the psycho ward? Pound, that's right. Hee, hee, hee. Those faces in the Metro, I remember now. Like they were strung along these pipes like petals—fucker knew how to write!"

She wondered if any of the goons had threatened Ben, and decided she didn't know. People were afraid of Ben because he was crazy or alien or both. But at that moment, he didn't seem either. He was just very different. "Push your head out, Ben. Let me draw you."

"I can't stop you; but I don't like it." Ben started to get up.

She leaned over and stared in Ben's gray, stubborn eyes. "I'll make you famous, like a movie star."

Ben made a noise that was half-croak, half-quake, and sat. "Famous? Make me immortal!"

"That's twice as hard." She picked up her charcoal, poised her hand over the blank paper, and started the sketch, thinking it would be easy, except it wasn't because Ben stuffed his head inside his coat. She put down her charcoal. "What do you think about this stuff?"

Ben withdrew deeper into his gray overcoat so only the bristles of his gray head showed and his voice came from the second button under the collar. "Immortality? The Christians made everybody want to die, for Christ's sake." Ben's head stretched out of his gray overcoat like an ancient turtle. "Hee, hee…die for Christ's sake, for Christ's sake. Hee, hee. What the fuck good is it living here, when the real stuff is up there." Ben's knobby finger struck upwards towards a pipe covered with decaying insulation.

"Fuck, no. I meant the goons, the invaders, the false residents, like Truck and Don. The invasion of the Rex. You have to know that."

Ben looked at her strangely. "You tell me: What difference does it make to stay or leave?"

"It's comfortable here, secure. People like it. *You're* here."

Ben shrugged. "TV, diversions. It's all lies, don't you see."

Ben seemed to think about what he'd said. Marcy picked up her charcoal and made another stab at drawing him. When she looked up, his head had disappeared. "Fuck." She regarded the top of Ben's head. "Okay Ben, come clean. Why are you the way you are?"

Ben looked at her quickly and shook his head. "I don't answer questions like that. Whence, whither. Can't answer them. Say why are you down here?"

Marcy sighed. "If you knew anything, you'd know that I fucked up a thug who looked like a fish. I thought he'd be arrested, but he hasn't been. I've been living a life of borderline panic."

Ben looked puzzled. "*You* fucked him up?"

"He beat up Mario and killed this guy Blondie. I guess I went a little crazy." The words soothed her, as if they trapped Kragen in some verbal, untraceable universe.

Ben chuckled. "I guess I'm not the only one."

"If you know you're crazy, you're not. We call that Catch-22."

Ben laughed out loud. "*We?* You don't seem panicked."

"I'm terrified, but I can't quit living, can I?"

Ben laughed his little laugh, then his "hee, hee, hee." It wasn't a bad laugh, just weird. "That was an interesting thing to do."

"Crazy, you mean."

"You know a lot more now, than you did."

"I'm not sure what."

"Limits," said Ben. "Who is this man?"

"I think his name is Kragen. He looks like a kangaroo with piranha head."

"And you went after him," said Ben, shaking his head. "I think I know him. He's lonely, isolated, violent, expert at what he does, thinks he's a god, immortal. There it is again. Can't help thinking about it. Well, if you need help, just yell." Ben got up and seemed to sniff the air as if he were an animal on a scent. Then he slipped out the door past the elevator housing and into the darkness. A few seconds later he reappeared in the oasis near the wooden stairs and climbed up, shaking his head back and forth, as if he were entering the world of the surface, a world he detested, but was required by a secret pact to enter every day.

Marcy looked at the maze of pipes, listened to the wheezing of the dryer, then the grinding of the elevator. She let her sketch pad slide to the floor hypnotized briefly by the thump of the dryer and clothes rotating and falling.

Kragen took his third hot shower that day. Hot water helped him with the pain, the steam with breathing. He turned off the water, stepped out, toweled off, and stood in front of the bathroom mirror. He scraped a large swatch of steam off the mirror with his hand. Through the smear he saw a monster, then his familiar face. His body was a triangle. His heavy limbs tapered to the point of his iron-gray widows peak. The small head had always bothered him; the large teeth made it worse. He'd rationalized this part and that, tried to see what people called good features. But *that* image had bothered him for days. He saw his finger reach up and touch his face. Bruised, swollen face, yellow bags under his eyes. His nose had a crick in it.

Marcy Benaventura.

Abruptly, he turned away from that image. He put on his black robe. He walked down the hallway to the front room, stopping briefly to look at his favorite painting, the woman in the room. He supposed he liked it because it symbolized how he felt about many things; but that day, he turned away from it and limped down the hallway.

Kragen stopped at the liquor cabinet. That day, he took out another favorite unblended scotch, Glenfiddich, poured three ounces in the small mug, and then poured a small glass of water. He walked over to his desk, then around it so he could see the park. There wasn't much to see at that time of day. The streetlights cast a shifting white barrier on the oaks and sycamores; the small pond was black; the trails were empty.

Kragen sat at the desk, pulled out his cordless phone, and punched out Tony's number.

"This is Tony. It's your dime, but my—"

"Cut the crap. This is Kragen."

"My main man. What's up, big boy?"

Kragen cringed. "Are you following Jack?"

"Sure I am. For four fucking days. It's boring. He's boring. I can see the condo from this little park. Most of the time he's on the roof staring into space like a zombie."

Kragen passed the phone to his right hand. "Listen, I don't want you calling Lansky all the time. This is a security issue."

Precisely an hour after he'd talked to Lansky, Tony called to tell him that he and the big man had gotten along like brothers.

"Hey man, we get along. I've got it covered."

Kragen sighed. "Don't call him, period. And don't let him tell you what to do about Jack. This has to be handled right."

"But Michael said I could call him."

Now it was "Michael." Fuck me, thought Kragen. "Listen, this is a secret assignment. You can talk to Michael later. We'll have drinks together and play golf."

"Cool. Fuck, I don't have any clubs."

Kragen shook his head. "I'll fucking buy you some. Just do what I told you."

Tony hadn't followed orders before and he guessed he wouldn't then. But his hands were tied. He had other things to worry about. His only solace was that as soon as the Rex was a pyre, he'd either cut Tony loose or kill him.

Next, he punched out the number of the Rex. He got a Russian. He'd gotten them before. It took an act of God to get them to understand anything. "Don in 502."

Don probably had a phone, but every room had a buzzer for the phone in the hall.

He waited a full minute, before Don picked up. "Hey, who is this?"

"It's a friend. I've got something to tell you."

"Oh yeah, well listen, I'm right in the middle of—"

Bunch of wise guys. "Cut the crap. This is Kragen."

"Oh, sorry Mr. Kragen. I didn't—"

"Just listen. Something is going to happen in the Rex Saturday night. Tell the boys to pack up and get out. And don't all of you leave at once."

"Shit. You—"

"I'm not here to argue, or discuss it. And you're not getting another wake-up call."

Kragen hung up. He didn't give a shit about Lansky's goons, but if any of them got hurt and were still alive, they might start talking. The best thing was to get them out. And he didn't want them scrambling over each other Saturday night.

Kragen tried to think of anything he'd forgotten. He stared out at the blackness of the park. He'd been busy that week. Despite looking like Leatherface's ugly brother, he'd met Rod, Lansky's guard. Rod seemed okay, but he made the meeting short and made sure, afterwards, that Rod didn't follow him. Fifty thousand bucks. It was a lot more than he expected. Fifteen for Casey, five for Tony, thirty for himself for meeting Casey and making sure Tony stayed on Jack, and generally making sure Lansky got the Rex. Oh Jack, poor Jack.

The next day, he talked to Casey and gave him the money. Last evening, Casey had slipped into the Rex and planted a firebomb in the basement.

Yes, everything was ready for Saturday night. But he wasn't happy. He obsessed about Marcy Benaventura. She was a fucking kid, a girl. And she got him. He still didn't understand it. She should be in Bellevue or packing her bags to leave the Rex or living with a boyfriend. But she was still in the Rex. He was still licking his wounds, walking from the kitchen to the front room, fingering his nose, checking his face in the mirror.

The major reason he wasn't happy was that for the first time in years, he was doing something he knew he shouldn't. He should stop, chalk it up to experience, and take off for Florida. But he was going to take a major risk to kill Marcy Benaventura. He couldn't explain it rationally. He guessed, finally, it was cloudy mix of revenge and professional pride.

Jack Kuhl leafed through the folder of "résumés." He knew what Lansky was going to do. It was perverse that he had to know for sure.

He found Casey's number and punched it out.

"Yeah, whaddya want," a voice demanded.

Jack took a deep breath. "Casey?"

"Yeah?"

"I'm working on the Rex for Lansky. I want to make sure we have the right date."

"Are you fuckin' shittin' me. Who the fuck are you?"

"I use George, but my real name's Jack. I worked on the Amsterdam and I work directly for Lansky. He wanted me to make sure everything was in place." Jack squeezed his eyes shut. Casey wasn't buying it.

"I don't like guys callin' me I don't know," Casey said, bluntly. There was another, shorter pause. "Yeah, Dombrey mentioned you. It's set."

"In the basement? The alley?"

"Who cares about where?" There was a longer silence. "It's in the basement, behind the laundry room, right next to cans of paint thinner. It's labeled 'important papers.' Latest technology; uses a chip; doesn't even look like a fire bomb. Should be a bonfire. I told Kragen. I set it for midnight on the twenty-first. Some kind of special day."

338

Jack felt hollow. *Kragen. Lansky was going to torch the Rex.* "Anything else?"

"Yeah. I'm gonna call the fire department after it goes off. Gotta limit the body count."

"Good. I'll call my guys. There may be another job."

"Yeah, sure."

Jack flipped the phone on the sofa. Lansky got Kragen to get Casey to set up the "dramatic" option. Jack Kuhl had been expendable for some time.

Jack picked up the phone and punched out Don's number.

"Don, Jack."

"Hey man. What's up?"

Don's TV was on. "About something big. I—"

"I know already. Kragen called and told us."

Jack felt sick. "Saturday, right?"

"We're all leavin' before that. I'm goin' to Mom's. I aint sure about the others. If there's anything left, we'll come back."

"Makes sense. I'll call you after."

"Sure Jack."

It was set up and he didn't have a thing to do about it. Lansky, Kragen. A fire. Everyone had been warned. Everyone except the residents.

Lansky gave him a week to get out. He'd packed and sent off most of his belongings. Tomorrow, he'd have to figure out where he was going, pack up the rest, and leave. The thought depressed him as he walked slowly up the stairs. He took off his clothes, lay on the bed, and shut his eyes.

That night he dreamed he was back in San Diego. He walked through the rooms of his house and finally opened a door and walked out. He was standing on a plain. His house had disappeared. There was one building out there. A hotel. It knifed the glaring white sky. Through a window, he saw a flicker, then a flare, then the fire. The fire was a presence, an entity. It crawled up walls, snaked across the floor, writhed like a mad dancer. Tendrils slipped up the stairs flanking the elevator, a volcano shot through the elevator shaft.

It was an inferno.

And Jack Kuhl couldn't yell for help. He couldn't scream. He couldn't stop it.

40

That September—gorgeous and strewn with garish deciduous colors—Kip's Bay holdouts fell like jacks. Bannon's, a once thriving Irish bar gone to warped tables, a broken jukebox, and rheumy, red-eyed locals, was bolted the third week of September, the neon shamrock switched off. The Wilsons told her Plato's Diner, Rose's favorite Greek diner, where, admittedly, you couldn't get fresh spinach pie anymore, was locked and bolted too. The construction crews had moved in, the windows papered with New York Times.

Through the slide of those anachronisms into the time pit, the Rex persevered, like the obelisk in "2001, Space Odyssey" waiting to be discovered as an eternal notion of birth, fall, and redemption. The Rex would persevere—at least for now—but it would change. Okay, call it a "boutique" hotel.

Frieda counted the changes, watched the soft light from her window, and worried about everything, especially about what she was going to do. She fielded calls from Toby, Rex residents, and especially Marcy. Dugan Peters called. She paid attention. Duggie. What did he want?

"Going away party. We have to have one. Everybody says so."

Frieda frowned. "Well—"

"Where?"

Frieda flipped through her calendar. "The Cave on either Friday or Saturday night. Saturday night is the solstice. Changing seasons, the Cave, the department—a coda. I can tie up part of my life in a neat bow."

"You can try," said Dugan. "But you won't believe it."

"When you want them to forget, they remember. I keep saying life is gray scale, not clean cuts across timelines."

"Don't worry it to death. I'll get back to you."

And that was that. She did worry about the party and she worried her future. It was odd how easy, in retrospect, it was to cut the cords to HRA, and how hard it was to plot a new path. She mailed all her papers, HRA forms, and the research on the Triple M to Toby. It would form part of the rat's nest on his desk. She listened to a symphony on the radio. Fittingly that week, they featured the Russians. Tchaikovsky, Rimsky-

Korsakov, the mystic Scriabin. She supposed with the Cold War over, the Soviet no longer a union, she could drag her feet through the stetle soil where the Korsokoff sisters played, schemed, and pined.

Frieda posed her foot in the air. It was still well turned with tiny blue vein nets making the whiteness alluring. A short distance beyond the admired foot, her books looked too well organized on their shelves; her bags cast clumpish shadows over the wall and the door.

Beyond the door was Sven's gallery—much smaller now owing to the depredations of Bert. Down further was the elevator, that spine which tied the residents to the world. And on every floor residents were going about their evening tasks with utter dependability. Frieda took out a cigarette, found her lighter. She didn't light it.

She was puzzled. Everything on the HRA side worked out. She would have her going away party and go away. She'd find a new place and start a new garden. She had the pension and she had a bit of money from Libby. She had a friend in Taos, New Mexico, Ruth, a former psychiatric caseworker turned potter, who asked her to come visit. She hadn't told anyone yet, because she wasn't sure.

Yet something puzzled her. She knew she shouldn't pursue it or didn't have to pursue it. She knew she would. She'd changed a lot in the last few months, but she hadn't changed her basic curious—occasionally called nosey—and confrontational nature. She made a stiff drink and finally lit a cigarette.

Now, what bugged her?

She flicked ashes into her man-in-the-moon ashtray and ran over everything that had happened since Rose stood in front of her with an IMD 209/code 333. That and that. There. Rodriguez. Morty. Resistance. That last HRA meeting.

Timing. The timing was off.

She called Fulvous Meridian.

"Fulvous, it's Frieda Berg."

"You're not still working, are you?"

Frieda frowned into the phone. Fulvous was right, but she had to do what she had to do. "Just trying to clarify something before I shuffle into the sunset."

"What then?"

"You had twenty 333 cases. Why didn't you report them earlier?"

"I asked myself the same question."

"And?"

After a pause, Fulvous said, "We did."

Frieda frowned. "Did what?"

Fulvous sounded irritated. "Report them! Jim, my second-in-command reported them directly to your boss."

"Toby?"

Fulvous laughed. "Have you forgotten already?"

Frieda let out a sigh. "I should have forgotten faster."

Frieda cradled the phone, shook her head. She felt oddly good, but what she'd just found out was not good. At all.

She picked up her address book and dialed Ramon Menes. "Ray, this is Frieda Berg."

"Hey, I'm coming."

"It'll be good to see you. Shit, we shared the same desk for five years and saw each other twice. What a world."

"Wait a second, while I finish this." She heard scratching on paper, then, "What's up?"

"Did Toby ever talk to you about the code 333 cases?"

"Everybody heard about them and what you did. It's over."

Frieda said, "I mean before. Maybe six months ago."

"He never mentioned it, until you started hammering away at it."

Frieda shook her head. Why was she doing this. "Anything peculiar going on in the office."

There was a long pause. Frieda wondered what that was about. "There was one thing." Ramon sounded hesitant, confused.

"What's that, Ray?"

"You won't say anything?"

What *was* that about? "You said it Ray, I'm leaving."

"Listen, I don't want to rock—"

"Ray!"

"Okay, okay. I don't understand it exactly. But Toby's been spending a lot of time with Morty Bennet. I saw them at lunch. You know that Chinese place on Hudson."

Frieda plucked her cigarette out of the ashtray and took a long pull. When she exhaled the smoke rolled out into her room, obscuring for a quick second the bags pulling on the door. "Okay. Thanks. That's all I wanted to know. See you at the party."

"What's up? Are you sure—"

"Forget it. It's a detail."

When she hung up, Frieda tapped the phone for a few seconds, then picked it up and dialed information.

"The Catskills Real Estate office in Roscoe," she said.

"That's 845-934-8899. Do you want me to ring them?"

"It's too late. I'll call tomorrow. Thanks."

Frieda hung up the phone. She felt empty, but curiously, she didn't feel bad. She didn't understand that exactly. She was outside the battle. Fulvous and Ray were right: She didn't have to do a thing.

Saturday, Frieda had a whirlwind day. She went to the Farmer's Market in Union Square and came back with armsful of leaves, ciders, apples, and honey. She tidied up, decorated, and spread leaves throughout her rooms. She tended her garden. She decided later, she was trying to keep her mind off the going-away party that night.

Late that afternoon, she called Marcy and asked her to come. "You've been inside too long. You've forgotten what life is about. There will be tough people there, at least one ex-cop, and Fulvous Meridian is an ex-Green Beret. Everyone thinks the guy who attacked you is in a hospital; if he's not, he certainly won't try anything now."

"I don't know," said Marcy, her voice trailing off, then quickening. "Yes I do. Can I bring Butch? I'm so lonely I could die."

"Bring him."

"I have to call him."

"Seven, in front," said Frieda. "I've got the cab."

That was better: she had a prop. She'd never been feted for anything, and she didn't like birthdays.

The rest of the day evaporated. She dressed in a killer burgundy outfit with a little more makeup than usual. When she arched her brows in the mirror, the scar faded, and Ava Gardner returned.

At seven, she met Marcy in the lobby and they walked out of the Rex into a cool, fall day. A few minutes later the cab drove up. They got in and drove off to Frieda Berg's going away party.

Frieda let herself relax into the back seat. As the cab turned on Park,

Frieda scrutinized Marcy. Just looking at her, you couldn't tell how fearless—reckless?—she was. Jack, Truck, Kragen, those notes. Marcy looked good, not worried. Auburn hair done up in "punk," classic bone-white forehead, dark eyebrows, startling green eyes, straight, short nose. Her thin lips, always a breath away from pursing into grim line, were made up with incandescent green lipstick. She wore short heels, no hose, a light green skirt and matching blouse, a light, black leather jacket.

"You look great," Frieda said.

"Bel's clothes from another era. I hate accessories. But Butch is coming. I want him to see what he's been missing. Dig the knife in a little deeper."

Frieda laughed. "I pity the man. You're reconciled with the bi-thing?"

"He's not bi-, just experimenting; shit, so was I. What I don't want is to get him involved in this shit with the hotel, with this asshole Kragen. I want to spend a week in bed with him." Marcy sighed, shook her head. "But I can't. I told him we'd meet there, then leave separately."

The driver turned on Fourteenth Street and headed west. "This has to end sometime," said Frieda. "Got your Mace?"

Marcy patted the jacket pocket. "Pepper spray. Never leave home without it."

Frieda traced the scar on her cheek with her fingertips. It wasn't big or deep, but it was there. She guessed it would always be there. "I've retired and I still can't fucking give up. I was checking something at the library yesterday and reread microfiche on the Cardiff and Amsterdam. I'd forgotten there were fires at both of them."

"Jesus. You think—"

"I don't want to think about it, but I do."

"Fuck. What can we do?"

"Be vigilant. Be cautious. Shit, I didn't want to think about that tonight. We're here. Let's try to forget that stuff for a few hours. I have my own little problem to work out."

"What?" said Marcy. She cocked her head in Frieda's direction.

Frieda wondered whether to tell her and decided not to. Sometimes it was tough to see exactly what Marcy might do. "Maybe later. When's Butch coming?"

Marcy grinned. "He should be here. I told him to come early, so if

344

Kragen follows me, he won't see Butch. I don't know how we're going to leave."

Frieda shook her head. "This has to end soon." The cab stopped across from the Cave. "Here we are. You go first. I have to calm down."

Marcy got out of the cab, looked in both directions, and walked slowly across the street. She was taller than usual because of the heels. Strong white legs, strong carriage. Slim and hard. She was striking. Of course, Marcy didn't care about that, except when she wanted to dig the knife in a little deeper. Marcy paused for a second, then walked down the stairs into the Cave.

Frieda paid the driver. She watched the crowds for a few minutes. Behind her, the street people in Christopher Park, brown bags sutured to their hands, were railing against some local injustice; the streams of people on Seventh Avenue were heading either uptown or down, or going into or coming out of the subway talking, laughing, and posing. It was a typical Saturday night in the Village with every possibility hanging in the cool air.

Frieda shrugged, crossed the street, held her breath, and took the plunge.

Butch looked the same. Black hair, black beard, amused brown eyes. Same construction worker/sculptor build. She hadn't realized she missed him, until she saw him.

"Place the same," she said, awkwardly.

"Still spewing out sculpture, hard and soft. It's still about sex. The Marcy nook is still there. Course there's no Marcy."

She slipped closer to him, looked up in his eyes, took his hand. It felt the same, as strong as the steel and iron he worked with. "That could change real soon." She felt his arm around her. She looked up at him, then twined her free arm around his neck, and raised herself up. She realized why women wore high heels. Got them closer to their guys. She kissed him. Same taste of slightly rusty metal. Same bulge in his pants.

"I don't know how much more teasing I can take," he said. "Let's sneak away for a month. It'll be over when we come back."

She held him close. "I'd obsess about it."

"You would."

"I want to think of something else, something positive."

He backed away a few feet, gave her an odd, quirky smile. "There's a show at the Crusty Eye. In a week."

"Cool. You got pieces in it."

"No. You do."

She frowned. She tilted her head, not sure whether he was putting her on. "What?"

Butch shrugged. "If you want. Craig, the owner, has a couple spots. I told him you'd be perfect. Brash, anarchistic, scary. An East Village van Gogh with attitude. He said bring her on. I'd said I'd try, but she's tough, does her own thing, doesn't like—"

"Quit that. I'm not that bad. Shit, really. Christ I don't know—"

"Don't be difficult. I'll help you frame the ones you want. Or, if you want to hide in the Rex, give 'em to me. I'll frame 'em."

Marcy grabbed his belt buckle, drew him towards her. "This is just a ploy to get some nooky, isn't it?"

"Whatever it takes."

Marcy laughed. "Shit I miss you. Listen, that's great. You sure?"

"Can't wait too long."

"Give me a couple of days."

Butch said, "Why?"

"Humor me. It'll be even better. Tonight, let's have a drink, stay in the corner and neck."

"I'll get the drinks."

When the smoke cleared, Frieda saw Marcy in the corner wrapped around a big guy with black hair and a beard. Butch. It made her feel ancient and motherly.

Then she saw the paper hangings: "Good Luck, Frieda" and "Our Last Hope."

"Oh shit." Frieda felt the tears start. She stopped for a few seconds, dried her eyes, and then started recognizing faces. They were all there: Danny, Dugan, John, Fulvous, Ramon, and a handful of caseworkers she hadn't seen in years. George, the IM chief with who she had recently locked horns, was hiding in the corner with Lenny. Borgan. Toby wasn't there.

"Thanks everybody."

They crowded around her. Champagne, friends, a last party. She felt intensely nostalgic. She supposed that was what that party was about.

John said, "Remember that time you went AWOL to France?"

Dugan said, "Remember when you threw the chairs at the cops."

"It's so embarrassing. We're going to visit all those Christmas pasts," said Frieda.

They hit all the high points: the fights with the police in the early eighties, her food stamp fight at IM13, with John the time the labor union struck and they were both there, with Danny a score of crises, the years of IM Investigations. After awhile, she began to see the disjointedness again. She'd started with the department out of idealism, but when that idealism had soured, she'd stayed. She supposed all that history shaped her character. But that night she saw it as ad hoc, fear of trying something different.

She had a fifteen-minute talk with Borgan.

"What about a fire," she said.

Borgan shook his head. "It's a trend. It seems insane to think about it after the articles, the police attention. But there's Lansky's reputation."

"There's not a lot we can do."

"He's toast if he does anything. He may be toast now with everything we've found, with the welfare scheme, with the ex-cons in the Rex."

Frieda shook her head. "That's not reassuring."

"On to more important things. What about a date?" said Borgan, smiling mischievously.

She put her hand on his arm. "Tonight I can't think. Call me."

"You know I will."

John told everyone to be quiet. He called everyone for a toast. "To our lovely, intelligent, Frieda," John intoned. "She kept us honest and she kept us in an uproar for twenty years. We already miss you."

Frieda raised her glass. "The Korsokoff sisters would have been proud," she said. She misted. She felt a tear slalom past her scar. And there were more tears. She couldn't help it.

After that, she made the rounds. She supposed that was a fitting leave-taking. Of course, the one question they asked, she couldn't answer. What was her next act?

She'd just finished talking with George—it wasn't much of a talk; she was sure George just wanted to make sure she was going to retire—when Marcy came up to her. "Butch is going to stay, but I'm gonna go.

We have to time this."

"Like a military operation," said Frieda, shaking her head. "Let me get an escort."

"You don't have to do that," said Marcy.

"Yes I do. Stay here."

Frieda walked over to Fulvous. "Fulvous, dahling."

"More champagne?"

"Later. Do me a favor. It'll take half an hour."

Fulvous frowned. "Anything—this is your night."

"Take my friend home. Someone is stalking her. A bad guy."

Fulvous, slightly drunk, leaned over and kissed her on the forehead. "For you, I'll take twenty people home. Where is she?"

Frieda motioned for Marcy to come over. "This is Fulvous. He's a very tough guy and a very nice guy. He's going to take you home. Okay?"

Marcy shook Fulvous' hand. "Glad to meet you, sir. And thanks. I'll be right with you."

Frieda watched Marcy go back to Butch, give him a big smack, then turn. She took Fulvous' arm and they walked out of the Cave.

Good. Marcy was safe. Now where was the party?

Saturday. Ten o'clock. Kragen dressed in a pair of dark slacks, dull black shirt, and black tennis shoes. He always worked in the same costume at night. Kragen strapped on his shoulder holster, re-checked the snubnose, and holstered it. He put on his dark overcoat and put his leather case in the inside pocket. The last item was a dark tennis hat. He checked the mirror. The hat tucked low over his forehead covered the top half of his face to his nose, the collar of his overcoat, hitched up around his neck, his jaw and neck.

Plenty of time. Everything was working like clockwork. He'd checked with Tony earlier. It looked like Jack Kuhl was packing up and leaving town. That was good. He told Tony to be extra careful, as if it would do any good.

Kragen walked downstairs into the garage. The Toyota was parked in the back. He got in, started it, and drove it up to the doors. His beeper opened the doors and a few minutes later, closed them.

He drove down Central Park West thinking about what he had done

348

and what he was going to do. Yesterday, he'd driven by the Odyssey and watched Marcy swinging through the booths with plates of food. Then he parked so that he could see the entrance to the Rex. He'd watched her trip up the steps of the Rex. His heart beat wildly when he saw her. She stopped on the top step. He wondered if she sensed he was out there. She looked up and down the block, and then looked right at him. Then she turned and vanished inside the Rex.

She wasn't afraid of him. It made him feel hatred, but also a kind of attraction. Love, hate. He'd never felt that before. He knew he should leave her alone, make sure the Rex was torched, and leave for Florida. He knew he wouldn't.

Marcy Benaventura. It had to be done that night, the Twenty-first. The fire would consume most of the Rex *and* Marcy. The timing had to be right. He'd take her in her room. He'd pick the lock, tie her up, mess her up, kill her, and leave her for the fire.

Kragen parked on Twenty-eighth on the west side of Park Avenue. In the distance, he could see the Rex and beyond the Rex, the Olympia. He waited and watched. Fifteen minutes. Thirty. Kragen looked at his watch.

There had been little activity at the Rex. He guessed that because it was Saturday night, the Rex would be half-empty. It was good for those people who had some place to go. If their night lasted after midnight, they might be alive to find another place.

He was about to get out, when a cab pulled up in front of the Rex. A big guy got out. There was a short heel, a leg. Marcy Benaventura! Fuck, she'd left the hotel! He could have missed her altogether. She stepped out, glanced up and down the block, and then they both walked up the steps of the Rex. Kragen shook his head. Was the big guy a boyfriend?

He waited a few minutes. The big guy came out. He looked around too, as if Mr. Kragen was going to stand next to the Rex waving his arms. Kragen waited five minutes after the cab scooted onto Lexington. Then he got out and walked slowly towards the Rex.

Marcy Benaventura was in.

Frieda saw Toby at the door of the Cave. He walked in slowly, gazed around the crowd, saw her, and went off in the opposite direction.

She was getting tipsy. She told the useless Frieda monitor to watch out. She tracked Toby to the corner.

Toby had on a coat that didn't quite fit, suspenders, and a ballooning blue shirt. He was the same seedy walrus she'd known for ten years. Emerson. Thoreau. Transcendental idealism and simplify, simplify, simplify. While she watched him, he clamped his pipe in his mouth and scanned the crowd.

"Mr. Minus. One would think you've been avoiding me."

Toby laughed. It was a tinny, forced laugh. His eyes searched hers for clues. "Not my favorite investigator."

"How's your house?"

Minus looked shocked. Then he recovered, looked past her, waved at Peggy, the bartender. She watched Peggy make a whiskey and soda and slide it across to Toby. Toby took a long pull on his drink. He looked at her meditatively. "How did you know?"

She didn't want to talk to Toby. It would have been so easy to turn around, let Toby leave, and forget about it. "Catskills Real Estate."

Creases threaded through Toby's forehead. He stuck his fingers in his mop of hair and scratched. Then his face fell, as if it had been held up with fragile props. He managed a shrug. "I saved my dimes."

"I don't think so. Let's talk about it."

Toby looked around, as if looking for an escape. "If you want."

"There's a free table near the juke."

They walked slowly towards the table in the corner. The Cave wasn't good with tables and chairs and that table looked older than the rest. Many battles had been fought at that table with its cigarette burns, glass rings, and chipped wood. Toby sat. She made sure her chair was solid and sat too. She opened up her bag, took out a cigarette, and lit it. She blew the smoke away from Toby towards the bar. That stream joined other streams and made a cloud, which hovered around HRA well-wishers and a few Cave regulars who had wandered in.

"Fulvous said one of his boys told you about the code 333 cases six months ago. Hobnobbing with Morty Bennet, calling those cases 'conversion' problems, sandbagging me at the last HRA summit. It all seems to fit together, just like egg-and-dart."

Toby's eyes drooped. He stared at the table, as if he'd lost something. "Just like egg-and-dart," he said, finally.

"I'm unsure of a few details such as why we played these cat-and-mouse games. And why, after putting in thirty good years, you throw it away."

He gulped his drink and set it down empty. "A year ago, Morty Bennet came into my office, sat down, and offered me thirty thousand dollars a building to cover up the code 333s. He didn't tell me much, except that it would only affect a few clients. He also said they'd reapply and get their benefits back. I wasn't sure until I had the money in my hand. When Fulvous's unit reported them, I deep-sixed the report. Shit, I don't know what's on my desk half the time."

It stunned her to hear Toby talk so casually about what he'd done. She respected him; they talked about the same things, felt the same about the world. Idealists betrayed. She took a long drag on her cigarette. The details didn't mean anything anymore, but she asked for them anyway. "If you knew, why send me to IM66?"

Toby shrugged. "I didn't know how they did it, or where."

Fulvous leaned over their table and said, "Too serious, too serious. Why aren't you partying my beauty?"

Frieda put her hand on his arm. "Did you deliver the goods, dahling?"

"Nice gal, but with a wild streak."

"I'll tell you what she did in a second."

"She told me. And she'd do it again."

Frieda shook her head. "I didn't want to hear that. Thanks dear."

Fulvous raised his glass to her and wandered towards the bar.

Frieda tapped her cigarette into the ashtray. She took a sip of champagne. The Cave had filled up in the last two hours. It felt good being in that crowd. Right after the divorce, she sat for hours—weeks—at the bar in front and watched the shoes, ankles, and calves of passersby, and wondered what had happened to her life.

She turned back to Toby. She didn't want to know, but had to ask. "Once you knew I'd stumbled over the code 333s and the scheme, why didn't you transfer me?"

Toby shrugged. "I tried. Remember? I couldn't try too hard; it would make you more suspicious. Did you forget what you're like when you think something's wrong?"

"You didn't know what they were doing at those hotels? The beatings, the harassment, the fires?"

Toby gulped and shook his head. "I guessed, later. It was such an insignificant part—"

"No rationalizations, please."

Toby grabbed the sides of his head. He looked miserable, defeated. "I think about it all the time. When I realized what they were doing, I couldn't do anything without revealing what I'd done."

"What about the Rex?"

"I couldn't stop them. I couldn't stop Lansky or this guy Jack you mentioned or the people they hired."

"I see," said Frieda. And she did. "One last question. Why?"

"When I saw the money in my hand, I saw what it meant. It meant a place in the country, retirement, it meant all those things I never had. I guess I did it because I got tired. When I got tired, I started thinking of all the time, all the wasted time and what I had to show for it." Toby looked miserable. "All that fucking time."

She'd never heard him swear before. She was surprised at his venom. But he was right. All that time. It happened to her. It happened to many of her friends. "What about the investigation? Will it get to you?"

"I don't think so. Rodriguez might implicate Morty, but Morty will get off. He certainly won't say a thing about me." Toby looked at her mournfully. "What are you going to do?"

Frieda sighed. If only she'd stopped. "In the words of the song, absolutely nothing. Why? Because of what you said. All that time. All that fucking time. Retire. Pen your legends, read *Walden*. As for me, I have a friend in Taos, New Mexico. She invited me and I decided to go. Odd, how were all leaving, and all because of greed, a bunch of goons, and the wrong fucking code. Maybe we've all been using the wrong cipher. Have a good life."

She got up and headed towards the bar.

The "Good Luck, Frieda" banner was hanging lower. She saw that as a good sign. She got another drink and turned in time to see Toby slump towards the door, then walk up the steps into the night. She felt sorry for him. He would worry about what he did. It was a cliché, but it was punishment enough.

Later, at eleven-thirty, she stopped and gave goodbye hugs to the people who were there. Then she walked up the steps of the Cave. On the sidewalk, people walked around her. She stood for a minute, looked back at the Cave. So many memories. So much time. She'd gone into her last welfare center. She'd gone into the Cave for the last time, too.

Time to move on.

There were still loose ends. If she could nail Lansky's butt to the wall. If she could stay until Marcy Benaventura was safe. If, if, if.

41

When Jack Kuhl woke up Saturday, his head was empty, dull, and blank. Jeanie was gone, had been gone for weeks, the other side of the bed as empty as his head. But through the void of time, space, and identity, he sensed that day would be the strangest of his life.

He threw back the covers, found his robe, and trudged downstairs. He switched on the light at the door. The apartment, always barren, was a desert. The only thing that seemed half-alive was his half-open laptop on the table under the Neiman print looking like jaws.

He made the coffee for, he realized, the last time. When the coffee was done, he took his metallic mug to the table. He sat, put his mug next to the laptop, and pressed the ON button. The laptop slowly booted up. A few minutes later, he stared at the diagram of the Rex. Eight floors, sixty-one residents—*before* he started. There were forty some odd left. The key word was *residents*. It wasn't a hole in the ground. It was an old hotel *with residents*.

Jack logged off. He got up and opened the drapes. The sun, the shimmering Hudson, the distant fantasy land of New Jersey mocked his inner, ragged state. He sat on the sofa and crossed his feet on the glass table.

Then it hit him.

It wasn't Lansky, the doomed project, his "agents," or that he'd been reduced to acting out a forgettable scene from the Jack Kuhl story.

Firebomb. Saturday. Midnight.

It lay like a boulder on his chest. The Jersey shore, already dim, wavered and disappeared. Intimidation. Blondie. Mass murder. Jack shuddered.

He left his mug on the table. He tried to stare at the river and couldn't. He had to move. He got up and paced to the work nook, then back to the window. He picked up his mug and poured more coffee, then left the mug on the counter. He picked up the paper and sat down on the sofa. He read listlessly for a few minutes and let the paper fall to floor.

If he called the Rex, told them about the firebomb, Lansky would call the police on Jack Kuhl. And what would stop Lansky from doing it again? Lansky could pick up the phone, call Casey or Kragen, and plant another firebomb in the basement. Yes, Lansky would get the Rex. And he guessed he'd get it sooner rather than later. Lansky was insane, amoral, a monster, but would live in the penthouse, while Jack Kuhl pecked out an existence in some backwater.

No, that wasn't it either. Not the rationalizations, not what he'd done. It was that red, burning image. It haunted his sleep. The fire snaked up the elevator shaft, snaked under doors, and coiled outside the fire doors. Fire danced in the windows like a grotesque monster. That nightmare seared his brain.

He could go somewhere, anywhere, and not read a New York paper. Fires happened all the time. When he thought about it, the Rex *was* a firetrap. It was a matter of time, before someone would fall asleep with a cigarette dangling from their fingers, a hotplate short circuit, or the tangle of plugs on a wall socket smoke and burn.

It wasn't his fault.

That was it. Pack and leave.

He punched out United's number and got a red-eye flight to Miami at two in the morning. Then he hurried upstairs and dressed. He spent the rest of the morning and early afternoon packing. He boxed Jeanie's clothes, CDs, Caribbean masks from Miami, a special blue glass ashtray.

UPS picked up Jeanie's box at five. He was almost done.

Finally, late, he checked the apartment from roof deck to the bedroom, to the garbage container under the sink. All done. Everything was shipped, the few clothes he kept in his pack. One last item. Jack unhooked the power cable off the laptop, looped it into the laptop case, then closed the laptop and fit it snugly into its black carrying case. He slipped it into his pack. He'd go to the airport and wait. Hurry, hurry, hurry.

One last glance over the burnished hardwood floor, at the Hudson, out the window, that garish print.

Jack stopped, frozen.

Fire. Midnight.

"Fuck me!" Jack slammed the door closed. He stood for a minute breathing heavily inside the door. Then he walked to the liquor cabinet. He made a stiff martini, propped his backpack on a chair in the nook and took out the laptop. He hooked up the power cable, and booted the laptop in the gathering gloom. Then, feeling like an automaton, he started jabbing out a history of the Rex project. He realized after a few minutes how mad he was. He'd questioned every step and he'd taken every step. But that night under the Neiman print in that Swedish desert, his doubts burst onto the laptop screen. Lansky, the Rex, goons, Kragen. The more he typed, the better he felt. He was typing himself into redemption.

He included every meeting with Lansky, the dates, what they talked about, what Lansky had said about razing the Rex. He used the name George for the last time, hoping that might protect him. He didn't mention Kragen. Finally, he noted the two fires at the Cardiff and the Amsterdam and said that Lansky was going to start a fire at the Rex, thanks to Casey and he included Casey's number.

Finally, he hooked up the printer and printed out two copies. One copy was for him; he wasn't sure why. The other was to Frieda—she'd know what to do with it. He slipped both into separate manila envelopes. In the one to Frieda, he included the folder of ex-con résumés. Then he addressed and put extra stamps on the one to Frieda. He slipped the other folder and the laptop into his backpack.

He paused a last time. Saturday, Jeanie was at Carismo's until midnight. He walked back to the phone and punched out the number.

After a few minutes, she came on. "Where are you," Jeanie said.

"The condo, staring at the Hudson. We used to do that."

"A thousand years ago. Don't be stubborn. I'm looking for a bigger place. You'll fit in nicely, as long as you give up 'hotel management'."

It was odd how she was up and he down. He supposed imbalance was a law of life. "I've given it up, but I have to figure out what's next. I'm going to miss you, the mornings."

"Me too, Jack. Me too."

"You know when you asked if I'd do anything to make it."

"Yes."

"It took me time to find the answer."

"I knew you would. Jack—"

"Gotta go."

Jack hung up. He glanced at his watch. He was so preoccupied he'd forgotten the time.

Eleven.

Firebomb. Saturday. Midnight.

He punched out the Rex's number.

"Da?"

"There is a firebomb in the Rex. Call the police."

"Da?"

He'd gotten a Russian, probably Ivan. Jack said, exasperated. "Let me talk to Rudi."

"Nyet. Rudi not here."

"Anyone who can speak English."

"Nobody. Everybody gone. Saturday night."

"Ring Don Breem's room."

Jack snapped off the phone after ten rings. He called the Rex again and asked for Truck. He waited another ten rings before hanging up. Of course they were gone. Fuck. What to do? What to do?

Jack shouldered his backpack and headed for the door.

The mirror near the front door trapped him a last time. He could see the clear line of jaw, the high forehead, and the long handsome face. But then there was the purple bruise, where Lansky's guard hit him, the band-aids behind his ears. His hair, normally impeccable, shot out at odd angles. He hadn't shaved in days. His eyes were grim and nervous.

Jack hitched up his pack, locked the door, and then walked slowly through Duane Square. The homeless woman in the dirty, brown knit cap was there when he arrived months ago, and she was there when he left. She was humming to herself and sipping out of a paper Starbucks cup.

Jack hailed a cab on Hudson Street. As he was getting into the cab, he saw a mailbox. He told the driver to wait. He fished the thick envelope addressed to Frieda out of his pack. His hand trembled. Did he really want to mail it? It could come right back to him. He could be signing himself into the New York prison system.

"Hey!"

Jack turned. Tony!

Jack stared at him for a second. Then he hurried back to the cab, threw his pack in, and scrambled after it. He fell into the back seat, trembling. He glanced over his shoulder and saw Tony running towards the cab.

"Hurry."

The cab took off slowly. "Somebody following you?"

Jack looked out the rear window. "The guy waving at a cab in your rearview mirror."

"Why?"

Jack scrambled for a story. "He's a detective. Dirt for a divorce."

"Fuckin' sneaky. I've always wanted to do this. Where to?"

He could take that cab to La Guardia. He could wait for his flight, leave, and forget. Jack took a deep breath. "Twenty-eighth and Park."

The driver gunned it. Places in the neighborhood flipped by as if on a diorama. Church, Hudson, West Broadway. He and Jeanie had eaten in that restaurant. Rainbow Redux. The Capriccio, where they'd listened to a Miles Davis imitator blowing lonesome tunes into the void. At Canal Street, he turned and saw Tony's cab three blocks back.

Jack dug himself into the cushions. He didn't know what he was going to do. He felt for the first time that he was going to die.

What a great night, Marcy thought. Life. Parties. Mixing it up with a guy she liked—but was ambivalent about. Always caveats. She supposed that was what would happen forever. Bel and her father, Bel and Mario, Marcy and Mickey, Marcy and Butch. Dueling couples. It looked like fate. And it felt like life.

She'd almost asked Butch to come with her, but it was too soon. After she watched Fulvous get in the cab, Marcy walked to the elevator, her thoughts on the Cave, Butch, what Frieda's little problem could be.

She saw Ivan at the desk. "How's the Rex, tonight?"

Ivan shrugged. "How is it!"

"Whatever. Anything going on? Any visitors?"

Ivan shrugged.

She decided to walk up, although her heels were killing her. She almost stopped on two to see Sid, but didn't. On three, she stared at Blondie's door the way she'd stared at it every day she passed it. She couldn't believe he was dead. She talked to him and a few days later he was dead. Over a piece of property, a location. She guessed a lot of wars were like that, over property that protected someone, had oil on it, diamonds, or something else. Or spiritual property, the property of minds and attitudes. She supposed you could take that metaphor as far as you wanted. That night, it was hard to reconcile that basic need to acquire with Kragen crushing Blondie's skull. But there it was.

She decided to see if anyone else was up. She walked up to five. She heard voices, but there wasn't anyone there she wanted to see. Six. She hesitated pushing open the fire door. Bel was leaving Monday. She felt tipsy enough to talk to her. She pushed the door open. She regarded Bel's door. No light under the door. Maybe she was at Mario's. Seven. She stopped in front of Mario's door.

Dark.

Didn't anyone party anymore?

She had half a bottle of wine in her fridge. She decided she would have a glass and run over the Cave night in her head. Butch. The Crusty Eye. She thought about the space. There was enough room for two sketches, one painting. They wanted van Gogh, she had van Benaventura. Take it or leave it.

She pushed open the fire doors on four. She was halfway around the elevator housing, when she saw someone bending over her lock. He stopped, turned, and stared at her.

Underneath the tennis hat, she saw Kragen. His small head looked different, bluish; there was a crook in his nose. He'd looked ugly before. They stared at each other for a suspended second. The tension between them was like a link, a link that was stronger than hatred.

"You asshole. HELP!"

She could tell it shocked him. It shocked him into turning and loping down the hallway after her. She sprinted towards the fire door and pushed it open hard. The fire door crashed into the wall. She was so distracted she went up, instead of down.

Seconds later, she heard the door crash into the wall. Then she heard steps. His shoes hit the steps like distant thunderclaps. On the fifth floor landing, she kicked off one high heel, but the other stuck. She hopped up three stairs, stopped, bent over, and flipped it off with her hand. That's when the pepper spray fell out of her jacket. She watched in horror as it made a "tink" on the stairs and flipped end over end down to the fifth floor landing.

"Fuck!" She turned and ran; her heart pounded so hard she could hardly breath.

When she hit the sixth floor landing, she wondered whether she should go into the sixth floor, down the fire escape. She decided that was a bad idea, considering she wasn't wearing shoes. She shot up the stairs.

"HELP! FUCKING HELP!"

Screaming and running didn't mix. She turned on the juice. She'd find something on the roof, something to fight him off with. If not. Fuck it. Everyone thought she had a death wish. Might as well show them they were right.

That's when she heard the elevator.

It couldn't be Kragen. She could hear his shoes slapping the stairs.

Jack had the driver drop him at off at Twenty-eighth and Park. *Firebomb. Halloween. Midnight.*

From the corner, he saw both the Rex and the Olympia. He stared at them for a few seconds, mesmerized by the juxtaposition. His stomach was empty, his head buzzing. He was scared shitless.

Jack glanced up and down Park Avenue. There were a lot of people on Park, but he didn't see Tony. He took a deep breath, hitched up his pack, and walked towards the Rex.

That night, the street was empty, the Moat quiet.

Jack bit his lip, then forced himself to walk up the worn steps. He opened the door and walked quickly over to the half-oval. Ivan looked up at him.

Jack searched for words. "I'm here...I'm here for Don."

Ivan shrugged and waved him on.

Somebody was using the elevator. Jack glanced at Ivan, who, bored, was fiddling with the radio. Jack took a deep breath and slipped around the elevator housing. He opened the door to the basement. He walked silently down the steps. He waited at the bottom of the stairs. The elevator ground away, the cables swinging back and forth.

Finally, he felt his mouth set grimly. He hurried around the elevator housing, past the laundry, and down a short passageway. He stopped at a small door. He opened the door and fumbled for the light switch. The bare bulb cast a weak yellow light over a tangle of old furniture, broken appliances, old files.

He took his pack off and walked into the center of the room.

It looked impossible. Where did Casey say he put it? Near paint thinner. An envelope. Or was it an envelope? There were layers on layers. He searched the room frantically. He couldn't see paint thinner. What did it look like? He pushed a chest out of the way. More junk. He pushed boxes aside. He threw over a pile of books.

"Fuck. Fuck." His hands fumbled over the tops of furniture. He peered inside a dryer without a door, behind a pile of magazines.

He gasped. Dirty bottles of brown liquid. Paint thinner! And paint! But where was the envelope? Jack blinked. There was a slim envelope leaning against a dusty bottle. Jack stared at it as if it were a coiled snake. It had "Important Papers" lettered across it.

Trembling, he picked the envelope up. It was slim, but heavy. He undid the clasp and peered inside. A timer clicked off seconds on a flat greasy-looking board. The time was eleven forty-five. He redid the clasp.

He had it. Now what?

A long shrill scream raised the hairs on his neck. Then there was a crash. He stared at the doorway.

Jack's heart bobbed into his throat. He couldn't think. He knew he had to get out of there fast. He grabbed his heavy pack and slung it over his shoulder. He sprinted out of the room, past the laundry, He carried the package in front of him, as if it were a religious object. He ran up the stairs and across the lobby of the Rex.

Ivan said, "Hey—"

Jack flung the door open.

Jack checked the street towards Park, then towards the East River. Sewer. He hurried towards the corner. He bent over to lay the package in the opening.

That's when his head split open. It was curious. Why? What happened? Why was the street rotating? Finally, he thought, as he hit the pavement, that he'd died.

Marcy raced up the last flight to the roof. She stopped for a split second when she saw Frieda's garden shears. She reached down, grabbed them, and then raced up to the door. The latch was on. It stuck. She swung the shears up from her waist and knocked the latch open. She kicked the door open, almost fell, and hopped onto the roof.

When she turned away from Frieda's broken trellis, she saw a roof of square palllets, scattered dark flowers, and empty stalks. The night was cool, almost brisk. Beyond the rim of the roof, city lights caromed off shifting banks of clouds.

She raced down the central path to the table. There were bottles on the table, an ashtray full of butts. She looked around, frantically, and decided she couldn't defend herself there.

Kragen appeared in the doorway to the roof. His shadow spread over the trellis, and blocked the light.

"Let's try this again," he said, as he started down the path.

"Asshole. Fishface."

"There must be something wrong with you," Kragen said, huskily. "A normal person would plead, make offers, and try to save themselves. You just dig in deeper."

"Fucking monster."

As Kragen walked, she edged around the table and backed up towards the fire escape. Kragen took something out of his pocket. It was a small leather case. She looked on in horror as he opened it. Scalpels and knives gleamed in the moonlight. Kragen took out a scalpel, closed the case, and carefully tucked the case back in his coat.

The fire escape. It would be tough to scramble down there without shoes. She turned to face Kragen. "All right, you ugly son-of-a-bitch." She held up Frieda's shears.

Kragen walked around the table. "Come here, little girl."

"You come here, Fishface."

She held up the shears. They were too heavy. She'd get one chance; then it would be over. She glanced over her shoulder and saw the fire escape railing. Eight floors down. She'd end up spread-eagled on the concrete where they kept the garbage behind the Rex. That thought made her turn on Kragen, furious. Then she saw the pots, where Frieda was working the other day. She switched the shears into her left hand, bent, and snatched at a pot. Her fingers dug in the dirt as she grabbed the side. She guessed where Kragen was and threw it at him without aiming. She grabbed another pot. That time she turned to face him. She saw dirt on his sleeve where he'd warded off the first pot.

Kragen walked around the table towards her. She threw the second pot at his head. When he ducked, she switched hands, backed up, and whipped the shears sidearm at his leg. The shears hit him right below the knee. She could tell it hurt.

"Fuck."

She turned and grasped the fire escape railing.

She felt his hand on her leather jacket. She shrugged out of it. The iron of the fire escape dug into her feet. She'd done three rungs, when she felt his hand on the back of her blouse. The material bunched around her neck strangling her. She saw her bone-white legs dangling in the air. Then she was in the air. Kragen dropped her in front of him. He held her by her blouse. The scalpel slashed down cutting through her blouse and opening a wound across her stomach. She was too hopped up to feel it. His hat lay on the skids. She saw his small bruised head, large teeth, a throbbing vein on the side of his neck. The scalpel glinted in the light.

She couldn't breathe, but her hands were free. She drilled her fist into his crotch.

"Jesus Christ."

His hand knocked her over, the scalpel nicking her face. She could barely see. His big hand grabbed her around the throat and picked her up. He slashed at her with the scalpel, but she caught his hand. He shook off her hand. That's when she registered someone else on the roof. She tried to kick Kragen in the balls and missed hitting him on thigh. The scalpel glinted in the cool night air. He was going for her face. Lights swirled around her.

"Truth is death."

Kragen hesitated. He turned. He held her in his left hand, the scalpel in his right.

They both stared at the grim form. Ben was almost as tall as Kragen. He had a frown on his face, as if he couldn't quite understand what he was doing, or what anyone was doing.

Before Kragen could do anything, Ben stepped forward. His arm shot out and up. He gripped Kragen around the neck. "Truth is death," Ben screamed. "Truth is death."

"Whaggaa dee fuckkaa." Kragen croaked.

Kragen dropped her. She crashed to the roof hitting her head on a pallet.

Kragen punched at Ben's face and missed. Then he slashed at Ben's arm with the scalpel. Ben didn't waver. He gripped Kragen's neck tight and pushed Kragen towards the edge of the roof. She couldn't believe Ben's strength. Kragen slashed and fought. Cuts opened on Ben's arm. But Ben kept pushing, pushing. In the middle of Kragen's flailing arms, there was Ben's unmoving arm, his hand embedded in Kragen's neck.

"Aaarghh. Aaarghh."

Kragen slashed and slashed. Ben pushed Kragen against the dead morning glories tangling over the roof ledge. Kragen's arms and legs jerked liked a spider impaled on a needle. Beyond his struggling body was the blackness of the night, lights from tall buildings on Twenty-third Street.

"Truth is death," Ben screamed. Kragen's face was a mix of horror and hatred. He slashed at Ben's face and missed. Ben punched Kragen's struggling form back and toppled him over the ledge.

Kragen's screams ripped the air.

The whole scene lasted a few seconds. Marcy shook herself. She couldn't move. She was lying on a pallet, her head in the middle of broken pots. She raised up. Her leather coat lay like a dead animal near the fire escape. She stared at Ben. Ben stood at the edge unmoving. His coat was in shreds, his arm leaked blood on the roof.

Then he turned. Ben looked at the cuts on his arm and the blood flowing out. Then he looked at her and shrugged. "You're bleeding."

The spell was broken. "Fuck me. So are you."

She got up, slapped at the dirt on her skirt, and went over to Ben. She leaned over the ledge and saw Kragen. He'd hit the shards of glass on the wall separating the Rex from the next yard. He lay ripped and crumpled in the Rex's small patio.

She was panting. Her feet hurt. She started feeling the pain on her stomach, the nick on her face. Pain: She was alive. She checked her stomach and saw she was bleeding from a foot-long wound. Ben was worse. It was time to wake up. She grabbed the bottom of her already ripped blouse with both hands and tore it apart. She shrugged out of the blouse, made a tourniquet, and wrapped it around what looked like Ben's most serious wound. Then she took his hand. "Let's get you off the roof, before anyone sees you and before I collapse. We'll fix your arm."

She led him down the central path. Ben. Their alien. Their troll. She thought it was the first time he'd ever been on the roof. She didn't understand why he had come up. She guessed she'd never know and that didn't make any difference.

Lexington Avenue swirled around Jack's head. He struggled to get up, but couldn't.

Tony's face appeared in the center of the swirl. He tucked what looked like a small club into his jacket. Tony bent over—what was he bending for? Then he held Casey's package in his large hand, laughed, and thrust it at him. "Ya can't mail it without stamps, dummy."

Tony kicked him in the stomach. He stared at Tony's foot, watched it pull back. He steeled himself for the next blow. Then he heard voices. Tony stopped; he thrust his finger out at someone. Tony ran across Lexington against a red light. A car horn blared in the night. A Chevy Nova rocked to a stop a few feet from Tony.

Tony ran down Twenty-eighth. Jack felt like running after him, telling him what was in the package, but he couldn't. Jack felt hands under his arms. He was dizzy. Then he was standing up with two men on either side.

"You okay," said the big guy with the cast, peering at his head.

"You were lucky," said the other. "Come into the hotel. We'll call an ambulance."

Jack looked into their faces. For a second he didn't understand who they were or what they were doing. Then he recognized Mario and Brucie. "No, no," Jack stuttered. Through the pain in his head, he realized he was embarrassed. "I'm okay."

"Guy who hit you looked familiar," said Mario. "Come on. You might have a concussion. We'd better call an ambulance."

"No, really. I'm okay."

Brucie bent over, picked up his backpack, and handed it to him. "Hope he didn't steal anything important. At least he didn't get this."

Jack shook himself. He saw blood on his shirt. "Nothing important. I'm okay."

"I've been mugged before," said Mario. "You have to brush it off. Get on with life."

Brucie patted him on the back. "Bellevue's just a few blocks. You want us to call a taxi?"

"Thanks, I'm all right now."

Mario said, "All right then."

Jack watched the two men walk slowly towards the Rex, up the front steps, into the building. Jack leaned against the side of the town house.

His head was full of gravel. He rested for a few minutes. Then he started walking clumsily down Lexington dragging his pack. Police cars sirened past him, making him think of the scream, the thud. Tony. Tony was taking the firebomb to Lansky. He saw the pay phone and stumbled toward it. He found two quarters, dropped them in, and carefully dialed the number. His hands were sticky with blood.

"Michael."

"Jack? Hold on. That's better. I see you Jack. You don't look so good. I can't help thinking it's going to get worse. Let's see, what would Kragen do first?"

Jack looked at his watch. Eleven fifty-nine. "Is Tony there?"

"Right here, Jack."

"Michael—"

"What is it Jack?"

Jack stared at the penthouse of the Olympia. Two figures. One tall, the other short, blocky. They gestured. Pointed. A week ago, two weeks ago, he was there pointing down.

Up, down. Outside the Tavern on the Green, in.

Metaphors of space overwhelmed, then eluded him.

He remembered. He should say something.

"Nothing."

Whump.

Fire sprayed out from the Olympia penthouse, then subsided. The two figures lit up like torches, then dropped away. Debris spread out in a plume from the penthouse, and glass fell like shiny drops of rain over the street and cars and pedestrians waiting at the stoplight. Small fires flickered over the low wall of the penthouse.

Jack didn't believe in spirits, afterlife, or weepy religiosity, and he wasn't sure he believed in redemption. But *that* was poetic justice.

He let the phone drop. There was something else. The confession. George's confession. Should he? He'd already made the gesture. He'd already felt remorse. The project had destroyed him inside and out. What would it mean, after all?

Sirens. People pointed up. A police car pulled up at the Olympia.

Jack stumbled towards the mailbox on the corner. He propped his backpack on the mailbox, unzipped it, and took out the envelope.

He shook his head, once, shrugged, and dropped it in.

42

Pale creatures swam lazily in glassy water. They were solid, but not solid. They were jellyfish, but their bodies ridged. Their mouths were soft, but then hard-seamed. She was immobile, waiting, watching. A creature quivered then whipped its long knobby tail. Light mirrored off its translucent scales as it slipped towards her. She stared into its vacant eyes and watched the seam of its mouth. Her limbs and skin were frozen, her eyes caught. She couldn't talk, yell, or scream. The seam cracked open; the teeth protruded. The eyes silvered and hardened. The teeth opened on a black space. A jagged tooth jutted out. She waited for the tearing and shattering pain, but it touched her cheek like a butterfly kiss.

Marcy Benaventura bolted upright. Bright light rimmed the window shade like the neon frame of a painting and cast a lunar rectangle, which stretched across the clear, waxed floor to the door.

Kragen!

Same nightmare. Same jagged tooth. Same kiss. And she knew Kragen was gone.

She put on her robe and opened the blind, and then the window. The Olympia was there, Lansky's hard-on, but the penthouse was silent, blackened and empty, rimmed in bumblebee tape. The last few days flipped through her head as if on a diorama: The chase through the Rex; the final confrontation with Kragen; Ben's bloody arm pushing Kragen off the roof. The final explanation was that Kragen was a stalker who tried to rape and kill her. It wasn't that far from the truth.

The Rex, the Rex. It stood like an old warrior who had by some alchemy vanquished a younger, better-armed enemy. In a few days the invasion that had bothered, harassed, and torn at their souls for months seemed suspended, drifting away like fallen leaves on a sluggish current.

Of course there were wounds. In two months, scores of residents were gone, hurt, or damaged spiritually. Carly, Harry, Meyer...the list was long. But the assault on the Rex went away as quickly as it came. Frieda said they'd taken the Rex back. Rudi said boutique hotel.

What next?

What next was the daily grind minus a few annoying goons making fake-whisper phone calls, breaking this or that, and staring down the residents. Not that the goons had gone away. She was trudging up the basement steps when she saw Tim—goon, or ex-goon—his face half-hidden in the desk clerk's half-oval. She paused and listened. He was complaining about a stopped toilet. A month ago, he would have caused it. The tables had turned or reversed or somersaulted. She wondered whether he would use the Rex as a base to jump-start his life, or whether he'd drift as many residents had drifted, waiting for fate, waiting for Godot, or just waiting.

She had talked to Ben, again—she couldn't explain it, exactly, but they shared a vision of life. It was in Ben's dire hopelessness of all he saw. It was the dark patches of her sketches and painting. They held hands somewhere on the dark side, on the side that knew about death, truth, and lies, that knew that the wedding cake spoils, the perfect couple divorces. So it was grim. It was who she was. Take it or leave it.

That Saturday, for better or worse, she was going to Butch's. She dressed, packed up her pack—double-checking her Mace, pepper spray, and lead club—grabbed her keys, and walked down the stairs. She said hello to Sid in the lobby, waved to Rudi, then walked down the worn steps.

She signaled for a cab and it glided to a stop in front of her. Before opening the door, she turned and looked back at the Rex. Slim, dark, a sentinel for sure, a haven. It wouldn't last forever, but she was glad it lasted that round.

She opened the door and slid in. As the blocks of Kip's Bay vanished in the rear-view mirror, she thought about the future. Next week there was a show at the Crusty Eye. She would have two of her sketches and a painting in it. She smiled, briefly, at Butch's description of her as a typically angry, neo-anarchistic artist.

As the cab swung downtown, Marcy tried to remember what Butch's was like. It was big and junky and you couldn't tell where the junk stopped and the art began. She'd sit on the sofa, sip a beer, and play with Butch. That's what she needed. She didn't need the Crusty Eye or fame, although she knew she'd go for it.

She tried to think of what she'd see in a few minutes at Butch's studio/apartment/gallery. But the Rex still bothered her thoughts. The Rex had survived, but many of the people there, the Bels and Friedas, finally realized the Rex was a dead end. Of course, it wasn't the Rex, it was all inside. And she supposed it would happen to her. And it wasn't just her pessimistic streak. Would she be stopped, halted, at the Rex or in the East Village or at Butch's? Would she go through the same cycle Frieda did, only to recognize, finally, that her location physically and spiritually was holding her back? Would she break out and leave on yet another quest? It seemed inevitable.

Marcy allowed herself a smile. Serial quests: If they were fated, at least she should try to accept them with a dash of humor.

Frieda Berg sat in her stuffed chair and stared at her bookshelves.

From that angle, she saw two streams of light. One, a few feet from her shoulder, made a bright ellipse on the floor near her feet, the other, in the other room, touched five boxes and cut a right angle shadow at the edge of the closest. She had spent much time—too much time—in that stuffed chair regarding her room and puzzling her history, or plucking her Art Nouveau mirror from the wall to scrutinize her image. She'd left the mirror alone for days and marked that as a sign, another sign, that her life had changed or more positively that *she* had changed her life. She supposed—she hated to think she was that cynical—that one day she would have a similar chair with a similar mirror in Taos, New Mexico, and that she would sit in that chair and muse about where she was and why.

But after all, how could she escape it? She would, once again, think of the Bronx, of her mother, the sisters, her white-cross chewing ex-husband, the department, Toby, HRA, and then the trail from Manhattan to Taos, to new friends, to new neuroses. Big deal. At that particular moment, she felt hope, free will, and change. The details reassured her. The bags were getting packed, the boxes shipped, the loose ends tied.

And it looked like the Rex would be around for a while as stopgap, or final stop. Physically, the hotel was tattered. Rooms had been closed, windows broken, sinks stopped. But Lansky was stopped too. The mysterious fire in Olympia penthouse had killed two people, one of them Lansky. When she got the bulky envelope that outlined Lansky's scheme—she was sure Jack sent it; only he would have known all those details—she realized how close they had come to dying. She showed it to the police and there was an uproar. Casey talked, finally, and implicated Kragen and Lansky, not that it made any difference. She wasn't sure how, but a West Side SRO Law project lawyer said that Rudi and Brendel could acquire Lansky's stake in the Rex. It would be a slow process of recovery, but Rudi and Brendel's crews were busy converting closed rooms into new spiffy units. Boutique hotel. No Rudi, she won't be here to see it.

Life at the Rex—most life, and not counting the missing Bels, Carlys and Harrys—continued. She supposed that morning Rudi would exit from the 6 Lex and walk over to the Rex to relieve Ivan. Ben—still a mystery, even after what happened—would wait at the corner for the cosmic juncture of lines of force and stars, or a whispered message from the ghost of Celine, which meant he could finally cross Twenty-eighth Street. Inside, the bathrooms would be used, the hot plates turned on, and the first flood of people, including goons turned residents—wasn't the point that we were all flawed human beings?—would start hurrying by the desk on the first leg of a morning routine that would take in the Times, coffee and breakfast at the Odyssey, or kick off the official work day. Residents would come and go, bring in take-out, have a solitary drink at five, pen a poem, or watching the flickering tube for signs of life in the republic.

But Frieda Berg was leaving. A few days ago, when she explained what she was going to do to Marcy or Maritsa or Rudi, she wondered if she was talking about somebody else. But that day, she knew it was true.

She was leaving the cocoon.

www.ingramcontent.com/pod-product-compliance
Lightning Source LLC
Chambersburg PA
CBHW071207250626
47159CB00001B/240